SONG OF THE DARK WOOD

SHEILA MASTERSON

BOOKS BY SHEILA MASTERSON

The Lost God Series

The Lost God #1

The Memory Curse #2

The Storm King #3

The Godless Kingdom #4

Standalones

Song of the Dark Wood

SONG

OF THE

DARK

WOOD

SHEILA MASTERSON

Ebook ASIN: B0D1M81771

Paperback: 978-1-960416-13-1

Hardcover: 978-1-960416-14-8

Cover Design & Illustration: Andrea Laguer

Map Illustration: Andrés Aguirre Jurado

Scene Illustrations: Charlotte Slegers

Editing: Erin Larson-Burnett at EKB Books

Proofreading: Tabitha Chandler

To my grandmothers, Hanna and Marie:
Thank you for the legacy of what it means
to make your way as a fierce woman.

And to all those who cultivate wildness
in a world made to tame.

Go forth and be a menace.

A NOTE FROM THE AUTHOR

Dear Reader,

SONG OF THE DARK WOOD deals with some difficult subjects including violence, death, death of a child, lack of bodily autonomy, blood, sexual harassment by a religious elder, religious trauma, and explicit sex. I've attempted to treat all sensitive topics with the utmost care, but this content might still be challenging for some readers. Please take care of yourself.

-Sheila

EIREIONE

WOLF'S KEEP

CRONE'S COTTAGE

HUNTSMAN'S HOLLOWS

DARK WOOD

BORDERWOOD

ASH AND ORCHARDS

MAIDEN'S TOWER

TEMPLE OF THE MOTHER

ELDER TREE

BALLYBRINE

"We live in the shadow of a forest full of secrets
haunted by footprints disappearing into freshly fallen leaves.
There is no hope for us here,
no hope but a woman in a cloak—
scarlet, like blood yet to be spilled
that somehow stains our hands already.

We are bound by what is promised
and cursed by what is taken."

– excerpt from the scripture of the Mother

————

"The Mother sees to the living.
The Wolf sees to the dead.
The Crone sees to the bargain between them,
and souls are ferried by Red."

– Ballybrine children's rhyme

PROLOGUE

When she was five years old, Rowan Cleary whispered her name to the Dark Wood, and the Dark Wood whispered it back.

Her mother had warned her never to speak her name so close to a forest full of vicious monsters. Names held power. But Rowan had been found out as a spirit singer and given over to the elders by her family. Her life as she knew it was over.

Rowan's power as a spirit singer meant that she would become the acting Red Maiden when she came of age. She would be forced to deliver on a bargain struck between two gods long before she was born. The Mother saw to the living. The Wolf saw to the dead. The Red Maiden was the bridge between two worlds, ferrying souls from the realm of the living, through the forest, to the realm of the dead.

It was reckless. She felt the wrongness in the magic of the Dark Wood, but still, it called to her—reaching out with icy fingers—beckoning her inside as if to say, *"Come play with me, Rowan—little red one. Come play!"*

One way or another, whatever lurked in the Dark Wood would get her. The rest of the world would know her as a Red Maiden and nothing else. So, she whispered her name and listened to the chilling echo of it in the darkness. It was the only rebellion she could muster at such a tender age.

She knew she would disappear in a matter of years, but at least the Dark Wood would remember her name.

1

ROWAN

There were things only the forest knew. A dark history woven into roots and soil and carried on the wind when the branches blew just right.

Now the trees seemed content to keep their secrets. In her twenty years, Rowan Cleary had never heard them so silent.

A cool breeze ruffled her red cloak, shaking leaves from the boughs above and along the mossy ground. The sun dipped low, shadows stretching as though the Dark Wood was reaching to claim her. Normally, a melody seemed to flow between her and the enchanted wood, but today it absorbed her whispers the moment they left her lips.

She'd stood on the edge of this forest so many times, her boots scraping but never quite crossing the invisible boundary, hands tenderly petting the leaves and branches like the hair of a well-loved doll.

There wasn't room for Rowan to feel much of anything at home in Ballybrine. Here, she could purge herself of all poisonous thoughts—rage, fear, and secret longings dumped into the only place that would hold them without judgment.

"I'm only two months away from becoming the acting Red Maiden, and I already feel like I'm disappearing."

The words wrenched from her lips. The secret stolen by grief.

Rowan rolled her shoulders, shaking off the stiffness of a day spent bent over her piano, practicing wielding her magical voice.

Turning her back to the Dark Wood, she looked at the lavender sky over Mother's Lake. Her two blessed hours of freedom before evening prayer and dinner were nearly over.

Footsteps crunched to her left and Cade appeared at her shoulder. She hoped he hadn't heard her. Though she trusted him implicitly, there were some things that were just between her and the woods.

"Are you really so eager to flirt with danger?" he asked, glancing at the Dark Wood.

Rowan rolled her eyes. "You're awfully skittish for a demon. I'm on the Borderwood side. I never cross over."

"I thought you were dreading meeting the Wolf, but you look like you're ready to move in."

Rowan bristled. "You may prefer the chaos of town like a good little demon, but I get tired of being gawked at. This clearing on the lake is perfect and I wanted to stop to see Sarai."

She turned toward the little cottage on an island at the center of the lake, the home of the Crone and her daughter, Sarai, one of Rowan's only friends.

Cade sighed. "Some days it feels like you drag me out here to punish me for your being found out."

Rowan laughed and ruffled his hair. Fifteen years earlier, her mother had found her speaking to Cade one afternoon. Rowan hadn't noticed until then that no one else ever spoke to him, and although he appeared to be a little boy her age, no parents came calling for him.

Instead of looking horrified, Rowan's mother had looked relieved. Rowan was the youngest of five children and her parents were eternally struggling to put food on the table. A spirit singer was only born once every five years, and while it might have been a curse for Rowan, it was a blessing for the rest of her family. Her becoming a Red Maiden-in-waiting granted them one of the nicest homes in town, elevated them to the highest social status, and offered a substantial monthly stipend for the rest of their days—all for the simple price of her sacrifice.

It was a bitter tincture to swallow as she was sequestered to Maiden's Tower, but Rowan couldn't hate her parents. Their bodies had nearly been broken by years of manual labor and they had little to show for it. She and her siblings rarely went a day without the incessant cramping of an empty belly. Still, she was relieved when they skipped monthly visitation days. It was hard to see their freedom when her life was so sheltered and controlled.

Rowan sighed. "You don't have to come with me if you don't like it here."

"I know, but I thought you'd want to talk." Cade dragged the toe of his boot through the mud.

"About what?" Rowan asked, looking away. Her gaze caught on a little white snowdrop flower that had pushed up through the leaf detritus on the forest floor, bright and pure against the muted background.

"About becoming acting Maiden."

Rowan tugged at the neckline of her dress, which suddenly felt too tight. "I have a plan."

Cade's grin widened and his eyes flashed momentarily red before returning to their usual hazel. "How can I help if I'm not in on the plan?"

"I have two months to work out the details. I'm going to ask the Wolf to strike a new bargain."

Cade stared at her. "You're going to ask—" He collapsed against a tree, clutching his stomach in a fit of laughter that sent a murder of crows in the canopy into panicked flight. "You're going to ask the god of death, the Wolf—who is supposed to devour you—to strike a new bargain? Why would he change a deal that offers him a pretty young virgin every five years?"

Rowan's shoulders sagged. "I suppose you have a better idea."

All the humor drained from his face. "I don't."

"I have to try," Rowan said. "I owe it to myself and to any future Maidens to change things."

Cade sighed. "It's a bad idea to make a deal with a god."

"Is it a better idea to die?" Rowan snapped. "Look, if I do what I'm supposed to and serve out my term, I force every Maiden after me to deal with the same terrible circumstances. If I can get the Wolf to remake his deal, I might still be on the hook to ferry the souls once a week, but I could have a life, friends—maybe even a family."

"And you can avoid the responsibility ever falling to Aeoife," Cade finished.

Rowan nodded as a breeze ruffled the hairs that had escaped her braid.

"Row, I don't want to discourage you, but don't get your hopes up. The Wolf is centuries old. It's hard to believe he'd make a deal with you that doesn't benefit him more. There was a time when the people of Ballybrine tried to break with tradition and the Wolf tore through town and killed every child on three separate streets in retaliation. He doesn't seem to like change."

Rowan wrapped her arms around her stomach, trying to settle its roiling.

Patting her shoulder, Cade gave her a reassuring smile. "I'm not trying to scare you. Just be very delicate about how you approach him."

They fell into step, approaching the wooden walkway that led to Crone's Cottage on the tiny island in Mother's Lake.

The cottage door creaked open and the Crone made her way down the rickety planks to dry land, casting a worried glance at the Dark Wood. Despite her title, the Crone couldn't have been older than mid-forties, and her brown skin showed little sign of aging other than the smile lines around her light gray eyes.

"You shouldn't be close to the forest alone, girl," the Crone scolded. Though she couldn't see Cade, her eyes narrowed on the space beside Rowan as if she sensed him.

Rowan shrugged. The Crone had been saying the same thing to

4

her since she anointed her as the next Red Maiden, but the woods were Rowan's birthright, and she wouldn't fear them the way everyone else did.

Of course, it wasn't just fear that kept folks out of the forest. The Crone had whispered stories of a time before she was born when women used to wander into the woods for inspiration. They'd come back with brilliant poetry, political aspirations, or a new wildness stoked inside them. It wasn't long before the elders condemned such wandering, certain that too many women with their own minds were a bigger threat to their way of life than the new religion rising in the north.

Wandering the woods seemed like harmless trouble to Rowan, but in their world, there was no such thing for women. Harmless trouble was reserved for men and boys. Whispers of such things spread like wildfire between women in the town square, laundress shops, and bakery lines. It was the only kindness the women of Bally-brine could offer each other—the truth of whose trouble was innocuous and whose was worth avoiding at all costs.

"I thought Sarai would be back by now," Rowan said.

The Crone shook her head. "She'll be along soon. The days grow shorter, but that girl loses herself when she's gathering herbs in the Borderwood."

Despite her posture hinting at disapproval, a smile tugged at the corner of her lips. The Crone seemed to admire her daughter's wildness, which would serve her well as the next Crone. Crones kept ancient wisdom, cast spells, and held the heavy responsibility of ensuring the bargain between the Mother and the Wolf was upheld. Their power required courage and an appreciation for the magic of the natural world.

"What's happening in the Dark Wood?" Rowan asked.

The Crone eyed her suspiciously. "What do you think is happening?"

Rowan rolled her eyes. "I don't know. Why won't you just tell me?"

"Because I don't know either, girl."

Everything the Crone taught Rowan about magic made her feel

closer to understanding her own power, especially since so much about her gifts was unknown and unspoken. Even the current Red Maiden, Orla, was forbidden from sharing her experiences with Rowan. Whatever happened between Orla and the Wolf was a mystery, but she must have been doing something right to have survived this long.

Rowan could get over her apprehension of walking into the Dark Wood alone, but it was hard to contend with not knowing what to expect from a god whose job it was to accept the souls of the dead into the Underlands and, according to scriptures, devour her. Her lessons suggested devouring was likely sexual and would probably lead to her death. It had been decades since a Red Maiden had lived beyond five years of service, yet everyone acted like it was so simple. *Ferry the souls of the departed. Keep the Wolf happy.* Rowan wasn't even permitted to hold a man's hand, so despite extensive tutoring in things the Wolf might like, she felt woefully unprepared.

Suddenly, Sarai darted out of the tree line, her hunter-green cloak flying out behind her as she ran. "Mother! Rowan! You must come. The Dark Wood is dying. The elders have gathered outside the Temple of the Mother."

Rowan fell into step behind the Crone and Sarai as Cade sidled up next to her.

"That can't be good," Cade said.

Rowan tried not to speak to Cade in front of people who couldn't see him, so she just shrugged, practically jogging to keep pace with the Crone and Sarai.

As the trees thinned and Ballybrine came into view, Rowan pulled up the hood of her cloak. Even the view of her full face was secret until she became the acting Red Maiden. It had taken Rowan a while to grow accustomed to walking around in her hooded cloak. The sheer panel in the hood cast the world in red and blocked most of her peripheral vision, but she'd trained her hearing to make up for it. The scriptures claimed her cloak marked her as a sacred vessel, but she knew it was really meant to ease consciences. Red Maidens were usually discovered when they were young, and it was hard to look at the face of an adorable five-year-old while promising her virtue and life to the god of death.

The scent of wood smoke from the wealthier homes and the earthy, pungent peat smoke from poorer parts of town filled the air. People rushed from their homes toward the Temple of the Mother, colorful doors slamming shut behind them. The bright paint corresponded to sails and ships so that families could be notified when one of their own was returning or lost at sea.

Ballybrine was constantly at war with nature. A team of huntsmen tended to the overgrowth weekly, but trees and ferns still pushed over the forest boundaries like they'd reclaim their territory if given the chance. The town was cut into the wilderness at the southern tip of Eireione, its isolation intentional as it had long been a haven for practitioners of the old religion. Refugees arrived weekly by the shipload from parts of the world where the new religion spread like wildfire, leaving violence in its wake. The Dark Wood lurked to the east, the Borderwood to the north, and the Huntsman's Hollows to the west. To the south, there was nothing but the sea, which was prone to sudden, dangerous storms.

Still, Rowan loved her untamed home. Both the forest and the sea reflected the wildness in her heart that sometimes felt like the only thing that truly belonged to her.

Cade nudged her, knocking her from her daydreaming. "This looks interesting," he said, nodding to the townspeople scrambling up ahead.

"You don't know what it is?" Rowan asked.

The Crone turned and raised an eyebrow but said nothing. Sarai just smiled—she couldn't see or hear Cade but liked to keep up to date on his antics.

"Just because I'm a demon doesn't mean I know every bad thing that happens around here," Cade huffed.

They cut through the dirt-packed side streets to the main cobblestone road that led to the square, where a steady buzz rose from just outside the temple.

Rowan paused, trying to adjust to the cacophony of the village.

Her magic meant she could hear human energy. The symphony of living noise was grating and hard to turn down. Even after years of training, she struggled. It was part of the reason she preferred the quiet melody of the forest, or even the ominous symphony of the Dark Wood.

As soon as they arrived in front of the Temple of the Mother, Rowan knew something was very wrong. She froze, her gaze resting on the spirit of Dylan McCray, a prominent fisherman who'd been lost at sea during a storm the week before. She was certain Orla must have already led him through the Dark Wood. Once a spirit crossed, they weren't meant to come back.

"What is it?" the Crone asked, sensing her unease.

"There are more spirits here than there should be," Rowan whispered.

The Crone patted her shoulder. "Run along and find Orla. We will figure this out."

Rowan nodded, making her way through the crowd. The townsfolk shifted nervously as she passed, giving her a wide berth, her very presence a reminder that the dead were close. Most preferred to think of the departed contained to the Underlands—a neat thing, tucked away behind solid stone grave markers in the cemetery.

But spirits preferred action. They liked to be where the people were, which was part of the reason the weekly Gratitude and Grieving Ceremony was held in such a public forum.

Rowan hurried toward Maiden's Tower, the tall, white, ivy-wrapped home she shared with Orla, who was five years her senior, and the youngest spirit singer, Aeoife, who was just ten. Taking the stairs two at a time with Cade on her heels, Rowan shoved her hood back from her face.

"You shouldn't come. You frighten Orla," Rowan said.

"I'll stay quiet. I swear," Cade insisted.

Rowan eyed him skeptically as they reached the landing.

"I don't understand why she doesn't like me. I've always been nice to her, and Aeoife likes me just fine," Cade complained.

"Behave yourself, or I'll banish you until the morning," Rowan said firmly. Learning to banish unwanted spirits was one of the first things she'd been taught, and although she often threatened Cade, she'd only ever acted on it three times.

"I'll be a perfect little angel," he said in mock offense.

They rounded the last staircase, stepping onto the floor that housed the three maidens' bedrooms and one vacant room meant for the yet-to-be-found spirit singer, who should have been born five years after Rowan and before Aeoife.

Orla's door flew open. "Rowan, thank the Mother! I was worried. Come quick!" Her gaze flitted over Cade, but she said nothing.

They followed Orla onto the balcony off her bedroom, where Aeoife waited, her thick strawberry-blonde hair twisted into twin braids.

"Rowie, the woods are dying," Aeoife said, her blue eyes wide as she slid her hand into Rowan's. Cade stepped to Aeoife's other side, and she leaned her head against his arm.

Rowan looked out on the scene far below. Sure enough, the edge of the Dark Wood, where the trail from the square to Wolf's Keep began, was full of barren, leafless trees. Their bark had turned a bright white, their branches like skeletal fingers reaching toward the moon, as if to scratch it from the sky. Heavy fog made it impossible to see how far the blight had spread.

Rowan looked at Orla. Though they weren't permitted to talk about anything important, Orla was like an older sister, always put together immaculately and brave in the face of chaos. But now her perfect facade was ruffled. Wisps of silky blonde hair escaped from her coronet braid and her cheeks were flushed in the autumn air.

"Is it the Wolf?" The question burst from Rowan's mouth before she could stop it.

Orla's dark eyes met hers. "I don't know. Maybe something happened to him."

"Happened to him?" Rowan almost laughed. "He's a monster, Orla."

Orla said nothing, but her hands were clasped together in a white-knuckled grip.

9

"Maybe he's not happy with the souls we've sent him," Rowan said. "I saw more than I've ever seen gathered down below."

Orla's eyes darted to Cade. "He has to go."

"He won't tell anyone," Rowan argued.

"I'm serious." Orla's voice was firm. "Please."

"Cade, leave," Rowan ordered.

"You know I'm great at keeping secrets," Cade said.

Rowan shook her head. "I know you are, but it's not my secret. It's Orla's." Cade didn't move. "I don't want to banish you, but I will if I have to."

Cade sulked away to wait in Rowan's room. She made sure he'd really gone before turning back to the other Maidens.

"What do you know?" Rowan asked.

In all their years together, Orla had said nothing to her about the Wolf. Even after she'd transitioned from the white dresses Rowan and Aeoife wore into red dresses that signaled the Wolf had claimed her, Orla had stayed silent.

Orla's gaze passed over the forest before coming to rest on Aeoife and Rowan. "He's not what everyone makes him out to be. That's not to say he isn't dangerous, but I don't understand why he would do this. I haven't done anything wrong." A crease formed in her brow, and she bit her lip. "At least, I don't think I have." She shook her head. "People here are too quick to blame their problems on the Wolf."

Orla squeezed both of their hands. Rowan wanted to ask a hundred different questions, and from the look on Aeoife's face, she was struggling with the same thing.

"Tomorrow is the next ferrying," Rowan whispered.

Orla swallowed hard. "Then I guess I'll find out what's happening soon."

Rowan should have taken Aeoife in for dinner, but they stayed beside Orla, as if their presence alone could banish her fear.

Three Red Maidens stared out at the withering Dark Wood and wondered what it meant for a forest full of dead things to be dying.

2

ROWAN

The dampness of the ground soaked through the hem of Rowan's dress as she knelt in the dirt of Sarai's garden outside Crone's Cottage. Autumn in Ballybrine was eternally wet, rain showers popping up so often that nothing ever seemed to dry fully. But even her sodden dress wasn't enough to stop her from worrying about Orla's ferrying later that night. She looked across the lake at the silent Dark Wood.

"You're distracted today," Sarai said. A gust of wind swayed the rosemary plant as she reached to snip it. She brushed her dark braids behind her shoulders. "Did Orla say anything about the Dark Wood?"

"It was so strange," Rowan said. "Orla has never told me anything worthwhile about the Wolf or the woods, and she looked worried. Then she told us that if there's something wrong, it wasn't the Wolf's doing. She suggested that something might have happened to him."

Sarai's eyes went wide. "Does she like him?"

"It's hard to tell. She said he was dangerous, but little else. It seems terribly impractical that Orla can tell us nothing about her experiences," Rowan said.

"It's because knowledge is power, and the elders like you weak,"

Cade called from where he lay by the edge of the water, pulling up blades of grass and tossing them to the wind.

Rowan frowned at him.

"It did always strike me as odd. Especially since the elders are so vocal about interactions with the Mother," Sarai mused.

The elders were originally messengers, meant to help spread the word the Mother shared via the Crone, but in recent years, they'd inserted themselves between the two. Not only had they stolen much of the Crone's political and theological power, but they'd slowly manipulated the messaging to suit their means.

Sarai bundled the rosemary in string, her jerky motions nearly splitting the stalks in half. "Honestly, their desire to control women in the community knows no bounds. Did you know they want to ban them from joining the huntsmen ranks?"

Rowan's eyes went wide. "How do you know that?"

"Raya told me," Sarai said, her cheeks flushing a dark berry color.

"But there are so many outstanding female hunters in their ranks. Do they just expect them all to resign?" Rowan asked.

"They don't care," Sarai said. "My mother is a fantastic Crone and they've made her a glorified ceremony master with no actual power. I worry there will be no need for me by the time I'm old enough to take over for her. It's maddening watching them constantly performing their devotion rather than actually feeling it. Don't you think?"

Rowan nodded. "I do, but you know how I feel. It's hard to feel connected to a religion that sends young women to a death god."

"I know," Sarai sighed. "And I know you hold no affection for the Mother who allowed you to be born to be a sacrifice."

"What an honor—to be a prize for a vengeful god," Rowan said, her voice tight with bitterness.

"You should be careful who you share those sentiments with," Sarai warned, laying sprigs of rosemary in her basket. "I may under-stand, but others won't."

Rowan tried so hard to be a perfect Red Maiden—to live a fric-tionless life—to be pleasant, compliant, and silent. Orla was frictionless, and everyone loved her. Rowan was chaotic and angry under a barely controlled exterior.

Sarai's gaze was like a brand, but Rowan kept her focus on the blooming lavender. It was not the season for lavender, especially with so much rain, but Rowan hummed quietly, listening to the song that flowed through the plant's roots and coaxing it to bloom.

She was forbidden from singing outside of the soundproof room she trained in, but the small rebellion was one of the few thrills in her life, and the Crone and Sarai made good use of their herbs. They made salves for wounds, herbal tinctures, and remedies for the poorest in Ballybrine.

Though Sarai knew about her power, Rowan had never explained the way it truly worked. She kept it to herself to prevent Sarai from being put in the awkward position of having to lie for her. Their friendship was always second to their responsibilities, though Sarai did her best to give Rowan an outlet when she could.

"The mint could use a song." Sarai gestured toward the pathetic-looking mint plant potted at the far edge of the garden.

Rowan smiled. "All right, but only one. If I give it too much, it will strangle the rest of the garden." She shifted her gaze over to Cade, who was distracted with digging worms from the wet dirt by the lake's edge.

She turned her attention to the plant and sang an old folk lullaby. Immediately, the mint plant perked up and grew before their eyes until it was lush and overwhelmed its pot.

"I've seen it so many times, but it's always amazing to watch," Sarai said. "Can Orla do that, too? Or Aeoife?"

Rowan shrugged. She'd never asked since she wasn't supposed to be singing outside of her training. She was pretty sure that neither of them would tell on her, but she didn't want to put them in the position of being forced to confess something to the elders. The punishments dealt by the elders were rarely commensurate with the alleged crimes committed. Rowan's gaze dropped to her hands, where she bore several angry red lines from being hit with a switch for asking questions out of turn.

Rowan couldn't quite explain her power. She just knew that when she sang, the resonance in her voice brushed up against the resonance of living things and made them grow. The same way a Red Maiden's song reminded the dead of life and lured them through the woods, Rowan's songs inspired living things to thrive.

Rowan gnawed on her lip, watching Sarai harvest some thyme. "I want to propose that the Wolf change his bargain with the Mother."

Sarai froze. She turned to face Rowan. "Are you out of your mind?"

"I told you so!" Cade proclaimed.

Rowan slumped. She'd hoped Sarai would support her idea more than Cade had. "Sarai, I don't know what else to do. I don't want to die. I don't want Aeoife to have to take over in five years. She'll only be fifteen! It's too young." She frowned. "It would help if we could find the Maiden who is supposed to come between me and Aeoife."

Red Maidens were born every five years, but despite the elders' best efforts, they hadn't found the girl who had been born five years after Rowan.

She felt a sick sort of envy for that girl. She must have had family looking out for her and remarkable control over her gifts. But Rowan couldn't fault her for wanting to duck her fate.

Sarai dusted her hand on her dress. "I have never even had an inkling of who she might be. It's as if someone has placed a veil over her and she's just gone."

"Is it possible that no Maiden was ever born between us?" Rowan asked.

Sarai shook her head. "No. I'm certain she's out there. I just don't know where. And while I think your idea is brave, I'm worried that the Wolf is already wound up enough with this blight. What if he makes it spread across the border into the realm of the living?"

Rowan sagged, frustrated. "I don't know."

Sarai laid a hand on her shoulder. "I don't want to discourage you. It's not a bad idea. Perhaps feel him out and wait a bit until you make requests."

Sarai gasped and went rigid as her eyes clouded over.

"Sarai?"

Although Sarai experienced visions with some frequency, Rowan had only witnessed them three times before.

"It creeps me out when she does this," Cade said, coming to kneel beside Rowan.

Rowan gave him a dirty look.

"What? Seers are strange. They see everything, but they tell us nothing of what to expect. If I could see the future..." He let his voice trail off, a look of envy in his eyes.

After a moment, Sarai's daze cleared and she blinked at Rowan. The color drained from her cheeks, and her eyes went wide.

"What is it?" Rowan asked.

Sarai swallowed hard. "I saw Orla."

"And?"

Sarai opened her mouth and then closed it again. "I saw Orla—so pale and bloodless—just lying on the forest floor. I don't think she was sleeping, Row."

"Wolf's teeth!" Cade choked. "Why doesn't she ever see good things?"

Rowan swallowed hard. "That doesn't mean it's going to happen for sure," she protested. "Remember last time? When you saw the Fellows boy drown in the sea? He didn't actually drown. He simply fell in the water and was rescued by a sailor."

Sarai nodded noncommittally, but she said nothing else.

The pounding of horse hooves nearby cut through the silence. Rowan pulled her hood up and looked toward the trail as Finn Ashand emerged like a fairy-tale knight on his white horse. Finn's face was unnerving in its symmetry, marred only by a few freckles that came out in the summers when he spent too long in the sun. His golden huntsman cloak draped over his broad shoulders, and his face was fixed in a broad grin. That smile and the openness on his face always made him stand out from the other huntsmen who tried so hard to look tough.

Rowan and Sarai had met Finn as children when they snuck away to play in the sea one day. Rowan had been caught in a current that dragged her out too far while Sarai watched, horrified, from the shore. Finn heard Sarai's calls for help, dove into the water, and brought Rowan back to the beach. After that, the three were fast—though secret—friends.

Finn was the eldest son of the Lord of Ashand, who owned the territory surrounding the Huntsman's Hollows and the Borderwood. He was also one of the few who had seen Rowan without her cloak and kept it a secret. She brushed her hood back and smiled at him.

Finn drew up on the reins and hopped down from the horse. "Thought I might find you here. By the Mother, Rowan, you look lovely today," he sighed.

Rowan felt a flush creep up her neck to her cheeks.

Sarai looked from Finn to Rowan with a grin. "I have to get these herbs hung up to dry." Picking up her basket, she winked at Rowan and disappeared into the cottage.

"You shouldn't say things like that in front of other people," Rowan scolded as Finn took her hand and kissed it softly.

"I know it's wrong to covet that which does not belong to me, but how could I not when you're so beautiful?" Finn said with a wink.

Cade made a choking sound. "He can't be serious. I'm going to vomit."

Rowan ignored him as she looked down at the lush grass, unable to meet Finn's gaze. She'd always been uncomfortable with the weight of his affection. It wasn't that she didn't care for him. She was simply aware that her feelings didn't match his, and it filled her with guilt. Still, she enjoyed the thrill of being seen as more than just an object.

Finn tucked a loose red curl behind her ear.

"What have you heard of the blight in the Dark Wood?" Rowan asked.

As a huntsman, Finn hunted game for the village in the Huntsman's Hollows, but he also led excursions into the Dark Wood when there were problems. He bore a special blessing from the Mother that allowed him to wander deeper into the Dark Wood than most since only Red Maidens and those with special magical blessings could travel more than a few steps inside. Those without that type of magic felt compelled to leave as soon as they set foot in the haunted forest. It was meant to protect the town, but Rowan couldn't help but feel it was another way to ensure that the Red Maiden was isolated on her journey to Wolf's Keep.

Finn furrowed his brow and ran a hand through his golden-brown hair. "I led an excursion yesterday. It was harder than usual for us all to withstand the heavy, oppressive energy of the forest. We only rode in a mile or so before we had to turn back, but as far as we made it, the trees along the trail were all affected by the blight."

Rowan swallowed hard. "What do you think it means?"

Finn shrugged. "It's hard to say. We didn't encounter the Wolf or any other beasts, but something was definitely very wrong. I can normally make it nearly the full three miles to Wolf's Keep before I feel a need to turn back. It was just a frustrating day, and when I have a bad day, you're the only one I want to see," he said.

"Why?" Rowan asked.

"Because you're my favorite person in this whole town. Just seeing your smile makes me feel lighter," Finn said.

Rowan brushed phantom dirt off her dress to hide how flustered she felt. "Finn, you shouldn't flirt with me. You should be out there courting a lady to marry."

"I'm going to marry you once you become a lady," he insisted.

Rowan rolled her eyes. "Finn, we both know that isn't going to happen. You're already of age to find a wife, and I haven't even begun my service. I could never ask you to wait for me. I have nothing to offer you."

"Nonsense," Finn said. "Once you hit your five years of active service, you'll become a lady. You'll receive the highest honor in the village. You'll be able to retire and be treated with the reverence you deserve. We'll have a family and a life. You'll want for nothing."

"I won't tempt fate by hoping," she said firmly.

Perhaps she would feel the same way Finn did if she lacked the sense to prepare for the worst. Rowan spent most of her youth on worthless hope. No one was coming to save her. Much as Finn might have liked to be her knight in shining armor, he was also a reverent rule-follower. He might bend rules, but he'd not break them.

"Then I'll hope enough for both of us," Finn said.

She couldn't help but smile. It did her no good, but Finn's confidence was contagious.

"Regardless, let me decide what I'm willing to wait for. I think you're worth it, and I could not care less what anyone else thinks," Finn said.

"Really? I've noticed that Lady Joy McCade seems to have taken a shine to you," Rowan taunted.

Lady Joy McCade was the exact type of person Finn should have wanted to marry. She was tall, wealthy, beautiful, and available.

Finn smiled. "Joy is a sweet girl, but she's not for me. My heart is set on someone else, and it's quite immovable."

Rowan looked away, willing Sarai to come back and save her.

Cade stepped up beside Finn, sizing him up. "Perhaps he should have been a poet instead of a huntsman."

"You shouldn't say such things," Rowan said, partly to Finn and partly to Cade.

"The Mother believes we should all speak our truth when we feel it. It's in her scriptures," Finn said.

"Yes, but your affection is wasted on me," Rowan sighed. "You shouldn't want me."

"Nonsense. He should be so lucky," Cade quipped indignantly.

Rowan flicked her fingers, her nonverbal sign of dismissal, and Cade crossed his arms before disappearing into whatever void he ran off to when she wanted alone time.

"Finn, there is a whole world out there for you. Just because I must spend my youth waiting for my time doesn't mean that I'm happy to doom you to the same. You're a good man, and you'll be a wonderful husband, but it won't be me," she said.

Finn ran a hand through his hair, but the gesture didn't hide the hurt on his face.

"I'm not saying it to hurt you. Your notions are terribly romantic, but I feel guilty taking your time and affection when it would be better spent elsewhere on someone who can give you what you deserve," Rowan whispered.

"And what do I deserve?" Finn asked, tilting her chin so she'd meet his eyes.

"You deserve a partner who can build a life with you. You deserve someone who will live a long life, who isn't forced to spend her youth serving a dark god," Rowan said.

"I disagree," Finn declared. "How could I do better than a woman who braves the Dark Wood to protect her people? Your character is far more important to me than your virtue. Even you won't change my mind."

He pressed a chaste kiss to her forehead. It was a tiny rebellion for both of them and as far into the realm of breaking the rules as he'd ever gone.

"Walk with me? I promise to have you back in time to see Orla off."

Finn offered her his arm. If Rowan had any sense at all, she'd keep him at a safe distance. Even if she wasn't a sacrifice—even if she didn't spend her time guarding her heart and the hearts of those she cared for—she wasn't sure her feelings would ever match his.

Rowan took his arm. Just once, she let herself pretend to be an ordinary girl with nothing to do but enjoy her huntsman and a wide-open future.

By THE TIME Rowan made it back to the tower, Orla was already in front of the mirror, braiding her hair and making final preparations for the Gratitude and Grieving Ceremony. People in town looked forward to the event that gave families of the dead an opportunity to grieve while also giving thanks for the bargain that kept balance between the living and the dead. But for Rowan the ceremonies were a precursor to a night of dread as she waited for her friend to return safely.

Rowan regarded Orla warily from the bedroom doorway. The memory of Sarai's vision was still fresh in her mind.

"Don't lurk," Orla said, meeting her eyes in the mirror.

"Sorry," Rowan mumbled as she stepped into the room.

Orla turned and smiled as her gaze passed over Rowan, taking in the mud caked on the hem of her dress. "You should get cleaned up. The ceremony starts at sundown."

"Are you scared?" Rowan asked.

Orla sighed. "Normally, I'm not, but I feel uneasy about this blight. They've asked me to take stock of it, discuss it with the Wolf and report back. I should be fine, but the look of those trees gives me the creeps."

"Just follow the rules, and you'll be fine," Rowan said. She tried to muster confidence she didn't feel, but her voice shook.

"Why do you look as if you're grieving?" Orla asked.

Rowan shook her head and looked away. "I wish you didn't have to go alone. If Cade didn't make you uneasy, I'd send him with you."

She hesitated to share about Finn. She'd mentioned him to Orla after the day they'd first met, but she tried not to say how often they saw each other for the same reason she kept everything else to herself. The less Orla knew, the less she'd be compelled to tell the elders if asked.

"Finn said that the hunting party struggled to make their way through the Dark Wood's magic."

Orla nodded. "I'd heard as much." She stood and buttoned her red cloak like it was an ordinary evening, ever steady even in the eye of a storm. Her calm stoked Rowan's urgency.

Rowan was a stranger to temperance. She only knew how to burn. Her life was a constant struggle to remain composed while she knew herself to be incendiary. Her indoctrination had been entirely about dampening the flames within her, and she didn't need the elders to see any hint that the embers in her smoldered still—not when they were confident they'd been well smothered.

"Orla, Sarai had a vision that something bad happened to you," Rowan said, her voice shaking.

Orla's eyes widened. She turned back to the mirror and licked her lips before meeting Rowan's gaze in the reflection. "It's not as if I can choose not to go," she rasped.

Rowan bit her lip. "Can you just stay overnight? Her vision was of you in the woods."

The line between Orla's brow softened. "I'll make sure that someone walks me back. I promise."

Rowan nodded. She refused to allow herself to overthink. She pulled Orla into a tight hug and whispered, "Please be careful. You and Aeoife are the only family I have."

When she pulled back, Orla's eyes were glassy. "Don't worry about me. Just keep Aeoife calm. You know how she always has nightmares on ceremony nights."

It was so like Orla to worry about all of them instead of herself when she was the one most in danger. Though she wasn't as emotional as Rowan, she insulated both younger Maidens from interacting with the elders. Yet each time Rowan tried to bond with her, Orla had an excuse at the ready for why she couldn't take part.

"I will." Rowan nodded.

She usually ended up with Aeoife asleep next to her in her tiny bed. Rowan didn't mind, even though the younger Maiden kicked. She didn't want Aeoife to grow up starved for human touch as she'd been, so she showed the girl as much affection as she could.

"Now go change and wipe that scared look off your face before Aeoife sees it," Orla said. She turned back to the mirror and pretended to keep working on her hair, though not before Rowan saw her hands trembling.

3

ROWAN

Rowan woke with echoes of Cade's eerie bedtime stories in her head and Aeoife next to her in bed. Perhaps it was a mistake to allow a demon to spin his tales, but Aeoife had been so restless the night before, with Orla off in the blighted Dark Wood, that Rowan ran out of ideas. When Cade offered to take over, she let him.

He'd told them a story about how demons made deals with the living in exchange for little pieces of their souls. It wouldn't have been Rowan's choice of a fairy tale, but it put Aeoife to sleep, so she couldn't complain.

Rowan rolled over and spotted Cade sitting by the fireplace.

"Was that story true?" she whispered.

His eyes lit with mischief. "All good fairy tales start with a heart of truth, Rowan. What do you think?"

"Does that happen still?" she asked.

If it did, maybe she could trade a part of herself to change her fate.

Cade's features darkened with something resembling pity. "I see you thinking you've found a solution. Don't even think it. To invite a demon to make a deal is to welcome trouble to your door every morning for the rest of your days. Demons don't make deals they don't come out on the winning end of."

Rowan sighed heavily. She'd known Cade long enough to know when to push and when to let things go. The only predictable thing about him was that his every choice was in his own best interest.

Aeoife curled closer to her side. Rowan had promised the girl's mother five years before—when her abilities had shown up—that she would take care of her. Unlike Rowan's parents, Aeoife's mother was clearly distraught that her middle daughter was a spirit singer. She'd needed to be dragged sobbing from the girl the day she was brought to the tower, and she came to every single visitation day along with Aeoife's two older brothers and her youngest sister. They were a beautiful family and a constant reminder of everything Rowan's family was not.

It was rare that Rowan's family showed up to visitation days, and when they did, they typically only caught Rowan up on gossip. No one asked how she was. No one doted on her, and they never brought her gifts.

The differences were glaring, leaving her sick with jealousy. Rowan felt foolish complaining about it, though. Orla had no family to speak of. A plague had taken her entire brood out when she was twelve.

A bell chimed in the distance, and Rowan reluctantly woke Aeoife for their morning prayers. They made their way down the hall to their rehearsal rooms. They spent their mornings in solitude in identical soundproof rooms.

As they walked down the hall, Rowan peeked into Orla's room. The bed was still made perfectly, the candles unburned. All signs that she hadn't come home yet. Rowan tried to convince herself it was normal. Occasionally, Orla stayed overnight in the keep. She ignored the fact that it only happened when the weather was bad, then thought back to Sarai's vision, and goosebumps prickled her skin.

"Where's Orla?" Aeoife asked, noticing her unease.

"She probably just stayed the night. It was...windy last night," Rowan improvised.

Aeoife looked at her skeptically, but seemed happy to have her anxiety explained.

Rowan guided her down to their practice and prayer rooms on the second floor, silently praying that Orla was safe at Wolf's Keep.

———

THE SUN BEAT down on Rowan as she looked at her reflection in the shop window. Aeoife stood next to her, finishing the last bite of her sticky bun and licking her fingers. Rowan brushed a smudge of caramel from the corner of her mouth, just below the edge of her hood.

When Orla still hadn't returned home by the end of their morning practice time, Rowan tried her best to distract Aeoife with a trip into town for sticky buns.

The din of deal-making vendors and the scent of fresh brown bread filled the air, and the curious gazes of townsfolk clung to the two hooded Maidens standing in front of Marie's Dress Shop. Beside them, Cade glared at all the curious onlookers as if they could see the threatening look in his eye.

A stiff wind blew between the buildings, ruffling their cloaks, giving reflected glimpses of the white dresses beneath. Their frocks were boring compared to the elaborate ones displayed in the window.

"I call the pink one!" Aeoife said, looking at a fluffy pink tulle monstrosity that Rowan wouldn't be caught dead in. Aeoife liked this game of daydreaming about dresses they'd never be allowed to wear. A little dreaming wouldn't hurt her, so Rowan played along.

"Have at it," Rowan laughed.

"I think the green one would look good on you," Aeoife said. "My mom always says that green brings out red hair. My sister Aileen wears it all the time because of that."

Rowan frowned. "I don't know how I feel about a skirt that big. It would get awfully muddy."

"You'd look like a cupcake," Cade taunted.

"Well, it's not for gardening, Rowie. It's for a ball," Aeoife teased, as if there was a scenario in which they'd be going to a ball.

"We should go back. I'm sure Orla is home by now," Rowan said. Suddenly, a murmur went through the crowd behind them. "Let's go see what the fuss is about."

They pushed through the pulsing crowd. The buzz grew louder the closer they drew to the Elder Tree in the center of the square. The magical tree had been transplanted from the Dark Wood years before and acted as a beacon for what was happening with the magic of the forest and the Red Maidens.

When they finally reached the front of the crowd, they saw what the fuss was about. Half the Elder Tree's branches were bright white with blight, the rest their normal, healthy brown.

But it wasn't the blight that had everyone whispering prayers under their breath.

Blood dripped like gruesome rain from the blighted branches of the Elder Tree.

Rowan stared in disbelief. Her mouth went dry and her ears rang. Her chest was too tight to draw breath.

"Rowie?" Aeoife said. Her voice shook with fear. "Doesn't that mean—"

"Doesn't that mean a Red Maiden is dead?" Cade finished.

Aeoife tugged on Rowan's sleeve, but she couldn't look away from the bloody branches.

After the third tug, Rowan snapped out of it. She looked around the square. Townspeople stood staring at the two Maidens. Aeoife's lower lip trembled under the hood and Rowan's protective instinct kicked in.

"Let's go," Rowan said, tugging on the little girl's hand. She pulled Aeoife through the gawking crowd toward Maiden's Tower. "Don't worry until we have to, okay?"

Aeoife nodded as she stumbled along beside Rowan.

Finn was waiting outside the tower doors. "Rowan, we need your help," he said solemnly. His gaze passed over Aeoife.

"Aeoife, can you go read in your room? I'm going to help the huntsmen."

The little girl hesitated.

"I promise I will come talk to you as soon as I know what's going on," Rowan said. She squeezed Aeoife's hand, and the little girl turned and made her way upstairs.

Rowan turned back to Finn. "It's true, isn't it? Orla's gone?"

"Row, I'm so sorry. I know you were close," he mumbled.

Rowan shook her head, blinking away tears. Having known for years that Orla would likely die young did nothing to soften the sting of her loss. She was just two months from the end of her term. She, Rowan, and Aeoife were a family of their own, and though her whole life brushed up against death, Rowan had never lost someone she cared about.

Evelyn, the Red Maiden before Orla, and Lorna before her, had always been cold toward Rowan, so she had never formed a close bond with them before they passed. Orla's death, however, touched something that lived in the secret part of Rowan's heart.

"Are you sure?" Rowan asked.

Finn swallowed hard. "That's why I'm here. Her body is just over the border in the Dark Wood, but the magic is so powerful none of us can bear to get close. We need you to go get her and pull her out."

Rowan paled. Things were happening much too quickly. She felt as if a clock had begun ticking down in the back of her mind. *Tick, tick, tick.* Orla was dead, which meant Rowan was the acting Red Maiden. *Tick, tick, tick.* Orla was dead, which meant Rowan would be dead soon, too. *Tick, tick, tick.* Orla was dead, and Rowan needed to retrieve her friend's body because no one else could.

She wanted to stay right where she was until her mind could catch up to the new reality. If she didn't see a body, it would feel less real. She wasn't prepared, and yet, in some ways, she'd always been prepared. This had been inevitable since the day she whispered her name to the Dark Wood. Rowan might have been able to pretend, but the knowing lived in the back of her mind like a recurring nightmare.

"*I can't*" wasn't a declaration she could make, even if the words screamed through her mind. "*No*" wasn't a word she had the luxury of using. She'd never had an option other than absolute obedience. There was only what the world required of her—which was everything.

"I know it's horrible, but I also know you wouldn't want to leave her there," Finn continued. "We will be close in case anything happens, but every time I've tried to cross the border into the woods, I get this horrible ringing in my ears, and I'm so dizzy I fall over. I didn't even want to ask, but I didn't know what else—"

"I'll do it," Rowan said, snapping out of her daze.

"I'll go with you," Cade said. She nodded at him, even though Finn couldn't hear the demon.

She followed Finn toward the Dark Wood. Her legs felt leaden, not with fear but with the dread of seeing with her own eyes that Orla was gone. Finn whispered beside her, but she couldn't make sense of the words—something about a lack of blood or obvious injury.

As they approached the trailhead, Rowan flinched at the sound of a loud, guttural scream. Her hands came to her ears, and she doubled over.

"Row, what is it?" Finn asked. He reached for her arm, but she ducked away at the last second. Finn looked chastened by the reminder that he wasn't supposed to touch her in public.

"You don't hear it?" she asked, wincing.

"Hear what?" Finn asked.

"The screaming," she whispered. Her eyes scanned the tree line in front of them.

Finn shook his head.

"It must be the spirits. Maybe she never made it to Wolf's Keep. If that's the case, the monsters of the Dark Wood could have stolen the wandering souls," Cade said solemnly.

"What does that mean?" Rowan asked.

Finn looked startled by her conversation with someone invisible. She'd never fully explained to him about Cade, and she would not make time for it now. It was unlikely he'd approve of her friendship with a demon.

"It means that those souls won't find peace unless they escape to town for the next ferrying. If they get lost in the woods, they'll become wraiths—shadow creatures that lose their sense of identity and are cursed to haunt the woods eternally. There are also evil entities in the forest that gain power by devouring lost souls," Cade whispered.

Rowan hurried to catch up with Finn as they approached a group of huntsmen waiting at the edge of the forest. The sea of huntsmen parted, and Rowan looked at the ground, allowing herself one more moment before her world fell apart.

"Red," the men around her murmured, hands crossed over the heart before they opened cupped palms to her—a sign of reverence toward the new Red Maiden.

Finally, Rowan forced herself to look down the trail.

Only about fifty feet into the forest, Orla's crumpled body lay in the center of the trail. Rowan blinked the tears from her eyes, quickly swiping away any that escaped with her fingers. The screaming was even louder as she moved closer, but the sight of her dead friend blotted out everything else.

"If it's too much," Finn started, "we can—"

"No, I can do it. She deserves the honor of a burial," Rowan said. She took a step over the border into the Dark Wood and waited. Nothing happened. She continued with Cade beside her.

"Anything unusual?" she asked him.

He gave her a half-hearted smile. "Other than the screeching, you mean?"

"Yes, other than that."

"Not that I can tell," Cade said.

Rowan closed the distance to Orla's body and paused, studying her friend. Orla's blonde hair was spread out around her like a perfect golden halo, and her arms were crossed over her chest with a rose trapped beneath them. Her red cloak was noticeably absent. The pallor of her skin was disturbingly ghostly. Rowan had heard people say that those who'd recently passed just looked like they were sleeping, but Orla didn't look like she was sleeping. She looked empty in a way that opened up a well of grief in Rowan's chest.

She tried to turn down the volume on her emotions and just focus on the scene. There was no blood on the ground around Orla, but when Rowan bent low, she spotted a bite mark on her neck. It wasn't large and deep, as if from the jaws of a wolf, but small and human. Blood crusted the mark, but there was no other sign of violence. Rowan was relieved that she hadn't been torn apart by one of the monsters that lurked off the main trail. Orla knew better than to wander from the trail. It was one of the first things they were taught when they were young Maidens.

It had to have been the work of the Wolf. Orla was just a few months from the end of her service. It seemed he wasn't content to let her live beyond it.

Rowan knelt and checked her friend's pulse, confirming what she already knew—Orla was gone.

"What happened to you, Orla?" Rowan rasped.

She crossed her hands over her heart and said a prayer to the Mother, then a prayer to the Wolf. Although they weren't popular, prayers to the Wolf existed, and Rowan figured if she wanted to pray for the repose of the soul of her friend, it made sense to pray to the god of death. She opened her hands in front of her heart, offering her sorrow up to whatever god or goddess might take it, but it brought her no peace.

She pulled Orla's body up to a sitting position.

"Mother help me. She's heavy," Rowan grunted.

"I can help," Cade said.

"Okay, but you have to make it look smooth, like I'm doing it. I just need to get her onto my back, and then I should be able to do the rest myself," Rowan said.

Still on her knees, she turned and pulled Orla's arms over her shoulders. Her body wasn't even rigid yet, and her skin didn't feel completely cold. Rowan tried to banish the thought that Orla could have been killed while Rowan was in her morning meditation or while she and Aeoife were walking to the bakery. She flicked her hands as though physically trying to shake off the thought.

Cade boosted Orla up, and Rowan came to standing. She bent forward slightly so that most of Orla's weight was on her back.

"Sarai's vision was correct after all," Cade said solemnly.

Rowan said nothing, but she'd been thinking the same thing since she realized Orla hadn't returned from her trip the night before.

Rowan's steps were heavy as she struggled under Orla's lifeless weight. Her hood tugged back from her face slightly, and she fumbled to tug it down. A scream erupted near her in the forest.

"Cade?"

"Just go," he said, turning to face the sound.

Rowan wasn't entirely sure what being a demon meant in terms of his powers other than his ability to spur on more gossip and increase jealousy and envy. If he thought he could help somehow, she wasn't about to argue with him. She staggered the last few steps to the edge of the Dark Wood, her hood nearly all the way off of her face. Most of the huntsmen backed away from her, as if death was contagious, but Finn stepped forward and carefully took Orla's body from her.

Rowan immediately tugged her hood back into place.

"Did you notice anything strange?" one of the huntsmen asked.

"Other than my dead friend?" Rowan retorted bitterly.

"I'll escort the Red Maiden back to the temple," Finn said.

The rest of the huntsmen murmured in agreement. They seemed relieved they didn't have to do it themselves. It was strange to be treated with both reverence and wariness—like a cursed object. Rowan supposed she should get used to it. She was the acting Red Maiden now, even if she hadn't yet been initiated.

She wordlessly followed behind Finn as he carried Orla's body up the stairs and into the Temple of the Mother, where the elders were already gathered. He laid her body on the altar and the elders shuffled closer.

"So it's true," Elder Falon said.

"Yes, Elder. None of us could cross the border to retrieve the body, but Ro—the new Red Maiden was kind enough to do it for us." Finn sketched a reverent bow as he settled Orla's body on the altar.

She looked like a true human sacrifice, which was exactly what she was to them. Orla was a twenty-five-year-old woman who should have had her whole life ahead of her after five years of hard service. She had courage, but to those men, she was an acceptable loss. Rowan was certain every single one of them lacked the fortitude to walk into the Dark Wood alone—to greet the Wolf and make their way back in the darkness with nothing to keep them company but the sounds of the monsters that lurked in the shadows off of the trail.

Rowan turned away and left them, unable to stand the hatred in her heart at the sight of them bent over her dead friend.

She emerged back into the daylight and found Cade waiting on the stairs. He refused to go into the Temple of the Mother. He insisted it wasn't because he couldn't, but because he simply didn't like it in there.

"What did they say?" Cade asked, falling into step beside her.

"I need to be alone," she mumbled, waving her hand to dismiss him. He disappeared without question.

She trudged toward Maiden's Tower with leaden limbs and opened the tower door.

"Rowan, wait—" Finn jogged across the cobblestones.

She paused on the threshold until Finn ducked inside.

"You can't be here," she muttered as she turned away.

Rowan didn't want him to see. She didn't understand what she felt, just that it was too much to bear, and she needed to get it together before Aeoife saw her. The years had made her adept at pushing anything too strong away and processing it when she was alone.

"Please, I just want to be alone," she pleaded.

Finn placed a hand on her shoulder. "Row, you shouldn't be alone. I'm so sorry I had to ask you to do that. You shouldn't have had to. I'm sorry about Orla."

He pulled her into a tight hug. Her first instinct was to push him away. They were standing in the open great room at the entrance of

Maiden's Tower, but she wanted comfort. After carrying her friend's corpse out of the Dark Wood, it was the least she deserved.

She let Finn hold her. She buried her face in his chest and sobbed. It felt good to have someone to cling to when her world was crumbling.

It surprised her how easy it was to relax into his touch. His hands were the ones that had saved her from a riptide when they met. The hands that had taught her to hunt with a bow and navigate the woods using the moss on trees and the stars. Finn's hands were the first hands that dared to reach out and treat her as more than just a sacrifice. She wanted so badly to believe the hope they held, but hope was elusive after such a terrible day.

"It's going to be okay," Finn said, brushing his fingers through her hair. "I won't let that happen to you."

If Finn wanted to believe that, he could, but they both knew the truth deep down. In a week, when she walked into the Dark Wood to ferry the souls of the dead to Wolf's Keep, she'd have to do it alone. Finn couldn't protect her, even if he wanted to.

Whether she liked it or not, Rowan was on her own.

4

ROWAN

Rowan stood in front of the mirror as a seamstress tucked and pinned the delicate white silk at her hem. Her grief showed in her wan appearance and the dark circles under her eyes. Sleep had been a challenge between Aeoife's nightly presence in her bed and Rowan's own nightmares.

The white silk dress made her look like a ghost. It was the first garment made specifically for Rowan instead of a hand-me-down. Something inherited wouldn't do for a new gift to the Wolf.

Rowan felt numb. She was so caught up in the whirlwind of becoming acting Red Maiden that there was little time to grieve Orla. Time marched on. Death stopped for no man or woman.

The village was restless over the blight. Frantic whispers followed Rowan whenever she walked through town. People looked at her like she was their salvation. She floated through her days like she was living a visceral nightmare.

Rowan winced as another needle jabbed her ankle.

"Sorry, dear," the seamstress mumbled. She blotted the blood before it could stain the fabric. She came to stand next to Rowan, and they both stared into the mirror.

"What do you think?" the seamstress inquired.

"Where is the rest of it?" Rowan asked.

She was meant to look tempting, but the dress left very little to the imagination. The delicate white silk did nothing to keep out a chill. Lace accented a sweetheart neckline that curved around her full breasts, and a slit up the right leg nearly reached her hip, leaving her assets more on display than ever.

"I'll freeze before I reach Wolf's Keep," Rowan murmured.

"Nonsense. You'll be moving quickly and singing. You'll have your red cloak, so you'll be plenty warm," Mrs. Teverin said.

Mrs. Teverin had tutored Rowan since she first came to the tower. She was a formidable woman, her family having served as the official tutors of Red Maidens for generations. The tutor had an air of authority that even urged the elders to sit up straighter. She was not known for her patience or kindness. Mrs. Teverin's idea of warmth was using their names instead of just calling them each "Red." Rowan looked at the deep creases in the woman's olive skin and wondered exactly how many Maidens she'd sent to their death.

Rowan tugged on the lace, trying to get it to cover more of her cleavage. She was grateful she'd left Cade to keep Aeoife company. She couldn't imagine what he'd say about her new look.

"Honestly, Rowan. I don't know what you're fussing about. You have a beautiful body that the Wolf is sure to find very pleasing," Mrs. Teverin scolded.

"It's just that I'll be in front of the whole town first," Rowan said.

Mrs. Teverin frowned in confusion. "You are a sacred vessel. If anyone from town has impure thoughts in seeing you, that's between them and the Mother."

Rowan shrugged, and the sleeves slid down her shoulders. She shivered as she stared at her reflection. She'd expected to somehow look different, but she was met with the same bright green eyes, wide with fear and anxiety. Her auburn hair was pinned up neatly in an intricate hairstyle to practice for the night of and for the elders to give final approval of the sacrifice before she was sent into the woods in a few days.

"Are you ready for me to let the elders in for their approval?

They're busy men, and they haven't got all day. I understand it's an adjustment, but you're probably as comfortable as you'll ever be, Rowan," Mrs. Teverin cautioned.

Rowan swallowed hard and nodded.

"Good girl," Mrs. Teverin said, nodding her approval.

Rowan stood still as Mrs. Teverin opened the door and the five elders entered. They circled her like sharks taking in pathetic prey.

Elder Garrett, the newest and youngest of the elders, paused in front of her. His gaze passed over her slowly, making her skin crawl. If he didn't look so delighted at her discomfort, she might have found him handsome. He couldn't have been older than thirty, with smooth, pale skin, dark brown hair, and even darker eyes. The predatory way his gaze followed her, even when her hood was up, had always made Rowan so uncomfortable, but this was much worse.

"Can we make the bust any tighter?" he asked the seamstress.

"Sir, if we make it much tighter, it might split when she moves," the seamstress said tentatively. Still, she moved behind Rowan and tugged on the strings at the back of the dress so that it clung to her breasts even more.

As the men nodded in approval, Rowan's cheeks burned and she wished she was anywhere else. The Dark Wood might have been preferable to being leered at by a group of men, most of whom were old enough to be her father.

"You've done a marvelous job, Mrs. Teverin. I'll expect Rowan to meet me in my office at noon on Friday for last-minute approval," Elder Garrett said.

Alarm bells rang in Rowan's head because the words sounded like a threat, but Mrs. Teverin nodded as if nothing was amiss, so Rowan simply clasped her shaking hands.

With that, the men filed out of the room, and Rowan let out the breath she'd been holding since the seamstress tightened her dress.

"No need to be nervous, dear. The worst is over," Mrs. Teverin sighed.

Rowan wished that was true.

"I HOPE you appreciate me making an exception to my rule of going into this monstrosity," Cade said as he stepped into the Temple of the Mother and sneered at the white marble aisle leading up to the altar.

"Thank you for suffering through the view of an extravagant temple, Cade. Your friendship knows no bounds," Rowan said dryly, making her way down the aisle toward the elders' offices behind the sanctuary.

They had jammed her entire week with final tutoring sessions on manners, etiquette, and sexual instruction. She'd learned more sex positions than she ever thought possible, and every time, she felt a strange humiliation for needing to be tutored in intimacy to begin with.

She fidgeted in front of Elder Garrett's door. She'd been dreading this final approval since he'd mentioned it on Wednesday.

A warning Orla had once given her rang in her ears. "*Be careful with Elder Garrett. Try not to be alone with him if you can avoid it.*" Orla had always been private, so it wasn't surprising that she gave Rowan no further context.

"I don't like this," Cade said, leaning against the doorframe. "Let's just go play in the woods. It's not like they're going to send Aeoife instead. They can't exactly choose to send no one, and the Wolf is clearly already pissed. You're their only option."

"What do you think happens if I ignore his request?" she challenged. "You didn't need to come."

Cade shivered, his hazel eyes shifting down the hallway behind her. "I know. This place gives me the creeps. It feels more like a tomb than a place of worship. I just have a bad feeling about this."

She sighed. Cade having a "bad feeling" was not a good sign, but she didn't see how she could leave now.

She knocked on the door and sighed as Elder Garrett's voice beckoned her in.

"Rowan, you're right on time." Elder Garrett smiled. "Come in. Have a seat on the settee."

He got up from behind his desk and crossed the room. He sat so close to Rowan that their thighs brushed. She scooted away so there was slightly more space between them.

"What do you need for your final approval, Elder Garrett? I'm sorry to say that Mrs. Teverin has me on quite a tight schedule today, and I need to be back for extra afternoon prayer and meditation soon," she said.

Elder Garrett smiled wolfishly. "How devout of you. You can take off your cloak. It's just the two of us, and I've already seen you."

She cautiously slid her hood back and loosened the ties on her cloak before shrugging it onto the settee next to her.

"That's better. Now tell me, do you feel prepared for your journey?" He rested a hand on her knee.

"Whoa, what's he doing?" Cade asked.

She shot the demon a dirty look.

"Sir?" Rowan looked at the elder's hand, unsure if this was some kind of final test she needed to pass. "No man is supposed to touch me before the Wolf."

His hand slid slightly higher, the heat of it like a brand, even through the thick wool of her dress. "Yes, but whose job do you think it is to give you a final inspection to ensure we aren't sending the Wolf a tainted Maiden?"

Rowan's mouth went dry. "I'm not sure I understand what you mean."

Even as she said the words, dread settled in her stomach like a stone.

"I need to inspect your body to make sure that no man has had what belongs to the Wolf," Elder Garrett said matter-of-factly.

Rowan looked toward the door, every muscle in her tensed, preparing to run.

He clicked his tongue. "Rowan, this is standard procedure. If it wasn't, Mrs. Teverin wouldn't have sent you here now."

If that was true, why hadn't Mrs. Teverin warned her this would happen? She'd prepared Rowan for likely scenarios with the Wolf. She'd learned how to please any appetite the Wolf might possess, but never once had anyone suggested that she'd be subjected to a final—apparently physical—inspection by one of the elders.

"Ah, you're just trying to be obedient, I understand. Mrs. Teverin doesn't tell the girls so that we can ensure that they've complied. It's about free will and a test of character," Elder Garrett said. "We need to know that our Red Maidens are chaste and pious without the threat of being found out. Choices matter, Rowan. You have free will."

She nearly laughed at the idea of choice. As if she'd ever had a choice to be something other than what she was. She would have chosen anything else.

"You could have easily experimented with a boy from the village by now," Elder Garrett continued. "You're twenty years old, and it wouldn't be unheard of for you to experience urges. You're a beautiful woman and a commodity. I'd be shocked if men hadn't propositioned you by now."

Rowan shook her head. "Sir, I assure you. I've never done anything like that."

Elder Garrett caught her trembling chin in his hand. "While I'm sure that you're telling the truth, I wouldn't be doing my job if I took you at your word. I wouldn't be doing my duty to the Mother and the people of Ballybrine if I didn't make absolutely certain. Now, I need you to take off your dress."

Rowan cringed. Only a man like Elder Garrett would think that his duty to the Mother required violating her.

"Sir, I really don't think that Mrs. Teverin would want me to. She was very emphatic that I shouldn't let any man touch me or see me in any state of undress. If this is some kind of test, I—"

Elder Garrett squeezed her chin harder. "Consider this a test of your obedience to your elders. Now stand up and take off your dress so I can inspect you. I won't touch, but I need to look."

Rowan stood slowly and clumsily tried to work the buttons on the front of her bodice. The elder's hungry gaze burned into her, and she closed her eyes to shut him out. When she reached the bottom button, she dropped her hand, bunching her fingers nervously in the fabric of her dress.

"Open your eyes and hold your dress open so I can see," Elder Garrett said. He took a step toward her, and she instinctively stepped back, bumping against his desk. The room suddenly felt much too small, and she wished she was anywhere else. "Rowan, hold your dress open so I can inspect your breasts—and open your eyes. You're making this more difficult than it needs to be."

She swallowed, but she couldn't bear to open her eyes.

"Fine," Elder Garrett barked. "Your hesitance is defiance. I'm going to need to do a physical inspection to be sure. Come here."

Rowan's eyes shot open, and she stared at him. "Sir?"

"This is insane. Don't do that," Cade snapped.

She looked at the demon desperately, her hand clutching at the gaping neckline of her dress, unsure what choice she had. She couldn't exactly storm out in such a disheveled state.

"What does the examination entail?" She hated the way her voice shook.

Elder Garrett smiled. "The Mother will give me the vision to see what I need to see—any sins."

Cade laughed. "No way, Rowan. Run! Get out of here! There's no way the Mother would sanction a creepy man looking at a young virgin to make sure she's pure. Ask him how he knows what the Mother wants."

"How—how do you know the Mother wants that?" Rowan asked.

Elder Garrett's brow drew in, and his face pinched. "You dare to question me, girl!"

He backhanded her so fast she landed in a heap on the floor. She sat up, rubbing her smarting jaw.

"Kneel," Elder Garrett gritted out.

Rowan met his gaze with barely contained fury. She forced herself to kneel.

"Pull your dress open. You should be grateful I'm willing to do this. I am a prophet of the Mother, and you'll do whatever I say, whenever I say to do it."

She choked down the shame as her hands came to the top of her dress. She couldn't get them to move. Elder Garrett swallowed hard as he watched. Rowan trembled so violently she worried she'd pass out.

"Look at me," Elder Garrett commanded. She blinked away humiliated tears as she met his eyes. "This is between me, you, and the Mother. Even if you tell someone else, they won't believe you. You're nothing but death's whore. Now open your dress."

Rowan was frozen in terror.

"No way! Don't do that, Row! This is too messed up, even for me," Cade said. "Tell him the Mother is speaking to you, and she's angry."

"S-s-sir, the Mother is speaking to me, and she's furious," Rowan said shakily.

Elder Garrett's eyes went wide. "You dare to blaspheme! You little liar! You're further gone than I realized! Don't worry. I'll give you a comprehensive cleansing—"

Before he could move, Cade shoved everything off of the elder's desk and threw a glass vase across the room.

"Goddess above!" Elder Garrett shouted. His wide eyes met Rowan's. "You did this!"

"Sir, I didn't. The Mother's will be done," Rowan said reverently.

Elder Garrett stared at her, his face red with fury, but his eyes showed a hint of fear. "Get out of my sight before I change my mind."

Rowan shot to her feet and stumbled out the door with her cloak in hand. She tugged it tight around her still-unbuttoned bodice and didn't stop to button it until she was safely inside Maiden's Tower. She leaned her head back against the wall in the hallway, and Cade stood next to her.

"Thank you," she whispered.

"That man is a problem," Cade grumbled. "These elders are all pretenders. *I'm* more devout than they are. He just wanted to jerk off on your virgin tits."

Rowan's stomach turned over at the thought of it. The act was one of the things she'd been taught about in tutoring as it was something the Wolf might demand, but experiencing the threat of it firsthand from another was degrading.

40

Her mind spun wildly. "I have to get out of here. I need air. I feel like I'm suffocating."

She fumbled with the rest of the buttons on her dress as Mrs. Teverin walked around the corner. She drew up short when she saw how disheveled Rowan looked.

"Mrs. Teverin, it's not what it looks like—" Rowan started.

"I wasn't born yesterday, Rowan, and I know enough to suspect what it is. Are you all right?" It was the first time the woman had been the least bit compassionate with her.

"I wasn't really supposed to let him do anything to me, was I?" Rowan asked.

Mrs. Teverin gave her a grim smile. "No, you weren't. Don't you worry. He'll keep his mouth shut because he knows what's good for him. If he doesn't, I'll have something to say about it. Forget your afternoon plans. Take some time for yourself and calm down."

"Thank you, Mrs. Teverin," Rowan said.

It was the smallest kindness, but it meant the world to Rowan. She took off down the hall before the woman could change her mind, swapping her red cloak for the plain green one she used when she snuck out. Then she tore through town until she reached Finn's apartment. She frantically banged on the door until it flew open.

"Rowan, what's wrong?" Finn asked. "Come in."

He beckoned her inside and peeked down the hall to make sure no one had seen her before closing the door.

"I need your help, Finn. I—" She felt ready to burst with rage and panic.

"What happened?" Finn asked.

Rowan burst into tears as she explained what Elder Garrett had done.

"He had no right to do that, and he should never have put you in that position. He needs to be held accountable." Finn jumped to his feet.

Rowan caught his hand and pulled him back down. "Finn, it's my word against his. No one but you will believe me. And if they find out, it could ruin me. He could lie and say that I'm impure or that I've laid with a man and confessed it to him. It would put both me and Aeoife at risk."

"We can't let this stand. We have to do something!" Finn said.

Rowan understood his outrage. He'd never met a problem he couldn't solve with wealth, influence, or courage. She might have been accustomed to powerlessness, but Finn was new to it.

"Finn, I can't move through the world as you do. You're the first son of a lord, and I'm no one. I can't count on anyone to listen to me—"

The furrow in Finn's brow softened and his shoulders relaxed. He cupped her face in his hands. "You're not no one to me," he said. "You're everything, Row. I—" He stopped himself, but she could practically hear the unspoken words.

It was selfish to want to hear them when she didn't feel the same way. Still, she longed for them. She clung to the hope in those words like it was an anchor.

He tucked her hair behind her ear and left his hand on her cheek, the tender touch in contrast to the rough, callused feel of his palm. She didn't mind that the only gentleness in her life came with its own rough edges. It suited her just fine.

Rowan wasn't certain that she wanted Finn as much as she was certain she wanted to choose something for herself. The words burst out of her before she could stop them.

"Finn, will you take me to bed?"

His eyes went wide in surprise, but he said nothing.

Rowan blushed and pressed on. "I know what you're thinking. Yes, I'm terrified by what happened, but you're the only person I trust with this. You'll be gentle and kind. I know you care about me, and I want this. I want just one thing in my life to be a choice."

Finn looked for a moment like he might give in, but then he ran a hand through his hair and shook his head. "Row, I'm sorry. It's not that I don't want to. Trust me, I do. But I would be no better than Elder Garrett if I did that."

Rowan stood with a start. "Yes, you would. I'm asking you to. He tried to take with no permission. I have no power over anything in my life. I've never asked you for anything. Please, just let me make this choice for myself. Everything else in my life just *happens* to me, but this is something I could *choose*."

Finn faltered as he stood and stopped her pacing. "You're going to survive this," he insisted. "You're going to make it to five years, and I'm going to make an honest woman of you. I want to marry you, Rowan."

Too many years had passed since a Red Maiden had survived her five-year term for Rowan to believe she'd be an exception, or that the words were anything but a romantic promise to a doomed woman.

She needed him to see reason—force him, even, to see the fact that she'd never particularly wanted marriage, which seemed more a prison than a boon to her.

Though Finn differed from most men in Ballybrine, she was certain they didn't want the same things. He saw her wild wandering as charming now, but it was clear he'd want her settled once they were married. All men wanted a wild woman until it was time to be tame. After being controlled her whole life, she couldn't imagine willingly agreeing to be docile forever. She couldn't imagine herself as the Lady Ashand, hosting stifling parties for fancy lords and ladies in Ballybrine.

Still, she let Finn entertain the fantasy because it was easier than trying to say goodbye to him.

Rowan met his blue eyes. He cupped her face in his hands, tilted her chin up, and kissed her. She'd never been kissed before. His lips were soft and warm against hers.

Finn tangled his hands in her hair as her heart beat against her rib cage like it was trying to escape. She gripped his shirt, pulling him closer. He tasted like peppermint—a fresh and invigorating taste that suited him so well she found herself eager for more. Her hands bunched in his tunic.

Finn's hands clasped around her wrists, and he pulled away.

"Rowan, I can't do more," he whispered breathlessly. He brushed a hand through his hair in frustration. "It's not that I don't want to. Trust me, I do. But I won't break a rule that could get you into trouble. I'm a believer. I'm not selfish enough to be the reason the Wolf is unhappy and comes to town to reap souls. My greatest fear is that you would be the one to pay for such a sin. Rowan, I want to, but I will not risk you or anyone else to satisfy a passing desire. I know you are afraid, but we will have plenty of time when your service is over, and I will make it up to you."

Rowan turned away and leaned her forehead against the cool, rough stone of the wall. Despair crept into her.

"I'm sorry," Finn whispered, placing a hand on her shoulder.

She shrugged it off. "It's fine. It was silly of me to ask," she said tightly. She grabbed her cloak and started toward the door, but Finn blocked her way.

"Please don't be mad at me," he begged.

Rowan frowned, stepping farther away from him. "Please don't ask me to give you absolution when I'm the one who's terrified. Tomorrow I'm going to march through the Dark Wood alone, with a bunch of spirits on my tail. I'll walk by the place where one of my only friends in this world died just a week ago. I'll go to Wolf's Keep, singing like my life depends on it. And then I'll be subjected to whatever depraved thing he wants. I'll never know what it is to be treated with compassion or gentleness. I may never get a chance to know what it is to be touched by someone who cares for me. If I have to deal with that knowledge, you may as well share the burden."

Rowan yanked on her cloak and pushed by him, slamming the door before he could say another word. As she cut through the cold afternoon, angry tears streamed down her face. She made her way back to the tower and snuck in through the servant's entrance, tucking her green cloak in its hiding place and making her way back to her practice and meditation space. She locked the door of the soundproof room and slumped to the floor.

Knees drawn into her chest, she buried her face in her hands and sobbed. She cried for the dream that Finn tried to sell her. She cried for the part of her that wanted to believe so badly that it could truly happen. Most of all, she cried because she wasn't even sure she'd want it if she could have it, and that made her feel like an ungrateful wretch.

5

ROWAN

Saturday blew in faster than a gale off the sea.

Dread crept through Rowan's bones like a winter chill as she lay in bed and stared at the cracks in the ceiling. Sleep had been elusive.

In some small way, it was a relief to have the certainty of knowing her time had come. She'd been waiting fifteen years for it, and at least she could find peace in the fact that her first trip into the Dark Wood would happen at sundown.

If the sunlight streaming through her curtains was any indication, she had very little time until her mother and sisters showed up to help get her ready for her presentation to the town and her journey through the Dark Wood. She dreaded seeing her family almost as much as meeting the Wolf.

Rowan knew they loved her as best they could, but it never felt like enough.

Her earliest memories were of her mother bragging to neighbors that Rowan had been born on the summer solstice—the brightest day of the year in Eireione—as if her birth alone showed her distance from darkness.

It was hard to pick one particular moment when her mother's

attitude had changed. Perhaps it shifted as they slowly starved, or when she realized that a spirit singer daughter would solve all of their financial problems at once. Regardless, somewhere along the way, her mother had stopped seeing Rowan as a daughter and started seeing her as a means to an end. Her mother's betrayal was like the sun, always hanging over her, blinding her to everything else.

Anger had always been safest for Rowan. Better that than the heaviness of grief or the startling emptiness of betrayal. The years since hadn't entirely trained the softness out of her, but they did bury it deep.

Rowan stood and crossed the room, throwing the curtains open. She opened the balcony door and stepped out into the daylight, casting a glance at Orla's balcony next door as though she expected to see her friend standing there.

The icy cold of the stone cut into her bare feet, but she welcomed the hurt. She gazed out at the Dark Wood below. The blighted trees stretched as far as she could see, but a dense fog still hung over the forest, preventing her from seeing how far it went. She puzzled over what it meant if the Dark Wood was dying and the monsters in the wood were gaining strength by devouring souls. Old magic should protect the trail she'd walk, but it hadn't protected Orla.

Perhaps it was the immediacy of her doom—staring down her mortality—her very proximity to death—that finally stirred something to life inside her. She felt desperate for more. Rowan wanted to dig her nails into her life and hold on. She wanted to learn everything that Sarai knew about herbs. She wanted to learn to sing more than just service hymns and local pub songs. Maybe no one else expected her to want more, but something inside her was growing too large to be contained. She was consumed by the fear that she would simply disappear from the hearts and minds of the people she loved the second she died.

She stepped back into her bedroom, closing the balcony doors behind her.

Cade slumped into the plush chair by the fire. He was always slumping into something, as if holding himself upright was impossible. His raven hair spilled messily over his forehead, and his unlaced tunic hung open, revealing a crisp white shirt beneath.

"You could run," he said.

"And go where?" Rowan laughed bitterly. "Even the Borderwood is impassable. It's too late in the season. I'd freeze before I reached another town," she lamented.

Cade frowned. "That's not necessarily true. Didn't Finn teach you how to navigate the woods? We'd just keep going until we found a new town. I would be with you the whole time."

"And together we'd wander into a new religious stronghold that executes those who practice the old ways," Rowan said. "Even if I ran, I couldn't manage myself and Aeoife, and if I left her behind, they'd have no choice but to send her in my place." She shook her head. "Is this a demon thing? Like you don't want me to go to the Wolf because it will somehow mess with the Mother?"

"No—I don't want you to go to the Wolf because you're my friend. If I were truly evil, I'd happily allow you to be devoured. That seems like the most evil thing," Cade sighed. "No, wait. The most evil thing would be letting that creepy elder have you."

Rowan paled.

"Too soon?" Cade asked.

"It doesn't seem very evil to save me," Rowan challenged.

"I never claimed to be evil or to want to save you," Cade said. "I just think it's fascinating that these people think they're holy for sacrificing a young virgin to save themselves from the Wolf's wrath. Death is part of life, and they know it. Just because they have some deal with him doesn't mean they should all be spared in exchange for giving him your virtue and life. The last time I checked, human sacrifice wasn't exactly virtuous."

Rowan lifted a brow. "You mean you wouldn't enjoy leading a Maiden to be devoured by a death god?"

"*Devoured*," Cade repeated, rolling his eyes.

That was the word that was used in the Mother's scripture. The Wolf would *devour* her. The elders believed in the importance of words, and they chose one that meant the Wolf would eat her greedily and ravenously—that he would use up and destroy her, or prey upon her and enjoy it.

She might have spent the last fifteen years being sculpted into a perfect sacrifice, but she was fairly certain that no amount of preparation would make her feel ready for that.

"What are you dreading more—the Dark Wood or your mother?" Cade asked.

Rowan laughed. "The Dark Wood."

He smiled. "I thought for sure you'd say your mother."

"She is not *that* bad," Rowan argued. She wasn't sure why she felt a need to defend the mother who had never protected her.

"Don't forget how my powers work. That woman is one of the most envious people I've ever met," Cade said, rolling his eyes. His proclivity as a demon tended toward inspiring envy, which also meant he could recognize it in others and help it grow, if he was so inclined.

"She wasn't always like that," Rowan said.

Cade cocked his head to the side. "Yes, but she got a taste of wealth all for your sacrifice, and now she chases after status mindlessly."

Rowan sighed. "I don't want to talk about this anymore. I'm not going anywhere. My mother is a necessary evil of this day. After that, I won't need to see her again unless she surprises us and attends a visitation."

"You're the one doing the big, scary thing. You shouldn't have to spend the day before pandering," Cade snapped.

"When have I ever had a choice?"

He opened his mouth to speak, but a knock at the door cut him off.

"Miss Rowan, your family is here for breakfast," a servant called through the door.

"Let the fun begin," Rowan said dryly as the door opened and the group of Cleary women bustled in.

Rowan took in her mother in her fine red wool dress. Her auburn hair was arranged immaculately, all hints of silver rinsed away with a beet wash. Rowan's sisters, Maeve and Shaina, paraded in behind their mother in elaborately embroidered scarlet dresses that brought out the red in their darker hair. Tonight they'd look the part of a proud family, even if they hadn't been to visit in months.

Maeve was four years older than Rowan and married to a wealthy man who ran fishing routes around the entire island of Eireione. They had two sons whom Rowan had never met. Shaina was two years older and newly married to a man whose family owned three pubs in Ballybrine, and she was pregnant with their first child.

"Darling, you look a fright," her mother said.

"I forgot how charming she is," Cade said from his perch by the fire.

Rowan's sisters awkwardly hugged her, as if she was a stranger and not the baby sister they should have spent their lives taking care of.

"Mother, honestly, is that any way to greet her?" Maeve placed a hand on Rowan's shoulder. "Ryan and Jack send their love. Ryan is running his own small fleet these days, and Jack is managing all of Megan's father's estate."

"Of course," Rowan said. "Life goes on."

Rowan wished she could have been alone, but it was the job of the new Red Maiden's family and a team of hair stylists and servants to prepare her for her inaugural journey.

Rowan crossed her arms. "I'm sorry that I didn't sleep well the night before my devouring, Mother. I suppose you all have your work cut out for you."

"Let's get to it, then," her mother said, and a team of servants and stylists descended upon Rowan.

———

ROWAN BLINKED SEVERAL TIMES, trying to recognize herself in the woman in the looking glass.

After her steaming hot bath, the servants buffed her skin and groomed her to painful perfection, plucking her brows and brushing and styling her hair until it felt like it might fall out. It was almost as bad as when they'd arrived two days before with a sugar paste to remove all hair from the lower half of her body. That pain alone was enough to make her fear death slightly less.

When the team of servants and stylists was satisfied with her appearance, they left her alone with her mother and sisters. She carefully dressed in the obscene white lace undergarments the seamstress had provided, and then her mother and sisters helped her into the silk dress, cinching it with ties at the back so that it clung to her curves.

Now, she stared at their handiwork in disbelief. Her long, curly hair was twisted into an intricate braid draped over one shoulder and woven through with tiny white flowers. They'd rubbed her lips with a beet stain to brighten them.

"You look beautiful," her mother said appreciatively, running a hand over the silk gown as if it was a wedding dress and not sacrificial garb for a virgin.

Rowan supposed that's what all wedding dresses were.

"You look like a doll," Cade said from where he leaned against the wall by the fire.

The clang of a bell outside—the first of three that let the people of Ballybrine know it was time to gather for the weekly Gratitude and Grieving Ceremony—saved her from having to respond.

"We should go," Maeve said. She and Shaina helped Rowan into her red cloak.

Rowan took one last look at herself and led them out of her room. In the hall, she found Aeoife waiting.

"Rowie, you look so pretty," Aeoife said, her blue eyes glassy with unshed tears.

"Thank you, Aeoife. You'll be okay on your own tonight, right? I'll be back when you wake up in the morning," Rowan said. She struggled for confidence she didn't feel, but she hoped that it was true for Aeoife's sake.

Aeoife's eyes passed nervously over Rowan's sisters and mother.

"Is it okay if I wait in your room until you get back?" She tried so hard to hold herself together, but her lower lip trembled.

Rowan pulled her into a hug. "Don't worry, okay? I'll see you in the morning, and if I can't be back, I'll send Cade."

Her mother's eyes widened in horror, her gaze darting around the room at the mention of the demon.

Cade chuckled next to her. "What, did she think I would abandon you like she did?"

Rowan gave Aeoife a light pat on the shoulder, pulled up her hood, and made her way out into the square outside Maiden's Tower.

Townsfolk were already congregating in the gathering dark. The elders waited on the dais by the temple stairs. Rowan led her family through the crowd of unfamiliar faces, all of them eager to get a glance at her.

Once she was on the dais, she took a breath and closed her eyes. She blocked out everything, connecting with the stillness inside her that allowed her to be an object instead of a person. She slid the mask of a perfect sacrifice into place—calm, confident smile, blank eyes, head held high. Rowan stood tall against her fear; against the assessing gazes of the town; against the terror that grew in her stomach.

You chose to stay. This was your choice, she reminded herself as a bell tolled overhead, calling the town to the ceremony.

As if there had ever been an option other than to stay and play the only role anyone had ever expected of her.

The crowd looked at her like she was their salvation and she hated them for it. The same people who'd fled religious persecution and death in places where the monotheistic religion was rising were content to see her suffer for their beliefs.

There, gathered for the ceremony, it was easy to see differences in the crowd. Though they wore varied clothing, had different skin tones and hairstyles, they were all united as much by their oppression as they were by their beliefs.

A chilly breeze rustled the leafless branches of the blighted trees at the trailhead across the square that led to Wolf's Keep. Rowan kept her hood in place with one hand, shivering as Elder Falon came to stand beside her.

"By the grace of the Mother, we are here today," Elder Falon said, his voice rising above the din of whispers. He waited for the crowd to quiet. "We've presented our offering, and our Red Maiden was deemed worthy of devouring by the Wolf of the Dark Wood. Let us rejoice about that."

A cheer went up through the crowd, lauding Orla's death. Orla wasn't a person to them. She was a magical object—a buffer between them and the evil that lurked in the Dark Wood.

Rowan was glad for her red hood for the first time in her life. It meant no one could see the horror on her face. Her stomach heaved. They would all cheer when she died, too.

Rowan wanted to scream. She wanted to rip her hood off and tell them all that Orla was a sweet girl who had loved apple cider buns and snuck into the kitchen of Hanna's bakery in town to bake scones in the little free time she had. That Orla once knitted one gigantic scarf because she didn't know how to knit anything else, but also lacked the patience to make a blanket.

She wanted to tell them that Orla had never dreamed of a life for herself because their people decided for her what her life would be when she was five years old. She wanted to tell them about Aeoife, who was still just a child, who'd cried for hours over the loss of the older Red Maiden without even thinking about the fact that she was now a heartbeat away from being a sacrifice, too.

But that was not what the people wanted to hear. Rowan's friend had died, but only the people of Ballybrine would receive comfort.

Elder Falon held up his hands in praise. "We are here to give gratitude for our health and safety. We also honor those who have passed on this week. Will the families of the departed step forward?"

A procession of people dressed in black and gray made their way to the front of the crowd and each of the elders took their time blessing the families and murmuring sympathies. When they were finished, Elder Garrett came back to stand beside Rowan.

"We are also here tonight to welcome a new Red Maiden," Elder Falon continued.

Rowan shifted as the weight of thousands of eyes fell on her.

Elder Falon placed a hand on her shoulder. "Blessed by the Mother from birth and consecrated by the Crone at five, she's been studying for fifteen years. Fifteen years of lessons, prayer, and meditation. We believe she's ready to take on the responsibility. However, if there are any who would speak against her worthiness, let them speak now or forever hold their tongues."

Rowan's eyes flew to where Finn stood with a cohort of huntsmen by the path to the Dark Wood. He opened his mouth and closed it. His arms remained helplessly crossed over his chest, knuckles white from their grip on his arms.

The silence was deafening. Rowan wasn't sure what she'd hoped would happen. If someone spoke against her, the mantle would pass to Aeoife, and that would be worse. She clasped her shaking hands to still them.

"Very well," Elder Falon said. "I now allow you to look for the first time upon her face. Let us all remember and honor the name—Rowan Cleary, your new Red Maiden."

Elder Falon lifted Rowan's hood, and for the first time, the people of her village saw her. The crowd went silent as they took her in. Hands crossed over hearts before opening to offer murmurs of thanks to the Mother. Several people went down on one knee once they finished gawking.

Their faith astonished Rowan, even though she resented it. She was the one making a sacrifice, yet it was always the Mother getting credit. All good things were attributed to the Mother, all uncertainty was soothed by the Crone, and all evil was the work of the Wolf. Red Maidens were simply the sacrifice to keep evil at bay. A small price to pay unless you were the one paying it.

Their beliefs were tidy; they didn't require critical thinking, just blind faith—something Rowan had never possessed. Maybe she would have if she was among the pretty young girls who were up for marriage this season, gathered at the front of the crowd in colorful frocks. Maybe if all she had to worry about was landing a husband and living a mindless life at his side, she'd not think critically about what her beliefs cost.

"We ask that the Crone, who is the mortal embodiment of the Mother's wisdom, step forward and give her blessing. She sees the truth in things. She sees what is for the good of all, and she steers us on this path of righteousness," Elder Falon continued.

The Crone stepped forward in her white ceremonial garb. Sarai's mouth was a tight line as she walked silently beside her mother, carrying some burning herbs. Her eyes were ringed in dark circles that mirrored Rowan's, and she wondered if her friend had been up all night as well. Only Sarai, Finn, and Aeoife felt that the people's gain was their loss.

The Crone came to a stop in front of Rowan, her eyes suddenly going cloudy with prophecy. Rowan wondered hopelessly if the Crone might see a way out for her, but her blessing was a formality. They had no one else to ferry the dead since Aeoife was so young, and as far as Rowan knew, the youngest acting Red Maiden in their history had been eighteen.

The Crone's vision seemed to sharpen and her eyes narrowed on Rowan before widening as she took a tentative step back. She swallowed hard but said nothing as she dipped her fingers in the bowl of water and blessed Rowan's forehead and heart.

At least she was blessed with a clear heart and mind as she marched to her doom.

"The Mother has given her blessing to Rowan Cleary," the Crone said with an unmistakable waver in her voice. "She will heal our dying wood and bring abundance to our village. She will please the Wolf."

A thunderous cheer rose from the crowd. Rowan watched the spirits of the departed that were scattered about the square. They seemed indifferent to the ceremony. Instead, they studied the people, trying to poke and tug at their clothes, confused by their lack of corporeal form.

She wondered what the people of Ballybrine would think if she told them how many dead crowded the square.

The Crone nodded, and Rowan turned to face her family. Her mother touched her cheek tenderly, a few tears streaming down her face in a perfect performance of elegant grief. Rowan turned away and awkwardly hugged her siblings and her father, who seemed the only one hesitant to let go. Finally, she caught Aeoife's eye and gave her a wink before turning back to the crowd.

The Crone and Elder Falon led Rowan from the stairs in front of the temple through the crowd and toward the Dark Wood. The crowd surged toward them, everyone reaching out to touch Rowan. Rowan had almost forgotten it was considered a blessing to be touched by a virgin Red Maiden.

"Thank you, Red," they whispered as their fingers brushed her hands, her shoulders, her hair.

For five minutes on the dais, she'd had a real name, but now she was simply "Red" again.

Rowan felt claustrophobic and panicked until they finally reached the edge of the Dark Wood, the crowd behind them.

"Bow your heads and pray for our sacrifice to be found acceptable. We give her up to the Mother and the Wolf," Elder Falon said. He nodded to Rowan.

Rowan met Sarai's glassy eyes and offered a half-hearted smile. They'd always known it would be this way, but it was still hard to swallow and Rowan had no idea what she would do if their positions were reversed. Sarai nodded toward the crowd, and Rowan turned to see Finn. His face was a picture of devastation, his eyes wide, his hands clenching and unclenching at his sides. She smiled at him like nothing was wrong. He tried and failed to return the smile.

The Crone placed a hand on her shoulder. "Sing now, girl."

Rowan took a deep breath, opened her mouth, and sang.

For a moment, there was nothing but the magic of her voice and the ancient song. An unnatural stillness settled in the air before the spirits began to drift toward her.

"*Follow me home,*

It need not be a lonely road.
Let your tears fall now
And wash away what came before," Rowan sang.

She turned to face the Dark Wood and shivered. She wished she was wearing something more substantial than a lace-and-silk dress, but the Wolf liked what he liked, no matter the temperature.

Rowan continued the song.

"The trail will rise to meet your feet,
Where the breeze is always at your back,
And the sun shines upon your face."

She took one last glance back at her friends before turning around and taking her first step into the dark.

6

ROWAN

Rowan forced herself to keep her eyes focused on the trail in front of her, despite the footsteps of the dead behind her and Cade beside her. The darkness swallowed up the glow from her lantern until she could only see a few feet in front of her.

Her gaze darted around the periphery, scanning the blighted branches that curved around the path like a tunnel. Dried leaves crunched under her boots, providing a percussive accompaniment to her song. A rustling to her right drew her attention, and she reminded herself of the first rule of her new existence.

Never stray from the main trail.

Her breath puffed out in front of her in tiny clouds as she sang. Rowan did not know how far she'd wandered and how much farther she had to go. The cold air of the woods seeped into her skin. She tugged her red cloak tighter around her to ward off the chill.

Rowan took solace in the fact that at least the horrific screaming that echoed through the forest a week before—when she'd retrieved Orla's body—was absent. She was left instead with an eerie silence.

She stumbled on a tree root and fell to her knees, dropping her lantern. She quickly picked up the lantern and launched back into the song, continuing her procession.

Rowan didn't dare turn toward the restless stirring of the spirits for fear of making eye contact with one of them and violating yet another rule.

Never meet the eyes of the dead or the monsters that lurk in the shadows.

If they looked into her eyes, they'd recognize that she was alive and could possess her. The song was enough to lure them in. It was a reminder of life meant to lead them to Wolf's Keep, where they'd find everlasting peace or judgment in the Underlands.

Cade trudged along, unusually silent, beside Rowan. The lack of incessant chatter from him was almost as unnerving as the Dark Wood itself.

She wondered if Orla was among the souls parading behind her and if the Wolf had killed her like everyone else seemed to think. Rowan's mind spun as she continued to lead the procession of souls.

A growl to her left ripped her from her thoughts. The hairs on the back of her neck rose, and she had the distinct feeling of being watched. It was almost impossible not to turn and look.

She froze as the third rule popped into her head.

Never bleed in the Dark Wood.

Rowan frantically checked her palms and knees for a wound from her fall. Her shoulders sagged in relief when she realized there was none.

"Easy there, Row. Take a breath and start singing," Cade said.

She shuddered as the growling grew louder. The Crone insisted that old magic protected the trail, and Rowan wouldn't be harmed as long as she stuck to it because the beasts of the dark couldn't wander beyond that boundary. If that was the case, it meant the Wolf had killed Orla and Rowan was about to meet her friend's murderer. It made little sense. Orla had insisted the Wolf wasn't what people thought he was.

Rowan drew up short. Perhaps he'd killed Orla simply for sharing what little she did with Rowan and Aeoife. It was technically a violation of the rules.

Her heartbeat pounded in her ears and her mouth went dry. It hadn't even been helpful information. It held no details at all, only meant to make her less afraid. Could the Wolf really be so vindictive that he punished Orla by taking her life for that?

"What's wrong?" Cade asked.

"Nothing," Rowan said, quickening her pace. She raised her voice even louder to drown out the growls around her. She was going to march right up to the keep, deliver the souls, and then she was going to figure out what happened to Orla.

Moonlight cut through the skeletal branches above, creating monstrous shadows on the forest floor.

"Rowan."

The voice was faint and came from just over her left shoulder.

"Orla?" Rowan asked. Her anger evaporated, leaving her with nothing but fear and confusion.

"Yes, it's me, but don't look," Orla whispered.

"I was worried that you wouldn't—" Rowan choked on her relief. She'd been afraid that Orla's soul hadn't been set free, that it would be trapped or had wandered into the woods aimlessly along with the others, destined to become a wraith.

"I'm okay now. I just wanted you to know I'm here," Orla said. "Keep singing."

Rowan sang a few more lines. They came out tight and tired as she tried to project around the lump in her throat.

"You look good, Orla," Cade said, giving her a wave.

Orla let out a surprised giggle. "Thanks, Cade."

The three of them walked side by side a few more paces.

"What happened to you?" Rowan asked.

"I don't know. It's all a blank spot," Orla said. "The Wolf told me once that souls that have traumatic deaths don't remember so that they can find peace."

Rowan could see her friend out of the corner of her eye. She looked like herself, just with a fainter, less corporeal form. Her blonde hair still moved as if rustled by the breeze.

"He did this to you. I'm going to ask him why," Rowan said.

"Row, I don't think he would do that," Orla argued.

"But he might have been mad that you told me something," Rowan countered. She continued singing the next few lines of her song.

"I think I would have remembered if it was him," Orla said. "I wish I could remember more, but I really don't. One moment I was walking down the trail, and the next, I was free from my body. I don't remember the in-between."

It was a relief she hadn't suffered, but Rowan still felt uneasy.

"I think I broke a rule."

Rowan wanted to ask more questions, but every single one vacated her mind as her gaze locked on the distant dark walls of Wolf's Keep.

"You're almost there. I just wanted you to know I'm here," Orla said.

Rowan slowed. "I'm scared."

"You'll be okay. Now make your way to the gate and bow your head and kneel as the spirits pass through," Orla instructed.

Rowan continued to sing as she neared Wolf's Keep. The blight reached all the way to its border. Large metal gates of intricately sculpted iron swung open as she approached. She tried not to stare at them, but they were the most beautiful and detailed things she'd ever seen. The winding metal vines and flowers looked more like they belonged at the entry into a beautiful garden than the realm of the god of death—or they would if it weren't for the fact that the design formed what looked like the jaws of a wolf.

Cade stilled beside her. He pressed his hands forward against an invisible boundary.

"I don't think I can go farther," he said, meeting her eyes. "There's some sort of magic to keep me out. I'm sorry, Row."

She swallowed hard and nodded.

"I'll wait here for you, I promise," he said.

She turned back to the gates and gasped. A dark shadow approached from the other side.

Rowan quickly lifted the hem of her silk dress and knelt. Her red cloak pooled on the ground around her like blood. The dead grass scratched at her bare knees as she bowed her head.

The mass of spirits surged around her, rustling her hair and cloak as they brushed by. There were only five to ten souls during most ceremonies. Tonight, there seemed to be some left over from the ceremony the week before who had made their way back to the town square when Orla passed. She estimated about twenty souls streamed by her.

Rowan wanted to lift her gaze and watch what happened to them. She wanted to watch Orla pass through the gates, but she wasn't ready to face the monster she'd been dreading her whole life. She wasn't ready to come face to face with her friend's killer.

Living with the knowledge of her likely fate her whole life had, in some ways, numbed her to fear. Still, all the angry determination and righteous indignation she'd felt earlier in the evening had cooled to dread as the Wolf's eyes bore into her, reminding her of the last rule.

Keep the Wolf happy.

She had never felt anyone's gaze on her so acutely. It felt like he was seeing through her, stripping her out of her scant clothing to glimpse the substance of her soul. She knew seeing what souls were made of was rumored to be part of his power. She wondered what he saw in hers.

"It's an honor, my lord," Rowan said.

She tried to hide the way she trembled, but it was no use. Even if she could have calmed her fear, the chill of the night bit into her.

The Wolf chuckled. "Liar."

She whipped her head up to look at him, and the air punched out of her lungs.

The Wolf wasn't monstrous at all. In fact, he was incredibly striking and entirely human-looking. His eyes were a light blue and gray, like storm clouds illuminated from within, and his dark hair was stark against his fair skin, falling over his forehead and curling around his ears. The god of death was due for a haircut. It was such an utterly ridiculous thought that Rowan laughed.

She'd imagined him so many ways, but never as an incredibly

handsome man who looked to be just a few years older than her. She was speechless.

"An amused liar, it seems," he said. His smile was a beautiful threat that she wanted him to follow through on, even if it meant her doom. She looked back at the ground. "What's your name?"

She narrowed her eyes, a flicker of anger curling in her stomach. "Rowan...and I'm not a liar."

The Wolf tilted her chin up with a finger, forcing her to meet his gaze. "We just met, and now you've lied to me twice, little Red. Didn't Orla warn you I can taste lies? Yours taste sweet, like burnt sugar. Harmless in small doses, but too much could rot my teeth. Care to revise your answers, lass?"

"Fine," she sighed. "It's not an honor. It's a curse that's plagued my whole life and robbed me of one of the few people I love. I'm not usually a liar. Only when I'm confronted with death himself."

The corners of the Wolf's lips twitched. "That's more like it."

"Do you look like this to everyone?"

"What do you mean?" the Wolf asked.

Rowan waved a hand at him.

"Yes, why?"

"I just thought—" She *just thought* Orla would have mentioned that he wasn't monstrous—that he was one of the most handsome men she'd ever laid eyes on. *Most handsome god*, she reminded herself. *He could wipe you out with a flick of his hand.*

"You thought I was simply appearing in a form you'd find appealing?" Mischief lit his eyes. "While I'm happy you approve, Rowan, I look this way to everyone, though I have another form that might be closer to what you were expecting. Something that mimics the worst fear of the beholder. Would you like to see it?"

Rowan shook her head mutely. She most certainly would not. She yanked her gaze away from his, feeling as though she had left part of herself behind in its snare.

"Did Orla make it?" Rowan asked.

The Wolf swallowed hard. "Yes, she crossed over. She'll be fine now. It was brave of you to come into the woods after what happened."

"Or perhaps foolish," Rowan said.

"That too."

Rowan shivered. The icy ground beneath her bare knees made it harder and harder to focus on anything but how cold she felt.

"You should come inside," the Wolf said. He reached out a hand, and she flinched. "I'm helping you up. You're very jumpy."

"I wonder why," Rowan muttered as she placed her hand in his.

She was shocked by the heat of his skin. Perhaps it was the chill of the night, but she swore his skin was nearly hot enough to burn. She stood slowly, allowing her stiff joints to move again.

"You're freezing. Let's get you inside," the Wolf said, guiding her through the gates.

She watched him out of the corner of her eye. Rowan was slightly taller than most women in Ballybrine, but the Wolf still towered over her and his strength was clear in the corded muscle that hardened beneath her hand on his arm. He looked fully human, but there was a deep stillness about him that rang of magic, though it didn't feel evil like she'd expected. In fact, the silence of his magic felt calming to Rowan.

He led her through several ancient-looking stone arches and up a set of stairs to a great wooden door. The entryway was so dim that Rowan couldn't make out much, except that the wing to the right appeared to be a black hole of darkness.

The Wolf guided her to the left, into a sitting room with a large, intricately carved stone fireplace blazing with a roaring fire. Silver moonlight sliced through large glass windows, casting shadows on the stone floor and expensive-looking carpet. A dark mantel covered in a collection of wood carvings—all various renditions of wolves—framed the fireplace.

Rowan took it all in as she tried to stop her knees from trembling. She turned slowly, surveying the entire room, trying to search for exits discreetly.

The Wolf caught the way her eyes lingered on the door on the far side of the room a second too long.

"You can relax. I won't hurt you," he said.

Rowan cocked her head.

"I know you have no reason to believe me, but if I kill you, who would bring me souls?"

Her anger rushed to the surface. "I don't know. That problem didn't stop you from killing Orla."

The Wolf's eyes narrowed on her, and he ground his teeth.

Rowan froze in place, fear locking up all of her muscles. "I'd like you to change the bargain you have with the Mother," she blurted.

The Wolf raised his eyebrows. "You think you know better than two centuries-old gods?"

Rowan swallowed hard. "I think I don't want to die to hold up a world that doesn't care about me."

The Wolf crossed his arms and leaned against the wall. Rowan shifted from foot to foot under the weight of his gaze. She clenched her hands in her dress, counting her breaths to settle her racing heart.

"That's a bold request for a brand-new Maiden."

Rowan gnawed at her bottom lip. She couldn't argue with that. It was bold, but waiting for something to go wrong was torture. It was easiest to get it out of the way now. Her mouth was so dry she could barely form the words as she forced herself to speak again. "So you'll consider it?"

The Wolf pursed his lips. "Everyone talks about the bargain, but no one seems to remember why it exists."

Rowan crossed her arms. "Enlighten me."

He closed the space between them in three quick strides and it took all of her self-control not to run. He tilted her chin up so she'd meet his gaze.

"There are more frightening things than me, lass. Our deal was made to give us the combined power to banish something sinister. Even if I wanted to change it—which I don't—it would require extreme caution."

Rowan's blood chilled as she considered what might be worse than death.

The Wolf sniffed, his eyes glowing faintly. He stepped away and left her trembling where she stood. "I'll consider it, but I make no promises."

It was noncommittal, but at least he hadn't tried to kill her.

Rowan's shoulders sagged in relief when a man appeared at the door holding a tray with two steaming cups and a plate of biscuits. He looked fully corporeal, but Rowan could tell he wasn't by the sound of his energy alone. He was tall and built like a warrior, with a scar that cut up his left cheek and disappeared into his hairline. Still, he was incredibly handsome with dark hair, tan skin, and pale gray eyes.

It seemed everyone in Wolf's Keep was extraordinarily good-looking.

The man grinned as if he'd heard her thought.

"This is Charlie," the Wolf said, gesturing to him. "You'll likely see him a lot, and he can help with any rogue souls that don't want to be corralled here. He's a—"

"Reaper," Rowan finished.

The Wolf whipped his head around to look at her. "How did you know?"

Rowan looked down at the ground. She couldn't seem to stop blurting things out. She'd kept her magic under wraps for years, and now she found herself unable to shut her mouth about it. "He just sounds like it."

The Wolf frowned. "*Sounds* like?"

Rowan wrung her hands. "He has a resonance that's between the souls and...um...you."

"What do I sound like?" the Wolf asked. There was a sudden vulnerability in his eyes that made her uncomfortable, as if he wanted her to assure him it wasn't something horrible.

She met his gaze and swallowed hard, worrying her lip with her teeth. "You sound like silence. Like a total lack of sound. Complete stillness."

The Wolf's shoulders sagged, and she reached a hand out, nearly touching him. She drew her hand back at the last second.

"It's not a bad thing," Rowan said. "It's actually quite nice. The village can be very loud for me. There's this frenzied song that runs through everything, and it's dissonant and grating. Being in the forest is quieter, more melodic. But being around you is pleasantly silent."

She blushed fiercely as she met the Wolf's gaze. "How many reapers are there?" she asked. Immediately, she clapped a hand over her mouth. "Sorry, I shouldn't have just blurted that."

She was royally screwing things up.

"What happens if you ask questions out of turn in Ballybrine?" the Wolf asked.

Rowan involuntarily tucked her hands inside her cloak, but he grabbed them and wrenched them into the light, taking note of the red welt that looked especially angry in the firelight.

"Bastards," Charlie breathed.

"It's fine. It barely hurts anymore. They say I'd be better suited with a less curious mind," Rowan said. She couldn't help that she wanted to know everything she could about the world around her. The more information she had, the better chance she had of surviving.

"That will not be happening here," the Wolf said. He ground his teeth and looked away. "You can ask what you like here. Whether you'll get an answer is another story."

It surprised Rowan that he cared about the marks. Maybe he wanted his toys to be pristine before he killed them.

"Here, put this on," he said, thrusting a bundle toward her.

She stared at the heavy robe in his hand for a moment before taking it. Did he want her to strip?

The Wolf sighed. "It's warmer than your cloak, lass. I'm offering you a trade. Unless, of course, you're so inclined to put on a show."

Heat crept into Rowan's cheeks as she unbuttoned her cloak and handed it to Charlie. The Wolf's gaze burned into her as she pulled on the robe. The soft material was luxurious and felt as if it had been wrapped in warming stones. It smelled faintly of whiskey and soap. It was only when she was cuffing the sleeves to free her hands that she realized it was the Wolf's robe.

Charlie looked from her to the Wolf before he smirked and made his way to the door. Rowan watched him go with mixed feelings. Part of her wanted the company, but the more daring side of her wanted to know what would happen if she was alone with the Wolf.

"The robe is mine, but it's considerably more practical than what you're wearing," the Wolf said, gesturing to her silk dress. "I don't know why they think I want that."

Rowan frowned, holding the robe open, and dropped her eyes timidly. "You don't find me pleasing?" She wished she could tug the question back as soon as it left her lips.

Are you really upset that the Wolf doesn't want to devour you? she chided herself.

Something about the entire evening had separated her from her common sense. She needed to reacquaint herself with reason immediately.

The Wolf closed the distance between them, and she met his stormy eyes. "I assure you, Rowan, I find you exceptionally pleasing." His gaze raked over her, and goosebumps rose on her skin. "I simply find it impractical for the chill of the season. I don't want you to be any more uncomfortable than you already are trekking into the Dark Wood alone."

Rowan looked at him, puzzled.

"I know they have educated you for the past—"

"Fifteen years," Rowan supplied.

"—on what to expect, but you should just forget everything you've heard about me. I don't relish your suffering, or anyone else's, for that matter. I don't want you to be anonymous and lonely."

Rowan let out a bitter laugh, turning to face him with her hands on her hips. "Then why was I taken away at five and forced to live at Maiden's Tower?"

"Harder to convince someone with something to lose to make a sacrifice. That's a choice the elders made for you."

"You mean—" Rowan couldn't speak. All her anger evaporated. Her throat clogged with emotion.

He meant she could have led a normal life until she became acting Red Maiden. She could have grown up with her family and friends, all while continuing her education, but she'd never even been offered the option.

Rowan narrowed her eyes at him. She wanted to argue, but it made too much sense. She felt deflated.

"So it's all a lie? The separation? The scriptures? The forced chastity?" Rowan asked.

The Wolf crossed the room faster than she could track him, and she took a step back. Her hand flew out in front of her to ward him off.

"Have you let another man have you?" he asked. His eyes blazed with barely contained rage. His entire body shook with anger.

She took another step back, and he relaxed slightly, as if realizing how contradictory it was to tell her not to be afraid and then be so aggressive about her first few questions.

He cleared his throat. "What I meant was—if you haven't been chaste, the magic might not be enough."

"That's kind of ridiculous, don't you think?" Rowan asked.

She expected him to be angrier, but the Wolf just sighed and shook his head. "It is. I think the idea was to make things more challenging for *me*, believe it or not."

Rowan stared at him.

"I know you have questions. I swear I will explain as best I can, but first, answer my question," the Wolf said.

"Yes. I've been chaste."

The Wolf's eyes glowed. Grays and blues swirled in his irises.

She blinked rapidly, unsure if she'd imagined it. Something about Wolf's Keep left her with that feeling constantly hanging over her—as if she was in another world where she couldn't entirely trust her eyes alone.

"You don't need to lull me into a false sense of security. You may as well just get it over with now," Rowan said, bowing her head slightly.

Did he simply like to play with his conquests? Was this fun for him?

When she met his eyes again, he looked both angry and amused. "Are you so eager to be taken?"

Rowan blushed fiercely. "No."

He chuckled, and a bitter rage erupted from her chest.

"I'm glad you find it funny that a lifetime lived beneath an executioner's blade has made me eager to end the suspense," she snapped.

The Wolf's eyes went wide and then softened. "You're right. I'm sorry. I don't mean to toy with you." He gestured to her steaming mug. "Drink and warm yourself."

Rowan nestled into the chair by the fire. "What about the blight?"

"What about it?"

"Why did you do it?"

The Wolf's face was inscrutable as he shook his head. "Don't concern yourself with the blight. I've already given you a lot to think about tonight. Just enjoy your drink. You'll need it so that you warm up enough to walk back."

Rowan eyed the mug and took a tentative sniff. Bright red pomegranate seeds floated in the golden liquid.

"Cider?"

A wide smile split her face. The monster in the woods drank warm apple pomegranate cider. She wondered absently if it was a bad idea to drink something offered to her by the god of death, but it seemed rude to refuse his hospitality.

The Wolf pursed his lips. "Did you expect poison?"

She shrugged and took a sip. It burned the whole way down. "Not just cider," she sputtered.

The corner of the Wolf's lips quirked up. "Yes, there's some whiskey."

Rowan coughed again, embarrassed by her innocence. "I've never had whiskey before."

The Wolf's eyes widened. "Seriously? You've lived your life in Ballybrine and never had whiskey? Drink up."

Rowan hadn't imagined it would be so easy to get him to answer her questions. He seemed almost too eager to offer her information.

"Am I really supposed to call you 'Wolf'?" she asked. "Also, why a wolf, anyway?"

He rolled his eyes. "Hundreds of years ago, I appeared as a wolf to one loud-mouthed bard and that was all it took. Not to mention that for years, wolves were the most feared and misunderstood creatures in these lands. You can call me Conor."

Conor, which meant "lover of wolves." It wasn't a common name since most people didn't give their children names that evoked the god of death.

Rowan clapped a hand over her mouth to stifle a laugh. "Of course."

"That's funny?"

"It's just so...ordinary," she said. "I expected something elaborate and less literal."

She knew she should take it slow, but instead, she gulped down the drink, relishing the delicious warmth that spread through her body. Taking off her boots, she tucked her legs up underneath the robe and rested her head against the back of the chair.

Without the adrenaline of fear keeping her going, Rowan felt suddenly exhausted. Using her magic for such a sustained period while walking just over three miles through the woods had taken more out of her than she expected.

The urgency she felt earlier faded away when Conor said he'd consider changing the bargain. It was a terrible time to lose her fire, but between her lack of sleep from grief all week, the warmth of the room, and the whiskey in her stomach, sleep felt more necessary than anything else. Before she could sort through the mess of questions in her mind, she nodded off.

7

CONOR

The new Maiden had a death wish. Conor stared at her in disbelief.

Rowan slept heavily, curled into the chair by the fire as though she was right at home in the lair of the god of death. She'd come in so fiery that he could practically taste her rage, but as soon as she realized she was relatively safe, she'd crashed. He couldn't imagine the life she led to feel at peace in his keep. She should have been scared out of her mind. Instead, she looked cozy, her full lips parted and her auburn hair catching the firelight.

He had plenty to do, but he simply sat in his chair and watched her. He tried not to think of the skimpy silk gown she wore under his robe, or the fearful, furious look on her face when he had tilted her chin up as she knelt at the gates.

He wanted to wake her and ask her so many questions about her magic. It hadn't occurred to him until after she fell asleep that all the past Maidens might have been able to hear magic, too. Their song enchanted and lured the dead to cross between realms. It made sense that their ears were attuned to more than what met the eye as well.

Suddenly, he questioned every moment when Orla had stood there in silence, eyes closed, as if she was waiting or listening for something. He wondered if she intentionally kept it from him or if she'd never mentioned it simply because he hadn't asked.

It felt like a bit of a betrayal, but as she'd proven many times before, Orla was hard to know. He'd tried to, but she was a very private person—guarded in the way those born of terrible loss were.

"Should I have Mrs. Kline clear out Orla's things and start on a wardrobe for the new girl?" Charlie asked as he bound into the room. He drew up short at the sight of Rowan asleep in the chair. "The new Red is a lightweight," he laughed.

"Don't call her that," Conor snapped. "Her name is Rowan."

He hated how everyone in town just called them "Red." It was dehumanizing, and it made him sick. He learned each of their names as soon as they trusted him enough to reveal it, though most were afraid not to. Years of being indoctrinated left them all confident that he was a monster. As if death wasn't necessary to balance the realms.

Charlie's eyes went wide. "Seriously? Her name is Rowan?"

Conor couldn't believe it himself. A Red Maiden named Rowan, which literally translated to "little red one." She had the red hair and a temper to match.

"So I assume I should have Mrs. Kline clear out Orla's room?"

"No," Conor sighed. "We'll put Rowan in the garden room."

Charlie's eyebrows shot up to his hairline. "Next to *your* room? Is that a good idea?"

Conor frowned but said nothing else. Moody silences were the easiest way to shut down Charlie's questions.

The reaper gazed back at Rowan. "She's certainly bright as a summer day."

Conor wished he could see what Charlie did. Reapers were gifted with extra sight that allowed them to spot and capture lost souls as well as perceive various aura colors to differentiate the dead from the living, the good from the evil.

"What does it look like?" Conor asked.

"Maybe the brightest I've seen," Charlie started. "She has lots of greens cocooned in red. I wouldn't be surprised if she was soft and sensitive underneath that fiery exterior."

Conor wished he'd asked Orla more about the younger Maidens. It was short-sighted not to have done so.

"Are you just going to let her sleep?" Charlie asked.

Conor shrugged. "I don't want to wake her yet. She's been through enough, and letting her sleep is the only kindness I can offer."

"She has courage walking into the woods with the blight and Orla's death. I'll grant her that," Charlie said.

"That she does." Conor eyed the sleeping girl warily.

Charlie stared at him. "Why are you looking at her like she's dangerous?"

"Because she is," Conor said, meeting his friend's eye.

Charlie's brows flew up. "Really? What changed? You were always fine with Orla. In nearly five years, you never had a slip-up."

It was true. Orla was a smart, beautiful girl. Despite her sheltered life, she understood people and possessed the natural distrust of the world that only orphans had. She was a survivor, and surviving was messy. Orla wasn't one to fear dirty hands.

She took a while to trust him, but she'd come around, and then she'd become an invaluable resource for finding out exactly what was going on with the Ballybrine elders. She had a natural talent for eavesdropping, and because she was such a fervent rule-follower in their eyes, she was privy to more information than most. The leader of the elders, Elder Falon, loved her and trusted her with more than most Red Maidens were told about the inner workings of the elder council and the Crone.

And in turn, Conor had betrayed the trust she placed in him.

Charlie stared at him, expecting more of an explanation. "You could—"

Conor narrowed his eyes in a look meant to eviscerate.

"That face might scare everyone else, but you forget who I am." Charlie laughed. "I know you think you can keep going as things are, but this blight is a sign that it's time for change. You might not want to know that, but that doesn't mean it's not true. Whether or not you like it, she might be your way to gain control once and for all—"

"It's out of the question," Conor said, cutting him off. "I'm not talking about this right now. I just need to get her out of here soon."

Charlie's gaze locked on to the sweat dotting Conor's brow and his white-knuckled grip on the armchair. The laughter in his eyes dissipated.

"Mother's tits! It's that bad?" he asked in a harsh whisper.

Conor tried to pretend it wasn't, but he could barely control himself. He was disgusted by the lack of restraint that had him practically vibrating with need.

All Red Maidens were tempting. It was part of the way the magic worked to ensure the power between himself and the Mother stayed balanced.

Most of the Maidens had a familiar, intoxicating scent and a loveliness that was unique and supernatural. Rowan smelled like goodness itself. She smelled so startlingly sweet and alive it was hard to even sit in the same room as her. She shifted in her sleep, and the robe fell open, offering a tantalizing view of the creamy skin of her neck and the swell of her breasts. She let out a soft, discontented whimper that curled Conor's toes.

She was tearing his self-control to shreds within a couple of hours. He wasn't sure how he'd make it five years.

As if reading his mind, Charlie spoke up. "Maybe it will get better over time. You'll get used to it."

"Maybe," Conor gritted out, panting as he tried to tear his gaze away from her.

Rowan sat with a start, choking on a gasp. Her wide doe eyes met Conor's, and she blushed.

"I didn't mean to fall asleep," she mumbled.

"Yes, we'll have to keep you away from the drink, lass. Can't have you falling asleep on the job," Conor said.

Rowan narrowed her eyes, as if uncertain if he was teasing her or actually disapproving. He wasn't sure himself. He was irrationally angry with her—for what, being lovely and tempting? It wasn't her fault. Magic made it so. She was no more able to control how she tempted him than he was to remain unaffected by her.

"I should get back. Aeoife will be worried," Rowan said, rising from the chair, shrugging out of the robe, and carefully folding it and smoothing it over the seat as if trying to erase her presence from the room.

"Aeoife?" Conor asked.

"The youngest Maiden. Orla didn't tell you either of our names?" Rowan asked. "By the Mother! Am I not supposed to tell you that?" She paled, and her hand came to her mouth. "They didn't teach us that in lessons."

Charlie laughed. "Relax, lass. Orla was just very private and protective of the two of you." He handed her the red cloak she'd arrived in, but not before his eyes raked over her slinky silk dress appreciatively.

Conor nearly growled at him.

Charlie cocked an eyebrow and chuckled. "Territorial," he whispered.

It was all a game to Charlie. He didn't know what it was to struggle like that. Worse, he'd likely forgotten what it was like when Conor was out of control. They'd both become complacent with the lack of temptation.

And he'd failed Orla. He shook his head, trying to blot out a vision of her lifeless eyes.

Still, Charlie had the lightness about it that only came from helping to clean up bodies he wasn't responsible for.

"I'll walk you out," Conor said. He held out his arm for her, as if it was nothing to be so close.

Both he and Rowan gasped when she wove her hand through his elbow, though he suspected they were breathless for different reasons. She was afraid, but he was fighting for control. He caught her watching him out of the corner of her eye. It was a novelty, since most people feared him too much to even be curious.

They stepped out into the chilly night. Rowan pulled her cloak tighter around her.

"You should wear something more substantial next week," Conor said.

She laughed. "I don't think the elders would approve."

"Doesn't it only matter what I approve?" Conor asked, even while knowing it didn't.

The ceremony of it all wasn't ever for the gods. It was for the people. For their compliance and homage—for their complacency to sacrifice beautiful young women to a monster in the forest.

"All respect, Conor, but they wouldn't believe me even if I suggested it was your idea. Men assume that their peers all want the same thing," she said.

"Don't they?" Conor challenged.

Her face was inscrutable. "I actually don't think they do."

Conor went utterly still. She said she was chaste, but that didn't mean that her heart didn't belong to someone else. The thought burned through him like a fever. He went momentarily blind with jealousy, but he could say nothing. It didn't break any rules for her to want someone else, only for her to give in to her desire.

"Be careful of those who would lead you to believe otherwise. It's a true monster that would lavish you with pretty words so you don't look at his genuine desire," Conor said.

Rowan flushed, and her face fell.

It was unnecessarily mean of him to jab at her when she was already scared and overwhelmed, but a primal part of him wanted her entire attention.

Still, she'd been raised to believe she was nothing but a sacrifice, and it was cruel of him to dash whatever small hopes she held onto.

He bent low, breathing in her scent—a delicious blend of lavender, vanilla, and spun sugar. The closer he got to her skin, the stronger it was. He was drawn to her on instinct—a moth to flame.

But Conor knew her for what she was—something dangerously beautiful. It would be foolish of him to get sucked in by her big, innocent green eyes and forget the way he could doom her—the way she could do the same to him.

Her breath went shallow, and she held stock-still as he kissed the inside of her wrist. His lips brushed over her pulse, making it kick into a frenzy.

It was a mistake. Conor knew immediately when he licked his lips because he tasted spun sugar and vanilla. She was temptation itself. The truth was, he'd been fighting the impulse to devour her from the moment he met her. Her essence sang to him—a torturous, intoxicating song. The urge to take had never been so potent with any of the other Red Maidens. He almost groaned. It took all of his self-control to pull back.

Perhaps he'd become accustomed to it, or it would lose its power over time like it had with Orla. After the first year, the moments he even remembered who she was were few. It could happen with Rowan, though that felt unlikely.

"Safe journey, Rowan," he whispered. "Stay on the main trail. Don't get lured from it. Nothing can touch you if you stay on the main trail."

"I know the rules," she said curtly.

"So did Orla."

Conor could tell from the suspicion in her eyes that she blamed him for Orla. He blamed himself. It was best for Rowan to maintain a healthy fear of him, for both of their sakes.

"I'll be happy to answer more of your questions next week," Conor assured her.

"What about the blight?" Rowan asked.

"I'm working on it," Conor said. "You can take that back to your elders."

She eyed him with scrutiny before she turned to walk back down the path. She looked back over her shoulder once before tipping her chin up to the brightening sky. Then she took off down the path. The urge to follow her was almost unbearable.

Conor wished he'd explained to Rowan that he hadn't hurt a Red Maiden in nearly ten years. He didn't have the heart to tell her that even though their blood was on his hands, he hadn't killed Orla or her predecessor, Evelyn. He also didn't have it in him to admit he was afraid that he was beginning a cycle that would end with Rowan meeting a similar fate.

It was better to keep his distance—to stay the monster. The

mystery and fear that surrounded him protected everyone else as much as it did him. It was even more dangerous for him to forget his own viciousness. He might not have been what Rowan thought he was, but he was a beast all the same. He'd done horrible things, and he'd likely have to do more. It was better that he remain monstrous for as long as possible.

8

ROWAN

Rowan hurried into the Dark Wood, her cloak billowing out behind her. If Aeoife woke before Rowan made it home, she might panic. Rowan would need to race dawn back to the tower. She'd just entered the strange, tunneled trees when a movement to her right made her freeze.

Cade burst forth from the tree line.

"Rowan, what took you so long?" he asked breathlessly.

"I was busy with the Wolf. Come on—walk and talk. I need to get back before Aeoife wakes up."

Cade fell into step beside her. "I tried really hard, but I couldn't cross over the boundary into Wolf's Keep. So I guess that's good. You won't run into any demons in there. What was it like? What happened? How was the Wolf?" He stopped short, grabbing her arm. "Did he—"

Rowan shook her head. "He didn't do anything except give me hot cider and whiskey, and then I fell asleep. I got to meet a reaper, though. His name is Charlie. He was actually really nice, and get this—"

Cade's eyes were wide with horror. "You fell asleep!"

"That's what you found most compelling about my tale?" Rowan laughed, walking faster.

"That you fell asleep in the lair of the god who is supposed to devour you? Yes, Rowan. That is my first concern," Cade said, running to catch up with her.

"It was fine. He let me borrow his robe to stay warm, and he seemed harmless—"

"He's not," Cade said. He grabbed her arm and pulled her to an abrupt stop.

A distinct air of danger clung to the Wolf. She wasn't naive enough to believe that just because he hadn't hurt her tonight, he never would, but she'd lost one of her only allies when Orla died.

If she wanted to protect herself and Aeoife, she needed to use every resource she could. The Wolf was tamer than she expected him to be. He was also her only real means of figuring out the mystery of the blight and what happened to Orla. She didn't trust him completely, but she trusted him more than the elders. Most of all, she trusted herself and her ability to sneak around. She knew she could figure out what happened to her friend and, hopefully, how to avoid the same fate.

She met Cade's worried gaze. "You know, for a demon who spends a lot of time convincing me he has no heart and no feelings, you seem awfully worried."

Cade frowned. "I don't have a heart. Just because I've learned how to act human doesn't mean that I am. It also doesn't mean I couldn't wander until I find someone else to talk to. I just prefer talking to you."

Rowan ruffled his hair. "I love you too, Cade."

He smiled despite himself. "Row, seriously. You need to be careful about who you trust. You shouldn't trust anyone completely—even me."

"I don't."

Cade had never given her reason to doubt him, but in her heart, she knew she could only rely on him to serve himself. Most of his interventions in her life had been for his own amusement, but something had shifted the day he saved her from Elder Garrett. She didn't know any other demons to whom she could compare his behavior, but Cade seemed strangely attached to her.

They walked on in silence.

Rowan's mind spun wildly. She'd expected Conor to, at the very least, kiss her. Now she wondered if she'd done something wrong. She'd been dreading his touch, but now she felt strangely offended that he didn't find her appealing enough to even kiss her.

She stopped. Perhaps he wasn't even attracted to her.

"What's wrong?" Cade asked.

A violent flush crept up Rowan's neck, and she shook her head. "Nothing."

"That's not a nothing face," Cade challenged.

"Do you think that I'm pretty?"

"In a boring human way—sure. You have the hair and the eyes, and, you know...the rest of it," he said, gesturing broadly to her body.

She frowned, and he rolled his eyes.

"Yes, Rowan, I think you're lovely. Though I'm not sure I'm an authority on beauty as much as jealousy. I covet you the way I covet all things that belong to someone else, so it may just be envy that makes you lovely to me."

She felt ashamed of needing the reassurance. Most of the time, it felt like men looked at her and saw a magical object instead of a woman. She knew from Mrs. Teverin's lessons that men found that which was forbidden more appealing, so she was never sure if the way the eyes of the men in Ballybrine followed her was because of how she looked, what she was, or both.

Even with Finn, she couldn't help but feel like he was in love with an idea of her rather than who she really was. He thought she was noble, but it wasn't as if she had a choice. So much of her life was simply things happening to her. She often felt like a passenger along for a ride. Now, she'd had a chance to take the reins and instead she'd fallen asleep.

Sarai was one of her best friends, but Rowan kept her at a distance because her mother was the Crone, and she would be the next Crone. As much as Rowan longed to fully be herself with some-one, she knew better than to let anyone see every part of her. She didn't want Sarai to be put in a position where she'd get in trouble for hiding Rowan's secrets.

Cade knew her better than almost anyone else. She didn't realize how much she cared about his opinion until that moment.

With no warning at all, she burst into tears.

Cade's eyes went wide. "Rowan, what are you doing? We have to get back."

"I just—I just need a minute," she said, covering her face in humiliation.

She felt pathetic crying in the forest because her only real friends were a ten-year-old, a seer, and a demon. All the stress and anxiety of the past week crashed down on her at once. She wished she could tell someone everything, to feel like there was just one place where she could fully be herself without needing to be on her guard. She wanted the kind of love that came so easily for everyone else. The kind she had never experienced and likely never would.

She didn't blame people. Loving Orla hurt. Losing her was a sharp pain that scratched against her heart like a splinter, aching at the most unexpected times. It was hard to love someone so ephemeral. No one wanted to lose.

Even the Wolf seemed indifferent to Rowan, and that was too much on top of the rest. He was supposed to want to ravish her. She didn't want to die, but she wanted to feel like some part of the many sacrifices she'd made served some higher purpose. Now even that had been stolen.

Rowan sobbed into her hands.

Cade tentatively patted her back. "It's okay, Row. But seriously, we have to get out of the woods. You need to walk and cry."

She used the edge of her cloak to wipe her eyes and continued to walk toward the lanterns flickering like distant stars at the end of the tree-tunnel trail. By the time she reached the border of the Dark Wood, her tears had dried into stiff, salty streaks on her cheeks. She drew up short when footsteps came from her right.

Both she and Cade jumped back as Finn stepped out of the shadows.

"Finn?" she choked out.

He held out his arms, but her gaze darted around the periphery. The risk of getting caught was too high. Instead, they stared at each other.

Finn cleared his throat. "I—I'm glad you're all right. I was so worried. Sarai wanted to stay too, but the Crone wouldn't let her."

Rowan almost started crying all over again as Finn stepped closer. His eyes were ringed in dark circles, and his hair was a mess, as if he'd been running his hands through it constantly—like he did when he was anxious. She was shocked and comforted that he'd waited to make sure she was okay. He took a step toward her, but she held up a hand.

He looked her over for injuries. "Are you hurt? Did he—"

She shook her head. "I'm exactly as I was before I left."

"I'm supposed to bring you to the elders," he said.

Cade let out an exaggerated sigh. "Can't those perverts wait?"

Rowan's shoulders slumped in resigned exhaustion. "Please, just let me go check on Aeoife. She's going to be so worried if I'm not there."

Finn nodded. "Go get some sleep. I'll say I nodded off and missed you."

She gave him a grateful smile, wishing he would hold her, before she turned and hurried to the tower doors. She paused on the threshold, turning back to look at Finn.

"Finn, thank you for waiting. It means a lot," she said.

He sighed. "I told you I don't mind waiting. As long as it takes."

She took one last look at him before she closed the door and rushed upstairs to find Aeoife.

ROWAN HAD JUST DRIFTED off to sleep beside Aeoife when a knock on the door ripped her from the dense fog of fatigue. Cade was gone, and Rowan was relieved not to have to face him after her outburst in the forest.

Mrs. Teverin burst into the room. "Thank the Mother! We were worried you didn't make it back. The elders need to see you at once. You need to—" She stopped short, taking in Rowan's puffy eyes.

Rowan held a finger to her lips as she extricated herself from Aeoife's arms. The younger Maiden let out a discontented sigh and rolled over. Rowan tucked the blankets around her.

"I'll be down in a minute," she whispered, finally meeting Mrs. Teverin's eyes.

"Why don't I stay and help you dress? What will we be wearing today—white or red?"

She looked so hopeful, and Rowan wasn't sure if the sudden rush of nausea she felt was due to lack of sleep or the fact that her long-time tutor hoped she'd been bedded by the god of death.

"White."

Rowan looked away, trying to hide her humiliation, but not in time to miss the disappointment on the old woman's face. Mrs. Teverin was silent as she pulled a white wool dress from the closet and helped Rowan into it. As she buttoned up the back, she finally spoke.

"You know, it took at least a month before it happened for Orla. I wouldn't worry," Mrs. Teverin whispered.

"I'm not worried. I just feel like the elders are going to blame me. I swear I did everything right," she said as she turned to look at Mrs. Teverin.

"Of course you did. I taught you. You're a gorgeous young woman. I'm sure the Wolf has his reasons," the older woman whispered as she wiped Rowan's face with a washcloth and got to work braiding her hair.

"How long did it take with Evelyn?" Rowan asked.

Mrs. Teverin wouldn't meet her eyes in the mirror. "Evelyn was a completely different case. It's not important."

"How long?" Rowan repeated.

"Her first night out," Mrs. Teverin said as she finished the braid and secured it with a red ribbon.

A new determination set into Rowan. Perhaps it was the fatigue, but she wanted to do whatever she could to get all her questions answered. She wanted to know about all the past Maidens and the Wolf's relationships with each. She wanted to know what the Wolf did about the blight and what happened to Orla. She'd do what she must to figure it out, so if that meant making herself more tempting to win over the Wolf, she'd do it. If it meant sneaking around the temple and searching the elders' archives, she would. She needed to do whatever she could to save herself and Aeoife. She took a fortifying breath and followed Mrs. Teverin out of the room and down the stairs.

Rowan pulled on her red cloak and was about to pull up the hood when she remembered she no longer needed to. Now that she'd been blessed and sent to the Wolf, she was allowed the small freedom of showing her face in town.

"I'll stay with you while you're with them," Mrs. Teverin said meaningfully. "There won't be any more issues with Elder Garrett."

Rowan smiled gratefully. She'd been so distracted she'd forgotten to dread Elder Garrett. Her mind could only process so many horrors at once, especially on so little sleep.

Ms. Teverin led her downstairs, across the square, inside the temple, and to the meeting room behind the altar. A large mural of the symbol of the Mother, hands crossed over the heart, painted in gold, hung behind the long meeting table. All five elders were gathered around the table according to rank, with Elder Falon seated at the head of the table and Elder Garrett to his right, then Elder Raymond, Elder Graves, and Elder Nasik.

"Finally," Elder Falon said, letting out an exasperated sigh, running a wrinkled hand down the front of his white and gold robes. "What took so long? Huntsman Ashand said he didn't see you return."

"Yes, as I understand, Huntsman Ashand nodded off and missed her. She was asleep after a very long night," Mrs. Teverin answered for Rowan.

"You've been returned to us—by the Mother's grace," Elder Garrett said with glee in his eyes. "We see you're wearing white still. I assume you failed in your endeavor."

Rowan gritted her teeth. "I suppose that depends on how you define success. I led all the souls to Wolf's Keep. They all crossed over. I can also confirm that the blight runs the entire length of the trail to Wolf's Keep, at least for the trees bordering the main trail."

She paused as several elders gasped.

"The Wolf says the blight is not what we think it is. I got the sense that perhaps he's not responsible," Rowan started.

"That's ridiculous. It's a death blight. Of course he's responsible. It would be naive to take him at his word," Elder Falon sighed. "Did he indicate how we could get him to reverse it?"

Rowan shook her head. She suddenly felt foolish for not pressing Conor further on the issue. It was easy for this room full of men who'd spent the night safely in their warm beds instead of in the lair of the god of death to suggest she should have asked more questions.

"I did not get a clear answer about Orla's death, but I—"

"We already know he's responsible. It's the nature of the bargain. The Maiden often dies, and it keeps the Wolf happy. There's no mystery there," Elder Falon said, cutting her off.

He shocked Rowan with his callousness about Orla. He'd taken a particular interest in her and allowed her extra free time in the afternoons, which she spent concocting recipes at Hanna's bakery.

The group broke out into a cacophony of murmurs and whispered arguments.

Rowan held up a hand, and several elders looked indignant that she was silencing them. "I'm happy to answer all of your questions one at a time."

"Was the Wolf satisfied with you?" Elder Garrett asked.

"Yes. He was very satisfied, but we had much to discuss, and his priorities were to the souls I brought, since there were many more than usual. By the time he saw to that, and we discussed Orla and the blight, it was nearly dawn."

She waited to see if anyone would challenge her and force her to admit she'd fallen asleep, but it was clear that none of them knew exactly how long the crossing took. They didn't seem to suspect anything. She sighed in relief.

Elder Falon handed her a leather-bound book. She flipped it open but found only blank pages.

"A journal," he said. "Each Maiden keeps them, and upon her retirement or death, they are passed along to the elders in case there's pertinent history or information."

Rowan's eyes went wide. She couldn't stop the words that fell out of her mouth. "So you have the whole history of Red Maidens? Can I read them?"

Several of the elders gasped as if that was a preposterous request and also because she'd asked a question without permission. She held her knuckles out for discipline, but Elder Falon waved his hand.

"That's not necessary," he grumbled. "No, you can't read them. They're sacred texts. The ones that have survived are kept locked away. They are invaluable to the elders."

Rowan stared at him. *The ones that survived?*

As if reading her thoughts, he spoke again. "Several Maidens felt a need to burn their journals upon retirement or just when they were full. We don't have a complete collection."

Rowan looked at the book in her hands. She couldn't imagine the elders reading her personal thoughts and experiences. Perhaps she'd fill it with some choice words. After all, if they weren't going to read it until after she was gone, she may as well get the last word and make it colorful.

"It's just a place for you to keep track of your experiences. Fill it with anything that feels useful or relevant," Elder Falon instructed.

Rowan nodded. As soon as she got some sleep, she would tear through Orla's room and then the rest of the tower to see if there were any journals hidden away. She needed to know what her predecessors had done.

"So the Wolf won't be coming to the village for souls, despite the blight?" Elder Raymond asked.

"No, sir," Rowan said.

"I don't like it. Perhaps there's something wrong with our offering," Elder Garrett proposed, his hungry eyes raking over her.

Rowan's mouth went dry.

"Nonsense. You know well that he doesn't always take the Maiden on the first night," Elder Falon said. "As long as he wasn't dissatisfied, we don't need to worry."

"But what of the Mother?" Elder Garrett challenged. "What if she's unsatisfied?"

Rowan almost laughed in disbelief.

Elder Falon frowned and the well-worn crease in his brow was more severe as he appraised his peer. "Do you have reason to believe that's so?"

"I know from our one-on-one time this Red is very stubborn, and at times, petulant," Elder Garrett started. "The bargain is between them both, remember? Not just the Wolf needs to be satisfied. You know how the Mother abhors selfishness and immaturity. I worry we may need to make an intervention."

"It's a bit early to discuss such a thing, is it not?" Mrs. Teverin interrupted. Half the men looked absolutely astonished that she'd dare interrupt, but the rest nodded with respect.

Rowan stared at her tutor. "What are they talking about?"

Mrs. Teverin shook her head. "It's not important, dear. We can talk about it later—"

"Oh no, let's talk about it now. The girl should know what's at stake if she doesn't fall in line." Elder Garrett pinned Rowan with a feral grin. "If the Wolf or the Mother gives the indication that they aren't satisfied, it's at our discretion to reconsecrate you and take care of the details ourselves."

Rowan wanted to scream. Instead, she looked around the room for a sympathetic face. "Why is this the first I'm hearing of this?" she asked, trying to make herself sound as timid as possible.

"I see what you mean about the petulance," Elder Raymond said with a sneer, wringing his liver-spotted hands.

Rowan felt like her fury might burn her alive. She'd done everything right, and she still couldn't win. If the Wolf didn't take her, this group of supposedly pious men would deem her unworthy and put her through even more trials than walking the Dark Wood. Half the faces in the room looked hungry for the opportunity. The rest—Elder Graves, who was about her father's age, and Elder Nasik, an older man who'd been appointed after leading a congregation across the sea—looked uncomfortable at the prospect.

Rowan took note of precisely who was on which side in case she needed an advocate later, not that she could count on any of the elders to dissent. They fell in line with each other with minimal argument. Even Elder Falon, who was usually so reasonable, had an inscrutable look on his face.

"I didn't realize I was on such a tight timeline. I assure you all I will do my best to press things on my next visit," Rowan said tightly.

"Is there anything else you need from Rowan? I'm sure she's quite tired," Mrs. Teverin said, as if reading the tenuous grip Rowan held on her temper.

"No, I suppose it's fair to say that we have everything we need for now. We will all sit in prayer with the Mother for her wisdom," Elder Falon said. He waved his hand in dismissal, and Rowan followed Mrs. Teverin out of the room.

"Breathe, girl. You look like a powder keg ready to burst," Mrs. Teverin whispered as they stepped out of the temple into the cool morning air.

Rowan let out her breath, trying to shake away the tension that made her chest ache. "What is the ceremony they were talking about?" she asked.

"It's best if you don't know, dear. Not unless it's going to happen for sure, at which time I will tell you everything. There's no use knowing and suffering the nightmare of worrying about it unless you have to," Mrs. Teverin said in the firm way that let Rowan know she wouldn't say another word about it.

Rowan sighed as they made their way back into the tower.

"I don't know what you did to make Elder Garrett so wound up, but perhaps you could patch things up," Mrs. Teverin suggested.

"Me? I've done nothing except deny him my body, as I was supposed to."

"Yes, but Rowan, you know well what powerful men do when you don't give them something they want. They try to take it. Justice is a lovely virtue, but one you shouldn't expect to find here," Mrs. Teverin sighed.

"And I'm supposed to do something about that?" Rowan asked.

"No—you're supposed to remember it, so you have a plan for *when* it happens," Mrs. Teverin replied.

The look in the older woman's eyes filled Rowan with grief because, suddenly, she wasn't speaking to her tutor. She was talking to a woman who'd had something taken from her.

"I'm sorry," Rowan mumbled, though she wasn't sure if she was apologizing for her outburst or Mrs. Teverin's suffering.

"Don't be sorry. Be smart, girl. That man has a bone to pick with you, and you'd be wise to have a plan for when he makes an issue of it."

Rowan nodded and wiped away a frustrated tear.

"Those tears won't save you. But perhaps a new dress will. I'll have the seamstress in to make something to entice the Wolf," Mrs. Teverin said. "Let's not worry about the rest of it until we have to. In the meantime, I'll let you sleep."

Even though Rowan had done everything exactly as she'd been told to, she still fell asleep feeling like a failure.

9

ROWAN

Rowan snuck into the Borderwood after her morning of lessons and meditation. She left Cade with Aeoife so the girl wouldn't try to follow her to meet the Crone. Rowan needed answers, and she obviously couldn't go to the elders for help. The boards creaked beneath her feet as she crossed the rickety bridge to Crone's Cottage. Her footsteps echoed across the Mother's Lake.

The Crone stood at the threshold, waiting for her. "Thought you'd be here sooner, girl."

The earthy smell of dried lavender and mugwort greeted her as she entered the cottage. "I need your help."

"I know," the Crone sighed, gesturing to the table, where a cup of tea waited for Rowan. She could tell from the smell it was her favorite lavender-chamomile blend.

Sarai sat on her bed in the corner, studying a huge tome with fraying edges. She smiled at Rowan before turning her attention back to her studies.

The Crone sat down across from her at the table. Rowan's gaze snagged on the ancient-looking book in front of her. The paper looked nearly transparent, so dry and delicate it would simply crumble in the wrong hands. She tried to read the words, but before she made any sense of it, the Crone carefully closed the book. *The History of Ballybrine Prophecy* by Crone Arietta LaFray was stamped on the spine in faded black ink. The book was written by the previous Crone, Sarai's grandmother.

"Why are you looking at old prophecies?" Rowan asked.

"You want to know about what the elders said?" the Crone countered, ignoring her.

"Could I just put on a red dress?" Rowan started. "No one would know if I had or hadn't—"

"Rowan, you know better. That's blasphemy in the eyes of the Mother," the Crone warned. Her eyes bore no judgment, just curiosity.

"I can't let those men use me like that. Isn't what I've done enough?" Rowan asked desperately. "Isn't it enough that I have given up everything else—family, love, all light in my life?"

"You need something beyond the Mother's light?" the Crone challenged.

Rowan scoffed. "As if her light has ever shone on me. I've spent my whole life in the dark about everything. Apparently, her light is reserved for those who relish in my misery."

The Crone's face was inscrutable.

"I really have to settle for being a sacrifice?" Rowan pressed. Her voice was as pathetic and small as she felt. "The Wolf said he and the Mother banished a greater evil with their bargain."

The Crone sat preternaturally still. She had a knack for weaponizing silences, whereas Rowan couldn't stand to sit with her thoughts. She spent enough time in meditation during the week, and she'd grown restless over the years, using much of her time to teach herself to play the piano.

"You should leave that alone, girl. Your sacrifice is bigger than just our town. There are sinister things beyond your wildest imagination," the Crone said.

Rowan huffed out a sigh and changed tactics. "Why can I sing plants back to life? What is the purpose? Have all Red Maidens been able to do that?" The words burst from her lips in a hushed frenzy.

The Crone looked at Sarai. "Leave us."

Sarai hesitated for a moment, worrying her bottom lip with her teeth, before laying down her book and leaving her mother and Rowan alone in the cottage.

The Crone pursed her bloodred lips. "No, all Red Maidens could not do what you can. You are a change-maker. You'd be wise to keep that gift between us."

"Why?" Rowan challenged.

"Because in the wrong hands, it could throw off the balance between the realms."

Rowan stared at her. "What am I?"

"You're a spirit singer."

"Please just tell me," Rowan begged.

"I don't know."

The Crone had seemed to hold the answers for every question Rowan had asked over the years. It was simply a question of whether she'd share them.

"Why did you look at me so strangely on the night of my first trek?" Rowan asked.

"Because I saw a glimpse of darkness in you—a power that could tip the realms. I wasn't sure if telling you would make it better, but it's likely worse for you to be ignorant of it."

Rowan's mouth went dry. She sipped her tea until her hands stopped shaking, and the warmth of it settled in her stomach, grounding her.

"So what do I do?" she asked.

"Keep it to yourself for now."

"What do I do about the elders?"

The Crone looked at her with something resembling pity. "You *endure* them, as only those of us who must answer to their whims do. You do your best to entice the Wolf, and you pretend to be ordinary and pliant."

"I cannot—"

"Rowan!" the Crone scolded. "Those who do not bend are broken. That is not a fate I wish for you."

Rowan stared at her. In all the time they'd known each other, the Crone had only called her by name in ceremony.

"Help me," Rowan pleaded.

"I am. I cannot save you. We all must save ourselves. Now finish your tea."

The Crone stood and beckoned Sarai back inside as Rowan drank her tea down to the dregs.

"Sarai, check the leaves," the Crone instructed.

Rowan grinned as she flipped her cup onto the saucer, spun it in a circle, and pulled it away so that Sarai could read the leaves. It was a recently emerged talent of Sarai's that the Crone did not possess.

Sarai stared at the pattern on the saucer, and her eyes unfocused. Her voice took on a strange, singsong tone. *"There's life in the darkness. Violence and blood. A song that's haunting, lovely, and full of longing. A bright light and a life-saving bargain. Take it."*

Sarai blinked rapidly, and her eyes refocused on the leaves before she looked up at Rowan.

"What was that?" Rowan asked. Panic crept into her voice. "What does it mean?"

Sarai stared at her. "What did I say?"

"Calm down, girl. Sarai doesn't always remember, nor does she know the exact meaning of prophecies. Some things aren't understood until they are set in motion," the Crone admonished her.

Rowan crossed her arms over her chest and sat back in her chair. She studied the tea leaves—the answers to all her questions were written among them in a language she didn't speak. Every answer and every new bit of information only led to new questions. There seemed to be no bottom to the well of knowledge she lacked.

Rowan stood and stormed out of the cottage. She walked down the wood bridge to land, listening to the hollow echo of her footsteps on the old wood.

"Rowan, wait!" Sarai's voice and hurried footsteps trailed along behind her.

Rowan stopped where the dock met the land and waited for her friend.

Sarai linked arms with her. "Let's walk. Tell me about the Wolf."

Rowan walked through the Borderwood with her friend and told her about everything that had happened. When she was finished, Sarai stopped walking and turned to face her. Sarai didn't judge her for falling asleep, and she seemed just as surprised that the Wolf and his reaper were so accommodating.

"So what are you going to do?" Sarai asked.

Rowan shrugged. "I don't know what choice I have. I have to entice him. As worried as I am about what will happen with him, I'm more worried about the elders. Elder Garrett has had it out for me since—"

"I know," Sarai interrupted. "Finn told me. He was distraught. He came to my mother hoping she would do something."

Rowan stared at her, jaw slack. "He did?"

It was so unlike Finn to ruffle feathers like that.

"She told him what you did," Sarai sighed. "That no one would believe you, and unless he witnessed it himself, the only one whose character it would hurt would be yours."

Sarai reached out and took her hand. "Rowan, I told Mama I don't remember my prophecies, but that's not always true. I do remember a part of that last one, but it's just a message for you alone."

Rowan stared at her friend.

"*Love is the thing that holds back the dark,*" Sarai whispered.

"What does it mean?"

"I don't know, but it's important. Maybe it's about Finn," Sarai teased.

Rowan cocked her head to the side. "Sarai, do you think that Finn really loves me?"

"I think he *thinks* he does, and in this world, that's all you can really hope for," Sarai replied. "Maybe that is the root of love that the big bloom grows from."

Sarai could be both eloquent and pragmatic, and the simplicity with which she viewed the world left Rowan feeling like a silly romantic. They walked in silence for a while, leaves crunching under their boots.

"I don't know what is happening, but something in our world is shifting, and it's not just the new religion in the north," Sarai said. "My mother has been poring over Grandma's prophecies and she won't tell me why. Regardless, I think your path will become clear the more you walk it. For now, you only need to see the next few steps ahead of you, like walking with a lantern. The path will reveal itself as you go."

Rowan had never been good at leaps of faith. She'd never been good at having faith at all, but she trusted her friend.

"Do you ever think about what you would be if your birth didn't decide for you?" Rowan asked.

Sarai shook her head and smiled. "I was always going to be what I am. I have the heart of a witch and the soul of a wild woman. I couldn't and I wouldn't want to be anything else. There's freedom in being feared and respected, even if I'll never be as powerful as I should be in Ballybrine. This world won't hand us power, Rowan. If we want it, we'll have to find our spots to take it."

"But how?" Rowan asked.

"You go back out there and control what you can. If you need the Wolf to want you, make him."

Rowan nodded and then pulled her friend into her arms. "I think your prophecy was wrong," she whispered. "I think you're the thing that holds back the dark."

She and Sarai stood there hugging each other for a long time—until twilight pulled ribbons of color across the horizon, the air chilled, and the forest stirred with the gentle rustle and chirp of wildlife—until they both felt anchored, if only to each other.

Rowan belted out her song as she marched down the trail toward Wolf's Keep. The Gratitude and Grieving Ceremony hadn't been nearly as intimidating the second time around, though she felt more uneasy than ever around the elders. Every glance from the men felt like she was being undressed by their eyes.

She'd spent the entire week sneaking through Maiden's Tower, looking for the journals of past Red Maidens, and had come up empty. She'd sent Cade into the Temple of the Mother to spy and look for hiding spots, but he'd also had no luck.

Cade was silent beside her, though he occasionally turned to check on the procession of spirits trailing behind.

There was very little moonlight, and the darkness felt more stifling than it had on her first journey. A stiff wind rustled the trees along the sides of the trail, and they groaned into motion. There was no growling to be heard over the sound of her song, but she sensed the beasts of the Dark Wood waiting for her to make one false move and stray from the trail. She didn't hear so much as feel the eyes on her and the tremorous crunch of claws in the pulped-leaf dirt on the forest floor.

It was a relief that the group of spirits following her was smaller and more manageable. It allowed Rowan's mind to wander as she sang. After turning Maiden's Tower upside-down looking for the journals, she was convinced they had to be somewhere in the temple archives. She'd avoided them all week for fear of running into Elder Garrett, but she'd have to summon the courage to explore the following week. She needed to know what her predecessors had known. Rowan was tired of being blind in the middle of the tempest brewing in Ballybrine.

She was so lost in thought that the sight of Wolf's Keep startled her. The mansion walls rose out of the misty evening, all rough charcoal stone and modest peaks. It seemed too grand a home for one god, with its massive, arched windows and stained glass.

Rowan finished the song and knelt, casting her gaze down at the ground as the Wolf's boots came into view.

Her mouth felt suddenly dry and her hands shook. Rowan did not know how she would seduce the Wolf, but she needed to control what she could and forget the rest. She'd found that waiting for something terrible to happen had always felt worse than the thing itself. At least now, she could try to steer things, even if it was in her own clumsy, awkward way.

She waited for the spirits to cross over before she lifted her eyes and looked at Conor.

"Come in and warm up. We should talk," Conor said. He reached out a hand, and she placed her chilly palm in his.

When they stepped inside, Conor helped her with her red cloak. She shifted so his fingers brushed the skin of her shoulders as he grasped the heavy fabric

Conor leaned closer, his breath ghosting over her shoulder as the cloak dropped away and revealed the plunging bias-cut back of the dress that draped just above her backside. The seamstress had taken Mrs. Teverin's advice and truly outdone herself with the new dress.

Rowan gasped as one of Conor's fingers trailed up her spine. He leaned so close his lips brushed the shell of her ear.

"This is a very interesting dress, Rowan."

She held perfectly still as he tossed her cloak on a chair and moved around her. Conflict twisted her stomach in knots. She was afraid of what he'd do, but more afraid she'd go back to Ballybrine a failure.

There was no mistaking the hunger in Conor's eyes as he followed the lace that dipped down between her breasts. It was easily the most scandalous dress she'd ever seen, let alone worn.

"Do you like it?" Rowan asked hopefully, stepping into the firelight and slowly spinning to let him take in the full view.

His gaze raked over her in a way that made her feel as if she was wearing nothing at all. She shifted to give him a glimpse of her leg through the slit up the side.

Conor arched a brow. "Do *you?*"

She frowned. "It's the finest dress I've ever owned. I think it's beautiful."

"But do you feel like yourself in it?"

The dress was a stunning work of art, but Rowan felt a bit like she was playing a character—a sexier, more confident version of herself.

"If you could wear anything, would you wear this?" he asked.

It was impossible to lie under the heat of his gaze. Rowan shook her head, and his lips quirked into a half-grin. Every smile she earned from him required a gallant effort. He always seemed to be fighting to maintain his stern demeanor.

"Why?"

"Well, I feel rather...naked," she admitted.

"That's a bad thing?" His tone was teasing, but her cheeks heated. "I must admit, I rather like the way you blush so easily. It's charming."

Rowan's eyes darted to his. Of all things for him to be charmed by.

"It's not an entirely practical dress," she murmured.

"I suppose it depends on what you're doing," Conor said.

Rowan tilted her chin down so her hair fell in front of her heated cheeks.

Thankfully, he said nothing else as he crossed the room and picked up his robe. He helped her into it, allowing his fingers to trail over her shoulders and up her neck as she shivered.

"Thank you. I was cold," she said, trying to cover up her reaction to Conor's proximity.

He turned and made his way to a chair by the fire. Rowan followed, easing herself into the plush velvet seat. There was already a mug of hot cider waiting for her. This time, as she sipped, she welcomed the harsh burn of the whiskey.

"The elders want answers about the blight. You said not to worry about it, but they've made it my problem," Rowan said.

"Aren't you all business?" he teased. "It's still spreading."

"Is there a way to stop it?" she asked.

"There is, but it's absolutely a last resort."

She swallowed thickly. "Do you *want* to stop it?"

He stared, his eyes almost animalistic in their assessment of her. She was used to hearing the rhythmic pulse of people's energy and could make sense of their feelings from it, but Conor was silent, unreadable. It was both terrifying and exhilarating.

"It seems to me it would be to your benefit for death to spread, no?" It was a bold question, but she was tired of dancing around things. She couldn't return to the elders without answers.

Conor gulped down his cider. The steam from it clouded her view of his eyes as he watched her over the rim of his mug.

"I can see why you would think that, but there's meant to be a balance between the worlds, Rowan. I have no use for the living," he said finally.

It wasn't exactly an answer. Rowan raised her eyebrows, waiting for him to say more, but he didn't.

"Did you kill Orla?" The question slipped out in a rush of breath.

Conor's expression was placid, but his eyes narrowed on her. She clenched her hands, waiting for his response.

"I may not have struck the killing blow, but I blame myself all the same," he said at last.

Rowan waited breathlessly for him to say more. Once again, he left her wanting, but if he was admitting responsibility, it was wise not to push.

He sipped his cider, his gaze fixed on her. "How was your week?"

She let out a surprised giggle.

"That's funny?"

Rowan clapped a hand over her mouth. "No, I'm sorry. It's just an abrupt deflection, and that's not what I was expecting." She considered pressing further. "My week was—it was terrible. Everyone is disappointed that you didn't take me to bed. I've never had so many people so interested in my virtue. It's quite uncomfortable. Worse, I found out there's—"

She cut herself off. If Conor didn't know about the journals, it was possible they held secrets about him.

"Yes?" Conor asked.

"An old tradition during which the elders attempt to make me more worthy of your devouring that sounds rather—" She searched for the word for it, but nothing felt quite right. *Repulsive? Harrowing? Needlessly mysterious?* "Unpleasant."

Conor waited for her to say more, but she met him with the same stoic silence he gave her when she showed interest in a topic. She held his gaze, allowing the robe to slide down her shoulder. Conor tracked the movement with predatory interest. She closed her eyes, trying to sense a magical melody around him, but still only found a pleasant silence.

He looked out the window. "You should probably go back soon, Rowan. It's late, and it will only be colder as the night drags on."

Panic surged through her body. She shuddered as she remembered Elder Garrett's hands on her. She could not fail again.

"You're right. Someone will be waiting for me."

Conor frowned, but he didn't take the bait. Maybe he was immune to jealousy.

She jumped to her feet, trying to think of any excuse to spend more time with him and find out if he'd given any more consideration to changing his bargain with the Mother. The oversized robe slipped off her shoulders, pooling on the floor.

He'd seen it before, but he assessed the dress as if he hadn't. It took an eternity for him to drink her in, from her boots all the way up the slit in the leg to the plunging neckline. Finally, he met her eyes and goosebumps broke out on her skin.

"I need more cider," she said tightly. She didn't know how else to buy herself time.

He offered her a lupine smile. "No need to panic, lass. I'm happy to get you more." He stood and left the room.

A moment later, Charlie materialized in the doorway between one blink and the next.

"There now, lass, I only have a moment before he's back," the reaper whispered. "I couldn't help but overhear you try instilling jealousy in the Wolf. Be careful what you tell him. He is quite possessive, and you wouldn't want one of your little friends to get hurt."

Rowan bit her lip and nodded. Though she'd conjured an image of Finn waiting for her in her mind, the warning didn't make her think of him first. Instead, she thought of Elder Garrett. Perhaps she could tell Conor about him, as Cade had suggested.

A smirk tugged on her lips as she imagined allowing the Wolf to rip Elder Garrett to shreds. Perhaps the Crone was right and there was darkness in her, but instead of feeling satisfaction, the idea filled her with dread. She didn't need to be in debt to a god.

"I'm afraid of whatever thought made you look so devious," Charlie said with a wink.

Conor came back into the room, cider in hand, and Charlie excused himself with a nod to the Wolf.

"I need to give you something," Conor said as he handed her the steaming mug.

Rowan stared at him in surprise. She'd never really owned anything. She'd worn hand-me-downs her whole life as the youngest of five children and then as a Red Maiden. Only the delicate silk gowns made to send her to the Wolf were her own. Outside of her inherited dresses, she was permitted no personal belongings or finery. The elders felt possessions led to greed and vanity and would chip away at her purity.

She held out her hand to Conor.

"It's not that type of gift. I want to give you my favor so that I can track you on your journey," Conor said.

"Okay. What do I do?" she asked.

He leaned close. Rowan trembled, nearly dropping her mug of cider. Conor licked his lips as he took the mug from her hand and set it on the table next to her chair.

He turned his attention back to her. She forced herself to hold perfectly still as he stepped so close that the fine velvet of his tunic nearly brushed against her dress. He bent low, his cheek almost brushing hers.

Conor hesitated a moment before kissing the place where her neck met her shoulder. Her skin beneath his lips tingled pleasantly. He trailed his nose up her neck, sending a shiver through her body.

He pulled back and met her eyes, both of them breathless and utterly still.

"How does it work?" Rowan rasped.

"It gives me a stronger sense of your location. I'll be able to find you wherever you are."

She swallowed hard and nodded as she brushed her fingers over the place where her skin still prickled from his kiss.

"You should head out now," Conor said.

"Are you sure that you wouldn't rather I stayed?" She tried to make the words sound seductive, but only sounded uncertain.

She ran her fingers over her collarbone, and Conor's eyes followed the movement with heated interest. She didn't really know how to be sexy. Rowan had spent years learning about every depraved and sexual thing the Wolf might want to do, but she felt ill-equipped to flirt. None of her training assumed that *she* would need to pursue *him*.

"Would *you* rather that?" Conor asked skeptically.

"Yes," she said, allowing her fingers to trail down the lace neckline of her dress.

Conor's throat bobbed as her hand fell away. He ran a finger down her neck to the center of her chest, pausing between her breasts—her skin tingling in the wake of his touch.

He froze as he ran his tongue over his lips. "Liar," he murmured. He shook his head. "While I enjoy the sweetness of those burnt-sugar lies, I don't like being lied to."

He looked away. His face shuttered and all the ground Rowan felt she had gained slipped away under her feet. She was entirely out of her depth with Conor.

"Go home, little Red. Get some sleep and stop trying to be someone you aren't."

A violent flush heated Rowan's cheeks as she turned away and dashed into the hall.

She scolded herself for being such a clumsy, awkward woman. She was mortified by her lack of experience. Worse, she was desperate to get it over with so that she could stop worrying about the elders—so she could stop worrying about the experience itself. The dread of it stalked her daily like a specter. She was haunted by a fate she knew awaited her, and unlike the actual spirits in her life, she did not know how to put the anxiety of what awaited her to rest.

Rowan opened the entryway closet and grabbed her cloak, pulling it over her shoulders. She froze, her gaze locked on something red in the shadows of the closet. Grabbing it, she held it up to the lantern light.

It was a Red Maiden's cloak. Rowan's mind drew up the image of

Orla splayed out on the forest floor without her cloak. Searching the neckline, she found Orla's initials along with a dried blood stain.

Rowan's hands shook. She'd believed Conor when he said he didn't hurt Orla, but now she felt foolish for taking him at his word.

She flung the cloak back to where it had been poorly hidden and dashed out of Wolf's Keep.

10

ROWAN

Rowan rushed down the stone stairs of Wolf's Keep and through the ornate gates, checking over her shoulder to make sure Conor hadn't followed.

The path to town seemed to stretch on endlessly. Her heart pounded and she wished there were markers to let her know how far she had to go. Fear coiled and uncoiled like a snake in her belly.

Conor hadn't directly said that he didn't kill Orla.

The hairs on the back of her neck stood on end as she felt the eyes of the monsters of the forest on her. She had the strangest sense that there was almost nothing holding them at bay. The usual symphonic pulse of the Dark Wood's magic had ceased once again.

The wood was nearly silent. There was only the whisper of leaves begging the breeze for mercy.

She hurried her pace, wishing she hadn't left Cade with Aeoife.

A loud crack sounded behind Rowan. She spun, hands uselessly held out in front of her, as if she meant to punch someone. Her eyes darted to the left, where the sound had originated, but she couldn't see anything in the velvety darkness. She turned back and continued down the trail faster. Another crack behind her sent her into a sprint.

She tore down the path, praying to the Mother that the lantern light of the trailhead would soon come into sight.

The cold night air viciously burned her lungs. Her heartbeat thundered in her ears as her boots pounded the forest floor. There was a distinct and horrifying sound of heavy footsteps behind her.

Rowan ran as fast as she could, but nothing seemed to put distance between her and whatever pursued.

Her mind spun. If the Wolf had discovered that she knew about Orla's cloak, he could have been coming to stop her from sharing what she knew with the elders. The only weapon she had was the lantern in her hand. It suddenly felt foolish to walk through the woods at night with nothing to defend herself.

A loud screech cut through the air, chilling her blood. It was more a screech than the howl of a wolf, but she didn't dare turn to look.

Claws closed over her shoulder and something barreled into her. She screamed as her attacker tackled her. Her bones creaked beneath the weight of whatever monster landed on her. She fought to draw in another breath and whispered a prayer to the Mother.

Rowan searched, hands clawing wildly at the damp earth. Her lantern had landed a few feet away, and she was utterly defenseless. The beast screeched again. She winced as hot, rancid breath and spittle hit her cheek. Tears streamed down her face, and she closed her eyes, too choked with regret to scream.

A brilliant light cut through the dark, and her eyes shot open. The light pulsed, blinding and golden.

The beast screeched, and its weight shifted off of Rowan. The relief was instant. She drew in a deep breath as she squinted against the light. One last guttural screech split the air, and then, the beast was gone in a blur of horror and claws.

Rowan tentatively pressed herself up to her hands and knees, brushing her sweaty hair back from her forehead. She turned to see the source of the light.

Standing in the center of the trail stood a beautiful, ethereal woman with bright blue eyes and blonde hair so radiant it looked nearly white. She wore a gown of golden silk so fine that it rippled in the whisper of a breeze.

The Mother.

Rowan stared, slack-jawed, completely in awe. She'd always thought that the elders lied when they claimed the Mother appeared to them, but here she was. Rowan wondered if she'd hit her head in the fall and was imagining it.

She blinked her eyes rapidly.

"You're not dreaming," the Mother said with a playful smile.

Rowan's lips parted in shock, and she shifted to her knees, crossing her hands over her heart and bowing her head. "Goddess."

She was shocked when a hand came to her shoulder. "Are you all right, dear?"

Rowan nodded in a speechless stupor.

"Can you stand?" the Mother asked.

Rowan took her hand and slowly rose to her feet. "Was that the Wolf?"

The Mother shook her head. "Just a beast of the Dark Wood."

Rowan brushed dirt from her dress before meeting the Mother's eyes.

"Rowan Cleary." The Mother smiled at Rowan's surprise. "You thought I wouldn't know the name of our newest brave Maiden?"

Rowan shook her head violently.

"I know what you think," the Mother began. Her voice was soft and lilting like a pleasant lullaby, in sharp contrast to her magic, which sounded like a dizzying, dissonant symphony. "You think I don't care about you, but I assure you it's very much the opposite. You don't know how many times you didn't feel me when I walked beside you. I've been there since you were a baby, so loud and vibrant and wild even then. I was there when you first started seeing spirits. I've been there for everything."

"Why are you just showing yourself now?" Rowan asked.

The Mother cocked her head, her blonde ringlets bouncing with the motion. "Because you're not a sacrifice, Rowan. You're a weapon. I need your help."

Rowan choked on a startled laugh. "What?"

"You're a *weapon*. I know there are flaws in the way they taught you. Unfortunately, speaking to the elders has its limitations. They force my words through the filter that occasionally distorts my true meaning."

Rowan's fatigue and the impossibility of the situation slammed into her at once. Her mind felt sluggish. "Then why not find a better filter? A better scribe?" She hadn't meant to sound so accusatory.

The Mother laughed. "I gave them more power, hoping they'd help our people grow and thrive in my light. It was foolish of me to add other players and expect that they wouldn't hoard what power I gave them. I thought they'd help support my people better, but they've focused solely on making themselves integral to the faith. That is why I need your help."

"Me?" Rowan squeaked.

The Mother nodded. "I have little time. It's hard for me to stay corporeal in the Dark Wood since it's not my realm. Walk with me."

She held out her elbow, and Rowan threaded her arm through.

"I know that this is a lot to take in," the Mother said as they walked toward Ballybrine. "You are very important. You must stay alive and survive this term, and you know what is at stake if you don't."

"Aeoife," Rowan breathed.

The Mother smiled sympathetically. "Yes. I know you care for her and I want to protect both of you. As you've seen, this blight is a problem. It's spreading toward town, and I don't know how much time we have to keep death from spreading to the land of the living. That's where you come in."

"But what can I possibly do to stop that? Please don't tell me to entice the Wolf into bed like everyone else," she sighed miserably.

The Mother winced. "Not exactly. It's not so simple. The Wolf is gaining strength, and his power is stretching past the boundaries of his realm. The blight has spread to Ashand Orchards."

"It has?" Rowan's mind spun. It had to have been recent—there was no way Finn wouldn't have mentioned his family's orchards were blighted.

"Just to a few trees, but it's a bad sign. I'm sure you don't need to be reminded that the Ashand farmlands are where most of Bally-brine purchases their produce. That's why, unfortunately, we need you to act with some urgency."

They'd reached the end of the trail. Rowan saw Finn sitting slumped against the door of Maiden's Tower, his head lolling.

The Mother followed her gaze. "I understand you've stolen the heart of the future Lord of Ashand."

Rowan blushed and shook her head. "Not intentionally," she murmured. "I don't understand. What can I possibly do to stop the blight?"

"You can kill the Wolf."

A hysterical giggle bubbled up from Rowan's chest. "Me? I don't know how to fight. He's much bigger than me. How could I—"

The look on the Mother's face stopped her instantly.

"You mean seduce him," Rowan said miserably.

The Mother stroked Rowan's cheek tenderly, and a flood of tingles lit her skin. "Child, the Wolf's power is tied to the bargain, just like mine. The Crone ensures that the bargain is sustained, but you are the token of the bargain. You can be a sacrifice, yes, one that gives the Wolf power, but you can also kill him."

"How?" Rowan asked.

The Mother sighed. "There's a little-known scripture. It's ancient, and they have ignored it. Unfortunately, the elders prefer for you all to feel powerless, so they exclude valuable scripture that speaks to your power, much to my disappointment."

Elder Garrett's face flashed through Rowan's mind. "Why not pick new elders?"

"Because change moves slowly. The elders are stubborn as mules."

"But you're the Mother," Rowan argued.

"And I gain strength through worship. I'm struggling. Rowan, this religion to the north affects me as well. My power is waning as the

Wolf's is growing stronger. I gain power and influence through the prayers of the faithful, and if I challenge the elders, they could easily turn on me. They've learned from the men who are spreading the new religion how to strip women of their power and ensure they keep the upper hand. These are delicate times for me and the people of Ballybrine. It's easier to believe in death when your life is so touched by it. It's much harder to ask for blind faith."

A tempest blew through Rowan's mind. It was too much to take in. She was too tired, too scared, too lost. Her gaze fell back on Finn, where he dozed against the tower door, his golden-brown hair falling over his forehead.

"How can I kill the Wolf?" she asked, turning back to the Mother.

Light flared in goddess's palms and a golden dagger appeared. A strange ringing sound pulsed from the blade. "You're a weapon, Rowan. The moment that the Wolf is taking from you, he's vulnerable. That is when you strike. That is when a victim becomes a warrior."

"You mean..." Rowan's voice trailed off.

"This blade plunged into his heart as he takes your virtue will end him," the Mother said.

Rowan took a step back. "He'll kill me. How am I supposed to get a knife into bed with us? Won't he be suspicious?" she asked. She pictured herself ripped to shreds by claws.

"Offer him some blood," the Mother said. She laughed as Rowan scrunched her nose in disgust. "It's an old custom to show trust and intimacy. It's a bond. It will also allow him to sense your feelings and make what's between you more intense and intimate. Trust that he will find it very enticing."

Rowan turned the dagger over in her hand. "So I bring this blade to bed, let him cut me and drink my blood. How much? What if I pass out?"

The Mother laughed softly. "It's very little blood—only a drop or two. When he's finished, I expect he'll be quite ravenous for you. He won't be able to resist. Just keep the blade nearby, and when the moment comes, it just takes a simple strike right here." She brushed her fingertips over Rowan's ribs. "If you press in here and drive up, you'll hit his heart."

Rowan swallowed hard. Could she really murder someone, even if he was the god of death? "What if I miss?"

"Don't miss," the goddess said with a gentle smile, as if it was that simple.

"And if I succeed, it will fix the blight?"

The Mother nodded.

"But what about the balance? Won't things go wrong if I kill the god of death?" Rowan asked.

"I have the power to replace him with a new god of death."

The Mother made it sound so simple, but Rowan was still skeptical. Gods didn't grow on trees as far as she knew, and she'd spent her whole life learning about the importance of balance between the realms.

"How?"

"Death is the pause before life. I'm the goddess above—the Mother of all life—and I can elevate another to take over. Best of all, we can strike a new bargain. One that doesn't require sacrificing a young woman or the rule of elders."

Rowan's jaw dropped. "Is that even possible?" Hope swelled in her chest. She hadn't even considered approaching the Mother to change the bargain because she did not know how to. Now she was offering exactly what Rowan and Aeoife needed.

"Of course it is. If there's a new god of death, I'd have to make a new bargain with him. He may even be so grateful to be elevated to power that the souls could be led by a group of huntsmen. Do this and the possibilities for your future and Aeoife's are endless." The Mother's gaze flitted to Finn. "*Anyone* you desire."

Rowan flushed. "I don't know what I want. I've never had a chance to want anything but the chance to live."

"Well, now you do. You have a week to figure it out. Here's a sheath. You can keep it on your thigh, and that way you'll have it if you run into issues with any of the elders as well," the Mother said.

"If you show them the dagger and its markings, they will know to remember that you are a sacred vessel."

Rowan didn't know why she still felt hesitant. The goddess was offering her everything she'd never let herself want. Maybe that was the entire problem. Rowan's father used to say if something seemed too good to be true, then it was, but she didn't need to trust the Mother to know this was her only viable option. Conor had been proven a liar the moment she found Orla's bloody cloak. Her back was against a wall, and any option that didn't mean her certain death sounded good, no matter how far-fetched her success seemed.

"I'll do it," Rowan said.

The Mother cupped her face tenderly. "I knew you'd do what's right. You have a good heart. I'll keep you safe as much as I can in the Dark Wood. You shouldn't be disturbed by a monster like that again. You have my blessing with that dagger. Be safe. Be courageous. Be decisive. And, of course, keep this our little secret. I'm sure you're eager to trust someone, but until we know where everyone's loyalties lie, it's not safe. We wouldn't want the Wolf to find out, and people talk."

The goddess kissed her forehead, and Rowan didn't know why it brought tears to her eyes. Her faith always felt fleeting, but now she felt a renewed reverence.

"I have to go, but I'll see you soon. In the meantime, think about what you want," the Mother said.

Rowan nodded. Between one blink and the next, the Mother disappeared in a flash of brilliant golden light.

Rowan stood suspended between the trail and the town, staring down at the goddess-blessed golden dagger with the power to end all of her suffering.

11

CONOR

The first evening stars punched through the darkened sky as Conor paced back and forth at the gates of Wolf's Keep. He couldn't remember the last time he'd felt so tense. The week before, he'd known his mistake the moment he'd kissed Rowan's skin. It took every ounce of self-control just to calmly walk away from her. Once she'd gone, he'd spent the rest of the night so feral with unspent lust he could do nothing but burn off all of the heat with anger as he searched the woods. He'd spent hours shredding demons and monsters that had escaped the Underlands, furiously trying to figure out how and why they'd managed to escape.

Conor gazed down the trail toward Ballybrine, wondering how long he had before Rowan appeared. He loathed the way the magic affected him and how hard it was to keep his hands to himself.

When he snapped his fingers, the torches by the gates burst to life with crackling flames, casting flickering shadows over the edge of the woods. Charlie still hadn't returned from his scouting mission, and Rowan was late. Conor squinted into the dark, worried something was keeping both of them. The blight had shaken up the monsters of the Dark Wood much more than Conor had anticipated. The shadows stretched menacingly toward the edge of the trail as the flames grew. After so many years, the gates seemed like too much—like he'd built them while trying too hard to seem threatening. In the early days, fear had served him, but now it seemed an old tool that had outlived its usefulness.

"Thinking of a redesign?"

Charlie's voice startled him. The reaper stepped out of the Dark Wood to the right of the trail.

"How is it?" Conor asked.

"All business," Charlie teased. "The blight has spread into the Ashand Orchards."

Conor nodded. "That's farther than I expected. How is the mood in the village?"

Charlie shrugged. "The whole town seems on edge. I'm not sure if it's bad enough that the elders of the Mother will be willing to bargain with us."

Conor shook his head. Though they'd never seen a blight before, he'd seen more than once how the people of Ballybrine responded to things that felt threatening. Their fear often transformed into violence. There was always upheaval when a Red Maiden died, but that transition coupled with the blight had stirred a frenzy.

"No. They're stubborn," Conor sighed. "It will probably have to get worse before they consider it. Was there any talk of Rowan?"

Charlie smirked. "Not much. Certainly, there's gossip about why you haven't taken her to bed, and there's some speculation that something is displeasing about her."

Conor laughed bitterly. "Don't they have eyes? What exactly would I find displeasing?"

Anytime Conor didn't take a Maiden immediately, the village buzzed with speculation that it was because she'd been with someone else. He should have anticipated it would be no different with Rowan.

He sighed and rubbed the bridge of his nose. "Demon's breath! This girl is going to be the death of me."

Charlie clapped a hand on his shoulder and laughed as he passed him, disappearing up the stairs to the keep.

A breeze blew down the trail from the Dark Wood, carrying Rowan's sweet scent like an omen. Her voice rose over the rustling of branches and leaves as she rounded the curve in the trail.

She made her way to the gates and knelt. Conor took care of crossing the spirits as she waited before helping her to her feet and walking her inside.

"I'd like to stay for the night if that's okay. It was a hard week," she said, her bright eyes full of apprehension. She slipped into this meek mask when it suited her, only to lose it the moment her temper stirred to life. He wanted to know which version of her was real and which was the disguise.

Declining her request would have been wise. It was the absolute worst idea to let her stay. It was idiotic, but he wanted to see what she would do. Her presence was the last thing he needed, with so much coming to a head at once, especially after he'd vowed to keep his distance. The blight was prolific. Conor needed to focus on how the town reacted—not on a Maiden prowling around his halls. Still, he couldn't handle any surprises down the line.

"Fine. I'll have Charlie get your room ready."

More than anything, he wanted to know why she was so keen to stay. He wanted to get to the bottom of her scheme.

It had been years since a Red Maiden had asked to stay so soon after starting her tenure for anything other than bad weather. Evelyn, the Maiden before Orla, had been a bit infatuated with Conor and sometimes stayed for a few days at a time. Orla typically spent hours in the keep but rarely stayed beyond sunrise unless there were storms.

Yet Rowan was comfortable enough to stay on her third trek. He couldn't tell if she actually wanted to stay with him or if she simply didn't want to go back to Ballybrine. The elders were exhausting, and Orla had often complained about how the townsfolk treated her like an object. His keep might have been grim, but it was likely better than what she was used to.

Rowan trembled as they made their way into the keep. Was she just cold? He couldn't tell. She seemed more anxious than last time.

Instead of bringing her to the sitting room as usual, he nodded down the corridor.

"Go on, have at it. I know you want to explore," he said, taking her cloak to place it in the hall closet.

Rowan's gaze lingered on the closet door, and she shivered in the darkness. Her face was inscrutable as she turned back to the candlelit hallway.

He let her lead the way, trying not to watch the way the white silk of her dress shimmered in the flickering light, or the way it clung to her backside. She explored tentatively until she realized he was giving her freedom to explore the whole western wing of his home.

Rowan wandered the halls like a lovely specter. He followed after her as she peeked into rooms until she found the library and stood in awe at the center of the room.

"I've never seen so many books," she breathed. She turned to face Conor, her eyes bright with joy. All of her earlier nervousness evaporated and he had the distinct feeling he was looking at the real Rowan. "Can I borrow one?"

Conor nodded. "Of course. There's not much else to do here, and that's why my collection is so extensive."

Rowan reached out to touch a book but stopped suddenly and drew her hand back as if burned.

"They don't bite," he teased.

She blushed. "Sorry. We don't have many books at Maiden's Tower, and the ones we do are mostly boring old scripture, and they're so delicate. We get scolded constantly to be careful, and we need permission before we take something."

She turned to face him, and his gaze instantly trailed down the column of her neck to the swell of her breasts beneath the fine white silk. She froze like prey caught in the sight of a predator. Instinctively, she wrapped her arms around her center. Then, as if catching herself showing vulnerability, she forced her arms to her sides and rolled her shoulders back, standing up straight.

"What are you doing?" he asked.

She chewed her lower lip. The maddening habit brought all of his focus to her mouth.

"I'm trying to be...desirable." She blushed, clearly mortified that she had to explain.

Conor bit back a smile. "That's not something you can try to be. You either are, or you aren't."

She swallowed hard, evident doubt tugging her smile into a frown. "And I'm not?"

"Not when you're trying," he said thickly.

She held his gaze a moment too long. Her awkward attempt at flirting was disarming.

"Which is your favorite?" she asked.

He moved toward her and she jumped when he caged her in, reaching for a book on the shelf just over her head. It was stupid and unnecessary. His chest brushed against hers, and the scratch of his velvet tunic against the silk of her dress was deafening. The heat of her skin emanating from beneath the fabric was too much. He was a reckless idiot.

He stepped back and placed the book in her hands, hoping she didn't notice the way his hands shook.

"*Pyrrha and the Wolf*. It's a bit narcissistic, no?" she laughed, flipping through the pages featuring pictures of a redheaded girl and a monstrous-looking wolf.

"Who doesn't love an origin story?" Conor countered.

Rowan's eyebrows shot up. "Is this a true story?"

"Based on one, I suppose. Certainly, it seems there's some artistic license taken," Conor said.

"Can I take it to my room?" she asked, as if it was a massive imposition. "I'd like to read before bed. I promise I'll be really careful with it."

"Relax, lass, it's just a book. Of course you can read it before bed."

She grinned at him, her smile like the dawn cresting the mountains to the north. He was surprised something so simple could bring her such delight.

"Come on. I'll show you your room," Conor said, holding out his arm for her to thread her hand through.

He led her up the stairs and down the candlelit corridor to her room. She stepped inside and took in the space tentatively. Her gaze lingered on the intricately carved bed. They both stood suspended just inside the doorway.

He could envision her there, pinned beneath him on the white linens, her thighs hooked around his hips, her wide green eyes peering up at him.

Conor shook his head, forcing his gaze from the bed. "There are spare clothes in the closet. You can take whatever you need for sleep, and the servants will draw you a bath in the morning and then bring you breakfast in here. I'm busy during the day, but you're welcome to stay as long as you need. Don't go outside without myself or Charlie."

Her eyes brightened with interest at that information. He'd have to keep an eye on her to see what she did.

"Good night, Conor. Thank you for letting me stay, and thank you —" She looked down at the floor. "Thank you for not asking why." She met his eyes again, and the vulnerability in them made his stomach plummet.

He nodded and turned away before he could do something more foolish than let her stay.

CONOR EXPECTED to find Rowan prowling the mansion the following day, but she spent most of her time in the library before returning to her room. Finally, in the evening, after she'd taken dinner alone in her room, his curiosity got the better of him and he went to check on her.

Finding the door cracked open, he crept inside. The sloshing of water in the bathroom drew him up short, though he figured it would be strange for her to be bathing with the door wide open. Instead, he found her bent over her white silk dress in the large metal bathtub.

Rowan scrubbed at the fabric with meticulous gentleness. Her brow was furrowed in concentration, and her teeth pressed into her lower lip. She huffed and threw the dress at the side of the tub.

"What did that dress ever do to you?" Conor teased.

She jumped as she whipped her head up to look at him. "Nothing...it's just—I need to get the soot stains out, and they're so stubborn. I accidentally touched the dress after I stoked the fire in the library. If I was back in the tower with my laundry supplies, it would be easier."

"You do your own laundry?" Conor asked.

Her cheeks pinked as she brushed a stray hair back from her forehead. "Well, technically, we have servants for that, but I have a tendency to get very muddy when gardening. I feel bad giving the maid my dresses when they're so badly stained, so I usually launder them myself first so that most of the stains are gone."

"Why are you blushing?" Conor asked.

"Because I'm embarrassed to be such a mess." She tucked a curl behind her ear. Her white linen nightgown clung to her skin, transparent in all the places the water had splashed. Conor shifted his gaze to her red, pruned hands. "I just don't want the next girl to have a stained dress. I try to leave everything how I found it or better."

She wrung her hands. He didn't understand her frenzied nervousness.

"I want the dresses to be nice when—" Rowan cleared her throat. "I want the dresses to be as nice as possible when Aeoife inherits them. It's not fair for her to get a bunch of stained dresses all because I'm so careless."

She began furiously attacking the stain again, and Conor was struck speechless. Despite her explanation, her nervousness suggested that she'd be punished for the stain, and that realization spread fury through his body like a fever. Anger was a catalyst for bad behavior, and he could not lose himself to her when he didn't trust her at all. She was probably just playing on his sympathies.

Conor stormed back to his sitting room. He would not let this girl into his head any more than she already was. Especially not when she was hiding something. She'd asked him to reconsider his bargain with the Mother, but he suspected that wasn't all she wanted.

He slammed the sitting room door and poured himself a whiskey before slumping into his chair by the fire. Several minutes later, Charlie cracked the door open and made his way into the room.

"You can't just ignore her, you know," Charlie taunted. "You can't just brood around, slamming doors, hoping she leaves you alone. Why are you letting her stay if she's too tempting?"

"Because she asked," Conor grunted.

"It's not a good idea. We were supposed to be working on the blight. This is not a time to be distracted."

"I know, Charlie. I know, okay?" Conor barked. "She wants something. I'm just going to figure out what it is so that I can get rid of her without issue. I cannot have her here long-term. Her scent is everywhere, and it's driving me out of my mind."

"You could always try—"

"I'm not going to bed her," Conor snapped. He ran a hand through his hair.

In the past, taking the Maidens to bed brought relief from the relentless desire temporarily, but he was almost certain it made it worse in the long term.

"It's taken the edge off in the past," Charlie chided. "I would be happy to be there just in case you lost control." He winked.

A low growl erupted from Conor's throat.

Charlie just laughed. "All right, easy, lad. I'm only teasing. Mother's tits! You're territorial about this girl." He crossed the room, placed a jar on the table, and sat in the other chair by the fire. "The Crone had that sent over. It seems she knew you'd be struggling with your new Maiden, or perhaps she's attached to the girl. I understand this one is good friends with the Crone's daughter."

Conor opened the lid, and the pungent herbal smell burned his nostrils. The Crone had made the tincture to help him resist previous Maidens, but only at his request. What did the Crone know that he didn't?

"I'm sure I don't need to remind you what happened the last time you felt that way about one of the Red Maidens," Charlie said, interrupting his thoughts.

Conor scrubbed both hands over his face. "The problem is that I've never felt—"

Charlie dropped his glass of whiskey on the table with a clatter. "Demon's breath! It's that bad?"

Conor grimaced. "I don't know. You don't smell her?" He used the jar's dropper to sprinkle a few droplets of the tincture into his whiskey.

"Of course, but all of them smell like that—you know, like life, daylight, springtime," Charlie said, waving his hand dismissively. "It's lovely, but I don't find it any more compelling than Orla or Evelyn or any of the rest."

Conor downed the glass. The whiskey and tincture burned all the way down. "Well, I do."

Charlie sighed and patted him on the shoulder. "If you change your mind, I'm happy to play chaperone," he said before ducking out of the room and leaving Conor alone with his thoughts.

Conor poured another large glass and leaned back in the chair. He took a fortifying gulp and began his torturous vigil.

12

CONOR

The following day, Conor gritted his teeth as he finished his second loop of the mansion. There was no sign of Rowan as he made his way back to the great room, the click of his boots echoing off the green marble floors.

He forbade her from going outside alone, but after one day of good behavior, she seemed determined to test the boundaries of his patience. He pushed open the heavy wooden door and stepped out into the gray morning. The air was cool and humid, and smelled faintly of Rowan. He crossed the courtyard, dried grass crunching beneath his boots.

A soft melody floated over the courtyard wall. Conor darted around the corner of the mansion, following the sound. Spirits huddled outside the garden walls. Several of them swayed from side to side at the haunting, lovely melody that floated on the breeze. One leaned against the wall, her ghostly white hands crossed over her heart, her eyes squeezed shut in rapture. She looked like she might cry.

The last thing he needed was the servant spirits acting up and wandering about when they had things to do. He cleared his throat, and all five of them jumped and then scattered in different directions.

He walked to the opening in the stone wall where the iron gate hung open, creaking gently in the breeze. Rowan stood in the center of the garden in profile. Her auburn hair was braided, but wisps of curls slipped free and blew in the breeze. She wore a charcoal-gray dress that was slightly too large for her. Conor made a note to have his seamstress see that she had some proper clothes made in case she needed to change.

Rowan's eyes were closed, her whole body swaying with the melody. Conor was unsettled by how at home she seemed in his world. She stopped her song periodically and brought her hands down to the soil beneath the brown, dilapidated flower beds. She was about to sing again when he stepped into the garden and she noticed him.

"Hi," she said with a smile.

"Good morning," he said. "I thought I asked you not to come outside alone."

"I thought that was more of a suggestion. I'm still within the garden walls." She smiled guiltily, and he shook his head as he tasted burnt sugar on his tongue. *Bold little liar.* She reached her hand up to brush the hair from her eyes, and in doing so, smeared mud on her cheek.

He stepped closer and Rowan froze, her lips parting in surprise as he rubbed the smudge away with his thumb.

He jerked his hands away. "You had some mud."

"What is this place?" she asked, climbing to her feet and brushing the dirt off the knees of her dress. She sighed heavily at the mud-stained fabric.

Conor swallowed hard. "The Dark Garden. It used to be that most of the grounds were gardens, but this section was particularly lovely, beautiful flowers of deep purples and scarlets, so dark they were nearly black. As you can see, they've all died off. It's looked like this for many years."

He didn't say that this part of the garden had been tended to by someone he cared for many years before. Someone he'd hurt with his monstrosity—a loss that still haunted him and served as a warning not to let his guard down.

Rowan looked around. "Maybe it just needs some love. That's why I was singing. Sometimes when I—" She stopped short, as if she caught herself sharing too much. "Plants like music."

Conor looked around at the dried-up, browned plants. She certainly had her work cut out for her, but he supposed it didn't hurt.

"You should be careful about singing like that. You had an audience of spirits outside of the garden wall that I had to chase back to their jobs," he said.

"I did?" Rowan's eyes were wide as saucers. "Wait, you have spirit *slaves*?"

"They aren't slaves. They chose to serve. Some spirits aren't quite ready to cross, or they have some sort of debt that they want to work off, or they simply want to be of service to me and the souls crossing over."

"Am I allowed to watch?" Rowan asked.

"Watch?"

"When you cross the souls?"

Conor nodded. "There's nothing to forbid it, although I expect you won't find it quite as exciting as you expect. The most interesting part is beyond the portal that opens and you cannot cross it because you're alive, Rowan."

She chewed her lower lip, looking contemplative.

Conor was about to say more when his gaze snagged on something bright green. He stepped closer to the rosebush. Sure enough, there was one green branch shooting up from the tangle of brown dead ones, and at the end of it, a cluster of buds, one of which bloomed into a dark scarlet rose.

"Mother slay me," Conor murmured.

"What is it?" Rowan asked. She stepped up next to him, looking at the bush.

"Nothing has bloomed here for years. I don't know how —" He stopped when he saw the look on her face. "What?"

She shook her head. "I swear it was like that when I came in."

He licked his lips and tasted burnt sugar. She'd lied twice in one conversation. Rowan was turning out to be a careless liar.

"Are you lying, little Red?" Conor asked.

She bit her lip and looked back at the rose. "Does it matter? I think we've established that we are friends—that we need each other right now to figure out a new bargain."

So that was what she was hoping to do—manipulate him.

Conor grabbed her by the shoulders. "It would be a mistake to look at me and see anything other than a monster."

"For you or me?" she asked, jutting her chin out defiantly. Her gaze dropped to his mouth, and he couldn't tell if it was calculated or accidental. It concerned him that he cared.

He smiled involuntarily, then immediately frowned. He couldn't remember a time he'd smiled so much. It was yet another sign of his lack of control.

"Is this the version of you that everyone fears?" Rowan asked, her fingers grazing the front of his tunic.

Conor almost laughed. She either had no fear or no sense of self-preservation, and he wasn't sure which was worse. "So eager to meet the Wolf everyone cowers for?"

"No." She bit her lip. "More like I've seen pretty faces that hide common monstrosity my whole life. I'm starting to doubt everything I've ever believed. I think maybe you're not as scary as you think."

That decided it. Rowan had no survival instinct at all. He could not have her being fearless when he'd spent every moment since meeting her thinking about ruining her. Her recklessness stoked his own, like a match to tinder.

It was a risk. Changing form made Conor wilder, and she was already irresistible. Still, she needed to understand who he truly was. She needed to understand the danger in thinking of him as anything other than the deadly menace he was. He could handle it. He'd taken the tincture that morning.

So he let the darkness in. He let it wash through him with its familiar heat. His power helped him take the form of whatever the observer expected and, if he dove deeper, their worst fear.

Her eyes went wide, and he waited for fear that never came. When Conor looked down, his hands were claws, his arms dusted in dark hair. It was what most people expected of him.

Rowan didn't cower. She reached up and brushed her hand over his cheek with tenderness so startling that he flinched.

No one had ever reacted that way. She welcomed the dark like it was her only friend.

He caught her hand in one of his clawed fists and wrenched it away. It wasn't safe to be so close when she smelled so good—when her heart kicked up and he heard the way the blood rushed through her veins like a symphony of life.

"I'm not the hero of this story, Rowan," Conor growled.

"I know," she said, jerking her hand away, careful not to cut herself on his claws. "I am."

Conor froze. What did she know? If she knew her true power, he needed to stay far away from her. "Now why would you say that, lass?" he challenged, brushing her cheek with his claw.

She held his gaze with a fierceness that sent a fever through him. "I'm the one who holds it all together. The hero is the one who has courage when they're scared but does the scary thing anyway. As far as I can tell, everyone else gets to stay safe while I do the brave work. That's what heroes do."

Conor studied her, looking for a lie, but her heart gave no false beat. Her breath was even, if a little shallow, and there was no hint of burnt sugar in his mouth. In this form, his sense of smell was even more powerful. She smelled like honesty, freedom, absolution. He leaned closer. If he could just taste her lips, he could—

He stopped himself and backed away. Years of cultivating self-control, and somehow he couldn't even think straight when he was this close to Rowan. How quickly he forgot when she stood there looking so small and vulnerable that she could just as easily hurt him as he could her.

"You need to learn how to defend yourself," Conor said.

"I know how to defend myself. Finn taught me."

Conor clenched his teeth so hard it hurt. Again, there was that hint of someone else in her life. "Who is Finn?"

Her courage suddenly gone, Rowan blushed, trying to hide behind wisps of hair that fell in front of her pinked cheeks. "My friend."

"You don't have any friends."

She flinched and he knew immediately it was much too harsh. He'd never worried about being too harsh with Orla, but Rowan was something else entirely. Though she had the same hard outer shell as her predecessor, it was clear she hadn't steeled her heart quite as effectively. Conor didn't like how easy it was to hurt her. He didn't like the way she looked when she was trying not to cry, her full bottom lip jutting out, her green eyes glassy with unshed tears.

"I know that, but what else do you want me to call him?" Rowan snapped. "He's a person who treats me like a human being, and he taught me how to navigate forests and throw a punch."

"And I suppose he did this out of the kindness of his own heart?" Conor asked. The way the men of Ballybrine gravitated toward the forbidden fruit that was the Red Maidens was one of the most enduring things through time.

"Actually, I think he did it because he's in love with me."

Conor almost laughed.

"Or, rather, he's in love with an idea of me," she corrected herself.

She really did understand the way the world around her worked, and any bit of humor or disbelief that tugged at Conor evaporated. He'd done exactly what everyone in Ballybrine did; he'd treated her as an object instead of a person.

He'd wanted her to see the truth, but now that she did, he could suddenly sense the potency of that fear in her—that she'd disappear and be nothing to anyone. She was achingly aware of how temporary she was without his reminding her.

Her eccentric behavior suddenly clicked—the way she scrubbed and scrubbed at her dress so she wouldn't leave a mark. The way she treated every library book as if it were an ancient document. The way she touched the whole world with the delicacy of a spring breeze, afraid to disturb the beauty around her with her very existence.

She'd bought into the belief that she was only worth what she could sacrifice, and so she actively participated in erasing her presence from the world on instinct.

Conor felt furious with her, with Ballybrine, with the Mother—mostly with himself. He'd fallen into the same trap as everyone else. He treated her with an impermanence that made her believe her value was inconsequential. Perhaps he'd been going about this all wrong. He was so afraid to get close, sure he'd lose control, but what had helped him numb away Orla and Evelyn before her, was taking the time to know them. In small ways, he'd let them in.

Somehow, he wasn't confident that caring about Rowan would help. He needed objectivity. She was a puzzle he needed to solve as soon as possible.

Instead, Conor tapped back into his power, pushing deeper into Rowan's fears. His form shifted again, and her eyes went wide in genuine fear. She wasn't seeing him as a monster. She was seeing something much worse. His power was both physical and psychological, so it could cause lucid hallucinations.

He closed his eyes, and he saw a family—he assumed hers—living happily as if she'd never been born, never died for their safety, never loved them even while they couldn't love her back. He saw a young woman with gray eyes and dark braids peacefully pruning her herb garden alone. He saw a handsome huntsman marrying a lovely blonde lady. He saw a happy, healthy, Rowan-less world.

When he opened his eyes, Conor expected she would be a helpless mess, sobbing on the dry grass like most of his victims after he showed them such things. Instead, she stood there blinking at him with just a few rogue tears on her cheeks.

"You think I don't know my own fear?" Rowan rasped. "You think I haven't looked at it every day? That I haven't known since I was dragged to that tower on the edge of the Dark Wood at five years old? Maybe I didn't understand fully then, but I've had a long time to befriend it. I know exactly what awaits me."

Conor opened his mouth to speak, but she just held up a hand.

"Fear is a worthless emotion because it won't save me. Fear is poison. If you take it all at once—if you let it surprise you—you're done for. But if you take a little bit every day, it loses its potency. Sure, it takes the light out of everything, but at some point, it's the only way to survive," she said. "There are only things I don't fear any longer and things I don't know to be afraid of yet."

Conor swallowed hard. The words were a knife slicing through his chest. He stared at her, stunned, speechless, as his magic dissipated. He'd been painfully wrong about her. She wasn't as delicate as she appeared to be. She was strong. It took courage to live with fear as a constant companion and still hold to the hope that she could outwit her fate. He felt ashamed for missing it.

"Rowan—"

"Don't. I don't want an apology," she huffed, turning back to look at him, the sun shining bright on her auburn hair. "You knew what you were doing, and you meant to do it. Don't apologize because you found out you were wrong. Don't apologize to assuage your own guilt. You're not sorry yet."

"I am," he said. He took her hand in his. "I'm sorry."

"You're not," Rowan snapped, wrenching her hand away. She pulled too hard, stumbling into the rosebush. She let out a soft curse as she pulled back.

The scent of lavender, vanilla, and spun sugar filled the air so strongly it nearly choked Conor. It mingled with a strange, coppery scent that took him too long to recognize.

Rowan held up her trembling hand. Blood dripped from the thorn pricks into the lines on her palm in a tiny river.

Conor met her wide eyes.

"Run," he growled. He tried to hold himself back, but he already felt powerless to the magic that demanded he devour her.

Recognition lit her eyes, and she turned and tore out of the garden.

Conor leaped to follow and was tackled to the ground by Charlie.

"Woah there, lad!" Charlie grunted. "You're losing it. I need you to settle down now."

"How did you know?" Conor gritted out. He didn't know why he asked. All of his reapers could sense his moods. It was their job to reap souls but also to protect the Wolf. He growled, half-fighting Charlie, half-fighting himself for control.

He couldn't lose Rowan the moment he realized how much he truly liked her. She might be the first woman in years strong enough to withstand what needed to be done to revive the Dark Wood and restore the balance between the realm of the living and the realm of the dead.

Charlie wrestled with him. "Fight it, Conor. I see the way you look at her, and you'll never forgive yourself if you—"

Conor tried with everything in him, but the pull to her was undeniable and so powerful it snapped what was left of his control. He threw Charlie across the garden and took off into the Dark Wood to hunt.

13

ROWAN

*N*ever *bleed in the Dark Wood.*

Of course the rule also extended to Wolf's Keep. Rowan tore down the trail back toward Ballybrine. She couldn't believe she'd been so clumsy. Now the Wolf really *was* going to kill her.

For all her talk of bravery, watching Conor lose control was far more terrifying than anything that waited in the woods. She'd broken one of the four critical rules, and she wasn't even confident the Mother had the power to save her so deep into the Dark Wood. She prayed to her anyway.

If Rowan didn't get back in one piece, Aeoife was the only Red Maiden left, and she would not leave the girl to that fate. Aeoife wasn't prepared for the forest alone, or the Wolf, or—worse—the elders.

Rowan wanted to pause and listen to see if Conor was behind her, but even a second's hesitation might be enough to get her killed. She kept running. She could only hear her heartbeat in her ears and her staccato breathing. The trees lining the trail like a tunnel around her were a blur of bony white spindles.

She chanced a glance over her shoulder but saw nothing. When she turned back, she found a man on the trail ahead of her.

"Bless the Mother! Help!" Rowan called.

He turned and grinned at her. "There you are, lass. You look as though you've had a fright."

He was on the trail, so he had to be a huntsman like Finn. He was tall and broad, and too far into the Dark Wood to be anyone else.

Rowan looked back over her shoulder. "We have to go. The Wolf is coming. I hurt myself, and he's tracking me." She tugged on the huntsman's shirt, urging him on.

"There, there, love. Take a breath. I've been looking for you. It's going to be just fine now. Look at me," the huntsman whispered.

Rowan lifted her gaze and met his bright amber eyes.

"Good lass," he said soothingly. A swirling, dissonant sound rushed around her and sank into her skin.

All the fear in Rowan's body dissipated as he spoke. *Everything was going to be fine.* She relaxed into his touch as her adrenaline faded. She felt tired, mesmerized by his eyes.

"How do you feel?" the man asked.

"Much better," Rowan mumbled. She was sure she should look away, but she couldn't. She was snared by the man's gaze. "What beautiful eyes you have."

"All the better to see you with, lovely." The man grinned, and she caught a flash of exceptionally pointy canines.

"What big teeth you have," she murmured. The fear that rose at the sight of them evaporated almost as soon as she became aware of it.

"All the better to eat you up, Rowan Cleary. You smell divine," he whispered.

Something wasn't right, but Rowan couldn't say what it was. The man brushed her hair over her shoulder, his fingers trailing up to rest on her pulse.

"How—how do you know my name?" she asked, her voice trembling.

"Because you whispered it to the Dark Wood fifteen years ago, and I heard it," he soothed. "I whispered it back. Don't you remember? I've listened to your whispers for years. I've waited for you."

"Waited for me?"

"Yes. To claim you just like you wanted me to," he whispered. "Why else would you give me such power over you by sharing your name?"

Rowan tried to shake off the soothing way his voice wrapped around her like a warm blanket, but she couldn't. She couldn't move or think straight.

The man lifted her hand to his lips, and his tongue laved over the blood on her palm. He groaned. "He's a fool not to take you. You are exquisite. Don't you want to be mine, Rowan? I can make you feel so good."

He's not a hunter. A hunter wouldn't touch you, Rowan.

The thought faded as he spun her, pulling her back flush to his front. A low growl rumbled in his throat, and his lips pressed to her neck.

"Good lass," he soothed. "Now don't scream."

Run, Rowan, run! Her mind pleaded.

But the message didn't get to her legs. His teeth grazed over her neck, and she shivered, trying to squirm away. His hand collared her, tilting her head to the side.

"It will only hurt for a moment, I promise," he whispered.

Before she could protest, he struck. Pain exploded from where his teeth punctured her skin. It was so sharp it stole her breath. The lightning-fast ache sliced into her, burning through her veins like molten ore.

Her mind spun until it caught on one memory—the bite mark on Orla's neck. A sick horror turned her stomach. This monster had killed Orla.

Rowan wanted to fight, but her body refused to move. He must have had some sort of magical influence. It was as if he'd placed her under a spell and all of her limbs were too relaxed to spring into action.

For all her courage with Conor, Rowan felt none now. She was going to die in the woods, just as Orla had. Aeoife would be alone. They'd send Aeoife in here, and this monster would get her too.

Tears streamed down Rowan's cheeks. She tried to yank herself away but only succeeded in squirming a bit.

"Settle, lass. The worst is over," the beautiful monster soothed.

The burn of the bite started to dissipate, and the monster pressed a kiss to the spot before pulling a long drag of her blood into his mouth. She felt like her soul was being rendered from her body in a warm tug that she felt all the way to her toes. It didn't hurt, but she was shocked at how quickly she felt weak. Her knees buckled, but the monster had a firm arm wrapped around her waist.

Rowan expected pain but only found a sinking emptiness and heaviness in all of her limbs. Her vision dimmed as her magic rushed out of her along with her blood. She didn't have long. Her consciousness was fading.

"Please," she whispered, but the man's grip on her just tightened. She had little left but surrender.

A thousand lives she'd never live bloomed in her chest. There were so many things she would have rather been than a sacrifice. The desire to live blew through her like a tempest, but she still couldn't muster a struggle.

Sing, a voice in her head commanded. *Sing!*

She opened her mouth and a strangled note came out—then another. The monster seemed unbothered by it. It took all her concentration to remember the melody and the words, to force air through her vocal cords.

Sing, her mind begged.

Several more notes came out, and the forest stilled as if listening. Rowan sang a song of angry grief. A song she'd written years before when her mother had missed yet another visitation. The melody was soft, but the words and notes were jagged and angry.

There was a strange pulse around her as the forest shifted. The trees rustled. Perhaps Conor was finally catching up. Maybe he would save her. The rustling grew louder, like the gusts of wind before a storm.

The fear and the fight faded, and Rowan surrendered. She didn't feel terrified. She felt peaceful as the monster drank from her. There was nothing but him and the warmth of his body pressed against hers. She looked up, trying to get one last glimpse of the sky through the spindly trees.

Suddenly, Rowan was struck hard from the side. She tumbled to the ground. There were sounds of a scuffle but she was too exhausted to move. She could barely keep her eyes open. She stared up at the blue sky before her eyes fluttered once, twice, and then closed.

ROWAN WOKE CHOKING ON A SCREAM. She sat up quickly and nearly passed out from the head rush.

Blinking her bleary eyes, she tried to focus on her room. It was a meditation technique meant to calm her. She looked at the detail on an elaborately carved canopy bedpost. Her hand brushed over the soft white linens, far finer than the ones on her bed back at Maiden's Tower. A roaring fire burned in a large fireplace, the frame of which was carved with floral patterns similar to those decorating the bed. Pale green velvet curtains layered with sheer fabric lined the windows, and two large, hunter-green velvet chairs sat by the fireplace, just waiting for her to curl up and read a good book.

She was in her room at Wolf's Keep. She wasn't dead.

The horror of the Dark Wood crashed over her. Despite her best efforts to fight it, she was caught in the memory of it. Her whole body trembled.

"Lass, it's all right," Conor said.

Rowan's head snapped toward his voice. He sat on the edge of the bed and took her hands in his.

"Conor?" She stared at him with wide eyes and, to her horror, she started crying. Loud, full-body sobs rocked her.

Conor looked as shaken as she felt. "Oh, lass, I'm sorry. Come now. It's all right. I really shouldn't be this close to you when you're like this." He awkwardly patted her hands.

She looked up and met his stormy eyes, her chin trembling.

"Ahh, Mother slay me," he grumbled. He sat on the edge of the bed and pulled her into his lap as if she weighed nothing.

She curled into him, tucking her face into his neck, and sobbed. She expected him to pat her on the head and pull away, but instead, he wrapped his arms around her and held her close.

"There now, you're safe," he whispered. He rubbed her back until her sobs turned to sniffles and her breathing calmed, and she drifted back under the heavy blanket of sleep.

She woke a few moments later, or perhaps an hour. She wasn't sure how much time had passed, but she was still in Conor's arms.

Touch was a luxury in Rowan's life. It was wonderful to be held while he rubbed slow circles on her back. She was ecstatic from the thrill of it. Like a child hopped-up on too many sweets, she was hopped-up on his touch.

He flinched away, realizing she was awake again.

"Please don't stop," she sighed. "No one ever touches me like this."

Conor winced as if the words hurt him the same way they did her. She instantly felt pathetic, like a stray dog waiting to be kicked for being so desperate for love.

Instead, he continued rubbing her back, his body taut.

After a while, he pulled back to look at her. She followed his gaze, and her hand flew to her neck. A bandage was wrapped around the wounds the monster had inflicted. Conor's eyes lit momentarily with hunger, but he shook his head and shuddered.

"What happened? How am I still here?" she rasped. "I thought I was dying—"

"No, lass, you just lost some blood and passed out."

Her mind was foggy. Her head ached. "Conor, how did I survive?"

"It was the strangest thing," Conor said. "Charlie and I had just spotted you when you flew from that monster's arms like he'd thrown you. He took off. Charlie gave chase, but he didn't want to go far when we didn't know how hurt you were. We got to you in time."

"Who was that?" Rowan asked.

Conor's eyes glowed with fury. "His name is Valen. He is a parasite who lives off the blood of others."

"Is he the evil you're holding back?" Rowan asked.

Conor sighed. "Among many others and one much worse."

"He killed Orla," Rowan choked out.

"I suspect he did, yes."

"What is he?"

"A powerful demon of sorts."

Rowan paled. Cade was a demon. Did he want to do that to her? If so, why hadn't he? She'd been young and vulnerable when they met. Perhaps the urge had been suppressed until she became Red Maiden. He *had* been distant recently. She shook her head, trying to shake away the bad thoughts.

"Is that what you want to do to me?" Rowan asked Conor.

"No. Rowan, I'm sorry I lost control. Your blood is just a much more potent version of your scent, and you smell like—" He sighed. "You smell irresistible."

"How are you keeping control now?" she asked.

"An herbal tincture that helps tame the urge. It's still there, but it's not nearly as powerful," Conor explained.

"How does it work? How do you devour me?" she asked.

He shook his head, his lips pressed into a thin line.

"No," she said firmly. "I almost died. Tell me how this works. I refuse to walk into the woods while you keep me in the dark. Tell me how it works."

"I don't. That's how it works for you. I don't devour you, and you live out your term."

"Conor, I've already been attacked twice on the trail where I'm supposed to be safe," she said. "I think you need to decide right now if you're going to trust me or not. If you don't, I'm going to die much sooner than we both would like."

"*Twice*?" Conor asked. His eyes were incandescent, blue and gray swirling like storm clouds in his irises.

Rowan realized her mistake too late.

"When? How did you get away the first time?" he asked, his eyes full of suspicious anger.

"My second ferrying. Cade," she lied.

"Who the fuck is Cade?" Conor asked. He licked his lips, and she knew he was tasting the lie.

"My best friend. He's—he's a demon," she mumbled.

Conor froze. His silence made her more nervous, and everything spilled out of her mouth at once.

"I wasn't trying to hide him. I met Cade when I was young. He's how I was found out as a spirit singer, and he's just always been around. I know he's evil. I get it, but he's different. You would have met him already, except he couldn't cross into the keep—"

"Of course he couldn't," Conor said. "The boundary magic is meant to keep evil things out. Which is what he is, Rowan. You'll stop talking to him immediately."

An indignant laugh bubbled out of her. "You may have dominion over my death, but you certainly don't hold any over my life."

"Don't I?"

Conor's eyes blazed, and the way he looked at her sent a warmth pooling low in her belly. His hand cupped her cheek, and he forced her to hold his gaze. He paused, as if waiting for her to pull back or to knock his hand away. It was a game of chicken she had no intention of losing.

"I bet I could get you to do anything I wanted right now, and I wouldn't need to use compulsion like that vile beast in the Dark Wood," Conor murmured.

He tipped her head back, and his lips drew over the curve of her jaw, sending a wave of shivers through her body. She should have pulled away, but instead, she tilted her chin up to give him better access.

"Mm, yes, I bet you'd be such a good lass for me, wouldn't you?" he murmured against her skin.

She swallowed hard. Conor drew back suddenly and lifted her so she straddled his lap.

She stared at him, stunned. "What are you—"

His fingers tangled in her hair, drawing her head back, and he brushed a line of kisses up the column of her neck. She gasped. The contrast between the pleasure that spun through her and the pain she'd felt earlier was staggering. Her heart beat wildly, trying to escape the cage of her ribs.

"Say it. Say you want it," Conor whispered. His breath danced over her lips, his words containing a desperation she couldn't fully grasp.

She was confused by his request for permission. Her whole life, she'd been taught that Conor had a right to her. She was his. But still, he wanted her consent. Control was a heady rush, but with it came responsibility for her actions.

Rowan knew what awaited her in Ballybrine if she didn't succeed in seducing Conor. Even more compelling was the relentless tug of attraction she felt whenever he was close. She wanted him to kiss her. Once again, she felt as though she'd lost her mind, perhaps for good this time.

"Kiss me," she whispered.

Conor cupped her face and roughly brought her lips to his. There was nothing tentative or gentle about it. He showed Rowan exactly what it was to be devoured, and she was surprised to find that she didn't want it to stop. She wanted him to raze her completely—burn through her like wildfire until nothing of what she was before existed. She was done being meek and obedient. She wanted to be something else entirely.

A growl rumbled up from his chest. He tugged on her hair—the bite of the pain perfectly complimenting the wild pleasure of kissing him.

His kiss was greedy and ravenous. His hands shook as he pressed Rowan's body against his, and she didn't know if it was nerves or restraint that he struggled with.

It was so very different from how Finn kissed her. Finn was soft and gentle, but Conor kissed her like he wanted to take everything from her and replace it with something new and better.

She slid her hands up his chest, enjoying the soft velvet of his tunic and the ridges of the firm muscle beneath. He went stiff at the touch before yanking her closer. One of his hands came to her lower back, and he pushed her hips down, giving her friction that sent chills through her body. She bit down on his lip, and he growled again, forcing her to roll her hips against him. His other hand went to the back of her head. She parted her lips, and he welcomed the invitation to take more from her.

He tasted like whiskey and cider, and she savored the bittersweetness. She let him open her up. After years of being bound, closed, starved for touch, she felt so completely overwhelmed by him. The momentum of what they'd started felt right. It felt unstoppable, inevitable, glorious. She wanted to drown in it.

Her hands threaded through his hair, and she tugged him closer. He groaned into her mouth, and it occurred to her that he felt the same way. He was devouring her, yes, but she was also devouring him. They exchanged the role of predator and prey in a precarious dance.

Conor pulled away suddenly, practically tossing her back on the bed. He crossed the room in great strides to put space between them.

She blinked at him, her mind too foggy with lust and fatigue to comprehend the sudden shift in his demeanor. He stared at her for a long moment before tearing out of the bedroom and slamming the door behind him.

Rowan giggled, her hand flying to her lips to stifle the sound. Her whole body still tingled with the pleasure of the kiss. Her laugh turned into something high-pitched and hysterical in her throat.

She knew the look on Conor's face before he stormed out of the room. The Wolf of the Dark Wood—the god of death—was afraid of *her*.

The Mother's words came back to her. *"You're a weapon, Rowan. The moment that he's taking from you, he's vulnerable. That is when you strike. That is when a victim becomes a warrior."*

If the Wolf knew that, it meant he wanted to take something from her.

Rowan's hand flew to her right thigh, where the dagger and holster the Mother had presented her with were still hidden. She let out a sigh of relief.

What if he'd felt it when he was kissing her, and that's why he ran? He could be preparing right now to kill her.

She stood and crossed the room on tiptoes. She tried to ignore the vicious spinning in her head. How much blood did she lose to feel so faint?

She ignored the not-so-subtle requests from her body to slow down. She cracked the door open and peeked out. The entire mansion was silent. She sharpened her senses as she stepped out into the hall. Her mind still felt fuzzy and her mouth dry, but she forced herself to focus on the magic that still curled and uncurled inside of her, like leaves reaching toward the sunshine.

Rowan was drawn down the corridor by the stillness that surrounded Conor. She found that she could follow its signature through the mansion with ease. She traced it down the stairs through the main sitting room to the foyer. She hesitated for only a moment at the entrance to the east wing, a place Conor had forbidden her to go. She walked through the dim corridor until it opened into a cavernous hall.

Arched ceilings and large glass windows cast the space in a strange, pale light that made the shadows appear twice as sinister and consuming. Rowan stilled. Sadness permeated the room, which must have once been quite grand. Nature had taken over, crumbling the dark green marble floor, which split to reveal a babbling stream and moss-covered rocks that led down to a dark tunnel. It was beautiful in a lonely, haunted way—the same way the Dark Garden was.

The impulse to explore was consuming, but Rowan forced herself back to the task at hand. She wasn't a princess in a magical abandoned mansion like in the fairy tales she read to Aeoife. Rowan was a lonely sacrifice in death's house. She could not afford mistakes.

She needed to confront Conor, and she was too lightheaded to be trusted on a hike down to an unknown dark place. She wanted to stay for a while and see why the space was forbidden, but the soft tinkle of piano music drew her attention.

Turning down the first hallway, she followed the passage as the music grew louder. Finally, she reached the doorway from which it emanated. She peeked through the cracked door and found Conor bent over the piano. The music was lovely—somehow sad and angry at the same time. His fingers flew over the keys, his eyes squeezed shut in concentration. He swayed as if the melody moved through him before he played the notes.

She couldn't explain why seeing him so consumed by the song made her want to cry. Rowan had never witnessed anyone else so overwhelmed by music. She didn't know anyone else felt what she did when she sang—like she'd willingly be swept away by it if it would take her. The same emotion she poured into the songs she made up—the songs that held all her loneliness, heartache, rage—he poured into his playing. It was mesmerizing.

When the song ended, Conor leaned his forehead against the keys and sighed heavily. It was too vulnerable. Rowan felt like the ignorant hunters who wandered into delicate habitats, not realizing the damage they might do.

Guilt twisted her stomach in knots. She ducked away and rushed back to her room. Laying down in her bed, her heart still pounding, she stared into the dark and waited for the confusion to subside.

14

ROWAN

Rowan stared miserably into her oatmeal, frustrated to be eating it back in her room at Maiden's Tower. Failure made her appetite elusive.

After she'd made it safely through the night at Wolf's Keep, Conor sent her back to Ballybrine without a second glance. He seemed wholly uninterested in her, and she'd never felt more aware of her lack of experience. When he left the room after kissing her, he'd looked afraid of her, but when he returned later, he was stoic and completely unmoved.

Now that she was certain he hadn't killed Orla, there was no barrier between them. When she thought about the kiss, a violent flush lit her from within and her skin prickled with goosebumps. She'd never felt so consumed by something. She didn't understand what she'd done wrong.

Conor was certainly distracted by things that he did not trust her enough to share. Rowan desperately needed to be more desirable.

Her thoughts spun like a tempest. Rowan barely noticed when Mrs. Teverin pushed into the room.

"Rowan, Elder Garrett wants to see you," Mrs. Teverin said. "I'll go with you."

Rowan nodded. She smoothed her dress and shuddered. She hadn't even seen the elder yet, but she already felt dirty.

"Relax, lass. I'll not let anything bad happen to you," Mrs. Teverin soothed.

Rowan followed her tutor out of the tower. Outside the sunlight was blinding. A cool pine-scented wind whipped across the square as they walked to the temple. Mrs. Teverin pulled the heavy temple door open and ushered Rowan inside. They paused in front of the large wood door to Elder Garrett's office.

Mrs. Teverin held her hand poised to knock and looked to Rowan, as if checking that she was ready. Rowan nodded.

The door swung open, and Elder Garrett was startled by the sight of the two of them. "Mrs. Teverin, this is a lovely surprise, though I'm afraid I have a private matter to discuss with Rowan."

Rowan kept her eyes focused on the gray swirls in the white marble floor, but still, she felt Elder Garrett's gaze like a weight on her shoulders.

"Yes, but I happened upon Rowan just after the last time I trusted you alone with her, and I understand some liberties were taken," Mrs. Teverin challenged. She crossed her arms and glared at him.

Rowan couldn't believe Mrs. Teverin addressed things so directly.

Elder Garrett, for his part, feigned confusion. "I'm quite certain I don't know what you mean," he said solemnly.

Rowan chewed her lower lip.

"I assure you that I would never behave inappropriately with a Red Maiden. This has to be a misunderstanding. Tell her, Rowan," Elder Garrett said.

Rowan finally met his eyes. A discordant sound struck the air around him, like a bunch of fiddles tuning up at once. Rowan tried not to cringe at the sound. Elder Garrett looked at her expectantly.

"She already knows the truth," Rowan said. "I'm not comfortable alone with you."

He frowned, his gaze focusing on Mrs. Teverin. His frenetic clanging energy surrounded the old woman like a bubble of sound. Rowan couldn't quite understand what was happening, but Mrs.

Teverin's entire demeanor changed. Her arms dropped to her sides, and her face softened to a pleasant smile.

"Mrs. Teverin, would you mind leaving us to a private scripture lesson? I'll take good care of Rowan," Elder Garrett said sweetly.

Rowan expected the same bluster as before, but Mrs. Teverin smiled cheerfully and nodded. "Of course, Elder Garrett. You know best," she said before turning and leaving Rowan alone.

Rowan stared blankly after her tutor.

Elder Garrett laughed as he grabbed Rowan's arm and pulled her into the office. "You think you're so clever. You forget who I am. I told you that no one would believe you. Does it feel better to have it confirmed?"

The shock rendered Rowan breathless as Elder Garrett locked the office door and turned to face her.

"You've been quite petulant. I think perhaps I haven't chosen the right type of discipline yet. But we'll get it right this time," he said.

Rowan stilled as he walked behind her, unfastening her red cloak and tossing it aside. His hands came to the buttons at the back of her dress. He tore it open. The air rushed out of her lungs all at once, her whole chest threatened to cave in on itself. A violent tremor went through her body as he ran his fingers down her spine.

"Such perfect porcelain skin," Elder Garrett whispered. She tried not to flinch as he pinched her. "Look at the marvelous way it pinks so easily."

He picked up a switch from his desk, and Rowan swallowed hard. It was stupid to feel relieved, but she had endured enough physical pain that she felt prepared. What was one more wound in need of mending? Better her skin than her soul.

He gestured for her to turn toward the wall, and she did so obediently.

"Kneel," he said. "Don't look so sullen. If you didn't want this, you would have done your job. I'm starting to suspect you enjoy our sessions." He clicked his tongue. "But the Mother's will must be done. It's a hard lesson to teach, but hopefully, this will inspire you to spread your legs and do your job."

Rowan knelt, closed her eyes, and put her hands against the cold stone of the office wall. Her fear was quickly swallowed up by fury. She bowed her head so that her forehead rested on the backs of her hands.

He struck so quickly she barely had time to register the first stinging blow of the switch against her back. She bit her lip to keep from crying out. She refused to give him the satisfaction. She hoped he feared the Wolf enough not to risk marking her permanently.

Rowan swallowed her helpless rage and prayed to the Mother to save her. She waited hopefully as the elder brought the switch down against her burning skin again.

The Mother never came.

BRIGHT SUNSHINE BLINDED Rowan as soon as she pushed out of the temple. The skin on her back ached every time her cloak brushed against it, and shame turned her stomach. She worried she'd vomit right on the temple stairs.

Cade waited for her, leaning against the wall by the door.

"Where have you been? Your timing is impeccable," she said, clenching her fists at her sides.

Cade's face darkened. "What happened?"

"Elder Garrett happened, and there was nothing I could do," she huffed, brushing by her friend.

"There's always something you can do," Cade challenged.

Rowan spun to face him. Her rage was incendiary. "Is there? Was I supposed to kill him? Fight him off? Beg for mercy?" she countered. "You should have been there. You left me alone."

"I'm not your savior, Rowan," Cade snapped. "I'm a demon. Mother's tits! What do you want from me? I can't be by your side every second of every day on pervert patrol."

Rowan stared at him, her lower lip trembling. "Where were you?" she asked. "Seriously?"

Cade looked away. "Sometimes, there are things I have to do. I don't want to leave. I'm sorry I wasn't there. It's not that I don't want to be. I hate Elder Garrett. Do you know who I really envy? Whoever finally gets to send him to Wolf's Keep."

Rowan blinked back tears as she looked away.

"What happened, Row?" Cade asked.

She shook her head. She was ashamed. She knew it wasn't her fault, but somehow, she was the one suffering under the burden of shame.

Cade's face grew serious. "No. Tell me he didn't—"

Rowan crossed her arms over her chest involuntarily.

"He did what he was going to last time?" Cade asked.

"He just beat me with a switch. It could have been worse." Rowan tried to lock everything up, but it sprang free. "I need a bath. I need someone to make sure it's not too bad."

For the first time, Cade looked genuinely worried. "You should tell the Wolf."

"Conor," she corrected.

"Whatever his name is, you should tell him."

"I'm not interested in being in his debt."

"Row—Elder Garrett, he's made a deal with a demon," Cade said.

Rowan froze and stared at him. "Like the bedtime story you told Aeoife? I thought you said that doesn't happen anymore."

"I said there's truth in every story. It happens less now than it used to. I'm not surprised that people aren't quick to explain that their successes are from deals with demons instead of hard work," Cade scoffed.

"How can humans make deals with demons if they can't even see you?" Rowan asked.

"We can appear out of necessity. For me, it feels like a sucking sensation—a magnetism that draws me toward a certain person. A normal human can only see us if they are in need of a bargain that plays to our particular gifts," Cade said.

Rowan stared at him in stunned confusion. "But no one else has ever spoken to you around me."

Cade arched a brow. "Doesn't mean they haven't seen me."

Rowan retraced all the times she'd been out around town with him, searching for proof that he was being honest. But she had no reason to doubt him and he had no reason to lie.

Her mouth went dry. "How do you know Elder Garrett has made a deal with a demon?"

Cade sighed and leaned against the wall. "I can smell it on him and see it in his aura. I don't know who he made it with or their proclivity, but it means that he has power, beyond what he has in Ballybrine with the elders. Without knowing exactly what deal he made, I can't say what it means, but if I had to guess, it must be some sort of persuasion. That would explain why even the elders don't see through him and how he's swiftly risen through their ranks."

"How is that allowed? What does it mean for me?" Rowan asked. "How have you never told me about this?"

Cade shook his head. "It never came up. Demons love to make deals like that because it feeds them. They get a little crumb of the dealmaker's soul—a touch of their life force. Something like that makes a demon more powerful while also giving the person a talent or gift they didn't have before or enhancing an affinity they already have. Row, they work in so many different ways it would be impossible for me to tell exactly what it is."

"Do you make deals like that?" Rowan asked.

"Not in a very long time," Cade said grimly.

"Why?"

"Because it's a gamble. I'm trading something, counting on the slice of soul giving me enough of a boost. Demons don't make deals unless they know they come out on the winning end of that kind of gamble. Also, my envy is such that it's hard to settle on one thing I want, which is kind of prohibitive to making deals. Whenever I think of something I'd like, I come up with something I want more. Anytime I get something I want, it instantly loses its luster. Being a demon isn't all it's cracked up to be," he said blandly.

Rowan stared at him. She tried not to look as horrified as she felt. They had rarely ever talked about the fact that he was a demon. It was the unspoken thing in every silence between them. It wasn't so much that Cade hid things, as she didn't bother to ask. She had no right to be mad at him for never sharing this particular inner working of his world.

Perhaps it was selfish of Rowan not to consider that the friend who'd spent years making her laugh and keeping her company might be someone else's monster.

"So what do I do about Elder Garrett?" she asked.

Cade threw his hands up. "You tell the Wolf."

"I've never needed someone else to solve my problems, and I won't start taking favors now. Plus, I have the Mother on my side," she said.

She hadn't told Cade about her deal with the Mother because she suspected he would disapprove and the Mother had asked her to keep it a secret. Still, the Mother's words restored her faith.

It was clear that Cade didn't know what to make of her newfound devotion to the Mother. "Yes, and what did she do for you just now? Did she save you?"

Rowan's anger was as bitter as unripened berries in her mouth. "No." They stared each other down. "She didn't save me from the monster in the woods, either."

"What monster?" Cade asked. His entire demeanor shifted from anger to curiosity.

"Some blood-sucking demon in the Dark Wood named Valen. Cade, he was on the trail. He wasn't supposed to be able to do that. I'd cut myself at Wolf's Keep, and Conor lost control and chased me—"

"You bled in the Dark Wood?" Cade asked.

Rowan held up her hands, exasperated. "Not on purpose. It was certain death with the Wolf or take my chances in the Dark Wood. I almost made it."

"Row, slow down and tell me everything from the beginning."

Rowan stopped and looked at him. "Tell me where you were first."

Cade's mouth formed a grim line. "I can't."

"Then I have nothing to say. I have to bathe and then take meditation and rehearsal time," she huffed. She arched an eyebrow at Cade, daring him to argue. They stood locked in a stalemate for a moment. When she turned away, he didn't argue or try to follow her.

It was what she wanted, but somehow, it felt worse than ever to be left alone.

———————

ROWAN SAT AT THE PIANO, trying to play a piece she knew by heart, but her fingers felt tangled up and her heart was too heavy to enjoy the levity of the music. Her wool dress scraped painfully against her tender back. The welts acted as a constant reminder of an invisible wound that threatened to pull her into a dark hopelessness from which there was no escape. She shook her head, trying to rid herself of the memory.

She felt a sinking flood of grief fill her chest. She wished Orla was there to talk to.

Rowan settled her fingers over the keys again. Her grief came in minor chords and staccato notes that struck out of nowhere. It swelled, simmered, turned into tinkling background noise, and then swelled again until she was left as breathless as she was every time she walked by Orla's empty bedroom.

The sound in the room warped and shifted. There was a bright burst of light as the Mother appeared next to her.

Rowan gasped, and her hand flew to her mouth as she bit back a curse. "Goddess," she said, crossing her hands over her heart and bowing her head.

"Yes, yes, thank you. I don't have much time. How did it go this weekend?" the Mother asked, waving her hand dismissively.

"He still wouldn't take me to bed. I swear I tried. There was an incident in the Dark Wood—"

"An incident?" the Mother asked, pursing her lips. Her golden curls bounced as she cocked her head to the side.

"I cut myself on some thorns, and the Wolf lost control and nearly killed me. I escaped into the Dark Wood, where I was attacked by a demon named Valen."

The Mother pressed her lips into a thin line. "I see." Her eyes focused on Rowan's neck.

Thanks to a salve from the Crone, the wound was already nearly healed over, leaving only a red imprint of teeth marks on her pale skin. Rowan stared at it in the mirror each morning. She'd expected the marks to be large and wild, the mark of a beast, but instead, they were small and neat and human. It was one more reminder of common monstrosity.

"You said you would protect me," Rowan said, her voice more accusatory than she intended.

The Mother wasn't angry. Her face was soft, conciliatory. "I'm sorry. Rowan, I'm going to tell you something that I'm ashamed to admit, but maybe it will give you an idea of the urgency of the situation."

Rowan nodded intently.

"Unfortunately, the rise of the new religion in the north has stolen many of my followers. We gods take our power from faith. It's what fuels us. Over the past few years, I've lost considerable power. It takes tremendous effort to keep the dark at bay. Things that used to be second nature now require intense concentration."

"Is that happening to the Wolf, too?" Rowan asked.

The Mother shook her head. "No, dear, people always believe in death. It's easy for him to hold onto his power because people die all the time."

Rowan swallowed hard. The Mother was becoming weaker as the Wolf's power remained unchanged. No wonder the Dark Wood and death itself were bleeding out into Ballybrine. Conor had been kind to her, but she was probably just naive to believe a few moments of kindness meant that he was innately good. Perhaps he could not help what he was, but that didn't make him any less dangerous.

"All of this is to say that I'm sorry that happened to you," the Mother continued. "I should have been there. I'm pulled in so many directions that I somehow missed it, and I shouldn't have. You are our greatest hope right now—our last good chance to stop what's already in motion. I'm counting on you, Rowan. Protecting you is my priority, and I will do better. How did you survive?"

The genuine curiosity on the goddess's face startled Rowan.

"I don't remember," she admitted. "I was dying, and I lost so much blood that I'm still weak now. The Wolf and one of his reapers arrived, but I hit the ground and lost consciousness. When I woke up, I was back in Wolf's Keep."

"That's all right. I was just curious," the Mother said. Her interest in Rowan seemed renewed. "I've never known him to save a Maiden before. Perhaps you've had more of an impact than you think."

Rowan blushed and looked away. Part of her hoped that was true, but underneath was a smaller, more insistent part of her that wished it wasn't. Saving the people of Ballybrine was a heavy weight to carry, even if it was one she'd been holding her whole life.

The burden of being Red Maiden was a passive one that required good manners and indifference to her own survival. Now the Mother wanted her to stand and fight; after a lifetime of being taught not to, it felt unnatural, even if the impulse to survive was one she'd always felt.

The idea of killing a god felt impossibly big. She couldn't wrap her mind around it.

Beyond that, it was frustrating to be raised in a community that asked her to only be strong at the exact time and in the exact way that it benefited them and to act meek the rest of the time. Her head spun from the dissonance between what she'd been taught to be, what they needed of her now, and what she knew herself to be.

"Stay the course, dear," the Mother said. "I know that feelings complicate things, but I trust you will find a way to make this happen. Now, I understand that Elder Garrett took advantage of his power. I promised to protect you and I let you down and for that, I'm sorry. It's difficult to be everywhere at once, and I was out saving one of the fishing ships from a storm. Your brother, Ryan, was aboard one, as I understand."

Panic swept over Rowan like a wave. Her older brother, Ryan, ran a fleet of fishing boats. "Is he all right?"

"Of course. But you understand, in the wake of my limited powers, I have to use my resources wisely. I assumed you would rather I save your brother's life." The goddess looked suddenly weary. "I hate that I can't save everyone from every bit of suffering, but the reality is that I have to make a lot of hard choices now. I'm sorry you were on the losing end of one of those choices today. I swear I'm doing my best."

Rowan swallowed hard and nodded. She was happy her brother was safe. Even if ensuring his safety came at the cost of her dignity, it was a trade she'd willingly make if given the choice.

The Mother's form flickered a bit. "Rowan, truly, I'm sorry that I could not save you. I swear I am working on Elder Garrett, but he has some additional power, and it will take me some time." Rowan was disturbed to hear Cade's suspicion of Elder Garrett confirmed, but the Mother forged on. "For now I can only heal the welts."

The Mother took her hand and a rush of warmth spread over Rowan's skin. Her back itched and tingled. When the feeling dissipated, the ache was gone.

"It's natural to have doubts. It's natural to feel sympathy for the Wolf when he treats you well, but I urge you to think of Aeoife, of your own survival." The Mother flickered again. "I'm afraid I'm being summoned elsewhere. I will do my best to keep that elder busy. In the meantime, remember our deal. The sooner you can act, the better it will be for all of us. I will gain strength, and I'll owe you a debt, Rowan. Be brave. I'll see you soon."

She faded into a shuddering flame and then nothing, leaving Rowan alone, feeling a strange mix of relief, bitterness, and tenacity.

15

ROWAN

Rowan cut through the Borderwood with Sarai at her side. The wind rustled the branches of the birch trees—bark scratching on bark an ominous sound heralding cooler weather. Autumn was always in a rush to give way to winter in Ballybrine, the ground damp from constant rain and frosting overnight.

The sunlight cast dancing shadows on the forest floor as Sarai squatted low to look at some mushrooms. It was the first hint of peace Rowan had felt all week.

Sarai's confident presence soothed Rowan. Rowan's head was spinning and she knew an afternoon gathering herbs with Sarai in the Borderwood would help ground her so she could see a clear path forward.

Sarai had always been braver, wilder, and more daring than Rowan. She was a world unto herself. Where Rowan struggled against the solitude of her life, Sarai embraced every sacred silent moment to herself. She kept her own counsel. Sarai had the kind of wisdom that came from being connected to something higher, something other, but she never lorded it over other people. She was generous with her time, her love, her joy. She lived as if the world owed her something, and she intended to claim it.

Sarai spoke as if feeling Rowan's appraisal. "I thought about what you said the other day—about what I'd be if I wasn't what I am."

"I thought you wrote that off."

"I did, but then I considered it, and I thought I owed you and me a better answer," Sarai started. "I love what I am. I love having a foot in two worlds and not fully belonging to either. I love reaching my fingers across the veil and pulling down ideas, thoughts, and inspiration from something much larger than myself. It's magical and exhilarating—but you know like no one else does that it can also be... isolating."

Rowan nodded.

Sarai ran a hand down her braid. "If I could be anything, I'd be what I am, but without the rules that keep me in line. I'd want no elders. I'd be a Crone like in the old days when there weren't a bunch of old men making the scripture more palatable for the wealthy and powerful. The Crone used to write the scriptures, you know, before the men wanted to claim power for themselves."

"I'd say I'm surprised, but that would be a lie," Rowan said dryly.

"The elders think that the tighter they hold on, the less traction the new religion in the north will gain, but I think they've taken everything pure about our beliefs and corrupted them. The world as we know it—this system that serves to crush both of our spirits—that aims to tame wild women—I want to break it."

Rowan grinned. "How?"

"I don't know yet, but the way I see it, you and I have power. It may not be much, but it's something. I can feel a change coming. I don't understand it, but I haven't missed the way my mother looks at you like you're a harbinger of something terrifying. I don't see it quite the same. I think everyone has light and dark, good and evil. No one is just one thing. I think if I could be anything, I'd like to be the person who rights this world."

Rowan grinned at her friend. For a woman who spent most of her life in isolation, Sarai had a remarkable grasp on humanity.

"By the Mother, let it be so. Is that all? Just that one small change?" Rowan teased.

Sarai laughed. "Well, perhaps I'd also like to spend some time with Raya Grange."

Rowan cackled in delight. "I knew it! I saw you staring at her at the last ceremony."

"She's quite lovely with all that wild blonde hair, and she kisses me like she's afraid I'll disappear." Sarai sighed whimsically.

Rowan's mind drifted to how it felt when Conor had kissed her the same way.

"You think that strange?" Sarai asked. She smoothed her dress, nervously playing with the end of her braid.

Rowan had always suspected that Sarai favored women from the way she perked up around Raya, but they'd never spoken openly about it. Just one whisper in the wrong direction could make her the victim of violent prejudice. Nothing was more threatening to a man than a woman who wanted nothing to do with him.

It made no difference to Rowan who Sarai loved, as long as that person knew how lucky they were and treated her with respect.

Rowan shook her head. "I find it strange that she wouldn't be as enamored with you. You are a brilliant, magical woman of astonishing beauty. She should be so lucky to have your heart."

Sarai sighed again. "I know it sounds frivolous, all things considered, but I think that love is the thing that adds the spice to life, gives it depth and peril and stakes. I just want to feel what I feel with her. I want the freedom to be something for which no mold exists." She went silent, looking down at her hands before taking Rowan's hands in her own. "I think if you hadn't asked me that question, I wouldn't have considered it. So thank you, Row."

Rowan grinned.

Sarai squeezed her hands. "Let's agree to keep asking each other the questions that challenge us to see beyond everyone else's expectations. Let's keep asking the questions that tear down worlds, Rowan."

Rowan nodded silently, in awe of her friend's intensity. Sarai had always played her cards quite close to the vest. This admission was the most she'd ever shared at once, and it meant the world to Rowan.

She tried to hide her emotions with a laugh, but Sarai missed nothing.

"What would you want to do, Rowan?" she asked.

Rowan wiped away a tear. "I want to break the world with you. I just have no idea how to do it—so you're in charge."

"And what about your handsome Wolf?"

"Goddess above!" Rowan sighed. "I know I'm inexperienced, but I genuinely do not understand how to get through to him or if I want to. I know I should be afraid, and yet I can't help feeling drawn in."

"Give it time. Perhaps all you've learned doesn't serve you well. Maybe you just need to be yourself," Sarai suggested.

"And who is that? It's not as if the life I've lived has cultivated a personality," Rowan grunted.

"And yet you still have one," Sarai said with a smile. "You are a woman of a hundred little rebellions. You have a wild heart hidden behind a pretty face. I think the question is, do you really want the Wolf to be interested in you?"

Rowan pulled her hands away and ran them through her hair. Her mind wandered unbidden to the memory of Elder Garrett. She cringed, trying to banish it from her mind.

"I don't know. Sometimes it feels like admiration is just another excuse for violence. Others, it feels like I can't believe I've gone so long without it. Either way, the Wolf has somehow become the lesser of two evils. I don't know what this ceremony the elders have discussed entails, but I imagine it's worse than Conor."

"What aren't you saying?" Sarai asked.

"A lot," Rowan said. Her lip trembled, and she was embarrassed by how quickly her composure slipped.

She admitted how Elder Garrett had beaten her. Sarai's face lit with fury as Rowan spoke and explained precisely what he'd done and what Cade said about his bargain with a demon.

"I don't know what to do," Rowan said, wiping away tears furiously with the back of her hand. "He can do whatever he wants, and there's nothing I can do to stop him because he's right—who would believe me?"

Sarai grabbed her hand. "I believe you." She spiraled a finger into one of her dark curls as she considered their options. "Maybe you should tell the Wolf."

"That's what Cade said," Rowan sighed.

"Then why don't you?"

"Because no matter how he reacts, there's no way it doesn't blow back on me," Rowan said. "Either Conor blames me for the elder's behavior, or he acts on it, and then the town blames me for the Wolf being dissatisfied enough to take it out on an elder. People are already upset enough with the blight. Tension is high in the village, and everyone looks at me in my white dress like I'm letting them down. I'm daily confronted with hundreds of stares that just remind me how I'm failing them. This morning, there were three more blighted trees in Ashand Orchards. A man yelled at me when I was on my way here that if I *'wasn't so frigid and stuck-up, the town wouldn't be at risk of starving.'*"

Sarai wrung her hands together. "I know you're right, but I hate that there's nothing I can do."

"Sarai, we've never been able to protect each other. I don't expect that of you, just like you don't of me. We do what we can when we can."

"Wouldn't you feel the same?" Sarai challenged.

"I'd want to burn down the temple if that happened to you," Rowan said bitterly.

"I know." Sarai smiled. "I will think on it. There has to be a way to protect you. Demon's bargain or not, Elder Garrett is only mortal."

Rowan nodded. It was a comfort to share the burden. To know there was another person who held the righteous anger with her. A burden shared was easier to carry.

"That's not it, though, is it?" Sarai asked.

Rowan laughed. "How do you do that? It is so unnerving how well you read me."

Sarai smiled in satisfaction. "You can't hide from me, Row. I'm all-knowing."

"Conor kissed me," she admitted.

Sarai squealed. "How was it?"

"It was—" Rowan took a breath and tried to settle on a word. "Consuming."

"And what of Finn?" Sarai asked.

"It's not as if I could choose Finn if I wanted to."

"And that's the only reason you won't give that poor boy your heart?"

Rowan sighed. "No. Sometimes I feel like Finn looks at me and doesn't see me at all. He sees someone who needs saving, whom he can project all his fantasies upon. It will always be better than any real opportunities he has because it exists purely in his head."

"You might be too hard on him. I think he can learn," Sarai said.

"Maybe," Rowan sighed.

"That's not important now, though," Sarai said. "I want to hear more about your Wolf."

Rowan explained all that had transpired in the Dark Garden, the monster on the trail and the bite on her neck, and what happened afterward.

"He kissed me like he was losing his mind, and then just as suddenly as he started, he stopped and practically threw me across the bed," she groaned.

"Sounds like you drove him crazy," Sarai laughed.

"Then I followed him downstairs and found him playing this beautiful song on the piano. I don't understand him at all. I don't know what he wants or why he's fighting against this. Everything I ever learned made it seem like the Wolf couldn't wait to get his hands on me. Now, half the time, it seems like he's afraid of me, and the other half he's indifferent."

Her mind flashed to what the Mother had told her and the blessed dagger strapped to her thigh. She wanted to tell Sarai about it, but the Mother asked her to keep it a secret, so she said nothing.

"It sounds like he just needs more time with you. Why don't you ask to stay a few nights? I'm sure if he has more time to spend with you, he will find you irresistible," Sarai said.

Rowan considered it. "Maybe you're right, and I've just been over-complicating things."

"The worst he can say is no, but it's supposed to be stormy tomorrow night anyway. Give it a try," Sarai suggested.

"I'm really scared, Sarai. I used to fear almost nothing, but now it feels like there is so much to lose. There are all these things I didn't know to want, and now I can't stop myself from wanting them," Rowan said.

"Why would you stop yourself?"

"Because I feel like I only have part of this story. When I found Orla's bloody cloak in his closet, I thought the Wolf killed her, but after being attacked by that other beast, I don't think that's true. And while I know Conor is responsible for the blight, I feel like there's more to that as well. I have all these puzzle pieces, and none of them fit together, and if I don't figure it out soon, I'm going to get hurt."

Sarai looked at the healed wound on her neck, still purple against her fair skin.

"*More* hurt," Rowan corrected.

"Just take a breath. One thing at a time. You said you're looking for the Maiden journals, right?"

Rowan nodded.

"Start there, and we will figure the rest out as we go. I'll try to see what I can get from my inspired meditation about the blight," Sarai said.

Rowan nodded. They spent another hour gathering herbs before Rowan snuck back to the tower, comforted by the plan she and Sarai had made.

16

CONOR

Conor stared out into the fading sunlight through his study windows. He had hunted to the northern edge of the Dark Wood but still found no trace of Valen. He didn't know how the vampire managed to evade him so easily. He was certain that Valen was responsible for Orla's death beyond the shadow of a doubt. He'd known the moment he saw her body, but Rowan's encounter only confirmed it.

It made him furious that a monster in his own woods felt confident enough to steal from him. Even the wildest beast in the Dark Wood knew the Wolf's scent and knew that the Maidens were his. It might not have protected them from his own impulses, but it was meant to deter everything else in the forest.

He couldn't escape the haunting memory of Rowan's dying song or the terrified look on her face when she woke up after the attack.

Valen had taken off by the time Conor and Charlie arrived. He must have heard them coming and thought it better to flee. Either way, they'd found Rowan bleeding on a bed of soft ferns.

Conor hated Valen for leaving him with these exhausting visions playing on repeat in his head of all the ways that someone like Valen could ruin Rowan.

Still, those visions were preferable to remembering how it felt to kiss Rowan. She was chipping away at the shield he'd built to protect himself and everyone else. He'd given up fighting the impulse to do it. Her near-death stoked his urgency. He'd kissed her, half-expecting to feel the burnt sugar taste in his mouth that indicated a lie in her action, but it never came.

She'd been just as eager, and not because it was her duty, but because she genuinely wanted to. Conor had quickly shifted from being the aggressor to the one who was falling apart. If he'd let himself continue, they would have ended up naked right then and there. No matter how badly he wanted that, he could not have it. It was a spectacularly bad idea.

Never before had he experienced such a loss of self-control so soon into meeting a new Maiden. It was reckless to both their health and safety.

He shook his head. *Get a grip, Conor. She's just a pretty girl with magic designed to make you want to consume her.*

Rowan, with her auburn hair, bright green eyes, and scandalous dresses. She would drive him out of his mind. He'd gone through more whiskey in the past month than in the prior six months with Orla.

Rowan would arrive tonight, and he already wanted to ask her to stay an extra night. Perhaps he'd been at this too long and he was tired. Maybe it was a desperate attempt to welcome his own undoing.

Conor needed to stay focused. Valen's ambition was evident, and his latest antics with Orla and Rowan were a clear sign of just how much Conor needed to show his power. The faith of the people of Ballybrine was what strengthened him, and thanks to the blight reaching the edge of the Dark Wood, along with Orla's death, it seemed everyone's faith in him was renewed. Still, people were fickle, and he didn't need them or Rowan to realize the power she had, or the way she could choose which god of death to serve.

He sat there for so long he'd missed the sunset. He felt the moment Rowan entered the Dark Wood like a skip in a heartbeat. The favor he'd given her alerted him to her nearness. He made his way out to the keep gates and waited. The evening was quiet, but it smelled like a storm. Dark clouds blotted out the moon, making the forest appear darker than usual.

A short while later, he heard her voice, angelic and serene as it sliced through the night. She turned the corner, her red cloak covering all but small glimpses of the white silk dress beneath as spirits processed behind her. She paused at the gates and knelt gracefully.

Conor tended to the spirits before reaching out to her.

"Conor," she said, meeting his gaze with a sly smile as she took his hand.

"Rowan," he said, forcing a frown.

She glanced over her shoulder at the Dark Wood. "It seems a storm is coming. Would it be all right if I stayed?"

On cue, the Dark Wood rustled, branches groaning as a gust of wind kicked up dried leaves from the forest floor and ruffled her hair.

Conor was spared from having to ask her to stay, but he couldn't seem too eager. She was growing more confident around him, and he wasn't sure it was a good thing.

"Well, lass, I'm not sure that's the best idea, but I wouldn't want you to get caught in a storm and ruin what I'm sure is a very lovely—though seasonally inappropriate—dress."

She grinned as she took his arm and walked into the keep.

Charlie brought her cider, and Conor gave her his robe. It was as if they'd done it hundreds of times before. Somehow they'd fallen into a pattern that was far too comfortable for Conor's liking.

"I'm afraid I'm very busy tonight, so you'll be on your own, but help yourself to the library or whatever else you need," Conor said.

"Is everything okay?"

"Of course. Just plenty to do."

"Grand. I'll take care of myself," Rowan said. She snuggled into the chair with her cider.

Conor left the room and waited. A while later, Rowan wandered from the sitting room to the library. Instead of tending to the many problems he should have been managing, like hunting down the monsters in his forest, he spied on her in the library until she meandered off to bed.

As she slept, he sat in his study, sipping whiskey and cursing himself for letting her stay. Her scent hung everywhere in the keep, and it enticed him to go find her in her bed. He could practically feel the softness of her skin under his hands, the way she'd gasp when he nuzzled her neck. He imagined the surprise on her face when he kissed her awake.

He forced himself to think of anything else, but it was too late. All the blood in his body was already heading south.

"Mother slay me," he grumbled, scrubbing a hand over his face as he settled in for another long night.

CONOR FELT the same thrill he did when hunting in the Dark Wood as he stalked Rowan around the mansion. If she noticed, she didn't let on. She bounced between the Dark Garden with Charlie and the library, where she spent hours lying in front of the fire reading books. She favored the romances. Occasionally her cheeks pinked and her eyes darted around the room as if she'd been caught doing something terribly naughty before she settled back in, riveted to what must have been the most scandalous part.

Conor had never read a romance, but he made note of each one she read so he could go back and read them later. The romance books in the library were the product of past Maidens' requests to Charlie, who could track down just about anything. Conor wanted to ask Rowan why she liked them, in part so he could watch her blush, but also because he hated to know how someone who'd been raised as she had held onto the hope of romance.

She flitted about the keep as if she owned the place, her tinkling laughter bouncing off the walls, her sweet scent haunting every room she visited like a magical memory.

After a full day of thinking about it, he decided to confront her.

Conor found her in the library. She stood on the first rung of the rolling ladder, reaching for a book on the shelf just out of reach. She looked more herself than she ever had in a simple green dress. Her hair hung loose in curls down her back, and all he could think about was wrapping them around his fist and tugging her head back and—

He shut down the train of thought before that side of him could take over.

"Good evening, Rowan," he said.

She jumped at his voice. Her hand flew to her heart. Suddenly all his good intentions of asking her about her literature preferences disappeared.

"Goddess above, you scared me," she huffed, stepping down from the ladder. "Hasn't anyone ever told you not to startle someone while they're on a ladder?" she scolded. "I could have—" She stopped speaking when she saw his face.

He said nothing as he crossed the room. Rowan retreated until she bumped against the bookshelves behind her.

So she had some sense after all—though not enough to run.

Conor bent down and claimed her lips. He had no idea how she'd react. He hadn't so much as gone near her since their first kiss. He hadn't even seen her in days, actively avoiding everywhere she went in the mansion as if she was the thing to be feared and not the other way around.

But now he claimed her once again, and she did nothing to stop him. Instead, she drew him in like a siren luring a sailor into the depths. He would gladly drown in the feeling of her. She let out a soft whimper, and he drew away.

He stepped back, burned by her intensity, by the surprise and desire in her eyes. She reached for him, and he knew it was a challenge. She wanted to see that he couldn't resist, and he hated himself for having centuries more experience and still being unable to control himself.

Conor scrubbed a hand down his face. "I hate kissing you."

Rowan cringed and blushed. "Am I that bad?"

"Oh no, lass," he chuckled. "Quite the opposite, actually. Your passion is terribly compelling. You kiss with your whole self."

Confusion stole over her face. "Then why do you hate it?"

"Because I can never tell if you really want to or if you feel obligated to."

She looked as surprised by his vulnerability as he was. Now it seemed she had the power to pull emotions out of him he hadn't ever expressed. If he had any sense at all, he would leave immediately.

"Don't you just want to kiss me because I smell delicious?" she countered.

"You look delicious as well," he said. His gaze dropped to her lips, and her cheeks turned bright red. "Especially when you blush like that."

She bit her lip and looked away. Conor hated that she shied away from compliments. It didn't suit someone with so much fire to be so demure.

"Do you?" he asked, prowling closer. "Do you actually want to kiss me?"

She nodded, and he couldn't drag his gaze from the indentation her teeth left on her lower lip.

"Why?" he pressed.

"I like the way it feels."

"And how does it feel?" He wrapped a stray auburn curl around his finger.

"Wild," she murmured.

"That's a good thing?"

She met his eyes and swallowed hard. "It's the only thing in my life that's ever been unrestrained—the only time I've let go."

Conor was so done for. Rowan couldn't have said anything else that would make him more ravenous for her. He practically pounced on her, kissing her almost violently before shoving her back against the bookcase. Her lips parted in a gasp, and he used the opportunity to slip his tongue into her mouth. She sighed as he tugged her hair, tilting her chin up more. One hand caressed her outer thigh and drew her leg up over his hip as he rocked against her. Her hands tugged at his waist, drawing him in.

It wasn't enough for either of them, so he grabbed her thighs and lifted her. She wrapped her legs around his waist. Her hands threaded through his hair with a roughness to match his, and he loved it. She dragged her teeth over his lower lip, and he groaned.

Conor wanted to claim her so badly it hurt. He had a primal instinct to take her right there, and the thought of fucking her up against the bookshelves made him even harder. If her current reaction was any indication, she'd probably love it. He cupped one of her breasts, and she arched into the touch.

"Do you like that?" Conor whispered against her lips.

"Yes," she rasped between kisses.

He rolled his hips against her, and she met the motion with her own. He growled. He was losing control. He needed to fuck her or leave immediately.

"I love everything you're doing. Please don't stop," Rowan whimpered.

Conor cursed and pulled away so abruptly she stumbled and nearly fell as he set her back on her feet.

She stared up at him, her cheeks flushed, lips swollen, hair a tumbled mess. "What did I—"

He didn't let her finish the question. He tore out of the room and into the east wing before she could follow. He flew through the corridor, his footsteps echoing against the tall ceilings. He rushed into his music room and slammed the door behind him.

He sat down at the piano and played furiously through loud, discordant pieces that drew out his rage. He jammed his fingers down on the keys, avenging himself against his lack of composure. It didn't quite work because he wasn't really angry. He was simply in turmoil, and once he burned through the little bit of frustration, he'd have to confront something much more significant.

In the past, he simply played what he felt. Where his words failed him, music was the way thought and memory and emotion poured out of him, seemingly effortlessly.

So Conor took a breath and played what he felt. It was violently unpredictable, sweeping, and dissonant before it crescendoed in an invigorating swell of sweetness. It was hard to put a melody to the utter chaos that filled him every time he laid eyes on Rowan Cleary.

The woman was a harbinger of destruction, and he wanted nothing more than to turn and run from her disarray. Instead, the magic that flowed through him seemed intent on drawing him into her orbit, burning everything he'd worked so hard for to the ground. He thought that part of him—the part that could care beyond duty—was gone centuries ago. He'd razed the bit of humanity that existed within him and salted the earth that allowed anything but mild affection to grow in his cold, barren heart.

And yet Rowan had managed to grow roots in a dark place where nothing else would. No matter how he twisted and turned, she shined a light into every fissure in him. It was maddening.

He played until his fingers cramped and his back ached and he'd sweat through his tunic.

An hour later, he finally emerged from his music room. Playing so furiously managed to take the edge off the desire to immediately seek out Rowan again, even if the thought of it still sank claws into his mind. He snuffed out candles as he walked back down the corridor when the sound of soft singing stopped him in his tracks.

He walked down the hall, careful to keep his footsteps silent. He didn't want her to stop. Her singing grew louder the closer he moved to the great room. When he reached the end of the corridor, he peeked around the doorframe.

Rowan sat on a rock at the top of the wilderness in the great room, high above the stream that cut through the floor. Unlike how she usually moved around as if trying to take up as little space as possible, her presence seemed to fill the entire space. She sat tall, her spine erect. Her long, auburn hair cascaded down her back. He couldn't see her face, but he didn't need to because her voice was expressive enough that he could feel the emotion in her words.

Conor recognized the song, though he'd never heard it sound quite so lovely. It was an old folk song about a powerful witch who could heal memories or steal them. When her land is invaded, she's forced to either let the invading king kill her love or use her magic to rob him of every memory of her. The song was about reliving their love story while enduring the pain of erasing it.

From Rowan's mouth, the song sounded powerful, vibrant, ethereal.

He sensed notes in her voice he'd never heard quite so clearly. His whole body buzzed with the pleasure of the song. The melody rolled through him like the very pulse of life itself. He had never felt anything like it, and if he wasn't so accustomed to his own stillness—as Rowan had described it—he might have missed it. Her voice filled him with a strange nostalgia for something he'd never known or couldn't quite remember.

She stopped singing abruptly, and he ducked behind the corner so she wouldn't catch him spying.

He wanted to ask her why that song. Favorite songs and connection to music was deeply intimate. He'd never had anyone to talk to about music. The idea of asking her those questions was thrilling, but he instantly shut it down. It would help no one. Getting closer to her would only make things worse. Even now, it was hard not to tackle her to the ground and ravish her in the middle of the hallway—such was the magical pull she had on him.

Conor needed to put distance between them before things got any more out of hand. As it was, he constantly felt on the precipice of pouncing on Rowan, and she seemed delighted to be plundered. Being out of control was his least favorite feeling, so he forced himself back down the hall and into his music room, where he played furiously until his control slid back into place and an idea formed in his mind.

He just needed some distance, and he had a good idea of how to get it.

17

ROWAN

Disorientation was the new normal for Rowan as she moved about the shadowy halls of Wolf's Keep. Since the day she'd been attacked in the woods, Conor had made a point to stay as far from her as possible—that was, until the day prior, when he kissed her in the library before once again making himself scarce. She sensed he was eternally right on the edge of losing control. The thought of causing that kind of frenzy in him made her feel strangely powerful.

Maybe it was normal for him to act so changeable, and she was simply too inexperienced to know otherwise. It wasn't as if Rowan had someone she could ask, and since she'd yet to find the Red Maiden journals, she was left in the dark.

She was still afraid to tell him about her issues with the elders for fear of how he'd react. Her whole life, she'd been blamed for anything that had gone wrong around her, and she wasn't sure that Conor had the temperament to handle the situation with tact. While he didn't seem as fond of punishment as the elders, she still didn't want to test things in case he blamed her for Elder Garrett's interest. They seemed to have settled into a precarious rhythm that she didn't want to disrupt.

Conor appeared at the library door. He looked both frustrated and nervous. Apprehension flashed in his blue eyes and he tugged on the sleeve of his dark green tunic, and rubbed a hand over the hair curling around the back of his neck. He still needed a haircut. The thought almost made her laugh, but Conor looked so serious she refrained.

"Good afternoon," she said, closing the distance between them.

She waited to see if he would kiss her or shake his head and walk away like he often did. His gaze dropped to her lips, and she leaned in slightly. Instead of kissing her, he took a step back.

"Come with me," Conor barked, grabbing her wrist and tugging her out of the room. She trailed behind him as he led her outside into brilliant sunlight.

"Have you given any more thought to changing the bargain?" she asked as she stumbled to keep up.

Conor stopped short so abruptly she nearly ran into him. "Rowan, please let that go. I heard your request, and I'm considering it. Do not push me on this."

The words held no menace, but she still felt chastised. She was asking more in the hope of selling him on her plan so he wouldn't suspect her deal with the Mother than of actually negotiating. Still, his easy rejection made rage curl in her stomach. She clenched her fists and reminded herself who she was speaking to as he led her around the corner and through the garden gates.

"The Dark Garden." Rowan smiled. She spun in a circle, taking it in. It had changed since her last visit. The late afternoon sun cast orange light on several new blooms on the rosebushes. Most of it still remained in dry neglect, but she could see the potential.

"What do you want me to do?" she asked.

Conor shifted on his feet and looked anywhere but at her as he dragged his boot through the dirt. "It's yours," he said so quietly she was sure she'd imagined it. "It belongs entirely to you."

"What?"

"The Dark Garden is yours—to do whatever you want with. If you need help or supplies, just tell Charlie, and he'll make sure you get what you need. I don't know what that might be, but I imagine seeds or bulbs or dirt." Conor ran a hand through his hair and gestured at the barren plots.

Rowan stared at him, her mouth clogged with words that felt too heavy to speak. Humiliating tears rose in her eyes without her permission. Her body seemed poised to absolutely lose it around Conor at all times. It was extremely inconvenient.

Conor took a step back and threw his hands up. "Mother slay me! Now what did I do?"

Rowan swallowed hard. "Nothing, I—"

It was embarrassing to even speak the words. Her clothing was all handed down, and she had no worldly possessions that were really hers. The lack reminded her of how ephemeral she truly was at all times.

She turned and looked around the garden in an attempt to compose herself. He probably meant to keep her busy and out of his hair, but with this one gift, he was also saying that he expected her to have time to grow something. Relief coursed through her as she turned back to Conor. He looked expectant, or maybe even afraid he'd done something wrong.

"I've never really owned anything before, at least not anything like this," she whispered. It was thoughtful not just because she loved to garden, but because it gave her a space in which she belonged.

Conor's face lit with recognition, and he gave her a sharp nod. He looked like he wanted to say something else, but instead, he turned and marched toward the gate.

"Conor," she called after him, and he paused. "Thank you."

He said nothing else as he disappeared through the gates.

Rowan looked around the garden. She saw its boundless potential. It just needed some love—something it had likely been sorely missing in Conor's broody presence. She laughed to herself as she began to yank at weeds, the dry barbs threatening to cut into her hands.

Can't make that mistake again, she thought, then said aloud, "Gloves first."

Instead of getting to work, she lay on the dry grass and looked up at the beautiful blue sky, dreaming up a garden of her own.

She stayed there for a long time. In the back of her mind, she knew that Conor's kind gift might have just been a clever way to keep her out of his business. The garden was just about as far as she could get from his sitting room while still remaining in Wolf's Keep. She didn't let it steal her joy, though, because—even if there was more than one reason to give her such a gift—she finally had something of her own.

ROWAN PADDED through the western wing of Wolf's Keep. She'd explored most of the rooms downstairs, but now she moved from guest room to guest room, wondering why the god of death required so many bedrooms.

Several rooms were occupied by the ghostly servants who worked for the Wolf, but most were empty—ghosts themselves—and covered in a heavy film of dust with furniture sheltered under white sheets.

Finally, Rowan reached the last room at the end of the hall. She cracked the door open and froze. The room was unlike most of the others in that it had been lived in recently. A familiar shawl was slung over the back of the plush chair by the empty fireplace. She stumbled back to the doorway.

"It was Orla's room."

Rowan startled, her heart jumping into her throat at Charlie's voice.

"Were you following me?" she accused, turning to face him.

Charlie shrugged. "Conor's out, and he asked me to keep an eye on you and figure out what you're up to."

"Snooping," she said with her most charming smile.

Charlie laughed. "Grand! Will you continue now that you've been found out?"

Rowan looked back at the room. He was offering her free rein of the space, but she felt suddenly guilty now that she knew whose space it was—or had been. For some reason, this room felt more sacred than Orla's at Maiden's Tower.

Charlie waved her into the room. "You can go in, lass. I doubt she'd mind. She was a very guarded person, but it was clear she cared about you and the little one. She didn't have many belongings anyway."

Rowan took in the red velvet curtains on the windows and the dark purple bedspread. Her eyes caught on a canvas in the corner where the sun poured in through the window. She took a tentative step into the room even though she felt like an invader.

"What's that?" she asked.

Charlie grinned. "Orla liked to paint."

Rowan blinked, stupefied. "You're kidding."

"I'm not. She painted every week. She spent most of the night here working on her paintings. If I'm not mistaken, she had some works at home, too."

Rowan stared at the reaper, trying to digest the fact that she hadn't known her friend as well as she thought. Suddenly Orla's long naps before ceremony nights made more sense. She was preparing to stay up all night and work. Rowan couldn't believe her friend had kept such a beautiful secret for so long.

Charlie spoke up. "I can leave if you want."

"No, don't."

Her grief was like lightning that struck with no warning or regard for the devastation it wrought. One moment, Rowan was fine, and the next, she felt as if the wind had been knocked out of her.

She'd grown up watching the people of Ballybrine mourn and wail publicly. But Rowan's grief was quiet, private—jammed beneath her lungs and felt every time she tried to take a deep breath. Her heart was haunted, the sorrow appearing out of nowhere then dissipating into nothing. There, and gone, and everywhere all at once. She wanted to hoard it to herself, but couldn't bear to sit alone with it.

"I don't want to be alone, and it's nice to know there were other people who treated her like a person and not just someone they could get something from," Rowan said. "She was always so stoic in the face of everything and so hard to read. I admired it so much. I walk around with everything written on my face. I just couldn't imagine what it was like to be so good at hiding it."

"You really do have a way about you," Charlie laughed. "It's entertaining to watch."

Rowan crossed the room to look at the half-finished painting. It was a landscape of the view outside the window: the walls of the keep, the dark forest in its fall colors.

"I don't know much about art, but I think it's quite good," Rowan rasped.

Seeing its unfinished parts filled her with such a potent sadness that she felt like she needed to sit down. Orla didn't get a chance to really be someone of her own making. Who would Orla have been if she'd gotten free of her life as acting Red Maiden? It was strange to mourn both a person and their potential.

"It's not bad. Although, landscapes weren't Orla's thing. She liked portraits. She did one for me and one for Conor too. You've probably seen his in the sitting room."

Rowan barked out a startled laugh. "She painted that? It's amazing." She had been shocked by the painting the first time she saw it because the artist had captured the eternal storminess in Conor's eyes. She couldn't imagine the talent it took to paint something so dynamic.

"She's had a long time to perfect her work. There are a few paintings over there she wouldn't let us look at," Charlie said, waving his hand to a bunch of canvases in the corner.

Rowan crossed the room and took them out one by one. There was a painting of Mrs. Teverin, one of Elder Falon, and several of people Rowan didn't recognize but knew must have been family members judging by their resemblance to Orla. She gasped as she pulled out a stunning portrait of Aeoife outfitted in a pink dress. Her smile was bright and lifelike, her strawberry-blonde hair painted into twin braids. Aeoife would have loved it.

Rowan stared. Orla had hidden tremendous talent. If Rowan had even a hint of such skill, she wouldn't have been able to keep it to herself. Unless, of course, it was her talent for bringing plants back to life.

There was one more canvas, and Rowan's hands shook as she pulled it out. She held it up to the light and immediately started to cry. It was a portrait of Rowan.

"That explains why she was so particular about her green paint order. She wanted to get your eyes right," Charlie said. "Had to travel beyond the mountains for that one. All the way to Solemnity."

Orla protected Rowan and Aeoife from prying eyes, even in Wolf's Keep.

Rowan stared at her own face in the painting. Her hair was unbound, and she was clothed in a dark green dress that she would have never been allowed to wear in Ballybrine. It meant so much to her that Orla had painted her as something other than a Red Maiden. In the painting, her arms were crossed over a book held to her chest. Orla was always teasing Rowan about her love of romances, reminding her they had no place in her life, no matter how handsome Finn was.

When she was young, Rowan hated that Orla burst her bubble, but as she grew up and worried about Aeoife in the same way, she started to understand it was an act of love. It grounded her in the reality that romance would spell disaster, regardless of whether it was with a man or the Wolf.

Rowan's face was somewhat serious in the portrait, her lips only half smiling, her eyes full of a barely contained fire.

"She does you quite a justice," Charlie said. "Don't tell Conor it's here, or he'll snatch it up so he can stare at those green eyes all day without you knowing."

Rowan's cheeks heated. "I don't think we need to worry about me telling him anything. You, on the other hand, can't ever seem to keep your mouth shut."

She went to set the painting down on the floor, and only then did she notice it weighed considerably more than the others. She flipped it over and there, tucked in the wood over which the canvas stretched, was a journal.

"Goddess above! Orla, you evil genius!" Rowan squealed.

She snatched the journal and pulled it open. A folded paper fluttered out, landing at her feet. She was shocked when she bent and saw her name on it.

Rowan swallowed hard as she looked at Charlie.

"Found what you were looking for, then, lass?" Charlie asked.

"I didn't know what I was looking for," she admitted.

Rowan was simultaneously eager to read the words and desperate to postpone their finality. They might be the last words that Orla ever shared with her, and the knowledge of that was too weighty to hold. She took a few steps and collapsed into the plush chair by the fireplace.

As she took a steadying breath, she unfolded the letter and started to read.

Rowan,

If you're reading this, it means I'm gone. Goddess above! That feels dramatic to write, but also maybe not dramatic enough considering the lives we lead.

A few weeks ago, I started feeling this strange sense of foreboding. I figured I could count on your nosiness, so congratulations on being at least a little bit predictable. I used to think the only predictable thing about you was your rage, which you don't hide as well as you think.

Rowan laughed out loud, brushing tears from her eyes. An ache formed in her chest like a fist clenching her heart.

Perhaps it's my imagination playing tricks on me with my tenure as acting Red Maiden coming to an end, but I can't help feeling that if there was ever a time to leave some final words, it's now.

Sometimes I regret hiding so much of myself away. I'm well aware that you tried your best to get to know me. I appreciate it, even when I seem like I don't. The truth is, I don't know how you bear loving people so much.

You're not as broken as you think you are. I believe you are actually better suited to this life because you've held on to your sense of rebellion.

I never had a sister, but if I did, I would want her to be like you—unflinching in the face of scary things. You stand up for what's right.

You've never asked me about him, but I saw the questions on your face hundreds of times. I'll tell you this—Conor can be maddening and cruel, but he does his best. He's so handsome it's easy to forget what he is. He doesn't care the way humans do. His care is possessive. It's ownership. Still, I think he wants to be good at his core. He's never been anything but honest and kind to me, but he is undoubtedly more than a little rough around the edges in all his isolation.

He likes to pretend he's so unaffected by everything, but I expect he will be quite taken with you. You have the kind of fire that matches his, and I think you could be good for him, as long as you don't forget that he's the god of death. He cannot care like you do, Rowan, but he can connect in his own way.

You and Aeoife are the two bright spots in my life, and I am so grateful for both of you, even if I never said so. Please take care of Aeoife. She's so much softer than you and I. I worry about what the future holds for her if she doesn't learn to protect herself as we have. The rest of the world will not treat her with such delicacy.

I don't have any regrets other than the fact that I haven't been able to fully unravel a mystery that I've been working on for quite some time. There must be a way to undo this bargain that puts us at the mercy of the gods. I've been researching for years now and haven't made as much progress as I'd hoped. I'd planned to request access to the former Maiden's journals once I finished my tenure and was made a lady.

Perhaps the answers are in the other Red Maiden diaries, wherever they may be. I know you'll be able to put it together.

Please help yourself to what little I have. I wish I had more to offer than a few paintings and this journal, but I also know what you need most and what you've been lacking your whole life is information. I've done my best to get everything I know into this journal. The one that the elders have is fake.

    All my love to you and Aeoife,
    Orla

"GODDESS ABOVE! I MISS HER," Rowan choked out.

The grief swallowed her whole. She could barely breathe around the ache of it. Charlie put a steadying hand on her shoulder, and she covered it with her own.

She felt compelled to start reading the journal right away but also unable to start. Instead, they stayed there for a long time: Rowan crying, Charlie a silent witness to her grief. Still, it felt better than grieving alone. Especially as the weight of all of it settled onto Rowan in one devastating revelation.

Orla had only allowed Rowan to truly know her once she was gone.

18

ROWAN

That night, Rowan woke to a great commotion. She sat with a start, and Orla's journal flopped onto the bed next to her. She'd fallen asleep reading it—not long ago, judging by the heavy dark outside her windows and the height of the candle on her nightstand. Flames guttered in the fireplace, threatening to go out. A tempest raged outside, pummeling the walls of the keep with vicious, windy fists. Sheets of rain furiously pounded against the windows, the storm begging to come in.

A loud screech cut through the din of the gale, chilling Rowan to the bone. She should have stayed safely tucked in her bed. Instead, she stood and pulled on her robe before cracking open her bedroom door.

Another screech echoed through the halls. The sound reminded her of what she'd heard in the forest after Orla died, when the Dark Wood resounded with the screams of lost souls being devoured by the monsters that lurked in the shadows.

Rowan hesitated at the threshold of her room before continuing down the hall. When she reached the top of the stairs, she heard murmuring between the agonized wails. She padded down the stairs, the soft sound of her slippered feet on the marble floor punctuated by low groans that she followed to the dining room.

Conor stood at the head of the table, bent over a spirit. His brow furrowed in concentration and his eyes glowed, staring down at the writhing spirit as Charlie and a dark-haired female reaper restrained it.

The soul didn't look like the ones Rowan led through the woods. Instead of the palish white-gray color with which she was accustomed, this one was nearly translucent, spotted with bright crimson —like spatters of blood. Rowan flinched as another keening wail burst out of it.

All three sets of eyes snapped to her.

"Rowan, you cannot be here. Go back to your room!" Conor barked. His eyes were incandescent, his presence somehow larger than usual, as if he could fill the whole room.

Rowan didn't move. She stared at the writhing soul. "I can help."

"Absolutely not. Out! Now!" Conor growled.

"I think you mean '*Thank you, Rowan, that's so generous of you,*'" she said.

Conor's eyes flared brighter. "I *mean* you have no idea what you walked into, and you're making things worse."

"It might help," Charlie intoned. "It might calm him. At least let her try."

Conor looked at the reaper with murderous intent, but Charlie nodded at Rowan. She closed the space between them, careful not to look at the soul's eyes.

"What's wrong with him?" she asked.

"He was attacked by a monster in the Dark Wood. What was left of his life force has been partially drained. We need to try to restore him so that he can cross over. Otherwise, he will become a wraith," the female reaper said.

Wraiths were souls trapped between worlds, forced to wander and never find peace. They were responsible for hauntings, and it was considered the worst fate for a soul.

Rowan shuddered. "Valen?"

Conor nodded.

Rowan took the soul's hand in hers, and she started to sing a lullaby she'd heard Orla sing many times when she thought no one else was in the tower.

The soul stopped screeching and writhing and focused entirely on her song. His gaze burned into her, but she didn't dare meet his eyes for fear of being possessed.

Rowan felt the heavy silence of Conor's magic fill the room. The soul squeezed her hand tighter.

"It's working," Charlie whispered.

Slowly, the soul filled in more evenly with color, and the red patches faded.

Rowan watched Conor. A strange blue glow pulsed beneath his hands where they rested on the soul's chest. He looked strong, powerful, and darkly sexy, with his hair falling over his forehead and his brow furrowed in concentration. She imagined having that same focus directed at her. She imagined his hands on her, and it filled her with a strange, fluttering heat. She clenched her thighs together.

Conor's nostrils flared, and his gaze snapped to Rowan. "Stop being distracting."

She looked back at the spirit's hand, trying to hide the mortified flush of her cheeks as she continued to sing.

After a few strained minutes, Charlie brushed her shoulder, indicating that she could stop. Conor grabbed the spirit and dragged him out of the room.

Rowan looked awkwardly from Charlie to the female reaper.

"I'm Petra. It's nice to meet you. Charlie's told me so much about you, but it's interesting to see that power of yours in action," she said, brushing her long, dark hair behind her shoulders.

"How many reapers are there?" Rowan asked.

Charlie laughed. "Plenty."

"What do you do all day?"

Petra's eyes narrowed on her. "Hunt down souls apprehensive about crossing. Help balance the realms. Keep Conor safe."

Rowan shivered, considering what the reaper might do if she knew about the dagger strapped to Rowan's thigh.

A moment later, Conor appeared at the door. He looked wrecked by the effort of restoring the soul. "Charlie, Petra, leave us," he said.

Charlie winked at Rowan on his way out of the room. "I'll keep an ear out just in case he loses his composure, lass."

Rowan turned and smiled at Conor.

"Don't smile. I'm very frustrated with you," he said. He ran a hand through his hair and rolled his shoulders back. Rowan didn't know someone could look so weary and dangerous at the same time. She stood completely still as Conor turned to look at her. "You do not listen."

Rowan stood tall with her hands on her hips. "Neither do you."

"It was perilous for you to be here during that process." He punctuated each word with a step closer.

"My whole life is dangerous," she whispered.

"You're foolish to be so brave."

"You're foolish to think I'd be anything other than what I am," Rowan countered.

Conor brushed his fingers over her cheek and down her neck. "I have no idea who you are, little Red. I'm not sure it would be wise of you to show me," he murmured.

He struck with no warning. His lips brushed over Rowan's as he drew her into his arms. She pulled him closer, her hands threading through his hair. Conor lifted her so that she sat on the edge of the table as he devoured her kisses. She moaned into his mouth, which only made him more ravenous. He tugged her hair, tilting her head back, trailing kisses over her jaw.

"It is dangerous for you to be here right now. I have very little control left after that," Conor whispered, even as he kissed down her neck and cupped her breasts through her nightgown. "Why must you tempt me?" His voice was tortured and his touch rough as he nipped at the delicate skin of her neck.

Rowan loved that he couldn't help himself. His desperation

spurred on her own. Shivers rushed through her body, and she wanted to be lost in the rawness of his touch.

His fingers expertly worked the buttons at the front of her night-gown until he slid his hands inside to palm her breasts. She felt help-less to his ministrations, but for once, she didn't mind being powerless.

Conor pushed her back so that she lay on the table. Her skin prickled in goosebumps as he kissed and licked a trail down her chest. He sucked one of her nipples into his mouth, dragging his teeth over it. Rowan arched up off the table with a surprised, desperate moan.

Conor jerked back as if someone had hooked him around the neck. His eyes flared with a bright blue and gray glow.

"Get out!" he barked.

She stared at him, dazed.

"Get out, Rowan!" he screamed again.

Rowan sat up and hopped to her feet. Her knees trembled as she hurried out of the room, grasping at the sides of her nightgown to cover her chest. In the hall, she bumped into Charlie, who gave her a knowing smirk.

"Best you stay in your room the rest of the night, little Red," the reaper said solemnly. "No matter what you hear, stay put. Seems he's a little out of control right now."

Rowan nodded and walked back to her room, locking the door and collapsing on the bed. She realized then that her dagger was still strapped to her thigh and she hadn't thought to reach for it once while Conor was kissing her.

ROWAN LAY IN BED, reading Orla's journal. Most of the early entries were simply about her interactions with the Wolf. From what Rowan could tell, Conor had been equally distrustful of Orla as he was with her. Then, the entries shifted.

TODAY, I overheard a conversation between the elders about the nature of power. I was so nervous, hiding in the shadow of the meeting room, listening to them speak. They reasoned that the new religion to the north was fueled by faith and belief in a singular god. Instead of faith being divided among multiple deities, it was focused on one, and since faith builds a god's power, it explained the rapid spread of the new religion.

ROWAN STOPPED READING and considered the words as she bathed and dressed for the day, pondering the questions of faith and power as she pinned her hair away from her face.

She gazed out the window at the daylight bouncing off the trees in the Dark Wood. She wondered if Aeoife was worried about her back in Ballybrine, but she needed to focus on the task at hand. What Rowan was doing was for both of their good. She wasn't entirely confident that the Mother's plan would really produce a positive result. Still, it was the best plan she had at that moment, so she had to stick to it until she knew more. She sat down by the fire with Orla's journal and continued to read.

IT IS time I write a secret that no one knows. I have a gift for spying. It took me a long time to realize, but I can lurk in peace where there are shadows. It is the strangest thing. As if someone can stand mere inches away and still not see me. It is how I have overheard many things I should not. Which has left me with the question: Do all Red Maidens have such a gift?

ROWAN STARED AT THE WORDS. Perhaps they all had secret gifts.

So far, Orla's journal brought Rowan as many questions as it did answers. She needed to find the rest of the Maidens' journals to see if they spoke of secret talents. Rowan read the words over again.

"You're quite entranced."

She jumped, dropping the book on the floor.

Conor leaned against her bedroom door. "I knocked, but you didn't answer. I was worried, so I just came in. What has you so enthralled, little Red?"

"It's private," she said with a frown.

Conor looked delighted by her answer. "Is it, now? You think you deserve secrets in my home?" His tone was playful.

"You think I don't?" Rowan challenged.

"I think you're up to something."

"I think you're overly suspicious. Have you been to Ballybrine? Would *you* want to stay there?"

Conor cracked a smile. "Fair enough. You should know, Rowan, nothing stays secret from me long."

"If you say so," she said.

"I think perhaps you've been here so long you forget who and what I am. I'm a vicious beast, Rowan."

Rowan frowned. "Is that why you put that poor soul out of his misery last night?"

Conor grimaced. "And why did you help him?"

Rowan was baffled by the question. "I helped him because he was in pain, Conor. It was a decent thing to do."

"By using your magic?"

"It's not just about magic. Music comforts people. Mothers sing to their babies. People sing at the Gratitude and Grieving Ceremony."

"So you sang to him out of pity?"

Rowan threw her hands up. "I sang to him out of *empathy*. Out of *mercy*. Is it easier to live as if every kindness is some secret weapon?"

Conor took a step back. "Do I do that?"

Rowan's kindness extended to Conor as well. It must have been hard to be a god, always feeling like people wanted things from you. She supposed everyone must beg him for time he could not give them. That at least would explain why he refused to take anything about her at face value. When the whole world wanted something from you, it must be hard to believe that someone could want nothing. For Rowan's part, the first thing she had done was ask him to renegotiate a centuries-old bargain. Still, she was exhausted and on edge from feeling the constant pressure of failing his tests.

"Charlie told me you found Orla's paintings," Conor said softly.

Rowan sighed. A fresh ache bloomed in her chest. "I didn't even know she liked to paint."

"She was a hard person to know."

Rowan only nodded, afraid speaking would reveal the extent of her grief. They stared at each other as an uncomfortable silence settled between them.

"Let me show you something," Conor said.

He led her down the hall to the eastern wing, carefully guiding her down the rocks that led into the dark tunnel cut by the stream. Rowan took in the smell of moss and wet grass as she followed silently behind Conor. Finally, they emerged into a dim hallway that opened into a large room with stained glass windows. The afternoon light shined through the windows, casting colorful patterns along the stone floor, which was marked with a mosaic forming the jaws of a wolf. It was Conor's temple.

Rowan followed Conor to the far end of the room. Small markers lined the wall, but Rowan didn't understand what they were until she approached the one Conor had stopped in front of. There was a glass jar splattered with paint stains and several paintbrushes.

"This is the shrine I made for Orla. There's one for each of the past Maidens," Conor said.

Rowan lost count as she looked back down the row, trying to take in how many shrines there were in total. It was startling to consider how many Maidens he might have killed. But she believed Conor hadn't killed Orla, and that was enough to settle the idea that perhaps he wasn't as violent as she'd been taught.

When she turned back, Conor looked as stricken as she felt at the loss of her friend. Everything frozen in her chest melted.

As if realizing how the shrine softened her heart toward him, Conor took a step away from her.

"Why did you bring me here?" Rowan asked.

"Charlie said how sad you were. I thought you'd like a place to come if you want to remember her."

He shifted between truth and lie so seamlessly he may as well have lied all the time. The stain of his deception tarnished all of his truths. She wanted to hang her hopes on his words, but she wasn't foolish enough. It seemed her life would have been easier if she was ignorant.

"Perhaps you think you can chase away your guilt for failing her by looking after me," Rowan whispered.

A coldness settled over Conor's face. His jaw twitched.

"Is it such a bad thing to care?" Rowan asked. She hated the desperation in her voice—hated that she wanted something from him.

"Death's gift is in taking. I have nothing to give. I'm not someone who can love you, Rowan. There's nothing but darkness where my heart should be."

"Who said anything about love?" Rowan challenged. She turned to face him head-on. They were so close the fabric of her dress brushed against his boots.

"You really want to do this here, little Red? You want me to make you lie in the temple of the god of death? Next to shrines for your fallen sisters? You want me to pretend that I don't see that desperate way you look at me like I'm the only person who can take care of you?" he taunted. He slipped into cruelty with surprising ease.

"I don't need you to tend to me. I can take care of myself," she snapped.

"Yes, lass, but should you have to?" Conor asked.

Rowan tried to hide any hint of reaction, but the words gutted her. She hated him using her fear as a weapon. "I've never been presented with much of a choice, Conor. I've done what was required of me."

"Are you so happy to be the perfect little victim?" he challenged.

The word made her feel ill. *Victim.* As if everything was

happening to her, and she was helpless to the momentum of life. She hated to look right at it, and she was humiliated that Conor saw her complacency.

"You taunt me for being a victim in a bargain *you* made. I am only what I am because you created a game with no thought of who might suffer for you to play it," Rowan rasped. "You know, the people of Ballybrine and the elders might be careless and cold, but you are actively cruel when it serves you and kind when you want something just the same."

Conor was content to pull her close when it suited him and shove her away if she touched a nerve. It was for the best that he kept reminding her that he was her enemy. The moment she forgot, she would be the only one who paid the price for it.

He looked equally frustrated and contrite, but she was too embarrassed to stay and hear his apology.

Rowan was no one's victim. She needed to take care of herself, and that meant walking away instead of standing there waiting to be wounded.

19

CONOR

Despite Conor's coldness in the temple, he enjoyed having Rowan in the keep. As difficult as it was to ignore the constant nagging pull to her, like a fishhook lodged in his chest reeling him toward her, she brought warmth to the place.

She'd spent the whole week with him, begging off on Friday morning so that she could go spend some time with Aeoife before she returned the following night with a new group of spirits.

Conor knew he was deluding himself. Playing house with a beautiful Maiden was fun, but they were avoiding reality. Things couldn't stay that way forever. Each time he touched her, she chipped away at the walls he'd built to protect himself. Talking to her was worse because she was clever, funny, and charming in a wholly natural way. It was lovely to see how she bloomed like some wild, exotic rose where most things came to die. She brought the mansion to life in more ways than one.

He'd felt a shift in the energy of the mansion, but it was confirmed when he was wandering by the old greenhouse and noticed that it had gone from dried-out remnants to its former blooming glory. It took him a day to put together that it was due to her sitting at the top of the east wing hall and singing. Even the luminaries—old plant spirits—had returned from beyond to enjoy the flowers.

Conor didn't understand Rowan's magic, but he knew it was something powerful. The house servant spirits seemed just as drawn to her as he was, sneaking away to hear her sing, each relishing the touch of life in her voice.

He should have interrogated her about her power. Several of the other Maidens had spent significant time at the keep, but none had brought with them such a frenzy.

Rowan was still shaken up from her attack in the Dark Wood, so Conor taught her how to fend off an assailant. It had been too long since he felt the adrenaline of a good fight, but the movements were still second nature to him.

Eventually, when being so close to her proved to be a problem, he taught her chess.

It seemed a platonic game. It felt safest to face Rowan with a table between them to keep her at a secure distance, especially with her looking lovely in a light blue dress his seamstress had made to compliment her fair skin and rosy cheeks. There were no innuendos in chess and no touching. There was only Rowan's brow furrowed adorably as she desperately tried to puzzle out how to beat him. At first, she was competitive and frustrated, but quickly got better—good enough that she could carry on a conversation as they played.

"Tell me about your family," Conor said, watching her face carefully.

"Tell me about yours," she countered.

Conor frowned and leaned back in his chair. He tried not to ever think about his family. "What makes you think I have one?"

Her full lips tipped into a half-smile. "The fact that you didn't immediately reject the idea."

Conor hesitated. Just talking about it felt like welcoming trouble. "I don't remember my parents, but I had a brother once. We were close—both of us warriors."

Rowan's eyebrows shot up. "So you were a mortal warrior?"

He nodded. "A very long time ago. So good at killing it made me immortal in the minds of men and then immortal in reality. Such is the power of faith."

"And your brother?" Rowan asked.

Conor looked away. He didn't want to think about that now. Perhaps it was superstitious, but he did not even think his brother's name. It was easier to think of him as a vague shadow that lurked at the back of his memory.

"My brother is gone." Saying it aloud felt like a dare. He could practically hear a hint of dark laughter echoing in his ears. His brother's voice saying, "*Then why don't you ever sleep?*"

He cleared his throat and focused on Rowan. "Have I earned the right to hear about yours now?"

"I suppose. I'm the youngest of five, and we were destitute," Rowan said. "When my mother figured out what I was, she only hesitated a moment before turning me over. I don't see them much, and it's easier that way."

Conor could hardly breathe around the fury as he tasted burnt sugar on his tongue. "That's a lie."

Rowan sighed, brushing a stray hair from her forehead as she leaned forward. "Fine. I don't know what's easier. I only know what I've experienced, which is that it is hard to listen to them talk about the lives of luxury that they enjoy for my sacrifice. I don't like feeling contempt toward them. Maybe easier isn't the right word, but neither option would bring me peace. If they are around, it's exhausting, and if they're not, it hurts."

They sat quietly as they exchanged a few more moves in their game.

Rowan waved her hand dismissively, as if trying to shake off her hurt. "I don't blame them. It's hard to love what you know you will lose."

"You excuse them?" Conor asked.

"No—I *understand* them."

"Why are you so content to be invisible?"

She recoiled. "What do you mean?"

"You scrub your dresses like you're afraid of leaving the slightest mark. You touch my books with a delicacy reserved for holding an infant. You deny yourself connection so the loss of you won't hurt the people you love. Are you content to disappear so easily?"

He wasn't mad at her; he was angry at the world, and the rage made him itch for his piano. He stretched his fingers toward phantom keys.

Rowan swallowed hard and blinked rapidly.

Conor froze. She was going to cry, and he felt an unnatural panic when that happened.

"I don't see what's wrong with controlling what I can." Her words were clipped.

"So it's about control?" he asked.

"I suppose."

"You don't like to feel out of control."

Rowan nodded.

How would she like Conor taking control? Would she enjoy it if he showed her how good it felt to let go, to let him take charge, to feel blissfully out of control? *Demon's breath!* He'd love to see her reaction to that. He wasn't sure if she'd slap him or give him one of those angry, heated looks of hers, all while letting him do whatever he wanted. He lived for those looks.

Rowan wrung her hands uneasily. "You judge them, but you don't even know them," she snapped, dragging him from his filthy thoughts.

Conor reached across the table and tilted her chin up. "I judge anyone who would look at this face and see only a payday."

"As if you see something different. All anyone sees when they look at me is what I can do for them. Don't pretend you're different when you just look at me like I'm your next meal," she scoffed.

Rowan's eyes burned with fury and a familiar heat spread through him. He wanted all of that rage. He could practically taste it. Her lies were sweet, but her anger was like a sharp spice that tingled on his tongue. He wanted to lick every smart word from her mouth. He needed some distance, or he would do something idiotic.

"I'm sorry," he said softly.

She was more startled by that apology than anything else.

He pressed on. "For presuming to know your life. I should have let you answer. Tell me about them."

"There's not much to tell. My mom found out what I was, and for about a minute, I saw conflict in her, but we were so poor, Conor. I'm not excusing it because, honestly, I would never dream of doing the same thing, but it's worth mentioning. I went to bed hungry...often. I can't imagine how hungry she and my father were. Anyway, she saw her chance and took it, and she never looked back. I didn't see my family very often after that. I've always felt a bit like—" She cut herself off and flushed as she looked away.

Her admission filled him with fury. She must have been wretchedly lonely. He'd always thought Orla was the loneliest person he'd ever met, but Orla was made for solitude. Rowan clearly thrived on connection.

"Please continue."

She hesitated. "It's horrible, but I always felt a bit like my mother went so far in the other direction to prove something to herself. The way she chases status and wealth is unnatural after what we've been through. But I felt like maybe she was just all in because she very badly needed to convince herself that she'd made the right choice. Maybe you're right, and I'm excusing her, but I can't help but think it still. Maybe there's a naive part of me that wants to believe that at least her motivations were good."

Rowan was so bright and analytical. Conor wasn't sure that he could have evolved enough to accept such a thing even after centuries.

"Anyway, I can't imagine my life any other way now. I am what I am because I've been without them for so long. I'm fortunate to have Sarai, and I was fortunate to have Orla for so long, and Aeoife." She was smiling at him even as tears filled her eyes; even as she sounded like she was trying to convince herself that was enough.

"Rowan," he whispered. "You're allowed to want what you want. No one can take that from you. You're allowed to want better for yourself even if no one else will."

"Wanting is for people who have futures," she said softly.

"No, lass. Wanting is especially for those who live short lives. You get to want more, want desperately. You have a shorter time to claim those desires, but it should not stop your trying."

Conor tried to pull her up from the depths with his words, but he saw her floundering. Grief followed death around and he was well acquainted with it.

Rowan had already grieved many times for what her family could not be, and he'd ripped open old wounds to satisfy his curiosity. It was unforgivable. He could not stomach her tears, even as she tried desperately to hide them, brushing them away with a vengeance reserved for someone who'd done her a great wrong.

Panic tightened his chest like a vise. He needed to fix this. He loved watching the way she brightened when he introduced her to something new, her eyes filled with wonder and fascination. She never seemed to think anything was strange, only delightful and unique. It might be the only thing to distract her from his questions.

"I want to show you something," Conor said.

"But our game," she protested, gesturing to the chessboard.

"We'll come back to it."

Her face lit up, though she also looked apprehensive. He would be the first to admit his surprises had been a mixed bag. It was his fault she seemed unsure whether to anticipate something pleasant or terrifying, but she showed no hesitance.

"It's a surprise, though," he amended.

She bit her lip but nodded as he held up a silk handkerchief. He tied it over her eyes.

"Also, I'll need to carry you because it's a little treacherous, and you can't get there blindly."

He chuckled as her pulse kicked up.

"Okay," she rasped.

With no ceremony, Conor scooped an arm behind her knees and swept her into his arms. She was clearly startled, but she still leaned into him. She wrapped an arm around his shoulder, her hand tangling in the hair at the nape of his neck. It felt divine.

"Sorry," she mumbled, drawing her hand back.

"No, it's actually nice. It just surprised me," Conor murmured as he started to move. "I like the way you touch me."

"Tentatively?" she laughed, running her fingers through his hair again.

"No. Gently—like you're afraid to hurt me."

She was struck silent by the admission. Of course, she was probably just afraid *he'd* hurt *her*. She'd lived her entire life one false move from being struck, and although he'd never given her the impression he'd do so, touching the entire world with that delicacy seemed a hard habit for her to break.

She leaned her head against his shoulder and rested her other palm on his chest. Her fingers skimmed the opening of his collar. Her hand was cold against his skin. It was mesmerizing how such a cool touch could inflame him so easily.

Conor's hands were made for violence and death. Even before he became the god of death, he'd been a fierce warrior. But the first time he held Rowan, he believed perhaps they were made for more. He didn't just want to consume her. He wanted to explore a capability for tenderness he'd never thought he possessed.

His footsteps echoed louder as they entered the eastern wing with its high ceilings and oppressive darkness. The stream trickled, and he could sense Rowan trying to get her bearings. Conor took several jerky and unsteady steps to climb down the mossy rocks.

He jumped, and she let out a surprised squeal and clung to him even tighter. Conor chuckled as he landed with ease a few feet below.

"It's a smoother walk from here," he whispered.

His footsteps echoed louder, and Rowan seemed surprised they weren't heading for the music room where she liked to spy on him. He let her watch and pretended he didn't notice because he spent the rest of his time spying on her. It was only fair to indulge her curiosity.

The air grew warmer as he walked into the greenhouse. He breathed in the scent of moss and the musty humidity of wet dirt and pollen.

Conor hesitated, enjoying the feeling of her in his arms, before he set her on her feet. He untied the blindfold and let it fall from her eyes.

She blinked, allowing her eyes to adjust to the dimmer lighting. Through the large glass windows, a neon sunset cast an array of pinks and oranges on the lush greenhouse full of ferns and huge, exotic flowers in bright reds, purples, and pinks. Rowan's eyes went wide as she spun to take in the whole room.

The entire greenhouse was vibrant with new growth. Vines climbed the large glass windows and hundreds of plants had either bloomed or were on the verge of doing so.

"What—what is this?" Rowan asked as she took a few tentative steps forward.

"It's the old greenhouse. These are some of the rarest and most unique flowers in our world."

"But they're *alive*," she murmured dumbly.

Conor smiled. "Not until recently. *You* did this, Rowan. They're alive because of you."

She turned and stared at him.

"I know you come down to the east hall to sing."

Her eyes widened in panic. "I know I'm not supposed to, but the acoustics are so beautiful with the tall ceilings—"

Conor held up a hand. "I'm not upset. I'm just hoping you'll explain."

She bit her lip and looked out the windows at the gathering dark.

"I promise I'm not angry. I'm just trying to understand how this is possible. The plants here have been dried up for a long time," Conor said. "I haven't done anything. The only change has been you and your singing."

Rowan swallowed hard. "My voice is magic. I don't know why. It's unique to me and not something all Red Maidens can do. When I sing, it brings things to life."

It explained why Conor found her so incredibly compelling. Rowan breathed life into his whole world. No wonder he was so helplessly drawn to her. No wonder she smelled and tasted like life itself.

"Clearly," he laughed, gesturing to the lush garden. "I can't even remember the last time I saw them bloom. I came down here the other day for the first time in a very long time and noticed. Also, the luminaries have returned."

"The luminaries?" Rowan asked.

"Yes, they're plant spirits who come to life at night and glow. You'll see them soon," Conor replied. She stared at him like she thought he was messing with her. "You'll see something pretty spectacular from the plants, too. I haven't seen it since I was younger."

"And when was that?"

His lips quirked into a smirk. "Some time ago."

"How old *are* you?" she taunted.

Before Conor could answer, the first glowing golden light caught her eye. Rowan gasped as she watched it float up from a large pink flower that was about to bloom.

20

ROWAN

Rowan couldn't believe Conor had brought her somewhere so romantic. The entire greenhouse looked like something straight out of a fairy tale. She hadn't even considered that her song might be reviving more than just the Dark Garden.

Suddenly, a bloom opened with a giant puff of glittering pollen in a rainbow of colors. It burst into the air and the light cast by the glowing luminary orbs made it sparkle as it floated down like iridescent snowflakes.

Rowan tipped her chin up, holding her hands out to catch the glitter as it rained down over her. The luminary moved to the next flowers, and she followed. Conor trailed wordlessly behind her as she stepped in front of a pearlescent white flower that bloomed the same way. Rowan twirled in the falling pollen, for once not caring that it might stain her dress.

More luminaries floated up from the ground in tiny, golden glowing orbs. She could almost make out minute bodies in the center of the glow, but they were too bright to look at for long. Seeing them scattered throughout the greenhouse reminded her of fireflies she, Sarai, and Finn used to spend breathless summer evenings chasing around in Ashand Orchards.

The luminaries bounced from flower to flower, and Rowan followed. The air filled with sporadic puffs of pollen, the entire greenhouse abuzz with magic and joy, and Rowan relished the thrill of it.

She jumped and spun, her hands in the air as she laughed. She almost forgot Conor was there until he caught her hand and drew her toward him.

"Will you dance with me?" he asked.

"Now?" Rowan laughed. "There's no music."

"I thought perhaps you could sing something."

"I thought you didn't like when I sang here. You said it attracts the spirits."

"I was wrong," he said as he drew her closer.

Rowan stared at him wide-eyed. "Are you feeling well?" she asked, pretending to feel his forehead for fever. "Can gods catch a cold?"

Conor laughed. "I have been wrong on very rare occasions."

"Let's mark down this one and hold a feast each year to commemorate this rarity, though one wonders if it's rare that you make mistakes, or simply rare that you admit to them."

He grinned as he pulled her flush to his body, one hand resting on her lower back and the other cupping her right hand. His proximity sent her heartbeat racing.

"What should I sing?"

"Do you have a favorite song?" he asked.

Rowan nodded.

"Sing that."

She couldn't bear to have his full attention on her at such close proximity while she sang. Instead of meeting his eyes, she leaned her head against his shoulder and started to sing a song about a witch who was forced to erase herself from the mind of the man she loved.

As she became more confident in the song, the entire garden erupted in a tempest of buzzing, pulsing energy, a symphony of rebirth. All the flowers started kicking up pollen in a frenzy, and the glitter floated around them in a stunning array of colors and patterns. It was too much—the beauty of the garden, the freedom to sing when she wanted, the way the plants reacted to her song, and the warmth of Conor's body against her. She'd never felt so at peace.

"Why do you like that song so much?" Conor asked.

Rowan sighed. "I like it because the woman in the song is broken-hearted as she steals the memory of herself from her love. He's so certain he couldn't possibly forget her. When he doesn't remember, she's crushed. But then he starts to notice that the absence of her left its own mark. He feels it even if he can't name it. He senses the lack of her. There's something beautiful about that."

She choked on the swell of confusion and peace that erupted from her chest. It took her a moment to realize that she felt safe. So much of her life had been spent in fear of saying or doing the wrong thing, of having something taken from her. It was strange to suddenly feel so entirely comforted and secure. She didn't even realize she was crying until she choked on a note and her vision went blurry.

"Rowan, what's wrong?" Conor asked.

"Nothing—I've never seen anything so beautiful in my life," she mumbled.

"Neither have I," he said, his intense blue-gray eyes fixed on her. He brushed tears from her cheeks and grinned. "You're so sparkly."

A giggle bubbled out of her as she brushed some pollen from his cheek. "So are you. I think it suits you."

"Does it?"

"Yes, I think it's a perfect look for you," she laughed.

Conor kissed her. The temperature in the room spiked, and Rowan's hand fisted in his tunic as she drew him closer. Conor cupped her face, tilting her chin so he could take the kiss deeper.

Rowan's fingers dug into his tunic frantically. She couldn't touch enough of him, couldn't get close enough. He tasted like whiskey and warm apple cider—sweet and bitter with the slightest hint of spice. She wanted to lose herself in it.

Conor trailed a line of kisses down her jaw and neck as she gasped. He guided her down to a bed of fern branches on the green-house floor. His arms bracketed her body, and her hands slid beneath the hem of his shirt. She paused, waiting for him to stop her, delighted when he didn't.

His skin was smooth and hot beneath her trembling hands. Theoretically, she knew what she was doing, but reading about something and actually doing it were two very different things. She hadn't counted on her heart pounding so hard, or the way she'd want him to keep kissing her, or the desperation she felt to feel him as close as possible.

Conor's lips trailed over her collarbone, and she moaned. The sound sent him into a frenzy. His kisses grew hungrier, more possessive as he slid the shoulder of her dress down. Rowan felt drunk on lust as she spread her legs wider, grabbing his hips to pull him closer. He rocked against her and her body responded on instinct, bringing her hips up to meet him the next time he moved. Conor seemed just as mindless with lust as he drew her into another breath-stealing kiss.

"Please," she whimpered.

"Mother slay me! You're killing me," he groaned, dropping his head to her shoulder.

He panted as she lifted her hips again, chasing something she didn't fully understand. He grabbed the hem of her dress, drawing it up over her thighs. She moaned as his hands skated up her bare skin. In all her hours of tutoring, she hadn't imagined that kissing someone could feel so good.

The magnetism between her and Conor took on a life of its own. It was a living, breathing thing. The pull to him was relentless. There was nothing but his hands and his breath hot on her neck, the searing heat of his kisses, the drag of his teeth, and the whiskey and the clean, soapy scent of him.

Conor's fingers dug into her thighs. It wasn't clear if he was holding on or holding back, but she didn't care. She wound a hand through his hair and brought his lips to hers, urging him to keep going.

"Is this okay?" he whispered as he trailed a line of kisses down the neckline of her dress.

"Yes, please don't stop," she begged.

His mouth moved lower, nipping at the skin at the very edge of her neckline, his tongue dipping underneath the fabric, and she sucked in a sharp breath, arching against him. He kissed down the front of her dress. She hated that she was wearing such heavy wool. She'd been so delighted to finally have clothes in colors, but now she longed for the scandalously thin silk dresses she wore when she journeyed through the Dark Wood.

Conor kissed down her stomach, and she tipped her head back and closed her eyes, just enjoying the sensation of the heat of his mouth, even through the heavy wool. His hands hiked her dress higher, and he pushed her right leg up, placing a kiss inside her knee. Her gaze snapped to his, and he froze. He was giving her a chance to stop him if she didn't want it, but she couldn't imagine halting the momentum of what they'd started.

"Don't you dare stop," she said.

Her voice was strange and husky in her ears. Conor smiled and kissed slightly higher, then higher, his teeth dragging over her skin. She moaned and her right hand shot to the back of his head, her fingers threading through his hair.

He paused again, startled by the contact. His gaze snagged hers, and she added the slightest bit of pressure on the back of his head to encourage him. She wasn't sure what he had planned. Her lessons had only explained how she might please him with her mouth, but not a single lesson had been focused on her pleasure. It didn't even occur to her that she might want something like that, but as he kissed his way higher, she got the sense that she might really enjoy it.

"Look at you. You are temptation itself, Rowan," Conor growled against her skin, and she whimpered at the way the vibrations sent a pleasant chill through her.

He bent her left leg up and gave it the same treatment. She tried to focus on his mouth and the sensation of his lips against her delicate skin instead of the fact that she was spread wide for him with nothing but thin silk and lace undergarments between them. He paused at the edge of the lace, his tongue darting beneath the fabric. She hissed in a breath, and he drew away, meeting her eyes.

"Rowan, please say you want this," he murmured. His eyes glowed with desire.

"I don't know what *this* even is," she rasped, suddenly self-conscious.

"Of course they wouldn't tell you about this." Conor sighed and shook his head. "I want to make you feel good."

"But it's my job to make *you* feel good," Rowan whispered. Her brain couldn't quite catch up, and the frenzy of kissing him had shut down all rational thought.

"This would make me feel very good. I want to kiss you...here," he said, running his fingers over the silk between her legs.

A violent flush spread through her whole body.

"Do you want that?" he asked.

She felt uneasy at the idea of Conor so close to such an intimate part of her, but she'd loved the feeling of his mouth everywhere else.

"I don't want to pressure you. If you're uncomfortable, we can stop right now—"

"No!" she interrupted with an urgency that made her cheeks burn even hotter.

Conor chuckled. "If I do anything at all that you don't like, just tell me. We can stop at any time. I'm a fool to tempt myself like this, but I just want you to feel something good."

Rowan wanted that, too. Kissing Conor was the most dangerous and best-feeling thing she'd ever experienced. Her whole body felt aflame. She was burning from the inside out, and she wanted to ignite.

"I want it," she rasped.

Conor grinned and kissed her inner thigh before hooking his fingers around her undergarments and tugging them down. She lifted her legs, bringing them together to make it easier. He spread her legs wide again. His gaze raked over her in ravenous hunger.

Before she could second-guess her decision, he brought his mouth down on her. Her head fell back, and her eyes looked up at the glass ceiling. The sensation was like nothing she'd ever felt before. She felt hot all over, but her skin prickled in goosebumps, and she shuddered, her entire focus narrowing to the wet slide of his tongue. The feeling fulfilled the promise made by all his past kisses. The hint of pleasure in them was nothing compared to the staggering, explosive warmth that surged through her.

She moaned loudly, and he chuckled against her sensitive flesh.

"Fuck," he murmured.

The vibration of his voice against her sent her arching into him. His hands came to her hips, and she wasn't sure if it was to help ground her or hold her still, and she honestly didn't care which as long as he didn't stop. Heated tension coiled in her body, her muscles tensing and relaxing as if trying to hold on or let go. With every ministration of his mouth, the pressure wound tighter until she thought she might break in half.

Her hands threaded through his hair, holding him in place. Conor groaned, moving more urgently. Her pleasure climbed higher and higher, the sensation more thrilling and exhilarating than anything she'd ever felt. He feasted on her like she was his last meal, and she'd never felt more vulnerable and free.

All the tension in her broke at once, like a wave on the shore. She arched off the ground and cried out. Her toes curled until her feet cramped painfully and her body felt suspended in contraction as he continued to work her. A rush of warmth and tingling satisfaction settled in her body and she relaxed onto the ground.

Conor sat up, looking stricken.

"Did I do something wrong?" Rowan asked.

"Quite the opposite. You were perfect—too perfect," Conor murmured. He looked pained as he licked his lips. His gaze slowly traveled over every inch of her skin before meeting her eyes again.

"You can have me," Rowan said. "I—" She felt suddenly shy and over-exposed. "I want you to."

Pollen still sparkled in the air around them, and for the first time, she noticed how Conor was covered in her glittering handprints. It felt possessive. He'd just claimed part of her, and the handprints signaled how she claimed him back in some small way.

He hesitated a moment before pouncing on her. Suddenly, his

hands deftly worked the buttons on the back of her dress as she fumbled with his belt.

Conor seemed unconcerned by her clumsiness as she reached for him. She stared for a moment, terrified of doing something wrong. She met his eyes as she wrapped her hand around his length and stroked him the way she'd been taught. He groaned and kissed her in a rabid, frenzied way that had her tearing at his shirt until he tossed it away and her hands could touch his skin.

He drew back and met her eyes. "Are you sure?" he asked, gritting his teeth as if pained.

She hesitated to answer. The brief pause sharpened her mind. Her dagger was hidden back in her bed. She couldn't kill him without it, and her mind was still so clouded with lust she wasn't sure she wanted to. How could someone truly evil bring out such intense joy and pleasure in her?

She stared up at him, unsure what to do. She desperately wanted to feel more of what he'd introduced her to. She'd never imagined feeling out of control could be so wonderful.

She wasn't thinking clearly. She should slow down.

She sighed heavily. The words of Orla's journal came screaming back to her.

He's so handsome it's easy to forget what he is. He doesn't care the way humans do. His care is possessive. It's ownership.

"I'm not ready," she mumbled at the same time Conor said, "I can't."

Relief washed over her. "I'm sorry," she stammered.

Conor shook his head. "No, I'm sorry. I didn't think you were ready, and I shouldn't have even asked. I also know it's a terrible idea. I don't just mean I can't now. I mean, I can't ever."

He rolled to the side, tugging her dress back into place as he fastened his pants. His face shuttered, morphing into something cold and indifferent. She cringed at how mercurial he could be.

"What just happened?" Rowan asked. "I'm fine. I loved what you did. I've never felt anything like that. It was incredible. I didn't even know anything could feel that good." She swallowed around the disappointment tearing through her.

Rowan had felt so little good in her life—pathetically little. She was inexperienced and foolish. She must have done something wrong for him to not want to continue, but she was frustrated that he wouldn't just tell her what. A lump formed in her throat and her eyes burned.

"Oh, Mother slay me, please don't cry. I don't know what to do when you cry." Conor ran a hand through his hair. "I can't, but not because I don't want to. In fact, it's almost all I can think about, especially with your taste still on my lips, Rowan."

She blushed and looked away. "Then why can't you?"

He brought his hand to her cheek, forcing her to meet his gaze. His eyes were stormy and incandescent, his face tortured.

"I can't take you because if I do, I'll suck the life force right out of you, and you'll die. That's how it works. That is what it means to be devoured by the Wolf."

21

ROWAN

The greenhouse went utterly silent, and the light from the luminaries faded to a soft glow.

"I don't understand," Rowan faltered.

"Devouring isn't literal," Conor started. "I'm not going to actually eat you, Rowan. I'm going to consume your soul."

Rowan choked on a gasp. Everything had led her to believe that devouring was about sex and murder, not having her soul rendered from her body. Was that what she'd felt when she'd been with Valen in the Dark Wood?

"Why?" she asked.

"Because I was careless when I made my bargain with the Mother. I didn't care what it cost to be strong. I just knew I needed the power." He rubbed a hand over the back of his neck. "Devouring a Red Maiden makes me more powerful."

"Then why not just devour us all right away?"

He looked resigned. "Because I am duty-bound to the dead. I need someone to ferry them, and the reapers can only handle rogue souls, not a weekly flock."

Rowan chewed at her lip. "What does all of this have to do with sex?"

Conor scrubbed a hand over his face. "One type of desire stimulates the other. Sex can take the edge off, and it has with other Maidens in the past, but I'm so drawn to you. I worry it would be impossible for me not to take it too far and steal your soul in the act. You would hardly feel it, as if I was just breathing you in. Red Maidens are always tempting, but it's as if you were designed to be the most desirable woman I've ever laid eyes on. What happened here can't happen again."

Rowan's head spun. She was comforted that his disinterest was an act and equally as disturbed that he spent so much time thinking about stealing her soul.

"What happens when you devour my soul?" she asked.

"I'll grow stronger."

"And to me?"

"You'll die," Conor said.

"And my soul?"

He swallowed hard. "It will cease to exist."

Rowan could not seem to wrap her mind around it. She'd expected claws and teeth—some sort of animal instinct that needed sating. Losing her life was one thing, but losing her soul was unimaginable.

In the blink of an eye she'd gone from the safest she'd ever felt to the most terrified. She wouldn't just die; her soul would be consumed. She'd never find peace or meet with her loved ones in the afterlife. It was a level of disappearing that she could not have prepared herself for. Fearful fury tore through her. It didn't matter what she felt for him because Conor wanted her soul.

Rowan needed her dagger. She had to kill him. If he devoured her soul, the blight would continue to spread. It could destroy the whole village in a matter of months. The crops and orchards would wither, and the wildlife would move on to the north, where there were plants to sustain them. Aeoife would become acting Red Maiden. Ballybrine would crumble.

Conor's admission strengthened her resolve in the Mother's plan. She needed distance from him.

Though every instinct in her body screamed for her to run, she stayed frozen where she was.

"Say something," Conor whispered.

Rowan shook her head. She needed to find the Red Maiden journals. While she could think of no reason for Conor to lie, she needed to be certain. She really would need to kill him. She tried to ignore the way her heart clenched.

It was too cruel that the moment she experienced the first true bit of affection, it had to instantly be ripped away. Her life seemed perfectly orchestrated to keep her from enjoying anything too much or forming any significant attachment. She'd been foolish to allow herself to want something—to allow herself to be crushed by the truth she'd always known—that she was meant to be alone.

She blinked away tears. She needed anger and her mind spun, trying to access it.

Conor had let this happen. He had been operating with all the information and was just telling her now. If he'd told her before, she could have been more prepared. Fury swelled in her chest.

"Rowan, I'm not going to let that happen. I won't hurt you, but we should probably take some space. You should go back to Ballybrine in the morning," Conor said. Everything that had been warm and heated in him had cooled to a steely, patronizing tone.

Rowan couldn't stand the way he pulled her close and then tossed her away with such ease. He had kissed her, knowing the risk he was taking. It was all a game to him—one where he knew the rules, and she was left blind to them.

"I'll go back now. Why wait until morning?" she said tightly.

"Rowan—" Conor reached for her, but she ducked his arm, using the evasion technique he'd taught her the day before. He spun, looking both impressed and frustrated. "At least wait until first light."

Rowan laughed cruelly as she turned and left the room. "Isn't it a little late to pretend you care if I'm in the dark?" She lobbed the words like a flaming arrow, and she knew they struck true when he flinched.

Charlie was already waiting for her in the foyer with her red cloak in his hand.

"I heard you're leaving," he said. It was disconcerting how the reaper always had a sense of precisely what was going on, but it seemed his magic was connected to Conor's.

Rowan pulled on her boots. She sighed, trying to push away the angry tears that threatened. "Yes, well, I just finished with the gardening, and I should get back before anyone gets worried," she said tightly as she grabbed her cloak and began to fasten it.

"Yes, it looks like you were doing quite a bit of gardening," Charlie teased.

She followed his gaze to the glittering pollen handprints on her pale blue dress, including several perfectly preserved handprints over her breasts. She crossed her arms over her chest.

"He got a little close, and now he's trying to shove you away," Charlie sighed, rolling his eyes. "Whether he wants to admit it or not, he needs you."

"He's just like everyone else. He only needs me for what I can do for him. He only likes me because I smell like dessert," she huffed.

"I don't think that's the only reason." Charlie cocked an eyebrow, and Rowan flushed and looked away. "Especially now that you've given him a taste. I think you're good for him, lass."

Rowan choked on a startled laugh. "He wants to eat my soul."

"Actually, him sending you away is a distinct sign that's exactly what he *doesn't* want to do. This would all be much easier if he did," Charlie pointed out.

Rowan could not think clearly about any of it. She needed space to clear her head.

"I'll see you next week," she said, pushing out the heavy front door of the keep.

She was almost down the stairs that led to the forest trail when Conor's voice rang out behind her.

"Rowan, wait!"

She paused and turned as he closed the distance between them.

A deep, desperate part of her hoped he wanted to apologize, but it was clear from the cold look in his eyes that he didn't.

"I just wanted to remind you that I'll expect to still see you in white next week," Conor said.

Rage burned through Rowan like a fever. For a moment, she seriously considered stabbing him right then and there, and the thought filled her with dark satisfaction. But stabbing him now wouldn't solve her problems; it would only piss him off.

She shook her head in disbelief. "I'm hardly untouched. What we did doesn't allow me to wear red?"

"No, lass. You're still intact, and you'll stay that way. Someday your future husband will probably be happy with that. The men of Ballybrine are small and archaic that way," Conor said, smiling at her as if waiting for a challenge.

"And you aren't?" she argued. "I seem to remember you asking with some intensity whether I had saved myself for you."

His smile only grew. "Well, now that I've tasted you for myself, I know it's true. As I explained then, it makes the magic more potent. Imagine the difference between eating a berry before its prime and one that's plump and ripe."

Rowan tore out of Wolf's Keep without looking back. She walked down the trail, and it took her a surprisingly long time to realize that she'd forgotten a lantern. The path was so dark it sent a chill through her. She thought about turning back, but she didn't want to see Conor again, so she pressed on.

She wished hopelessly for Orla. She had no idea what to do, and she just wanted someone more experienced to give her the answers. She wanted the comfort of a big sister or a mother to tell her that she was okay. She'd felt like she and Conor shared something intimate and special, but he had so quickly shut off any sense of feeling afterward. Maybe that wasn't the act. Perhaps the act was the part where he pretended to actually care for her at all. Perhaps it was all a game to trick her into giving him what he wanted. The way he'd switched off any feeling was disconcerting.

She stopped suddenly. He could be lulling her into a false sense of safety until she let her guard down. She looked back over her shoulder, but she'd gone far enough that she couldn't see the lanterns of Wolf's Keep any longer. She turned and continued down the moonlit trail.

The branches above cast eerie shadows on the forest floor. The glimpses of silvery moonlight seemed few and far between. Rowan looked up at the trees but saw no sign of the blight.

She spun wildly. All of the tree trunks had healed to their usual brown. Each branch held new growth and large plumes of leaves. She laughed nervously, bringing her hand to her mouth. Her lips were still tender from Conor's rough kisses.

She ran down the trail until she reached a place where the moonlight was easier to see. The blight had healed from Wolf's Keep about halfway back to Ballybrine.

Rowan woke bleary-eyed. She could tell that it was at least midmorning by the slant of the sunlight slicing through her windows.

Despite her frustration, a pleasant satisfaction settled in her body, leftover from her time in the greenhouse with Conor the night before. The whole thing felt like some sort of dream. The sparkling pollen, the pulse of life in a space usually reserved for dead things. Conor had implied that everything there had once quivered with life. It was his blight that had robbed them of their vibrance, just like the Dark Garden. It made no sense for him to destroy his own world, but it could have been a byproduct of his growing magic.

That made the most sense. As Conor's power grew, its potency would also become more concentrated and could easily produce such unexpected consequences. Perhaps it was as Charlie suggested, and the real reason Conor had thrown her out was entirely out of fear of losing control. Maybe that fear was more warranted than she realized.

She rolled over and stretched her arms overhead, remembering the way it felt when Conor had used his mouth on her. She'd never imagined anything could feel so good. Her hands skimmed down her body, brushing over the cotton nightgown.

As frustrated as she felt, she wanted Conor's hands on her again, and she wanted him to teach her how to find that same satisfaction herself.

"Row, I should probably let you know I'm here before you get too involved with yourself—"

She jumped at the sound of Cade's voice. Her gaze snapped to where he sat by the fire, bent over a book.

Her cheeks flamed as she sat up.

"Good dream? Or is this a result of your time with your big, bad Wolf?" Cade taunted.

Rowan frowned at him. "That's none of your business."

Cade laughed. "I'll take that as a yes. Good for you, Row. It's about time you had a good experience. How was it?"

Rowan covered her face with her hands. "Absolutely not! I'm not talking to you about this! Get out of my room!"

She threw a pillow at him, but he disappeared in a puff of smoke and reappeared on the edge of her bed.

"Why are you here?" she huffed.

"Because my mission to find the journals has been fruitless. I have searched every drawer, chest, and crevice of the temple and the elder offices, and I have not found a single Red Maiden journal," Cade said.

"Every crevice, you say?" Rowan asked, arching a brow.

"A little bitty tumble with the Wolf and now your mind is straying to dirty places. Naughty Rowan!" he taunted.

She swung her pillow at his face as he laughed.

"I'm kidding. Even if I wanted to search every crevice in that place, those old geezers are way too tight-assed for me to even get a peek."

Rowan collapsed in a fit of giggles.

Cade grinned. "It's good to see you laugh. I thought you might not forgive me after the other day with Elder Garrett. I thought maybe you weren't coming back. You've been spending a lot of time with good old Wolfie."

Rowan sighed. "I have, but it's not to avoid you. It's more to avoid the elders. But it's also because I really need the Wolf to like me. This is my one chance to—" She cut herself off, realizing she almost tipped her hand about her deal with the Mother.

"Yes?" Cade prompted.

Rowan shook her head. "I have a chance to actually do something instead of just waiting around for my life to happen to me. It's the first time I've really been able to take on any semblance of control. I don't want to mess it up, and I certainly don't want to give the elders any reason to cause more trouble for me."

Cade nodded solemnly.

"Cade, I'm so close. Since I was five, my entire life has been devoted to this, and as unpleasant as it might be, I can actually see the light at the end of the tunnel."

"Yes, but isn't that the most dangerous place to be?" he questioned.

"Of course, but I'm not any safer here anymore."

Cade bristled.

Rowan held up her hands. "That's not a jab at you. You were right. I shouldn't need you to protect me, and it's certainly not your job. You didn't create the world that put me in this place. I wasn't even mad at you. I was frustrated with the whole situation. I'm tired of being powerless, and being at Wolf's Keep is the one time that I'm actually in charge of something, at least a little bit."

"Is your Wolf housebroken yet?" Cade taunted.

Rowan rolled her eyes. "He's unpredictable, but I'm learning what he likes."

Cade quirked an eyebrow. "And you're one of those things?"

She narrowed her eyes. "You're awfully curious all of a sudden."

"I'm always curious. Do you expect you'll soon be able to start wearing red dresses?" he pressed.

He was dancing right on the border of what she was willing to share with him. He might have been one of her closest friends, but it was strange to talk to him about romance.

"Cade, give it a rest! Are you so eager to see me devoured?" Rowan snapped.

Cade frowned. "What's wrong?"

She rolled over in bed. "I don't want to talk about it with you. It's weird."

"Whatever you say," he sighed. "You should spend some time with Aeoife. She's been very restless with you gone."

"I'm sorry I was gone for so long. I just need to try to get through to the Wolf. If I can change into red dresses soon, it will get the elders off my back and give me some time to untangle this mess."

"What mess?" Cade asked.

She'd said too much. "I just mean the mess with the elders."

He nodded, but she could see that he didn't buy her lie. He knew her too well, and years of friendship meant he knew every expression on her face just as she knew his.

"You know you can tell me anything. I don't judge," Cade sighed.

Rowan swallowed hard, tugging at a loose thread on the linen sheets. "I know. I'm just not ready yet."

"I'll be here when you are," he whispered.

ROWAN WALKED into the tower kitchen just as Aeoife exited her meditation and practice session.

"Rowie!" she shouted, throwing herself into Rowan's waiting arms. "I was worried when you didn't come home."

Aeoife's sweetness brought her to tears. "I'm sorry I was away for so long. I'm trying to make everything better for the two of us," Rowan said.

Aeoife pulled back, reaching up to cup Rowan's face in her small hands. "Someday, I want to be brave like you."

Rowan swallowed hard. She didn't feel brave. She felt lost. "I got to see Orla's room at Wolf's Keep, and guess what? She knew how to paint."

Aeoife's eyes went wide. "Landscapes?"

"Even better. She painted portraits, and she painted a beautiful one of you in a pretty pink dress. I promise I will bring it to you as soon as I figure out where we can hide it here, okay?"

Aeoife clapped her hands and jumped in delight before her face grew grave and her eyes went glassy.

Rowan knelt so she was at eye level with the girl. "What's wrong?"

"Did he hurt you? I heard Mrs. Teverin talking, and she said that —" Aeoife cut herself off, unable to finish as her lower lip trembled.

Rowan sighed. "No, I'm perfectly fine. See, I'm even still wearing white," she said, gesturing to her dress.

"Then why is your heart so sad?" Aeoife asked.

Rowan stared at her. "How do you know my heart is sad?"

Aeoife looked down, dragging the toe of her boot over the stone floor. "Sometimes I can feel things that other people feel."

"What kinds of things?" Rowan asked. Her mind flew to what Orla had written about her unique abilities. If anyone found out what Aeoife could do, they were bound to exploit it.

Aeoife finally met her eyes again. "Well, I could feel when Orla was lonely, or when you were sad that your parents didn't come to visitation. I could feel it when you were afraid to go see Elder Garrett. And now I can feel that you're embarrassed and sad."

"What does it feel like?" Rowan asked.

"It feels like it's in my heart and also like it's not. It's hard to explain. I just have learned what most of the sensations mean," Aeoife said, her gaze darting around the room.

"Aeoife, look at me," Rowan said sternly. "Do not tell *anyone* else what you can do, all right? Your secret is safe with me, but other people could take advantage of your gift. This is our secret, okay? Don't even tell Cade."

Everything Rowan had learned about demonic bargains chipped away at the long-established trust she had with Cade. It wasn't that she thought he was evil so much as opportunistic. Still, his close relationship with Aeoife meant that he had more pull over her than most, and Rowan didn't want to risk it.

Aeoife nodded.

"Good. Now I'm sure you've been lonely, so why don't you tell me everything you've been up to, and we can get sticky buns at Hanna's before we catch up on some reading."

Aeoife's face lit up. She took Rowan's hand and tugged up her hood so they could walk to town.

Rowan spent the whole day with Aeoife, walking through town and then reading to her for hours until the girl finally fell asleep, clinging to Rowan.

Cade had been mysteriously absent. Aeoife said he'd been gone a lot while Rowan was away.

Rowan was about to nod off despite her worry for her demon friend when the sound in her bedroom warped and the Mother appeared with a bright flash of light.

Rowan stared at the goddess. Her sudden appearances were so disorienting. She carefully extricated herself from Aeoife's arms and crossed her hands over her chest before opening them in front of her and bowing her head.

"I don't have long. What news do you have?" the Mother asked.

"I am making progress, but the Wolf seems intent to stop me at every turn."

The Mother frowned. "He *still* hasn't taken you to bed? What is he waiting for?"

Rowan shrugged. "We got...close."

"How close?" the Mother asked.

"He danced with me and then kissed me," Rowan said.

"A kiss? That's all?" The Mother looked forlorn.

"Not just on the lips," Rowan continued. She gestured to the rest of her body.

The goddess's eyebrows shot up. "Oh really? And how did you like that?"

Rowan flushed. "I liked it a lot."

The Mother arched a brow. "I bet you did. And how did he like it?"

"Enough that he almost took me to bed afterward, but I stopped it because I didn't have my dagger. I think I can do it next week," Rowan said, trying to summon confidence she didn't feel.

The Mother flickered slightly and said nothing.

"On my walk home, I noticed that the blight is healing, and the Dark Wood is healed almost halfway back to Ballybrine. It seems a clear sign he's losing power," Rowan continued.

The Mother still looked disappointed.

"I thought you'd be pleased," Rowan said.

Her face softened. "Dear, I don't mean to seem ungrateful. I already knew it was healing. The problem is that it doesn't matter if it's healing. The Wolf is still getting stronger. If there was ever a time to strike, it's now. I just need you to understand the urgency. The new religion is a threat to me and to all of us. Right now, it is my will alone that holds back death. Even if the blight is healing in the Dark Wood, I'm not strong enough to prevent it from continuing to spread into Ballybrine. Several more apple trees in Ashand Orchards went barren with blight just this morning."

Rowan swallowed hard and nodded.

The Mother touched her cheek tenderly. "All isn't lost, dear. You can save us. I believe in you, and I know you can do it the next time you are there."

Rowan was bolstered by the Mother's confidence.

"His resolve is nothing for you, Rowan. You are a beautiful, talented woman. He won't be able to resist," the goddess said softly.

"I'll find a way," Rowan said, her eyes darting to Aeoife's sleeping form. She didn't need a reminder of what was at stake. She didn't want Aeoife to have to suffer the same life she'd led.

"I'll be watching over you, and I'll see you soon," the Mother said. Rowan nodded and watched her fade into a flickering flame before disappearing.

Rowan climbed back into bed next to Aeoife and promised herself she'd go into her next visit with the Wolf with as much information as possible. In the morning, she'd tear the temple apart to find the Red Maiden journals.

22

ROWAN

Rowan poked around the elders' drawing room behind the temple altar but could not find the Red Maiden journals anywhere. Though Cade had already checked, she needed to see for herself.

She walked down the aisle of the temple and slumped into a pew, looking around for any other obvious hiding spots. She was running out of places to look.

The back doors opened and Elder Garrett stepped into the temple, as if summoned by her dread. She felt the phantom ache of his lashes on her back as he walked down the center aisle.

"I see you've failed again, Red." His lips quirked up in a feral grin. "That's too bad, though you mustn't worry. We've devised a backup plan, as previously discussed. Come with me."

Rowan hesitated. She wished Cade was with her, but he had checked in at breakfast before making himself scarce again. She had asked where he wandered off to, but he had just deflected. Now, she wished she'd waited until he was around to start wandering the temple.

"Rowan, am I to take your hesitance as defiance?" Elder Garrett asked. The threat was clear in his tone and the look in his eyes.

She shook her head and made to follow him. He led her to a dark stairwell behind the raised dais at the front of the temple. It was so well hidden that she'd missed it when she was poking around before. The stone stairwell was dim, with just the light from a candle held by Elder Garrett to light their way. She followed a few steps behind, careful to stay out of arm's reach.

When they reached the bottom of the stairs, she followed him down a long, dark tunnel. Dread pooled in her stomach. The air in the space was stale and oppressive. She rubbed her arms, trying to stave off the chill.

Finally, Elder Garrett pulled a lever on the wall and a door creaked open, revealing a large, open room. Rowan followed him inside. The space was slightly brighter, smelling of moss and spiced incense. Several lit torches lined the walls around the periphery, but the focus of the room was on the ceiling at the center. Thick roots grew out from above a stone altar, most of the roots cascading around the domed ceiling but several cutting straight down, wrapping around the bottom of the altar.

"The Elder Tree," Elder Garrett said before she could ask.

"What is this place?" Rowan inquired.

His eyes lit with menace, and she immediately regretted the question. "It's a ritual room, of course."

She swallowed hard, following his gaze to the altar. She stepped closer. There were carvings along the side in the old language that read, "*Under the watchful gaze of the Mother, as witnessed by the Crone, for the sake of the living, we sacrifice to the Wolf.*"

Intricate carvings of a wolf and the sigil of the Mother wrapped around the front of the altar.

Elder Garrett ran his hand over the cold stone affectionately.

"I don't think I should be here," Rowan said, wringing her hands.

"Oh, I think this is exactly where you should be. You see, when you return from the Wolf again this Sunday morning untouched, we'll prepare this room for the following week, and here on this altar, you'll be tended to by an elder as chosen by the Mother."

She took a step back. "That's blasphemous."

"I assure you it's not. We've already decided among the elders, and the decision has been sanctified by the Crone, who will bless you here and witness your *sacrifice*."

Rowan tried to hide her horror because it was clear that it only served to please Elder Garrett.

"You look like you want to say something," he said with a lupine smile.

Her mouth went dry. "The Mother's will be done."

Elder Garrett looked disappointed by her tepid reaction. He bent down, reaching behind the altar and lifting two silk ropes. "These will be fastened around your wrists so your arms are stretched overhead."

Rowan nodded, holding his gaze, willing her breathing to stay steady, willing her heart to stop racing. Sadly, her will was no match for the adrenaline coursing through her.

He frowned. "That doesn't worry you?"

"The Mother's will be done," she repeated.

A part of her withered to dust like a desiccated flower. She retreated as she did when anything horrible and unavoidable happened. She went in and in and in—descending blindly into the dark, bottomless well inside her. There would be time to feel later. Now she simply needed to endure. Survival was an ugly choice, but Aeoife was relying on her.

"Well then," he said. Dropping the ropes, he grabbed her arm.

She desperately wanted to wrench it away, but she didn't dare. She was underground with a predator, and she knew no one would be able to hear her scream. One false move was all it would take.

Elder Garrett shoved Rowan back so that she lay on the altar, looking up at him. Then he yanked her wrists overhead and wrapped them in the silk ties before pulling them tight. Her heart pounded in her ears along with the discordant sound of the energy around him.

An awful, pulsing hatred coursed through the air. It tried to wrap around her. She could feel the press of it, but it could not touch her skin. She looked around the room wildly for anything that could help.

Against the wall on the left side of the room was a large chest next to an armoire. They probably just held supplies for rituals, but she made a mental note to try to sneak back later and check for the journals.

"You look perfect like that. You're right where you belong. You'll then be spread wide by two of the elders. And do you know what will happen?" Elder Garrett asked. He stepped closer so his hips pressed against her knees. "Then I'll be right here."

Finally, Rowan couldn't temper her reaction any longer.

He grinned at the horror on her face. "That's right, Red. My peers unanimously chose me to taste what the Wolf isn't interested in. I'm going to enjoy every minute of it."

Rowan shook her head, squeezing her eyes closed in disgust, but it just made it worse as she pictured everything he was saying.

"When I'm done, we'll take your blessed blood and anoint the Elder Tree and pray to the Mother. If the sacrifice is accepted, the blood will be drawn up the roots, and we'll know it's successful."

Rowan's eyes snapped open, and she stared at him in abject horror. How had he convinced the elders this was a good idea—that the Mother would approve of such a thing or that the Wolf would want it?

Rowan desperately wished for the Mother. Her protection felt surprisingly flimsy.

Cade's warning about Elder Garrett spun through her head. If he'd truly made a deal with a demon to be more persuasive, perhaps that was exactly how he'd convinced the elders this ceremony was a good idea and that he should lead it. Dizzying nausea spun through her.

"I need air. I think I'm going to be sick," Rowan rasped.

Elder Garrett made a disgusted face, but it was clearly the right thing to say because he quickly unbound her hands, and she hopped up and followed him up the stairs. Once she recognized where she was, she rushed past him and tore out of the doors of the temple.

Rowan sucked in huge gulps of air so cold it turned to pins and needles in her lungs. She only paused for a moment before contin-

SHEILA MASTERSON

uing through the square. Elder Garrett called out behind her, but she just kept walking. Her head spun. Her knees were weak. She had no idea what she needed, but she couldn't seem to calm her shallow, rapid breathing.

She tore through the town square nearly colliding with a burly man who stepped into her path.

"This blight is on you, Red! You need to do something! The Wolf is killing our food supply because you won't give him what he wants!" the man grumbled.

Rowan took a step back as a woman joined the man.

"Yeah, give the Wolf what he wants, girl. Or do you think you're too good to work for your living? Are you just content to live off the backs of this community?" the woman demanded.

"You owe it to this town to do your job, girl. People are trying to sacrifice children that aren't even spirit singers. I heard they dragged three crying girls from the temple just yesterday," the man said.

Rowan's stomach heaved. How could things possibly be this frenzied in such a short time? Her eyes darted around the square. More people were starting to gather, drawn to the shouting. The crowd swelled and pressed in from all sides.

"I have to go," she said. She turned, shoved her way through the mass of bodies, and ran until she reached Finn's apartment on the edge of the Ashand property. She banged on the door relentlessly. He probably wasn't home. He was probably out on a hunt, but she needed something or someone to ground her.

Everything was spinning out of control too quickly.

The door swung open, and Finn's eyes went wide at the sight of her. "Rowan, what—"

She pushed past him, into the foyer, and leaned against the wall. She bent forward, her hands on her knees, still struggling to catch her breath.

"Goddess above! What happened?" Finn put an arm around her and guided her into the sitting room to a chair in front of the fire. "Put your head between your knees and try to breathe deeper." He placed a hand on her back. "Try to breathe deep, down to my hand."

Her breath slowed along with her heartbeat. As the dizziness abated, she sat up and looked at Finn. His golden-brown hair was mussed, his shirt unbuttoned at the collar, revealing more of his skin than she'd ever seen on display. He followed her gaze and quickly buttoned himself up.

"I can make some tea," a voice said from the small kitchen.

Rowan jumped as her gaze shot to Lady Joy McCade, who flushed and looked away.

"I'm sorry. I didn't know you had company," Rowan said, springing to her feet.

Finn grabbed her hand, and both she and Joy gasped. He quickly let go, remembering that he wasn't supposed to touch her. "Rowan, don't run off, please. Just have a cup of tea and tell me what happened," he said softly.

Finn's eyes pleaded with her, but she wouldn't tell him anything in front of Joy. Strange jealousy twisted in her stomach. She didn't feel the same way for Finn that he—supposedly—did for her, but still, she'd always taken him at his word, and he had sworn he would wait for her. He said he wasn't interested in Joy. It was highly inappropriate for her to be alone with him in his apartment.

"It's fine. I won't tell anyone about this," Rowan said, gesturing to Joy.

"It's not what you think," Finn said.

Rowan crossed her arms. "I don't think anything."

She had no right to be mad. Still, it felt like a bit of a betrayal for him to swear that he only wanted her, that he'd marry her when her term was done, and now she'd barely begun and Finn was already sneaking around with someone else.

"I'm only here to talk about a special ceremony after the Gratitude and Grieving Ceremony in two weeks," Joy said. "Finn will be there to attend the Mother as a guard, and I'll be there to attend her as a lady-in-waiting. We were just discussing things because we've both been given so little information."

Rowan's mouth went dry and her stomach lurched. She brought a hand to her mouth. "I think I'm going to be sick."

Finn jumped up and brought her a bowl. She bent over it and tried to slow the swirling thoughts in her mind.

"They expect the Mother to actually be there?" Rowan asked, not looking up from the bowl, afraid the loss of focus would make her vomit.

Finn sighed. "They're being extremely tight-lipped, but for some reason, they've asked us both to be there. Sarai is supposed to attend also, along with her mother."

Suddenly the dam burst, and Rowan started to cry. "They don't think I'm worthy of the Wolf."

"What?" Finn looked astonished. "It's only been a few weeks."

"I know. I don't know what they want," Rowan choked out. "I've gotten so close—"

Finn winced at the words.

"If I don't succeed next week, they're going to do some insane ceremony in this secret room beneath the Elder Tree where they—" She looked from Joy to Finn as realization dawned on both of them.

Joy looked as ill as Rowan felt. "*That's* what they want me to witness?"

Finn shook his head violently. "They can't do that."

"They can. The Crone approved it. It's going to happen unless I can somehow succeed in winning Con—the Wolf over next week," Rowan said.

"Oh, Rowan, that's horrible," Joy said. For her part, she looked genuinely distraught. She walked toward Finn, seeking out his support as if she was the victim. "Finn, you can't let them do this. There's never been this kind of urgency before."

"It's because of the blight," Rowan said hopelessly. "Even though it's getting better, they don't care. It's still visible here, and the townsfolk are restless. It doesn't matter what *is* true. It only matters what *feels* true."

Joy looked about to collapse. Finn pulled her into a hug and Rowan stared at them. There was no denying that they looked good together.

"This week, several families offered up daughters to the elders.

Girls with no gifts. People are desperate for a solution and panicked for next season without those trees. Some of the women in my quilting circle were saying that they heard men shouting at the younger Maiden over the weekend," Joy said.

Another wave of nausea rolled through Rowan's stomach.

"I will talk to the elders," Finn said.

Rowan stood, slamming the bowl down on the side table. "Don't you get it? They do what they want! They make the rules. They think that if they make the sacrifice, it will fix everything. But Finn, Elder Garrett has been bargaining with a demon—"

"Rowan! You can't make such accusations," Finn said, horrified.

"It's true," Rowan said. "I can't explain how I know, but I do. Those with magic can sense it. You can probably even feel it with your blessing from the Mother, Finn. He's not right. He's stirring this frenzy among the rest of them. It's supernatural. Think about it— Orla didn't ever experience this pressure, and it was more than a month before the Wolf took her."

Rowan was beginning to doubt anything had ever happened between Conor and Orla. Perhaps he'd just approved of Orla changing into red garb. Maybe if Rowan explained about the elders, he would allow her to do that. It was a victimless lie, but if Elder Garrett held such power, they might go through with the ceremony anyway. The frenzy in town was too much to ignore and Elder Garrett was opportunistic.

"The elders are corrupt," Rowan whispered.

"Row, if they were corrupt, the Mother would interfere," Finn said.

"You're naive!"

"And you lack faith!" Finn countered.

Joy looked back and forth between them. "Perhaps I should see myself out."

Finn snapped out of his daze and turned to her. "I will take care of this, Joy. I'll make sure that none of us has to experience or bear witness to such monstrosity."

Joy bit her lip and nodded as Finn kissed her hand and ushered her out the door.

Finally, he turned back to Rowan.

"Talking to them won't work," she told him.

"It will," Finn insisted.

"It won't," Rowan said. "I already have the Mother on my side. I have been trying to figure this out for weeks and have made no progress. You have no idea what it's like."

"I can help!"

"You can't. You've just begun to have to face this monstrosity, but I've been dealing with it alone for weeks. I don't need you to save me," Rowan said coldly.

Finn threw up his hands. "Yes, Rowan. Punish me for not being able to bear the thought of what is asked of you. Hate me for not being able to think about what you will need to endure at that monster's hands."

"I hope you're not talking about the Wolf," Rowan quipped.

"You know I am," Finn sighed. "Goddess above, Rowan! Every week, I watch you disappear into those woods, and every time, I wait for you to return. If you could feel what I feel, you'd understand. It's agony to wait for you. To not be able to follow you without risking your life. To know that he could hurt you however he wanted for his own amusement—"

"He's not like that," Rowan sighed.

"You haven't the faintest idea what he's like, Row. You've known him for a few weeks."

"I know he's treated me far better than our supposed *holy* leaders," Rowan snapped.

Finn's anger vanished, and something like desperation settled in his eyes. "Do you love him?"

"What?" Rowan choked on her surprise. "No, of course not."

"Do you love me?" Finn asked.

Rowan swallowed hard.

A frantic knock on the door saved her from having to break Finn's heart. Finn opened it and found a breathless Sarai with Raya slumped in her arms. Sarai's cheek was swollen, her lip split, her eyes red and puffy, but Raya's shirt was soaked with blood, her body bent from pain.

"What happened?" Rowan asked as she helped Raya to a chair.

Sarai turned and looked from Finn to Rowan. "The elders caught us together and had us whipped. I got off easier since I'm the Crone's daughter and they're afraid of her, but they want to cast us both out for our deviant behavior." She shook her head, wiping her eyes. "Raya can't travel like this. Her back is a mess. She needs time to heal."

Fury surged through Rowan. "How dare they! How dare they take love and make it something ugly and shameful! How dare they lay a finger on you!" Her anger was a life force pounding through her like a beating heart. "What do you need? What can we do?"

Sarai paced the room as Finn brought Raya some water. "I don't know. It's possible we could make it through Huntsman's Hollows, but it will be weeks before we can leave. And I need calendula, marshmallow, or chamomile to try to heal the wounds. I don't—" She broke into a sob as she collapsed to her knees in front of Raya. She brushed the hair back from the huntswoman's face. "I'm so sorry. I should have been more careful."

Raya smiled weakly. "We were both there and knew better."

"I could talk to the elders for you," Finn offered.

Sarai shot to her feet and stormed toward Finn. "You have been willfully ignorant long enough, Finn Ashand. You know better and yet you remain blind. What will you say to those bigots? How will you convince them? And what good is their mercy if it condemns me to my knees to plead contrition for the rest of my days? What was my sin? She is to me what Rowan is to you, Finn. How can it be wrong to love someone?"

Finn swallowed hard. "Sarai, you know I don't care who you love. I love you no matter what, but the scriptures say—"

"I don't care about the goddess-damned scriptures from those blasphemous morons!" Sarai screamed. "I care about Raya! I have asked you for nothing in all our years of friendship, Finn. *Nothing.* I have kept your secrets and given you advice. I have told you exactly how to get what you want."

Finn shook his head. "I know. I owe you so much, Sarai, but I cannot do this right now. You don't understand. Everything with Rowan—"

Sarai's gaze shot back to Rowan. "The secret ceremony?"

Rowan nodded. Despite the fact that she appreciated Finn's loyalty, she couldn't help but be disappointed in his lack of imagination. He had more power than she and Sarai combined, but he was unwilling to use it.

Rowan stepped behind Raya, carefully lifting her hair from her back and braiding the blood-stained strands out of her face. "You could hide them in your hunting cabin."

Finn frowned. "And what happens if they're caught?"

Sarai let out a bitter laugh. "Don't worry, we wouldn't dare sully the name of Ballybrine's Mother-blessed golden boy. We would say we snuck in without your knowledge."

Finn threw his hands up. "Goddess above, Sarai, that's not what I meant, but if they're this on edge and they find out I helped, there won't be anywhere left to run."

"The goddess above is no goddess of mine. I've had about enough of her absence," Sarai snapped.

Rowan held up her hands, trying to settle them both. She crossed the room and took Sarai's hands in hers. "I won't let them hurt you again. I'd sooner see them dead."

Sarai's face softened. "You're not a killer, Rowan."

Rowan took a deep breath. "I don't think we know yet what I might become to protect the people I love."

For weeks those words had been a poisonous specter that haunted her mind. Saying them out loud and having witness to them, strengthened her resolve.

Finn looked startled by the admission, but Sarai's shoulder straightened, and hint of satisfaction lit her eyes.

"We'll hide until Raya is healed and make a plan. We're not going to run. I'll not leave this town to festering hate that will hurt other women." Sarai's eyes blazed with fury. "I'm going to burn it down, just like we talked about. I'm going to burn out every bit of infection in this town and I'm going to be the kind of Crone that brings people together instead of tearing them apart." She leveled her glare at Finn. "You better know what side you're on when it comes time, Finn. Choose wisely! Because I'll remember this, and I might be quick to forgive, but Row holds a grudge."

Sarai helped Raya to her feet and the duo stormed out the door, slamming it so hard the entire building shook.

23

CONOR

Rowan leaned back in the plush chair in the sitting room. Her green eyes narrowed in concentration on the chessboard in front of her. Fading sunlight streamed through the window, highlighting the red in her curls. She propped her chin in her hand, brow furrowed as she nudged her bishop to a new square.

Conor frowned at the move. It was a beginner's mistake to go along with the ones she'd been making all game. She was obviously distracted, and it bothered him that she wouldn't share what was on her mind.

She'd asked to stay the night before without bothering to explain why. He was going to deny her—he didn't need the temptation—but she'd looked at him with such desperation in her eyes that he couldn't bear to send her away so soon. He didn't like the weakness she pulled out of him and she'd been so sullen since she asked if she could wear red and he'd turned her down.

Even now, she just stared at the chess pieces as if expecting them to move of their own accord. Rowan typically relished the opportunity to try to beat him at chess. Conor found her determination charming, but now she seemed strangely withdrawn. Even her posture was slouched, as if life had taken the air right out of her.

He replayed everything that happened the last time she was at Wolf's Keep. Perhaps it was just a reaction to his admission about devouring. She'd left in a huff, but he'd noticed that her temper tended to burn hot all at once and then reduce to a simmer.

Conor moved his queen. It was an idiotic move, one that she should have pounced on immediately. Instead, she just stared at the board like she'd never played before. When she moved a pawn instead of taking advantage of the huge mistake he'd made, he finally spoke up.

"What's on your mind? You seem more than a little distracted."

Her eyes scanned the board, and she slapped a hand to her forehead and shook her head. "I'm sorry. I don't know how I missed that."

"If you don't want to play—"

"I do. I just think that my mind is not all here tonight. Perhaps I should just have some tea and go to bed," she said.

She stood, and Conor grabbed her hand.

"Please stay and play. We can start over."

She hesitated before sinking back into the chair and resetting her pieces. Then she just stared at the board.

"What do you want, little Red?" Conor asked.

Rowan looked dumbfounded by the question. She wrung her hands. "Why are you asking?"

It was an accusation, and it made sense from a woman the whole world only saw as someone from whom they could get something.

He sighed and shook his head. "Has anyone ever asked you that?"

"No," she admitted. She leaned back in the chair and closed her eyes. "I think I'd like some peace. I'd like to live a simple life with a garden and a little cottage." She shook her head. "It sounds so pathetic when I say it."

"I don't think so," Conor said.

She blinked her eyes open and glowered at him. "Says the god who lives in a creepy mansion in the woods. As if you're a paragon of normalcy."

"I suppose you're right," he admitted. "Still, I imagine that for you, the village is noisy and overwhelming. Plus, you've spent most of your life being stared at. I can understand the desire to blend in—to move about without notice. What else?"

She ran her fingers over her collarbone as she considered. She did it every time she thought hard about something. It was the most innocuous movement, but catching her small habits filled him with warmth—when she wrung her hands nervously or brushed a phantom hair behind her ear when she was embarrassed.

It's just magic designed to draw you in, Conor thought. Still, he found every little habit incredibly compelling. He wasn't sure he'd ever been so fixated on someone, and he was certain it was unhealthy.

"I'd want to grow herbs, of course, but also frivolous flowers that are just beautiful. I'd read books, as many as I could." She smiled and her cheeks pinked.

"And would you live there alone?" Conor asked.

The glimpse of light in her eyes winked out, and her face shuttered. "I'd like to go to bed now," she said flatly.

He'd pushed too hard. *Stupid, Conor, always trying to peel away her layers when you hate having your own peeled.*

Still, he couldn't curb the impulse. He wanted to know and understand Rowan. Beyond that, she deserved to be treated like a person with hopes and dreams. The more he could humanize her in his own mind, the more he might be able to withstand his impulses.

"Rowan, you can tell me if something's wrong," he said softly.

She sighed. "Something more than the fact that I've lived my whole life waiting to die at your hands? You want to know what I want? I want to change the bargain to protect myself and Aeoife."

Conor scrubbed a hand down his face. "I cannot give you that, Rowan. It's so much more complicated than what I want."

He wanted to argue with her, but the truth was he knew what it was to live with a near-constant dread. Dread was his new companion every time she set foot in the Dark Wood. Still, he wanted to remind her that fear meant she had something to lose.

He met her eyes, and a familiar heat sparked in the air between them. "I don't think you're mad at me right now. You're just picking a fight to deflect. You can tell me anything, little Red, when you're ready."

Her gaze dropped to his lips. She sighed and turned away, leaving him with nothing but silence and the scent of lavender and vanilla on the air.

THE NEXT DAY, Conor followed Rowan around the Dark Garden as she told him where to move sacks of fertilizer, baskets of seeds and bulbs, and buckets of water. She grumbled about how it was far too late in the season to get started before pausing with her eyes closed, as if listening closely to some phantom sound. It was a relief to see her in better spirits.

"What do you hear when you're in there? Why are you so drawn to this garden?" Conor asked.

She worried her lower lip between her teeth. "It's like I can hear the melody of the dormant flowers. It's sad and lovely, like everything else here. Whenever I get close, it tugs on me like it just needs a little help to bounce back. It calls to my magic."

"Will you show me how to plant?" Conor asked.

Rowan stifled a giggle. "You want to plant flowers?"

"I want to plant flowers with you, yes," he said. "I may as well after I got you all these fancy seeds and bulbs."

She grinned, her eyes lighting up. He'd finally stopped trying to resist the way she drew smiles out of him. He was worried that allowing feelings for her to develop would feel like being sucked into an undertow, but surrendering to it felt more like floating along with a gentle current than drowning. As long as he could keep some space between them, he'd be fine.

Rowan brushed her hair back from her face, smearing a bit of dirt from her gloves on her forehead. Conor rubbed it away with his sleeve.

"I'm not sure what exactly is planted in this portion, so I'll need to grow that a bit to find out before we know exactly what to plant," she started. "But over here, there's no music at all, so we can really go wild. I'm thinking of some of these tulip bulbs. It might be a little bit late in the season, but if I help them along, they should survive the winter and be really beautiful in the spring."

Conor followed her lead as she dug small holes for the tulip bulbs, evenly spaced at the front of the flower bed. He considered the impracticality of planting flowers on the precipice of winter, but the determined look on Rowan's face kept him from sharing his concerns.

She laughed at his technique, placing her hands over his. "Slow down. You're not trying to murder the soil. You're just trying to dig down a few inches. I know you're not exactly made for delicate things, but I think you can learn," she whispered.

Her words were laced with innuendo, but he caught no hint of teasing on her face. She pretended as if she'd said nothing as she handed him a few more bulbs and watched him plant them. Once she was satisfied with his technique, she went back to work.

When they finished with the tulips, they interspersed those bulbs with allium bulbs, black dahlia tubers, chocolate cosmos, black pansies, black magic hollyhock, black velvet petunias, and dark purple calla lilies. Rowan was entirely in her element.

"How did you learn so much about flowers?" Conor asked as he pruned back the rosebushes.

"Some of it I learned from Sarai. Some I just know because I can hear things when I listen to them. Here, give me your hands, and I'll show you. It's like every plant has its own melody, and from that, I can tell how much space they need, or how deep they need to be planted, or if they like the spot I put them."

Conor knelt in the dirt as Rowan removed her gloves. She placed her hands over his and guided them over a tulip bulb. She was so close he could hardly focus on anything but her scent and all the places her body pressed against his. Her eyes fluttered shut, and a faint smile tugged her lips up.

"This one will need a little extra coaxing. It doesn't like how cold it is right now."

"What does it sound like?" Conor asked.

Rowan listened and then hummed a fluttery melodic tune softly. Conor felt her magic brush up against his hands as she hummed a little louder. He felt the melody—not just in his hands, but in his whole body. It was pleasant and bright, like the first warm days in springtime, when the frost breaks and things melt and the crocuses shoot up from the thawing earth. He closed his eyes and enjoyed the sensation.

After a moment, Rowan drew his hands back, and he blinked, startled as a tulip shot up through the ground and, a moment later, bloomed.

Conor stared at it in shock. He knew what she was capable of, but it was another thing to see her power in action with so little effort. Very little surprised Conor after centuries of existence.

"Can we do it again?" he asked.

She nodded, guiding his hands to another spot. "This one is a dahlia. Let's see, it sounds like—" She closed her eyes and started to hum again.

This time the melody was slower, winding. It reminded him of a violin concerto. Her magic pulsed through his hands and then spread through his body as she sent it down into the ground. This time the magic felt like lying in the sun on a warm day and feeling the warmth spread over his skin and sink into his muscles.

Once again, Rowan shifted his hands to make room, and he blinked his eyes open in time to watch a stunning black dahlia bloom as if it was the height of summer instead of late fall.

He turned to look at Rowan. "What are you, love?"

She shrugged. "I'm just Rowan."

Conor pushed her back into the grass and kissed her. His body still buzzed with the aliveness of her magic. For someone who was always surrounded by death, it felt like a high. It was as good—if not better—than devouring. He told himself that, but it had been so long since he'd done it, he wasn't certain that was true.

Rowan opened for him like the bloom, and he sighed in relief. She'd been so bound up and worried. Seeing her relaxed felt like a reward. Not only did she let him touch her, kiss her, steal all the breath from her lungs—she pulled him closer, like he couldn't take enough from her. Like she couldn't get enough of being had.

Her fingers curled like claws in his hair as he bit her lip. They played a strange game of chicken. He advanced, bunching up her dress, and she helped him hike it higher.

He caught glimpses of her face between kisses. Her eyes were full of questions and anger, like she was frustrated by her lack of control.

Conor blessed the recklessness that let him kiss her fiercely, all while he cursed himself for the restraint it took to not suck the life out of her as he drank up her gasps and sighs.

He wanted to drag Rowan down into the dark with him. He wanted to watch her react to every dark thing he introduced her to. It was wrong, but he couldn't stop thinking about her in all manner of compromising positions—tied to his bed, bent over his desk, on her knees, looking up at him, waiting for instructions.

Would she give him the same petulant pout she did when he sent her away, or would her eyes light with excitement? Where would she draw the line? Would she draw it at all?

He thrilled at the thought of having to draw it for her—having to teach her exactly where it was. She'd enjoy those lessons so much more than the ones she'd been taught by tutors growing up. He wanted it too much.

It was all wrong. Rowan was warm, sweet, ethereal, angelic, and he wanted to dirty her up. Conor never realized how utterly starving he was until the first time he'd kissed her. He'd drawn enough power from people's fear and faith alone that he hadn't needed to devour a Maiden in a long time. Now, he felt like he might lose his mind if he didn't taste every part of her.

It's just magic, Conor. She tastes like everything you've ever desired because of magic. You've seen it before. You'll see it again. Get it together. She's just a pretty girl with a lot of fire.

She sighed against his lips and slid her hands up his shirt, and he flinched away from her.

"Stop! I don't want this, and even if I did, it's just magic. You can't trick me into taking you to bed," Conor bit out.

The defensiveness was a reflex, like ripping a hand back after touching a hot pot.

Rowan looked surprised by his casual cruelty, which made it clear that was the exact thing he needed. The harsh words were a violent flail in the dark, less to remind her that she should resist him than to prompt her to want to. She didn't look wounded, but she took a breath, scooting away from him, her hands fisting in the dry grass like it was the only thing anchoring her to the earth.

The sweetness of her in his mouth turned to sour regret. Still, he knew it was the right move. He needed control more than ever, and Rowan shredded his to bits. Even now, as she looked at him with eyes full of familiar frustration and pouty lips bruised from his kisses, he faltered.

She read the shift in his body, her own coiled for action, though it was unclear if she meant to fight, run, or just let him kiss her senseless.

What he wanted wasn't really relevant. What he *needed* took precedence, and right now, he needed that beautiful woman and the feral look in her eyes as far from him as possible. Her proximity was dangerous, like sparking a flint near a powder keg purely for the thrill of seeing if it would spark. It was foolish, but he couldn't seem to stop chasing the high of it.

"You have to go home now," Conor said. He rose to his feet, and she stared at him in disbelief.

She stumbled to standing, looking around the garden. "How will I take care of my garden if you just send me away again?" she said after a long time.

The fear on her face was not at all commensurate with fear for her garden. There was something else that she was afraid of. He cursed himself for shoving her away yet again when he wanted to know so badly what weighed on her.

In some ways, he'd been right about Rowan when they first met. She was delicate, but not in the way that she would break under cruelty. It was more like alchemy. She took a delicate touch because the wrong move could be explosive, and that volatility was incredibly compelling to Conor. He wanted to cultivate it, wind her up, and watch her melt down—not to drive her mad, but just to watch the ease with which she accessed passion—like she had an endless supply of it.

Living for centuries had a way of taking the fire and urgency out of everything. Rowan was a reminder of what it was like to be so blessedly, vibrantly alive. He was mesmerized by it.

"Okay." She said it as if she was trying to convince herself.

Conor studied her, searching for what was different.

She wouldn't meet his eyes. "Are you sure I can't stay, just for a few more days?"

Conor hated the desperation on her face, the racing of her heart, the high, tight pitch of her voice.

"What aren't you telling me, little Red?" he asked. He tilted her chin up, but she stepped back out of reach.

"Please—please just do this for me, Conor," she murmured. "Please just let me stay." She took his hands in hers.

"I've already told you what will happen. Why are you so intent on welcoming oblivion?" he asked.

She shook her head and turned away from him. She looked toward the garden gate, and he caught the scent of fear.

"What are you afraid of?" He grabbed her arm.

He knew it wasn't just him. She'd already shown him over and over that she had far too little fear when it came to him, even after he'd admitted exactly what would happen if he took her to bed.

She yanked her arm away, but as soon as he tuned into his power, his mind came alive with her new fear. No longer was it disappearing. Instead, he saw her tied to an altar, held down by elders in some sort of gruesome ceremony.

"What the fuck is this?" he gritted out, lost in the illusion.

"It's what will happen if I go back a virgin," she said. "So, if you don't mind, I'd prefer to make the only choice available to me."

Conor wanted to strangle the life out of every man who'd taken what little joy she held on to. There was no end to her courage, but he wouldn't abide her making the best bad choice. He had never taken a woman to bed who didn't want to go, and he had no intention of starting now.

It put Conor face to face with the thing *he* feared—that she'd never want him for real or that he wouldn't know if she did. It was one thing for her to think she wanted it, or to want the way he made her body feel, or to want it because the alternative was worse, but it was another thing entirely that he couldn't strip her indoctrination from her. She would never be neutral when it came to him.

"How dare they!" he growled.

"They're scared, Conor," Rowan huffed. "I'm not excusing it, but they're worried about the blight. It's healed here, but it's still along the fringes of the Dark Wood. It's still in the Ashand Orchards. They think that this will stop it and satisfy you. You don't know what it's like in the village right now. People yell at me every time I walk through town. I'm afraid of what they say to Aeoife. The elders and the people of Ballybrine think something is wrong with me and that you don't want me."

Conor swallowed hard. Charlie had informed him of the tension, but Conor had no idea things had spun so out of control.

"You know that's not true."

Rowan laughed bitterly. "It doesn't matter what I say, Conor. They don't listen when I speak. Such is the nature of the men who make the rules. It doesn't occur to them that anyone else could know more than they do, even if they've never met you or set foot in the Dark Wood. Elder Garrett has taken issue with me from the beginning."

He knew he should take a breath, but Conor raged like a wildfire with no thought of the ash.

"I'll be happy to straighten that out for them right now."

Rowan grabbed his arm, trying to hold him back. "Conor, no—stop! This won't affect you, and it won't make it better. It will only make things worse for me," she pleaded.

He wasn't hearing her anymore. He shrugged her off, taking one last glance at her over his shoulder as he tore out of the garden.

He ran blindly down the trail toward Ballybrine, Rowan's terrified face frozen in his mind. He hated the men who'd made her feel powerless, objectified, fragile.

It was archaic and ridiculous for him to feel so possessive of her. She didn't belong to him—and yet also she did. Their fates were tied together, wrapped in each other like roots. He felt a responsibility to her.

He didn't care what Rowan said. He couldn't let an elder threaten to take what was his. The moment common men thought they could take from the gods was the moment he lost his power entirely. He didn't care what kind of bloody mess he left or who would clean it up, as long as they remembered who their fear belonged to.

24

ROWAN

Dread hung like a chain around Rowan's ankles as she made her way down the path toward Ballybrine. She had no idea what awaited her, but she could assume it would be gruesome.

When she finally reached the place where the trail met the town, several huntsmen and Elder Falon were waiting for her.

"Lady Rowan, please forgive us our mistake," Elder Falon said, his eyes cast downward.

Her gaze lingered on a fresh bruise on his throat. She tried to pretend it was normal for him to extend deference of that title, but it was typically reserved for Maidens who had completed their service. Elder Falon could barely meet her eyes.

"What mistake was that?" she challenged.

The elder shifted. The rush of power was heady, and she almost smiled. Instead, she kept her face placid as she looked over the men. She stayed calm until her eyes locked with Finn's. He looked stricken.

"Lady Rowan, there's something you should see," he murmured.

She walked by the elders and followed Finn into the temple. Several hunters trailed behind her. The energy song around the group pulsed frenetically. They were afraid, and their fear was contagious.

"What happened?" Finn whispered.

Rowan peeked over her shoulder. The hunters trailing them gave her a wide berth.

She cleared her throat. "The Wolf can sense people's worst fear. He sensed that mine had shifted."

"He's seen it before?" Finn asked.

"Yes," she murmured.

He silently led her into the ceremony room.

She was instantly assaulted by the coppery scent of blood, and as her eyes adjusted to the dim light, she narrowly avoided a red puddle on the floor. Blood painted the walls in bright red splotches, and on the altar, what was left of Elder Garrett made a gruesome center-piece. His eyes bulged, his face frozen in a shriek of terror. The red silk ties he had shown Rowan were wrapped around his neck.

Rowan wasn't nearly as horrified as she should have been by the sight. A vindictive part of her she hadn't known existed until that moment took a small bit of satisfaction in knowing he'd felt fear as potent as that which he'd inflicted on her.

She met Finn's gaze, and he nodded at the wall to their right.

Touch her at your peril.

The words were written in blood on the wall above the large wooden trunk at the far side of the room.

"Well, I suppose there's no mistaking this," Rowan mumbled.

Finn looked startled by her calm. "Rowan, I think you're in shock."

She crossed the room to the trunk. She lifted the lid, and inside, she found a bunch of brown leather-bound journals. She flipped the first one open and found notes from Evelyn, Orla's predecessor.

"Finally," Rowan breathed.

"Row, how are you so calm?" Finn whispered.

"Because someone who wanted to hurt me is dead, Finn."

"How can you condone such violence?" he asked.

She could hardly breathe around her outrage. "Probably the same way you did: by telling myself it's for the greater good and assuming it's the will of the gods."

247

Finn's horror only made her angrier. He was so blind, and the longer he refused to look at the hypocrisy, the more her rage swelled.

Rowan had been silent and steady when she wanted to scream and fight. She had done *everything* they asked of her. She had given them so much and still, they wanted to take more. For so long, she'd been certain Finn could get there—that when he saw her suffering, the issue would become more personal.

Now, the realization that he would never confront the discomfort of his own complicity made her cold all over.

"What has that monster done to you?" Finn asked.

She rolled her eyes. "He hasn't done anything except give me autonomy."

Finn shook his head. "You're so cold now. What happened to the sweet girl that I fell in love with?"

Rowan blew out a disbelieving laugh. "She never existed."

She turned to face the rest of the elders huddled by the entrance. "I'll need someone to bring these journals up to my room in the tower."

"Lady Rowan, we'd be happy to pack these up for you to bring to your tower. We do feel, though, that it may be best...to appease the Wolf, of course...for you to go and stay at his keep," Elder Graves stammered.

"I don't think that's what he wants at all." Rowan laughed in disbelief. "I'm certain that's not what he meant. He just didn't want me to be ritually *blessed*."

The elders averted their eyes.

"Please, Red, we just want the Wolf to be happy. If he comes back, we have no idea what souls he will reap," Elder Raymond said.

It was unfathomable for them to ask for her mercy after what they'd planned. If she was a different person, she'd send Conor back for the rest of them.

Instead, Rowan tipped her head back and sighed heavily. Before, she was their sacrifice, and now, she was their savior, but she still wasn't someone they'd listen to.

Cade strolled into the room as if summoned by the chaos. He

whistled, tapping his foot in a blood puddle. "I'm impressed. I take it Wolfie wasn't a fan of whatever deviant plans the elders dreamed up for this hall of nightmares?"

Rowan said nothing, pinning him with a glare.

"Mother's tits! This is a mess! I wonder what the Mother thinks of this. I suppose he kept the blood out of her house, at least. She seems to like a tidy space," he joked.

Rowan bit back a laugh. She didn't realize how tense she was until Cade teased her.

She turned her attention back to the elders. "Fine. I'll select several journals to go with me, but I expect every single one of the rest of them to be in my room when I return before the ceremony in a week," Rowan said. "I'm counting them now, and if any are missing, I will know."

Elder Falon nodded emphatically.

She walked back to the altar. The stillness in the room grew heavy as she paused in front of Elder Garrett's body. She felt nothing for him—no pity or empathy, just relief. She looked forward to Conor receiving his soul, though she hoped she wouldn't have to ferry it herself.

She crossed the room and paused in the doorway. "I want this room sealed up permanently. There won't be any rituals again or any talk of them. You'll wipe the records of such a thing from our history and never even think of suggesting one again." She paused. "The Wolf will know if you don't follow through. And—more importantly —*I* will know."

Rowan didn't even need to turn to sense their agreement. She climbed the stairs, walked through the temple, and back out into the cold air with Cade on her heels.

"That was so badass!" he laughed. "'*I will know.*' You're scary when you want to be, Row."

"Good," she whispered.

She didn't know if she should be as worried that she didn't feel pity for the dead elder or fear of the Wolf. She felt oddly light, like she was coming back to life, or maybe just living for the first time.

There was a large crowd gathered in the temple courtyard. Huntsmen shouted over the group, trying to get them to disperse. Clearly, word of Conor's display of violence had already spread through town. It had done nothing to settle the tension in Ballybrine.

Rowan pinched the bridge of her nose, trying to rub away the beginnings of a headache.

Cade ducked back inside the temple and reemerged a moment later holding a leather satchel filled with journals. He offered it to her. Rowan slung it over her shoulder, turned, and started toward the Dark Wood trail.

"Rowan," Finn said.

A cold gust of wind ruffled her cloak as she paused at the edge of the trail.

"I promise I'll get you out of this. I promised I'd save you, and I still will," he continued.

"It's a little late for saving now, Finn."

She walked swiftly back to Wolf's Keep. The Dark Wood was strangely still, as if recovering from the Wolf's explosive violence.

Cade was just as quiet beside her.

"I need you to keep an eye on Aeoife. The frenzy in town makes me nervous," Rowan said.

"What about you?"

"I can take care of myself," she replied.

Cade sighed heavily but nodded and turned back toward Maiden's Tower.

A few moments later, she climbed the stone staircase and pushed through the heavy wooden door of Wolf's Keep.

Charlie stood in the foyer. "Surprised to see you so soon, lass."

"I'd love a word with him," she said.

Charlie offered her a grim smile. "I don't know if that's the best idea. He's a bit wound up from the bloodlust."

"Sounds perfect to me."

Rowan pushed past Charlie into the sitting room. Conor paced in front of the fire, his hair still wet from his post-murder bath. He froze when he saw her.

"Glad you had a chance to clean up from your foray into finger painting—or is it called *claw painting* for you?"

"Get out," Conor gritted out through clenched teeth.

"Sorry, but you scared them so badly they don't even want me in town anymore. Looks like you're stuck with me unless you want to leave me to the creatures of the Dark Wood."

Conor sighed miserably. Apparently, her company had become unbearable. She wasn't sure what to make of him. One moment he seemed obsessively focused on her, and the next, he was trying to ignore her.

"I suppose I'll be expected to help Elder Garrett's soul cross over next week?"

Conor huffed out a breath. "Charlie will take care of retrieving him tonight. You'll not need to see the man again. You may go to your room," he said dismissively.

She narrowed her eyes at him. "And if I wish to stay here and enjoy my cider?"

He clenched his fists at his sides. "It's not a time to test me."

"Funny—I feel much the same about being bossed around, especially after I warned you that you wouldn't help anything," Rowan quipped.

Conor stood with a start, the chair clattering to the ground behind him as he advanced on Rowan. She stood her ground as he towered over her. "You have a death wish!" he barked.

"And you have an obsession with control," she countered. She should have been scared, but his passion only stoked her own, no matter how reckless it might have been.

Conor's nostrils flared and his gaze dropped to her lips. She hated that she wanted him to kiss her. It was exhausting wanting him all the time when he was so unpredictable.

They stood there, chest to chest, both breathing in short, shallow gasps.

Rowan met Conor's stormy eyes. "I'll take my cider now."

Conor took a step back, shaking his head. "Demon's breath!" He sighed, turning away from her and righting his chair before sitting and returning to his reading.

Rowan grinned in triumph as she sat in her chair by the fire. A moment later, Charlie appeared with her cider. She sipped it slowly, watching Conor over the rim of her mug. He wouldn't look at her, but she could tell he also wasn't reading. He was just staring at the book so he could ignore her.

Taking another long swig of her cider, she relished the burn of the whiskey. She rested her head back against the chair and tucked her legs under her.

She didn't mean to fall asleep, but she woke when Conor lifted her into his arms and carried her up to her bed. He removed her boots and tucked her beneath the blankets, and before she settled back into sleep, she heard him whisper so softly she thought she might have imagined it.

"I'm sorry."

She wasn't certain if he meant for killing Elder Garrett, for not listening to her, or for getting her banished, but she was too exhausted to ask, and when she woke the next morning, she was certain she'd imagined it.

25

ROWAN

Rowan was tired of waiting. For days, Conor avoided her as she prowled around Wolf's Keep, reading journal after journal so she wouldn't lose her mind.

Despite Elder Garrett's death, Rowan still felt uneasy. She knew that Conor's attack had raised the fear and anxiety in Ballybrine to a fever pitch, and she didn't like being away from Aeoife. She couldn't stop hearing the frenzied voices of the people gathered outside the temple.

Were they harassing Aeoife? She wanted to go back and bring the younger Maiden to Wolf's Keep, but she was worried that would be no safer for the girl.

Most of all, she was tired of Conor's games. She wanted answers.

She marched into the library to confront him, breathing in the scent of ink and parchment. Normally, she found it soothing, but today, she was too frustrated to enjoy it.

"What am I to you?" Rowan asked.

Conor looked startled by her abrupt entrance and the question. He slid his chair back and closed the book he was reading, but said nothing.

"You don't want me, but you also want no one else to have me,"

Rowan began. "You keep me here but treat me like I'm equally desirable and aggravating. It's disorienting not to know if you're going to pounce on me, hate me, or ignore me altogether. You give me pleasure, and then you won't even come within a few feet of me. You didn't want me to stay here, and now you don't want me to leave, but I'm alone all day except for the few moments you deign to pay attention to me. I'm just *lonely*."

The word hollowed her out. It was a feeling she'd lived with so long that it was shocking it still had the power to steal her breath. Speaking it into existence gave it more power, and she felt a black hole open inside her, the vacuum of it threatening to suck her down into an abyss. It was absolutely not the time for self-pity, and yet her rage had burned itself away, and she was only left with a strange, empty grief.

No—get it together, Rowan.

Conor was her enemy. The dagger in the sheath on her thigh was the reminder. She could not forget that loneliness was reliable. She could only count on herself. The Mother was counting on her. Bally-brine was counting on her. Aeoife was counting on her.

She wrung her hands nervously. The vulnerability on Conor's face stripped away her resolve.

Conor ran a hand through his hair and started to pace. "That's not what I want for you, Rowan. I want you to have more than just people who look at you and see an object. It's safest for you here. Until I understand better how you fit into this."

"You think you know what's best for me. How are you any different from them?"

For the first time, she saw the hurt in his eyes.

"You're right," he said.

Rowan was so startled by the admission that she took a step back. She had expected him to argue with her. She'd become so accustomed to the world treating her irrationally simply for having her own thoughts that validation was a foreign concept.

Conor sighed and leaned back against the bookcase, squeezing his eyes closed as he rubbed the bridge of his nose. He laughed suddenly, startling both of them. "I've been trying so hard to hold on to my own control that I've resorted to simply controlling you—or at least trying to. It's proven to be a futile effort."

Rowan smiled.

"I'm sorry that I made you feel that you don't know your own mind or that you don't know what's best for you. It's not an excuse—I've lived for a long time, and I've become accustomed to working alone. I should have simply been honest with you from the beginning. I should have just given you all the information and let you decide for yourself how you want to handle things. I didn't trust that you could handle that, and selfishly, I didn't want—"

He fell into silence, meeting her eyes across the room. She felt like he was looking right into her soul. A flash of heat pulsed through her.

"You didn't want?" she asked breathlessly.

"I didn't want you to stop looking at me with curiosity and start looking at me with fear. I wanted you to be on my side so badly that I made you feel like I wasn't on yours."

Conor was afraid of the same things she was. The words emboldened her.

She crossed the room to him. He stood frozen, his stormy eyes locked on her face as she ran her hands down his velvet tunic. Her gaze followed the touch, as if to validate that he was truly letting her do it. Conor's breath was shallow under her hands. Her heart raced as she met his eyes.

Her mouth was dry, her voice small and frail as she spoke. "What would I see right now if I could see *your* fear?"

Conor said nothing. He squeezed his eyes shut and grimaced as if picturing it himself. "I don't know if you'd see anything, but I know what you'd hear."

He grabbed her hand and dragged her out of the room, leading her into the east wing and down to his music room. He sat down at the piano and snapped his fingers. Hundreds of candles in the room fired to life.

In the brighter light, Rowan's gaze fell on a bed under the large windows. "Have you been sleeping down here?"

Conor laughed. "I don't sleep."

"Ever?"

"Ever. I don't need to."

Rowan had no way to confirm that. It wasn't as if she'd shared a bed with him. She looked around the room, which she'd only lurked outside of before.

Most of the keep was neat and tidy, but this space was much homier. Sheet music was stacked on the bookshelves, while pages and pages of scattered notes in surprisingly neat penmanship littered the piano's surface.

She tucked her legs under her and snuggled into the plush chair facing the piano.

Conor sat down on the bench. He fidgeted with the sheet music, his gaze drifting to her several times before he flexed his fingers over the keys. For the first time, the stillness around him broke apart, and tiny fissures of buzzing anxiety broke through like frenzied bells.

Rowan welcomed the noise. It was the first sign that he felt anything at all.

"You know I've heard you play before," she said.

"Of course—when you were spying," Conor said dryly.

"So why are you nervous?"

"Because this matters. It's—" He licked his lips. "I've never been good with words, but you asked what you were to me. When I see you, this is what I hear. This is what I think of. This is what my fear sounds like, Rowan. You told me that I sound like stillness to you, but this is what you sound like to me."

He started to play.

Rowan didn't realize she was holding her breath until he'd been playing for a full minute and her chest began to burn. The music was beautiful—lovely and tinkling in some moments and loud and bold in others. It swelled and crested and soared, all while a strange melancholy thrummed through it. There were lines that sounded like the frenzied longing in the breathless kisses they shared, the sharp fury she felt when she first stood up to him in the garden, and the true contentment she'd felt when he danced with her in the greenhouse. It was a song of joy and hurt and savage longing.

Beyond the song, Conor looked pained as he laid all of his feelings bare. She could clearly hear his struggle in the music, and she was stunned at how closely it mirrored her own. She didn't realize she was crying until he stopped playing and looked at her, startled by the sight of her wet cheeks.

"I'm sorry," he mumbled.

Rowan closed the space between them and pulled his lips to hers. She kissed him with everything in her, climbing into his lap and running her fingers through his hair. He only hesitated a moment before wrapping his arms around her, crushing her against his body.

It felt so good to be held like that—like he never wanted to let go. If he kept doing it, she might never want him to—she would lose herself.

She could not afford to forget who he was and what he meant to her—destruction.

Rowan brushed a hand over the sheath on her thigh. She brought his hands to her breasts so he wouldn't notice it. She didn't want to give him any reason to stop kissing her.

Conor pulled back breathlessly. "I take it you liked the song? I must admit this is the best review of my music I've ever had."

"Yes, you could say that." She cupped his face in her hands. "Conor, it was so beautiful."

His face grew solemn, and he looked at her with reverence. "I know—" He swallowed hard. "I know what you think—that you'll disappear...but Rowan, I'll remember you. Rest assured that you've left a permanent impression on me. I'll never stop hearing that song. I'll never stop playing it. I'll never stop wanting to hear it."

Rowan blinked away tears. It was so beautiful and personal. He spoke directly to her deepest fear. It was far from a profession of love, but it was, perhaps, the only kindness the god of death could offer her. They were who they were. He could no more stop wanting to devour her than she could stop being drawn to him.

It's just magic that weaves us together. That makes me feel this way, she tried to remind herself. But still, her heart raced as he kissed the tears from her cheeks.

She needed to end this now. She needed to kill him tonight. If she got any closer, she'd never be able to detangle herself. Even as she tried to convince herself it wasn't the case, she felt herself growing roots in a life there in Wolf's Keep.

She liked the quiet darkness of the space. She loved her garden. She loved Conor's music and playing chess with him.

But Conor had said it himself: the only thing there for her was death. She couldn't build a life where everyone else's ended, and she could not protect Aeoife unless she killed Conor and the Mother made a new bargain with a new god of death.

Her hands trembled where they rested on Conor's chest, and she squeezed her eyes shut, trying to summon courage. She needed to end him before she lost her nerve.

She blinked her eyes open. "Take me to that bed right now."

His eyebrows shot up. "Rowan, I—"

"Don't say no. I want you to. I want this. I get to choose nothing about my life. Let me choose this. I want you. I trust you."

"You shouldn't," he gritted out.

"I know, but I have to choose to trust someone eventually, and you've been nothing but honest with me."

Conor squeezed his eyes shut, his fingers digging into her hips, then opened them and laughed. "Demon's breath, you are stubborn."

She had to push it. She hiked up her dress and unsheathed the dagger. "I want—"

Conor sucked in a breath and froze, his gaze trained on the blade. His eyes became incandescent. "What *do* you want?"

"I want you to take some of my blood. You've kept me safe, and I trust you. I want you to bond with me—"

"How do you even know about bonds?" he asked.

"The Red Maiden journals," she lied. "Evelyn wanted you to do it with her, but you didn't like her enough."

"What makes you think I like you?" Conor challenged.

She laughed. "Your song."

"I suppose you have me there," he sighed. "You need to understand what it will mean. I'll be able to feel what you feel. I'll be able to sense when you're in danger. But, my tempting little Red, it will be very hard to hide anything from me." Conor studied her carefully. "Are you sure you want that?"

Aching desperation pulsed through her body. "Only if you'll take me to bed. Only if you'll finish what you started in the greenhouse. I don't care about what anyone else thinks. I only care about us. I'm tired of dancing around this. I want something that I choose. Something that's mine," she rasped.

"And you trust me?"

"Yes."

"Rowan, *I* don't even trust me." He looked pained as his hands drew the hem of her dress higher.

His mouth said one thing, but it was clear from the way he looked at her that he wanted her. He was trying to talk himself out of it, but she could see his resolve sliding away. She had him. She couldn't believe it. The feeling of holding sway over someone so strong was a heady rush. For the first time in her life, she felt truly powerful. She wanted more.

"Do you trust me?" Rowan asked.

He laughed. "Against my better judgment—yes."

She leaned closer so that her cheek brushed against his, and they both shuddered. Her lips brushed the shell of his ear as she whispered, "Then take me to that bed right now."

Conor growled as his hands came to her bottom, and he lifted her. She reflexively wrapped her legs around his waist as he began to kiss her in a maddening, harried way. She kept her grip on the dagger in her hand, careful not to cut either of them as he carried her to the bed, where he laid her down as if she was the most delicate thing he'd ever touched.

He kissed down her jaw to her neck as he unbuttoned the front of her dress. His mouth followed his fingers, greeting every new bit of skin with soft kisses. She brought her free hand to the back of his head and moaned.

"Mother slay me, you taste so good, it's like your skin is dusted in sugar," he whispered into the space between her breasts.

"Don't stop," she begged.

His restraint broke all at once, and he ripped the front of her dress open. She was startled by the display of strength, but it was more out of surprise than fear.

Rowan reached for him, and it wasn't until she saw her hand on the hem of his tunic that she realized she'd dropped her only weapon. She didn't dare look at it for fear of him noticing.

Focus, Rowan. He's not your friend. He can't be, she reminded herself.

Conor dragged what remained of the dress down her body and froze. His eyes raked over her, and she held perfectly still as he took in the delicate lace underthings. He unstrapped the dagger's sheath from her right thigh, his gaze slowly wandering back up her body.

"What on earth are those?" he asked. Although he'd seen her undergarments before, she hadn't worn anything quite so elaborate.

She giggled nervously at the ravenous look on his face. "I was apprehensive about being completely nude under my dresses, so the seamstress made them for me. Do you like them?"

He bent down and kissed along the edge of the lace at her hips, alternating between soft kisses and nips with his teeth. The competing sensations of pleasure and pain sent her heartbeat into a frenzy. She fought to hold on to her sanity as he kissed his way up her stomach, pausing at the lace that covered her breasts. He dragged his teeth over one nipple through the material before darting his tongue under the edge of the fabric.

She felt like a puppet, helpless to the ministrations of her puppet master. Her breathing was shallow and her skin buzzed everywhere his hands and mouth drifted.

It's just magic, Rowan. It's not real. It's just the bargain trying to ensure that it's completed.

Still, the chaos in her body was incredibly compelling.

"This lace is very pretty, but I've been dying to see you naked," he murmured.

She blushed as he deftly peeled away the lace underthings. His fingers brushed over her delicate flesh, and she shivered.

"You're so soft—every part of you," he murmured as his tongue laved over one of her nipples.

She cried out in surprise, and he chuckled against her skin. She was losing control, and all the power she'd felt before seemed to have transferred to Conor. She could not have that. Not when she was so close.

She hiked her legs up around his hips and rolled so that she was on top. Conor stared at her in stunned admiration, but she was unsure what to do with the position change. She leaned forward and kissed him, letting one hand roam down his bare chest as he groaned into her mouth.

"Tell me what to do," she whispered.

"Rowan, don't rush. We have to go slow. I want it to feel good for you, which means we need to slow down so I can get you ready."

She knew what he meant in theory from her years of learning about the Wolf's appetites, but she felt suddenly self-conscious. She unbuttoned his pants tentatively.

"Do you want me to—"

Conor grabbed her wrist. "I would love that, but this isn't about me, lass. This is your first time, so why don't you let me steer?"

She bit her lip and nodded.

"As appealing as this position is to me because you look incredible, it doesn't work for what I want to do," he said.

"What...what do you want to do?" she asked.

"I want to do what I did in the greenhouse," he said, letting his fingers trail up and down her side in a mesmerizingly soothing pattern.

She tried not to look too eager as he flipped her onto her back and sat back on his heels. Her skin heated under his gaze. He'd seen parts of her before, but never all of her naked at once.

"Are you okay?" Conor asked.

She nodded. "Just nervous."

"Don't be. I'm going to be as gentle as I can."

"And if I don't want you to?" she challenged.

Conor scrubbed a hand over his face. "Mother slay me, Rowan. Are you trying to kill me?"

She froze. *How does he know?*

He laughed and shook his head, and she let out a shaky breath.

Before she had a chance to calm her hammering heart, Conor kissed up from the inside of her knee with a patience that was both wonderful and maddening. By the time he reached the apex of her thighs, the anticipation stole her breath.

Just like before, she squirmed under his touch. He was so attentive to her every whimper and moan, so expert with his mouth, that her mind emptied of every thought. She couldn't tell if she wanted to run toward or away from the sensations building in her body.

She tried to ground herself by glancing at the dagger on the sheets beside her but was instantly distracted by the wet glide of his tongue. It was only moments before she couldn't stop bucking her hips in rhythm with his movements. She was so close to release that she almost cried when he drew away.

Conor chuckled at her discontented whimper. "Relax, I'm going to keep going. I know you're close. I just wanted to use my fingers to warm you up a little more. Is that okay?"

Rowan nodded, her mouth too dry from panting to speak.

He kissed her as one of his fingers slid inside her. She moaned, her head falling back against the bed. The competing sensations of his finger and his mouth were almost too much. He played her as expertly as he played the piano.

"Conor," she whimpered.

His name on her lips was enough to send him into a frenzy. He pumped his fingers faster as her muscles drew taut with pleasure.

"Please," she begged in between sounds of utter nonsense. Suddenly the tension snapped, and she felt suspended in time as she fell apart.

Conor didn't stop moving until she settled back to the bed, feeling boneless and satisfied. He kissed her inner thigh and then her hip, slowly making his way back up her body until he found her lips.

"You're so beautiful," he whispered between kisses.

"Don't stop," she begged. She couldn't think straight. Her mind was shrouded in a pleasant lustful fogginess.

Her hand brushed the dagger, and her thoughts snapped into focus. *Get him to take you so that you can take something from him, you idiot,* she chided herself.

She held the dagger out to Conor. He sat up and took it from her before taking her left hand in his. He brought the tip of the blade to her pointer finger.

"Are you sure you want this?" he asked. "This is your last chance to back out. I won't be upset—"

"I want it," she interrupted.

Still, he hesitated.

"What's wrong?" Panic sharpened Rowan's mind.

"I'm just worried that you wouldn't want this if you hadn't been told to make me happy. I don't like feeling you've been pressured to want me," he said.

She sat up so they were eye to eye. She brought her right hand to his cheek, and he leaned into her touch before kissing her palm. It was something lovers did, something so intimate, yet he did it as casually as if they'd done it a hundred times.

"Conor, I don't want you because of that. I want you because everything I believed was wrong. Because of the greenhouse and the library. Because you saved me when no one else did. Because of that beautiful song. Because you speak to my fear with tenderness. I could worry that you only want me for the same reasons, or because I smell like dessert."

He laughed, and it broke all the tension between them. "That you do. All right, if you're sure. I'll just take a drop, and then you have to say that you accept the bond."

He pressed the dagger into the tip of her finger, and she winced at the tiny bite of pain. He drew the blade away and dropped it on the bed beside them. She tracked where it landed but was instantly distracted as he drew her finger into his mouth and sucked gently. His eyes closed, and he groaned. A flare of heat shot through her body.

"Fuck," he murmured. His eyes glowed brightly, swirling blue and gray as he looked at her. "Say it."

"I accept the bond," she whispered. She waited for something to happen. "I feel the same."

Conor closed his eyes and smiled. "Well, I don't. I feel how turned on you are, so I suppose I should stop making you wait."

He kissed her fingertip and released her hand so she could lay back. She glanced the dagger in her periphery, only an arm's length away.

Conor stripped out of his pants and climbed between her legs. He was strong, beautiful, and ethereal. His entire body was toned—as if he did nothing with his time but heavy manual labor—with a smattering of vicious-looking scars. Her hands raked down his chest, the muscles rippling under her touch as he prowled over her. His eyes glowed with power as he drew her into another kiss. His hips rolled against her, and she groaned at the friction.

"Rowan, look at me." She blinked her eyes open and met his gaze. "Are you certain this is what you want?"

"Yes," she said breathlessly. Rowan was surprised at how utterly desperate she felt for it while at the same time dreading what she'd have to do.

"I'm afraid I'll lose control," he murmured. He looked so ashamed as he said it.

She brought a hand to his cheek. "You won't. I trust you."

Conor brushed a stray curl back from her face and kissed the tip of her nose. "It might hurt, but I promise I will make it feel good for you. You just have to try to relax, okay?"

She nodded as he started to press into her. It was slow going. Though her mind was fully on board, her body seemed unwilling to yield to him.

Above her, Conor clenched his jaw in concentration, studying her face as if waiting for any sign of pain. His hands wove through her hair. It felt so nice to be touched that way.

"Breathe, lass. Just try to relax," he murmured, kissing her between words.

She hissed in a breath. Even though she was expecting some discomfort, she was startled by the ferocity of it.

"I'm sorry," he whispered, covering her face in kisses. "Just breathe. It will pass."

She slowed her breathing, and he slid in deeper until he was fully seated inside her. He paused, allowing her to adjust.

"You're okay?" he asked.

Rowan nodded. She was startled by the raw vulnerability on his face—by the intensity of his attention. She hadn't expected him to be so careful with her. Despite his words, she thought he'd be rougher. Everything she'd learned from her years of training and even from his own threats had set her up to expect something vicious. Instead, he touched her like she was made of delicate porcelain he was afraid to break.

She looked at Conor—really looked at him. His brow was furrowed in concentration, and his arms shook with the effort of holding back. Once he started to move, she would need to act quickly.

"What are you waiting for?" she asked.

"I'm waiting for you to be ready," he said through gritted teeth. "I don't want to hurt you."

"I'm ready," she said, bringing a hand to his face. "You won't hurt me."

She wasn't sure it was true. If he didn't die right away when she stabbed him, he might hurt her. She couldn't exactly blame him. Still, she felt that whatever wound he dealt her would pale in contrast to the wounds the rest of her life had inflicted on her.

He relaxed and began to move his hips. Rowan's head fell back as she moaned. It still stung the slightest bit, but pleasure swelled up, eclipsing the ache. She closed her eyes, wanting to commit the rawness of the feeling to memory.

"Rowan," Conor groaned, his lips skimming her jaw. "Eyes on me."

She snapped her eyes open. He looked wrecked, gazing at her as if welcoming his undoing.

"I need to see your eyes to know that you're okay," he whispered.

Conor moved his hips in a steady, slow rhythm, and she found herself involuntarily lifting hers to meet each movement. Tension wound through her like it had before, but this time, it was much more intense. She dug her heels into his back, trying to draw him closer.

He paused. "Are you sure you're okay?"

"Wasn't the point of this," she said, holding up her finger, "that you know what I'm feeling?"

He nodded.

"And what am I feeling?" she asked.

He squeezed his eyes shut and shook his head. "Too much for me to discern any one thing."

"Are any of them bad?"

He squeezed his eyes shut in concentration. "Just some fear."

She held her breath as her mind spun. He couldn't know what she was going to do, only what she felt, but she needed to act soon.

"This is a new experience. Of course I'm nervous. I'm not afraid of you as much as the unknown," she whispered. "Please don't stop." *Please don't figure out that I'm about to kill you.*

"So demanding," he chuckled.

She held his gaze as he started to move again. The intensity of looking into his eyes as he moved—the kindness reflected back—nearly brought her to tears.

She clung to the last threads of her resolve as she slid her hand out to the side, her fingers brushing the cool hilt of the dagger. It slid into her palm, and her heart pounded in her chest, both from the building frenzy in her body and the racing torrent of her mind.

Just stab him, Rowan. End this. If you do this, you and Aeoife will finally be safe.

Conor kissed her neck, groaning into her skin as she hugged him close.

Now, Rowan—you have to do this now. The dagger trembled in her slick grip.

Conor nipped at her neck, and she nearly dropped the dagger. He did it again, and she shuddered as shivers danced over her skin.

You won't get a better chance. Do it now, you idiot. This is bigger than you.

Rowan thought of the elders. She thought of the Mother, who hadn't bothered to save her from Elder Garrett. She thought of her own family, who'd given her up. No one could truly make her safe, and maybe now she was close enough to get Conor to renegotiate without actually hurting him. Maybe she could convince him to change. He'd already changed so much with her. She'd never felt secure anywhere in her world. Could she really kill the only person who might have the key to the freedom she wanted so badly for herself and Aeoife?

She dropped the dagger and brought her hand to Conor's shoulder. He pulled her into a kiss that stole her breath as he moved faster.

"Conor," she moaned.

"Mother slay me! I'm going to lose it if you say my name like that," he grunted.

His movements became more frenzied. He pushed her knees up higher and slid deeper, and she groaned so loudly she worried the whole keep would hear her. She didn't understand what was happening, but for once, her lack of control felt good.

She hooked an arm around Conor's neck and drew him close as all the tension in her body broke. Her back arched, and she cried out. Conor kept moving until he grunted, shuddered, and collapsed with his head tucked into her neck.

They lay together, panting, in silence.

"I don't know what you were so worried about. I feel fine," Rowan whispered. "Actually, I feel incredible." Her body buzzed pleasantly in the wake of her climax, and all her limbs felt heavy and relaxed.

Conor laughed and kissed down her neck. "I don't think you appreciate the amount of restraint it took to be gentle like that." He rolled to the side, propping himself on an elbow. He brushed his fingers over her collarbone. "Do you feel different?"

Rowan shook her head. "Not really, just pleasantly sleepy."

Conor smiled. His smiles were rare, but that was part of their beauty, and Rowan found herself chasing them more and more.

His gaze trailed over her body, frowning. "Are you sore?"

"Just a little bit." She followed his gaze and, for the first time, felt the blood sticky on her inner thighs. She knew to expect it, but it was still startling.

"I'll draw you a bath so you can clean up."

She grabbed his arm and curled into him. "Just relax for a moment."

He seemed to sense what she needed. She wasn't sure if it was the magic or just his experience, but he pulled her close, tucking her against his chest, and kissed the top of her head.

"I'd nearly forgotten what it's like," he whispered after a long silence.

"Sex?" Rowan asked, trying to contain her surprise.

"Yes. It's been a long time."

All at once, the puzzle pieces clicked together in Rowan's mind. "Goddess above! You never slept with Orla?"

Conor shook his head. "We were friends, but I never took her to bed."

"Then why did she change to red?"

"She asked, and I gave her my blessing."

Rowan propped herself on an elbow. "Then why wouldn't you let me?"

He stroked her cheek. "Oh, my lovely, fiery little Red. It's quite complicated."

"Wait, if you didn't sleep with Orla, that means—" Her mind spun wildly.

It meant that Evelyn was the last Red Maiden he'd taken to bed. She'd written extensively about it in her journals. Evelyn had been a little bit in love with the Wolf, but unless Rowan had missed something major, it was a short-lived affair, and she spent the next few years of her service being bitter. No wonder she hadn't been kind to Orla and Rowan. They were the next in line to win over the god Evelyn was in love with.

"Yes, it means I haven't been with anyone in many years," Conor sighed. "If I was a better god, I wouldn't have taken you, but I'm not. Now let me draw you a bath because I may have had enough tincture to hold on to control, but I can't keep laying next to you when you smell like blood and sex and dessert. I've already stretched myself as far as I can for one evening."

Rowan tried to hide her disappointment, but Conor knew what she felt now, so there was no point.

Conor laughed as he kissed her cheek. "Settle now, lass. Who knew you'd be so insatiable?"

As he made his way to the washroom, she tucked the dagger under her pillow and prayed that she'd made the right choice not to use it.

26

CONOR

Conor stood suspended in the doorway, staring at Rowan asleep in his bed, feeling as afraid to leave as he was to stay. He'd temporarily lost his mind to lust and let her curl up to sleep in his bed once she'd bathed. Now his fresh sheets—and likely his whole room—would smell like her. He'd allowed her to take over the only Rowan-less room in the entire keep.

He feared if he blinked, she'd disappear. Rowan was too good to be true, and he was certain he was moments from waking from a rare, pleasant dream. Still, he felt her contentment as his own through the bond she shared with him. At least he hadn't shared his blood with her. For now, their connection remained one-way. The last thing he needed was for her to know everything he was feeling. If she knew the extent of what he felt, she'd be impossible.

Rowan's full lips tugged up in a gentle smile even as she slept. Her auburn hair pooled around her like a halo. She shifted, and the blanket slipped down, revealing the pale skin of her shoulder.

Desire perked to life at the hint of her nudity. He was not even mildly satisfied with the little of her he'd allowed himself.

Conor cursed and dropped his head back against the doorframe.

"Afraid of your little conquest?"

He startled at Charlie's voice.

"How did you know?" Conor asked.

Charlie chuckled. "As if I could miss all that moaning. Sounded like she enjoyed herself."

Conor narrowed his eyes at his friend. He didn't like that anyone else had witnessed it. The territorial way he felt about Rowan was unnatural.

"I thought you'd be more relaxed, considering," Charlie said, waving a hand at the bed. "I just wanted to check in on you. It seems you were successful in not sucking the life out of her."

Conor nodded. "I don't know if I can do it again. It was hard enough to keep my composure, and she seems determined to tempt me until I lose my mind."

"By sleeping?" Charlie challenged.

"She offered to bond with me."

Charlie choked on a laugh. "And you took it? Are you truly out of your mind?"

"Yes. That's what I'm telling you. I think I made a mistake. Even right now, all I'm thinking about is fucking her and devouring her life force. Once she's awake, I'm going to feel everything she does."

"And that's a bad thing?" Charlie asked.

Conor grimaced.

"Mother's tits! You actually have feelings for her."

Conor shook his head violently.

Charlie laughed. "You *do*. Little Red is under your skin."

Conor scrubbed a hand over his face. He did care for her, and that would not do at all. He needed to stop caring as soon as possible. His emotions had only ever served to create destruction, and it would be no different for her.

The best he could do was approach her with the same cool indifference he had in the beginning. The problem was that was what he'd been trying and failing to do for weeks. He only succeeded in popping up out of nowhere, kissing her, and then disappearing again to stew in his own self-loathing.

It would be so much easier if he hadn't killed an elder, if they hadn't sent Rowan to stay with him, if there was anywhere on the island that was safe for her.

He'd cursed himself for the deal he'd made with the Mother so many times he'd lost count. He'd been a different person then, a mortal-turned-god, hardened by centuries of fighting and loneliness. Conor hadn't counted on the way the Maidens had taught him about kindness, duty, compassion. He'd become dreadfully soft.

Rowan needed him to be who he once was, yet even though he knew he'd be her destruction, all he could think about was climbing into bed and curling around her.

That sweetness competed with the darkness inside him that wanted to kiss her awake and make furious love to her in the way he'd held back from doing earlier. He wanted to show her who he really was. He wanted to drag her down into the darkness with him. He was afraid she'd go—that she'd like it as much as he did.

If one of them didn't act as the voice of reason, things would spin out of control fast.

"What are you thinking about?" Charlie asked with a grin.

Conor rolled his eyes. "How to stay in my right mind."

"Just have some fun. You've been way too tense, boss. You deserve it, and she certainly seems a spirited girl. No reason not to enjoy yourself. It would only help—"

Conor narrowed his eyes. "No. It's out of the question."

Charlie sighed, shaking his head. "If you don't, you might not be able to protect her much longer anyway."

The words settled in Conor's stomach like a stone. As much as he hated to admit it, Charlie had a point. The magic in him surged at the thought.

CONOR SAT in his chair facing the bed, not sure where to begin. He needed to be himself. Maybe that would serve a dual purpose in giving him what he needed while also scaring her away.

Rowan sighed as she rolled over in bed and stretched, pushing her wild hair out of her eyes. She grinned at him, sitting up and letting the sheet fall away from her full breasts.

"I want you again," he said.

Instead of looking apprehensive, Rowan's eyes lit up. "How?"

Of all the questions in the world, she asked the one that sent all of his focus south. *Of course she'd ask that. It was what she was taught to ask*, he reminded himself.

"You're just saying that," he accused. "You were taught to want that."

"Am I?" she asked. She climbed out of bed and crossed the room until she stood right in front of him. She lowered herself to her knees in front of his chair, and he swallowed hard at the sight.

"Perhaps I simply want to make you feel as good as you made me feel," she whispered. "Perhaps I know you were holding back and I want all of you like you've had all of me."

Conor stared at her. "I held so much back before."

"I know."

"I'm afraid of hurting you. I don't want to get carried away."

"Conor," she said, sliding her hands up his thighs. He flinched at her touch. "I want you to get carried away. You've been in control so long, and so have I. I want something else, and I don't care if it's dark. Neither of us are afraid of the dark."

Conor groaned. "That may be true, but I still don't want you like this."

"Then how do you want me?"

"I want you to tell me what you want," he said. He was losing his nerve.

She blinked up at him and bit her lower lip. "I want you wild—how you really are."

He tugged her to her feet and tossed her back on the bed. She let out a squeal of delight and surprise. He slid off his pants and prowled between her legs.

"Rowan, Rowan, Rowan...where do I even begin with you?" he murmured as he kissed the inside of her ankle, her inner knee, then up her stomach.

She whimpered, arching into his mouth. She had the unique ability to separate him from his sanity with just that sound. How had he ever felt the predator in their relationship when he was so obviously prey to the exquisite woman in front of him?

Her green eyes were bright and full of fire, and he'd willingly let her burn right through him. At times, she seemed unaware of the power she held, and at others, she asserted an effortless command over it.

He wanted her in every position, on every surface of that room, but for now, he'd settle just for seeing her face as he moved with her. In all his years of celibacy, Conor had forgotten what it was like to be with someone.

In the back of his mind, an even more frightening revelation reared its unwelcome head. He'd never once felt the kind of connection he did with Rowan, and it intensified every kiss, every touch, every glance. The bond made it even stronger.

He slid inside her, and they both groaned in unison. He was certain nothing had ever felt as good as being so close to her.

"Okay?" he asked, brushing hair from her eyes.

"Goddess above, Conor! Stop checking on me. I'm fine, and I'll say if I'm not. Now move!" she huffed, lifting her hips, seeking friction.

The words broke his restraint, and his hands gripped her hips hard enough to bruise as he pulled back and thrust into her. Her nails dug into his shoulders as he did it again, but her eyes showed only desire and not a hint of pain.

He pulled her into a scorching kiss, swallowing up her moans as he moved rhythmically. She tried to meet his movements, but he held her in place, exactly how he wanted her to take him. The shift in power made her wild. Her hands gripped his arms, and she tossed her head back, sitting right on the precipice of release.

Conor kissed her neck as he moved, dragging his teeth over her skin. He was still holding onto the gentler side of himself, but barely. If his restraint slipped, he wasn't certain he wouldn't take too much from her.

"Conor," Rowan whimpered. He met her gaze. "Let go."

He shook his head.

"Fear is poison. Don't let it steal the joy from this," she whispered.

He remembered the day he'd first looked at her deepest fear when she'd said those words. She was right. Every time he feared losing control, he gave that fear power. He, of all people, understood that.

The ravenous, unrelenting desire took over as he let go, his hips churning faster. His hands were everywhere. He couldn't touch enough of her, even with the soft curves of her body pressed flush against the hard lines of his, even with her clinging to him just as tightly as he did to her.

Conor was absolutely starved for her—for love, for touch, for life itself—and Rowan was every single one of those things. His movements became frenzied, jerking, relentless, and she arched into him. A sound between a scream and a moan ripped out of her as she came undone. It was so beautiful, but even the animal in him needed to see her eyes, needed to know she was okay.

He slowed and sat back on his heels, drawing her up to straddle his lap. He had all the power, but he was handing her control.

Her eyes lit up as understanding dawned on her. She covered his face in kisses. In all of Conor's years, no one had ever been so sweet with him.

She paused, tentative as she rolled her hips. Her eyes were glued to his face, watching every reaction. He didn't expect to ever find anything he liked as much as control, but at that moment, he liked Rowan being in control more than anything else in the world.

Her back arched, and her breasts thrust forward as she moved her hips. She looked wild and lovely, and he wanted to lay the world at her feet.

It's just sex, he reminded himself. *Don't be desperate, Conor.*

But in the back of his mind, he knew it was more than that. He was falling for this wild, magical woman. He liked her sharp edges and her rage as much as her humor and warmth. She wasn't afraid of wounding the same way she wasn't afraid of the wounded. There were moments when she seemed untouchable, even to him. Parts of her would always be unknowable, but it didn't stop him from wanting to know them.

He shoved those thoughts away. He tucked the feelings deep inside him as she curved into him and squeezed so tight around him that he followed her over the edge. He devoured her mouth with a passionate kiss and she let him, smiling breathlessly when he finally pulled away.

"That was more like it," she laughed as he laid beside her.

Conor laughed in disbelief. "You'll be the death of me."

Her smile faltered momentarily. "That's impossible," she mumbled.

Conor was about to lob a comment back when he licked his lips and tasted burnt sugar.

Rowan was *lying*. She somehow knew it was possible for him to die. Through their bond he sensed a slight buzz of nervousness buried under heavy fatigue.

"Rowan, what do you know?" he asked. He needed to know exactly what she was planning so he could save her from herself.

"Hmm?" she asked as her eyelashes fluttered, sleep carrying her away.

She curled into Conor, and against his better judgment, he let her. He tried to kiss her back to consciousness, but she stayed asleep.

He smiled at how sweet she looked asleep beside him. The feeling of soft skin against his was a sensation he'd all but forgotten.

Rowan might have been exhausted, but Conor felt wired, powerful, energized. He extracted himself from her arms, worried he would wake her, but she remained heavily asleep.

Conor hadn't had true companionship in years. Though he was surprisingly desperate to connect, he had no idea where to begin. He feared that everything he'd held back was bound up inside him in a hopeless knot. If he let any part of it free, it might all unravel at once, and he could not abide a loss of control.

Pulling on his robe, Conor felt better than he had in years.

A knock on the door drew him away from the bedside. He opened the door and found Charlie holding a tray of tea and biscuits.

"Thought you could use some refreshments." Charlie stopped suddenly. "What did you do?" he demanded, his wide eyes looking through Conor.

Conor frowned.

"Your aura, it's brighter than I've seen it since—"

Horror crashed over Conor in a great wave. It couldn't be true.

He dragged Charlie into the room. The tray clattered to the floor, the teapot and cups shattering with a loud crash. Rowan didn't stir.

Conor raced across the room to her side. He sighed with relief that she was still breathing.

"What about her?" he demanded, looking at Charlie's stricken face.

"Hers is faded. What did you do?"

Conor cursed, raking his hands through his hair. "I must have lost control. I must have accidentally sucked out some of her life force when I—" The guilt punched the air from his lungs.

Rowan had tried to meet him as wild as he was, and he'd nearly killed her for it. All she had succeeded in doing was proving for sure how little control he had over himself. He needed to get as far from her as possible as fast as possible.

No wonder he felt so good. He'd stolen from her.

"Calm down," Charlie said. "She's fine. She's only slightly faded, so you must have only taken a little bit. She'll wake up and be no worse for the wear. You'll just tell her what happened, and everything will be fine."

Conor shook his head. "It's not fine! Everyone in her life has looked at her and only seen what they could take from her. I convinced her that I saw more, and then I did the same thing. I stole something."

"But you didn't mean to," Charlie argued.

"I'm not sure intention matters when it comes to stealing someone's life force."

"The lass is quite forgiving—"

"I'll not make hope a noose from which to hang myself," Conor interrupted. "Hope is not for me. I'll only become a bigger danger to her if I believe it is."

"I don't see how you being a martyr for an honest mistake changes things," Charlie quipped. "Just talk to her when she wakes up. Let her stay a bit."

Conor paced the room. "No. She has to go. I'm sending her back to the tower. I'm no better than those elders. I'm just as much of a risk to her."

Charlie grimaced. "Would it be the worst thing if—"

"I don't want to doom this woman," Conor hissed.

He didn't know how to tell Charlie that Rowan had been let down by all of the people she cared about most. He didn't know how to explain why he cared. He closed his eyes and tipped his head back. He could not believe he'd been so careless.

"It's worse because I knew better, and I still let her convince me to do this. She's dangerous to all of us, Charlie. I don't need to remind you. I think she knows she can kill me."

Charlie shook his head. "But you're safe now. There's nothing else for you to take from her."

Conor met his gaze. "Isn't there? The way I see it, there are two more things I could take from her. Her heart and her life."

The two stared at Rowan as if they could see through her to her true intention.

"Then let the elders or the Dark Wood have her. Mother's tits, Conor! Don't you have any sense of self-preservation?" Charlie said.

"And then what?"

Charlie huffed out a breath and banged his head back against the wall. "Then finish the job. Take all of her life force now. She is a sweet girl, but there's so much more at stake." He ran a hand through his hair. "You've been dreaming again, haven't you?"

Conor stared at him and said nothing. Contrary to what he'd told Rowan, he did sleep—and more so lately. He'd only dreamed a couple of times, but that was all it took.

Charlie shook his head. "Well, I have."

Conor froze. That was alarming. If Charlie was dreaming, all the reapers would be. The problem was much worse than he'd thought.

"You could do so much with that power. It's my job to protect you and there are things even I cannot save you from. This is your time. If not now, *when*?" Charlie pleaded. "Will you wait until the nightmare is stronger?"

The words stirred something cold and ancient in Conor, but he shoved it down.

"You'd have a ten-year-old guide spirits across the Dark Wood? Aeoife is still a *child*. I won't have her terrified and walking through the Dark Wood with a group of spirits," Conor said bitterly.

"What about the fifteen-year-old Maiden?"

Conor shook his head. "She's gone."

A crease formed in Charlie's brow. "Dead?"

"No. Just gone. I know she's out there, but she's much farther away than Ballybrine."

"I could hunt her down."

Conor cocked a brow. "Have you not been trying to do that for years?"

Charlie threw up his hands, his eyes glowing. "I'm telling you, she's magically protected somehow. Every time I think I have the trail, it slips away."

They fell into a tense silence.

"I'll go to meet the little one and guide her," Charlie said. "It's unorthodox, but there's nothing preventing it."

Conor shook his head. "I'm not going to devour Rowan. End of discussion. When she wakes up, I want her things packed, and then you will take her back to Ballybrine, kicking and screaming if need be."

"You know she'll just come back. She's the most stubborn Maiden ever," Charlie groaned.

Conor sighed and walked to the window. There had to be a way to convince her. He leaned his forehead against the cool glass.

The answer came to him like a dagger to the heart. The only way to ensure that she stayed away would be to hurt her.

It was far from what he wanted. Centuries had taught Conor that clear communication was best, but Rowan was the type of wild that did not respond to reason. The only way he could attempt to keep her safe would be to keep her away.

"I will convince her. Don't worry about it," Conor sighed. "Go pack her things up. I have no idea how long she'll sleep, but I want her out as soon as she's awake."

Charlie gathered the shattered tea set in a huff and left the room.

Conor gazed miserably from the spiderwebbed frost on the windows to Rowan asleep in the bed. Already her color looked better. Her cheeks were pink, and her lips, red and swollen from being well-kissed, were drawn up in a slight smile.

Mother slay me. She's beautiful, he thought.

He was a fool to even risk taking her to bed. It appeared there was no end to his foolishness. When she woke, he'd give her up, but while she still slept, he wanted to hold her one last time.

Climbing into bed, he pulled her against him, burying his face in her neck. He breathed in her sweet lavender-vanilla scent and cursed the Mother, the elders, and magic itself. He cursed himself for tempting fate with his happiness.

27

ROWAN

Rowan blinked her eyes open. She was momentarily disoriented until the black curtains and dark red bedspread and the stacks of sheet music on the nightstand reminded her that she was in Conor's music room. She stifled a laugh as she realized it had the look of a villain's lair. It could do with some brightening.

She wanted to snoop, but first, she wanted him. The embers of desire still smoldered at the thought of his touch, but when she reached out, the bed was cold beside her.

She'd slept like the dead, heavy and dreamless and, judging by Conor's absence, likely for a while. Her body was pleasantly sore, and she smiled, remembering the way it felt when Conor gave her control —his eyes full of awe. It was such a rush. It was ironic that she'd never felt more alive than when she was in the arms of death.

"Grand, you're awake."

Rowan whipped her head around to see Conor sitting in a chair across the room by the fire, sipping whiskey.

"Come back to bed," she said, patting the space beside her.

"You have to go," he said without meeting her eyes.

The coldness in his tone was in startling contrast to the warmth in the way he whispered her name as she fell asleep in his arms. Perhaps she'd imagined that tenderness.

She swung her legs out of bed and stood, crossing the room to stand naked in front of Conor.

His nostrils flared, but he didn't look at her. "Rowan, please don't make a fuss," he said. "I know you're young and maybe you don't understand. I got what I wanted from you, but I don't do aftercare. You should go back to where you belong."

She laughed in disbelief. "Really? You want me to believe that you just wanted to sleep with me? After you killed an elder for me? After that song?"

He said nothing as he finally met her eyes.

"I don't believe you," she said.

"I killed an elder because he wanted to take what belonged to me," Conor said with a harsh laugh. "I killed him, and then I took what I wanted from you. I have centuries of experience, little Red. Do you really think I couldn't convince you to give something up to me with some sappy story about a song I wrote for you? I've played that same song for the last eight Red Maidens. You all fall for the same story. The god of death with a heart of gold. I understand. It's very compelling to be told you're different than all the rest, but I'm afraid you're exactly the same, Rowan. A pretty little virgin who let me convince her this was her idea. It works every time."

The cruelty of his laugh opened a crack in her mind through which doubt grew like a weed through cobblestones.

"Don't get me wrong—you were fantastic. You're very well trained. I enjoyed every moment of it. I told you before that death's gift is taking," he taunted.

"You're lying," Rowan said, blinking away humiliated tears. Whether he was being honest or not, it was a disturbing reminder that cruelty came naturally to Conor.

"I'm not. Why do you think I made you sleep so long afterward? I didn't want to deal with the waterworks that always come at this point," he said.

Rowan's resolve faltered. She'd slept like a stone, and that never happened. He had to have used some sort of magic on her. She usually dreamt in wild, vivid colors and lucid stories, but there had been nothing but darkness this time.

"You've been asleep a full day, lass."

Rowan stared at him in disbelief. A full day. She wanted to deny it, but the grumble in her stomach suggested he was telling the truth.

"I'll have Charlie bring you some tea before you go. I've laid out a red dress on the bed for you. You should have no issue with the elders now. You're welcome for that, by the way."

"Conor, what are you doing? This isn't you."

He gave her a patronizing glance. "You have no idea who I am, little Red. But right about now, you should be figuring out what *you* are. You're simply an object to be used—a magical little doll to satisfy me. The sooner you remember that, the better off you'll be."

Every word was drenched in ice. He'd kept her at arm's length, and the first time he did anything remotely kind for her, she'd thought he was different. It wasn't her fault that her concept of caretaking was so flawed. She was as the world made her.

She went back over the course of events. She'd begged him not to go after Elder Garrett, but he'd still done it. He hadn't wanted her to stay with him when the elders sent her. He'd acted like she was a disease he might catch. Then he'd avoided her, popping up only occasionally to kiss her before disappearing again. She'd basically thrown herself at him.

Rowan met Conor's eyes, expecting to find contempt, but she was met with something so much worse: indifference.

She felt gutted. How could she have been so stupid as to not have just stabbed him when she had the chance?

Dressing in the red clothes he'd laid out for her, Rowan was disappointed she couldn't even rejoice in the fact that she could finally wear red. Everything felt hollow. She laced up her boots and buttoned her cloak.

Conor handed her the dagger that the Mother had given her.

Anxiety spun through her, but there was no sign on his face that he knew her original intent.

"Don't forget this, lass. You might need it out there. I'm glad to see you've started carrying a weapon. Can't always expect me to come and save you. Like I said before—"

"You're not the hero in this story," she rasped.

She couldn't believe the man who'd been so sweet and gentle with her the night before could so easily switch to cruelty once he'd taken what he wanted.

"Oh, that's right. *You're* the hero. Think what's between your legs is sweet enough to save your people? What would you do to save them, Rowan? To save Aeoife?"

Rowan stuffed down her horror and met his eyes. She clung to what little anger she could wrangle. Everything was made so much worse by the fact that he felt everything she did, so even if she succeeded in hiding how broken she felt, he'd feel every bit of her despair. She flipped the blade in her palm, slipping it from the sheath and pointing it at him.

"You know *nothing* of what I'd do," she gritted out. "Say what you want about me, but don't dare to speak her name, or I'll—"

"You'll what, Rowan?" he taunted. There was a distinct challenge in his eyes. Perhaps he did know what she intended with that dagger. "Will you fuck me into submission?"

Rowan swallowed hard. "No. I'll end you without a second thought. I might have been foolish, but I'll not make the same mistake *ever* again."

A flicker of what looked like pain passed through his eyes, but it was gone as quickly as it appeared, and she was left with the cruel god of death once again. He grabbed her arm and practically dragged her down to the foyer and out the front door. She had to jog to keep up with him, taking in lungfuls of fresh, snowy air.

She paused when they reached the gates, staring out into the snow-covered forest. The Dark Wood looked like it had been dusted in powdered sugar.

"If something happens to me, it's on you," she said.

She didn't look back as she passed through the gates and into the Dark Wood for the first time in days. She walked quickly through the forest, blinking away hot tears that froze in the cold air.

Footsteps crunched in the snow behind Rowan. Her heart leaped into her throat as she spun, hoping for a contrite Conor. Instead, Charlie stood there, a grim smile on his face in the fading daylight.

"I'm to see you back, lass."

"I don't need a babysitter," she huffed, starting back down the trail.

Charlie rushed to fall into step beside her. "It's for the best, lass. Much safer for you to be back in Ballybrine."

Rowan laughed bitterly. "Charlie, I'm not safe anywhere."

"Yes, but what about that little lass you take care of? If those elders will hurt you, do you imagine they'd leave her be?"

The words sent a chill through her more vicious than the icy wind ever could. In her own selfishness, she'd completely forgotten Aeoife. She was probably terrified on her own with so much turmoil. She deserved better than being abandoned by Rowan when so much was in flux.

Rowan pushed her pace even faster, the red dress swishing around her legs.

Everyone would be delighted to see her in red. She'd been eager for it herself. Now it seemed silly. Before she met the Wolf, before she'd been the Red Maiden, she'd been so foolishly eager for experience. The rebel in her was always so ready to run free. Now, that rebellion was responsible for the savage pain in her chest.

She reached for anger, but it was stubbornly elusive, as if she'd used the last of it to try to wound Conor on her way out. It wasn't as if she'd been in love with him, but she'd at least felt the stirrings of something. The idea that someone could look at her and truly see her had been dangled in front of her—having it wrenched from her grip was cruel.

The song Conor had played for her still reverberated through her chest. She swore he understood. She let him close because she thought he did. Rowan pushed, and she'd been the only one burned by her foolishness. She only had herself to blame.

She brushed a rogue tear from her cheek. Charlie gave her a pitying look.

"I'll not take pity from the likes of you. Your job is literally to reap souls," she barked.

Charlie didn't look hurt by it. His eyes were fixed on the trail in front of them until he abruptly stopped. She followed his gaze and found Cade standing in the snow a few yards ahead of them.

"Row, what did he do to you?" Cade asked. He seemed to be looking through her, but his eyes were full of fury.

"What do you mean?" she asked.

Cade glared at Charlie, but the reaper shook his head. Something unspoken passed between them.

"I'll take it from here, reaper," Cade said with disgust.

Charlie opened his mouth. "I don't think—"

"Charlie, you've done enough. Run back to your keeper," Rowan said, reaching for Cade's arm.

As they walked away, she felt Charlie's eyes on her back. She supposed he felt the same way about demons that Conor did.

Good, she thought, *go back and tell your master*.

"You're wearing red," Cade noted.

"Yes," Rowan said, failing to keep her tears at bay.

"Do you feel okay?"

"Yes. Just exhausted."

Cade only nodded in response.

"Thank you for coming to get me."

"Of course," he said. "You're my best friend."

"How did you know I needed you?" Rowan asked.

"I told you before that I can feel when the Dark Wood shifts. All demons can."

"It's no less creepy hearing it a second time," she sighed.

He grunted. "What happened?"

"I told a lie that only I ended up believing," she whispered.

"Row, for what it's worth, I'm sorry that it was a bad experience," Cade said.

"That's the problem," she rasped. "It wasn't."

"I take it you didn't succeed in killing him?"

Icy shock tore through Rowan. She stopped walking. She hadn't told anyone about her deal with the Mother for fear that the Wolf would somehow find out. There was only one way Cade could know.

The revelation rended her from the one friend she'd had her whole life. She was well and truly alone.

Cade's eyes went wide as he realized he'd tipped his hand.

She yanked her arm away from him and stumbled backward, nearly to the edge of the protected trail. Maybe staying on the trail meant the Mother's magic would protect her body, but it did nothing to protect her heart.

"Rowan, be careful!" Cade called.

"How do you know I was supposed to kill the Wolf?"

"Row—"

"*How?*" she screamed. "You don't know from me. Which means —" She brought her hand to her heart. It felt like her chest was caving in. "No." It was barely audible, the word lost with the air that punched out of her lungs.

Cade stared down at the snow in shame. The only one who knew her mission was the Mother herself.

"What did she promise you? Why would you help her?" Rowan asked.

Cade ran a hand through his hair. "Demons aren't the only ones who make deals, Rowan. I used to work for the other side, you know. I used to be one of the good guys. I made one mistake. That was all it took. One mistake for a lifetime of darkness. She said if I kept an eye on you, pushed you in the right direction, I could get back what I'd lost."

The icy burn of cold air in her lungs was the only thing keeping Rowan anchored to her body. She half-believed she was still asleep and trapped inside a nightmare. She pinched herself on the off chance she might wake up.

"How long?" she asked.

Cade winced like it hurt to confess. "She's a planner, Row. She likes to have contingencies. She knows how to play a long game."

"*How long?*" Rowan shouted.

"Since you were turned over to the elders," he mumbled.

Rowan stumbled back a few steps to the very edge of the trail. The only sound was the swirl of snow through the branches above them and her heartbeat in her ears. The grief hacked at her, but she could not fall apart in the middle of the Dark Wood. Conor was probably back in his keep, feeling her broken heart as clearly as if it were his own. She didn't know if that was a comfort or something to fuel her humiliation.

She sank to her knees, the snow instantly soaking through her wool stockings. She bit her lip to focus.

Cade's eyes darted around the periphery. "I know you're mad, but we should get out of the forest. Your grief, misery, betrayal—all of it will attract danger."

Rowan couldn't seem to focus on anything but the way her life had been blown apart in a matter of moments.

"Say something," Cade said.

She finally met his eyes. "I banish you, Cade. I banish you from my presence. I banish you from Aeoife's. I banish you from my entire life. Begone, demon."

Cade swallowed hard as he faded into smoke, and she was left alone in the Dark Wood. It wasn't permanent, but it bought her time to figure out how to force him to leave her for good. It would give her time to figure out what to tell Aeoife, who'd become quite attached to the demon.

A rustle in the brush behind her urged her to her feet. She stood and tore down the trail back toward Ballybrine. She sighed in relief between sobs when the ivy-covered Maiden's Tower came into view.

Mrs. Teverin opened the door of the tower and took in her teary eyes and red dress. Her mouth formed a grim line.

"There now, love, let's draw you a bath," she said.

Rowan surprised herself when she wrapped her arms around the woman and sobbed into her shoulder.

"Shh, let's get you into the washroom. If Aeoife sees you like this, there will be no consoling her. Just a few more minutes, okay? Then you can tell me everything."

Rowan nodded miserably and followed the woman into the tower.

28

ROWAN

Rowan didn't leave her room in Maiden's Tower for two days. She was too exhausted and depressed to face the world, and as restless as the town was, she wasn't sure she could face them in her red dress and keep her hurt under wraps.

Mrs. Teverin was good enough to leave her to her sulking, only stopping by to drop off meals and detangle her hair.

Rowan couldn't muster the enthusiasm for much of anything. She made time to read to Aeoife at night, but other than that, she stared at the wall and wondered how she'd ever been so foolish to trust Cade. She'd always known he was a demon. He'd told her repeatedly not to trust him.

It was easier to cultivate her anger toward him than to think about Conor.

Rowan had the dagger within her grasp, had been presented the perfect opportunity to use it, but she'd let Conor live. She'd believed him. He'd convinced her that she was worthy of gentleness the world had never shown her, and as soon as she relaxed into it, he yanked it away. It was unbearably cruel.

She didn't ask the Wolf to be anything other than himself. She'd gone in expecting nothing but cruelty. He'd been the one to convince her there was another option. He'd given her a garden, told her things could be different for her. It was a lot to offer her just to use her.

Every time she tried to make sense of his betrayal, she ended up more lost. Her anger at Conor warred with her rage at Cade.

She knew that Cade would always do whatever served him best, but she'd never suspected that their entire friendship was based on what it could get him. She'd always thought that they kept each other company—a means to a lonely end for both of them. But now, she was the same to him as she was to everyone else; a pawn to use for some larger gain.

At the bottom of it all, she was mostly just furious with herself. She'd let the first glimpse of kindness in her life throw her off course.

"You're not a killer," Sarai had said, but that was before, when they were talking about Elder Garrett. Perhaps her friend was right, but if Rowan wanted to live, she would need to make herself into one.

Cade's betrayal had broken her, but Conor shattered her. Now she needed to sharpen herself into a weapon to wield against them both. It was with that purpose that Rowan dragged herself to her practice space on her third day back at Maiden's Tower.

Rowan sat at the piano. She stumbled through several pieces she knew very well, but her fingers felt too heavy and her voice was tight with grief. Nothing worked as it was supposed to. She jammed her fingers down on the keys in frustration.

The air in the room warped and bent, and there was a flash of light as the Mother appeared.

"You've got some nerve showing up here today," Rowan snarled.

"Ah, I see we're finally beyond formalities," the Mother said.

"You tricked me!" Rowan snapped.

"You are an investment of my time and resources. I wanted someone to keep an eye on you. I'm sorry that I kept it a secret. I know it feels like a betrayal. I've found that people have a tendency to act in a performative way when they know I'm watching. I wanted to know who you really were and what you were made of."

Rowan shook her head and sighed.

"I needed to know that you could manage this," the goddess soothed. "I've known this crisis of faith was coming for some time now, but I needed the confirmation that you were a Maiden who could handle herself. You've always had to be a fierce little thing. I wanted to see if that fire burned deep—that it wasn't just sparks."

Rowan sighed. "Well, now you know."

"You might not like the way I work, but the reality is this: the Wolf can only survive another season if he devours you. If he doesn't, a new god of death will rise."

Rowan stared at the Mother, wide-eyed. Never once in any of the scriptures had she read about such a thing. It was one thing to accept that the Mother had the power to create a new god of death, but another to know that Conor could lose out to some other beast without her help.

Rowan shook her head. "Is he getting stronger or weaker? I've lost track," she said with a curt smile. "You contradict yourself every time we speak."

"He is stronger than I am, but make no mistake—he'll not make it through another season without you. And I don't know if I will if you don't manage to end him. Right now, his blight is growing, but this is his last-ditch effort to inspire the kind of fear and faith that strengthen him."

The Mother's words sobered her.

"How can a new god rise?" Rowan asked. "How will that be better?"

"By my grace, of course. And it will be better because we can renegotiate our deal. The people of Ballybrine can bear witness to such a deal, and that will restore faith and rebuild my strength," the Mother said.

Rowan stared at her, waiting for more. The truth felt just out of reach. "That's not much in the way of an explanation."

The Mother frowned. "Have you not already seen how cruel the Wolf can be? No matter what he might want to be, he's still a monster who can only survive off the souls of innocent young women. He'll kill you whether he wants to or not. Whether he means to or not. The reality is that the Red Maiden can choose which god of death to serve. I will make a deal with him that does not include your sacrifice. It might still require your weekly service of ferrying the souls, though there's no reason why you couldn't be escorted by some brave huntsmen as well."

Rowan stared at the floor, trying to untangle the thread of what the goddess was saying.

"You think he cares for you," the Mother sighed. "You think he's a misunderstood monster."

"I think no such thing. Don't pretend to know my mind," Rowan said.

"Ah, I see you've grown some thorns," the Mother said. Her face changed, and Rowan swore she saw a flash of regret in her eyes. "I'm sorry that you had to."

Rowan said nothing. Her mind was a mess. At times, the Mother seemed gracious and kind, but she was always pragmatic.

"Dear, it doesn't really matter if you believe me. I don't need you to love me or honor me. I just need you to do what's right, and that is a thing I know you will do, Rowan. You know what is at stake if you fail."

Rowan swallowed hard. *Aeoife*. Aeoife was at stake. Whether Rowan wanted to rebel or not, she wouldn't. Her responsibility went beyond herself, and if there was any way she could save Aeoife the same pain, she would do it. What was one more sacrifice in a long line of them?

She might have felt something for Conor he didn't feel for her, but she still didn't want it to be true. She wished there was another way, but the only way to end the exchange of Red Maidens for peace between realms was to kill the Wolf and let a new god of death rise in his place.

It was foolish of Rowan to ever dream that her life with the Wolf could be a fairy tale. It was a scary story, a tale of horror in the woods. The only real trick had been the one she played on herself in believing it could be anything else.

"I'll figure it out," she said. "Until then, you'll keep Cade away from Aeoife and me."

"As you wish," the Mother said. "You should know he feels quite distraught at your banishment."

"I don't care how he feels," Rowan snapped. She wished it was true, but deep down, she felt Cade's absence acutely.

Satisfied with her response, the Mother nodded and blinked out of the room in a bright burst of light.

Alone in the silence of her practice room, Rowan's mind spun too fast. She jumped up and left the tower in a huff, unsure what she was searching for.

As Rowan walked through the square, the stares of the townsfolk made her want to peel off her own skin. No one yelled at her, but hushed whispers still rose as she passed. She cursed her stupid red dress—the dress that made it feel like all of her pain was on display for the world to see.

Look at me and my broken heart, she thought. Conor may as well have cleaved her open and left her in the town square. It would have been kinder.

She cut down alleyways to get away from prying eyes until she found herself pleasantly lost in a part of town she wasn't as familiar with. Rounding a corner, she bumped into a group of men.

"Excuse me," she mumbled, stepping around them, narrowly missing the slosh of beer from their mugs.

"Aye, Red! See you finally let the old Wolf into your magical twat," one of the men taunted.

Rowan bristled as another stepped into her path. "Where you off to in such a hurry? You've not given him enough yet, apparently. The blight is still spreading in Ashand Orchards," he said, grabbing her arm. "Can't even do a good enough job of lying on your back to save your people."

He pushed her into a third man, who held her firmly by the shoulders. "What do ya say, boys? Should we have a taste of the Wolf's leftovers?"

Rowan struggled to free herself from the man's grip when another man stepped up in front of her and pulled her into an alley. He shoved her against the wall, knocking the air from her lungs, and began to hike up her dress. Rowan scratched at his face, trying desperately to get free.

There was so little she had left to offer. She'd sacrificed her childhood, her family, her heart. It struck Rowan that they wouldn't be happy with her life, either. There was nothing she could offer that would be enough. Worse, they felt entitled to her pain. There was no sacrifice too great for her to make, and if she didn't decide where the line was, they'd never stop demanding more.

"Leave Rowie alone!"

A red blur burst around the corner, launching at the man grasping Rowan's arm. He let her go out of sheer surprise as he shook off his attacker.

Rowan stumbled back, shocked to see Aeoife standing there, her hood pushed back and her little fists held out in front of her like she was ready for a fight.

The man took a step back, averting his gaze before turning back to Rowan. "You should get that one home. She's too young for this."

"But not too young to venture into the Dark Wood alone. This is the face my death condemns," Rowan said, thrusting her hand toward Aeoife.

The men stepped back, looking more startled than truly chastened.

Rowan's hands itched to beat the man bloody. A feral, impotent anger rose inside her and she clenched her fists to try to hold it back, but it was futile. She cocked her fist back.

"Rowan!"

Finn's voice startled her into stillness. He came between her and the group of men as she lowered her hand.

"Be gone or the huntsmen will make sure you go painfully," he snapped. The men scattered as Finn turned to face Rowan and Aeoife. His eyes lingered on Rowan's red dress. "Are you well?"

"I'd be better if these people would leave me alone."

"They're scared, Rowan," Finn sighed.

"And I'm not? What have they to be afraid of? It's me that stands between them and the Wolf."

Finn shook his head. "We're isolated here. They're worried for the future and the food supply."

Rowan took a step toward him, but Aeoife slid her hand into Rowan's and gave it a squeeze, and all her anger fled. "I have no future," she whispered.

"That's not true," Finn said. "You have belonged with me since the day I pulled you from that riptide. I looked into those beautiful green eyes and I was done for. I didn't leave you to the sea then, and I will not leave you to the Wolf now." He leaned closer. "I love you."

Rowan turned away from him, pulling her hood up to hide the tears streaming down her face. Aeoife walked beside her, whispering comforting words the whole way back to Maiden's Tower. But nothing could soothe Rowan.

She cried because she desperately wanted to hear those words from the lips of a god who would never say such a thing. She was caught between a Wolf who used her and a huntsman who desperately loved an idea of her, and she didn't know how to free herself.

29

CONOR

Rowan was sick with grief, which meant Conor was, too. He cursed himself for ever bonding with her because he'd been cruel the first opportunity he got. It didn't matter that it was for her own good. She hurt, and Conor did, too.

He'd been so desperate to own some part of her, so feral and territorial, that he let himself get roped into it. Now it was nearly impossible to separate what he felt from what she felt.

His own grief meant he'd become much too attached. He'd forgotten himself, and if he didn't remember now, she'd be the one to suffer for it.

He was unaccustomed to such intense emotions. Centuries of life had dulled everything, the monotony turning down the volume on joy, sadness, and lust evenly. But they all tore through him like a tempest now, and it was hard to sort hers from his. His emotions seemed to shift and make room for hers, reacting and responding to each one. When she was sad, he felt guilt. When she was angry, his temper stoked to match hers. On and on it went until he felt like he was ready to crawl out of his immortal skin.

He shifted in his chair, staring into the roaring fire in the ornate fireplace in his sitting room.

"Doing all right, lad?" Charlie asked.

"Some mistakes were made," Conor gritted out. He was so lost in thought he'd forgotten Charlie was sitting next to him. *Where Rowan belongs.* He shoved the rogue thought to the back of his mind.

"Curious mistakes, I'd say." Charlie gave him no grace at all. He was relentless in his encouragement to lure Rowan back and apologize. "For what it's worth, I know you've lived a life that's made you accustomed to misery, but the only one who will change that is you."

Conor finally looked at the reaper. "What kind of future could we possibly have?"

"We could speculate, but there's only one real way to find out," Charlie said. "I've always been a fan of playing it safe myself. I'd certainly prefer to keep things as they are, and the easiest way to do that is for you to destroy her instead of pining for her. But I think that you deserve more happiness than you'll let yourself have. I think that girl is tougher than she looks, and I think she probably deserves the truth, as hard as that might be."

"You've certainly come full circle," Conor laughed darkly.

"Well, a week of watching you brood around the mansion is about all I can take," Charlie teased. "Think it over. She'll be here tomorrow for the weekly delivery. You've got time to decide how to handle it."

CONOR HELD his breath as Rowan walked to the gates and knelt. Her red cloak stood out against the freshly fallen snow. He felt her fury radiating off her like heat off a summer meadow.

The souls came in a flurry of activity, but mercifully they all seemed at peace, and made a swift transition. When he was finished and the portal was sealed, he came to stand in front of Rowan. She kept her eyes averted.

"Rowan," he murmured.

She met his gaze and stole the breath from his lungs. If looks could kill, Conor would have been immediately eviscerated. She looked affronted that he dared to speak her name.

"Come in for some cider," Conor said.

Rowan laughed bitterly. "I'd rather run naked off the trail into the Dark Wood."

Conor bit back a surprised chuckle. "That's a sight I'd like to behold."

Her eyes narrowed as she climbed to her feet, ignoring his outstretched hand.

"Come inside, Rowan," he said more gently.

"Is that a command, O great Wolf?" she asked with faux reverence.

He knew that Rowan was attempting to scold him, but her viciousness only succeeded in turning him on.

"Does it need to be?" Conor asked. He felt pathetic pleading, but he'd been desperate for the sight of her. Now that she was in front of him, he didn't want her to run off so soon.

"If you want me to come in, it does," she ground out.

He considered the options. If he let her run back to Ballybrine, he wouldn't see her again for a week. The thought made him feel sick. Conor didn't think he could take another week of knowing how upset she was when he could do nothing to comfort her. He couldn't take another week of knowing he was the cause. Maybe Charlie was right, and he should just tell her everything from the beginning. Maybe he simply found her anger incredibly compelling, and he enjoyed playing with fire.

"Fine, consider it a command, little Red," he taunted. "It's only fair after I've been forced to endure your heartache all week."

Rowan blushed. "How lovely to have all of my worst hurts on display for your amusement," she rasped as she walked into the keep.

Her scent was an assault on his senses as she brushed by him. Desire pounded through him relentlessly as he followed her inside. He clenched his fists to try to tamp down what he felt.

Rowan furiously unbuttoned her cloak and tossed it on a chair, standing before him in a red wool dress. She hadn't even bothered to make herself up, though that did nothing to reduce his desire for her.

Her open rebellion against her role only made her more unexpected and fascinating.

In the firelight, he could see the toll his carelessness had taken on her. Her eyes were puffy and rimmed in dark circles. Her hair was unusually messy, fastened in a loose bun at the nape of her neck. He wanted to pull it out and scatter the hairpins around the room. He wanted to messy it with his fingers while he kissed her.

Her eyes narrowed as his gaze dropped to her lips.

"I'm afraid I'm not thirsty this evening. What can I do for you?" she said coldly.

"Perhaps I should ask what I can do for you, lass. You seem tense."

Rowan looked ready to slap him. Conor met her fury with flirtation because he was uncomfortable with the weight of his affection for her. He knew he was already too far gone. Humor was the only bit of levity left in him.

"I don't see how that's your concern," Rowan sighed. She kept her gaze militantly focused on the fireplace behind him.

He took a step closer to her, and she held perfectly still. Another step, and her gaze flew to his. One more, and she stumbled back, bumping against the sitting room wall. Her anger faltered momentarily, her gaze dropping to his lips.

Conor struck like a viper. He pressed his body flush to hers and kissed her feverishly. Her anger only made his desire for her more intense, her scent more tantalizing. He wanted her so badly.

Rowan was just as swept up. She poured every bit of rage into the kiss, all while he poured in every bit of contrition and sorrow. Her fingernails dug into the nape of his neck, and he groaned.

She tensed and shoved him away, then slapped him—surprisingly hard.

"Stop playing with me, Conor," she said, blinking back tears. "I'm a person, not a toy you can wind up for your amusement."

He'd taken it too far. He'd hurt her worse. He had nothing to say. He stared at her, wondering how he'd managed to screw up so spectacularly so quickly.

"Is that all, or do you need further services?" Rowan asked. He saw the genuine worry on her face.

She actually thought he'd make her service him after rejecting her and hurting her as badly as he could. He might have behaved monstrously to protect her, but it still stung that she thought he could be that type of cruel.

"Rowan, I can explain everything—"

"Yes or no?" she interrupted. She blinked furiously, trying to stave off tears. He wished he could hold her.

"No, I don't need anything else," he rasped.

The truth of his feelings choked him even as he was desperate to share them. Even if he hid the words with silence, it made them no less true. He was in love with Rowan Cleary. *Love.* Not an imitation or obsession. He felt the kind of love that stole his breath when she laughed, made him want to burn the world down when she cried— and that made him the most dangerous thing in the world to her.

Instead of saying what he really wanted, he bit his tongue to keep silent.

"Good," she said. She turned and grabbed her cloak from the chair where she'd tossed it, then stormed out of the keep without bothering to even pause and button it.

He waited a few moments before starting after her, but when he came to the gates, he found nothing but silence and her small foot-prints in the snow.

Charlie appeared at his shoulder. "Con, you should know. Her aura was back to normal."

"Are you certain?"

"Yes."

"How is that possible?" Conor asked.

Charlie shrugged. "I have no idea. I only know it's true."

Conor stared down the path toward Ballybrine. He wanted to go grab Rowan and bring her back to his keep where he could be certain she was all right, but after his cruelty, that was impossible.

"I'll follow her home," Charlie said.

Conor nodded and watched the reaper tear off down the trail

toward Ballybrine, leaving him alone with the soft patter of snowflakes on his now-living garden and the thought that he'd only succeeded in making things worse.

———————

THAT NIGHT, Conor woke with a start. His sheets were soaked with sweat and his brother's face was fresh in his mind.

After Rowan left, he had forced himself to rest for the simple fact that it would put him out of his profound misery for an hour or two.

That was a mistake. A strange sinking feeling filled his chest, a queasiness settling in his gut.

He tried to sense Rowan. Confusion and grief and a distinct sense of foreboding turned his stomach. Something was wrong, but he couldn't put his finger on it. He shoved out of bed and pulled on clothes, and the dread only heightened.

He stormed down the stairs and to the gates of the keep before pausing. The Dark Wood felt strange, wrong, even to him.

Charlie appeared beside him so suddenly that he jumped. "What's going on out there? It woke me up. The beasts are restless."

Conor's mind churned. "Valen took her blood, and he knows her name. If he's strong enough now, he could lure her right into the Dark Wood."

He couldn't believe he hadn't thought of it before. Valen could nearly match Conor's strength now. When she was in Conor's bed, Rowan was safe from the pull of Valen's compulsion. But in Ballybrine, on her own, she'd be helpless. She might not even wake up in time to realize what was happening.

The two of them took off down the path.

"Can you sense him?" Conor yelled over the howling wind.

Charlie grunted confirmation, and Conor turned to follow him into the trees. The two of them moved as fast as they could, snow whipping by them, making everything blurry. The large flakes stung his eyes and made his face feel raw, but Conor didn't slow down.

Finally, he caught a stronger hint of her scent on the wind and followed. Horror sliced through him when they spotted her a moment later.

One of Valen's arms wrapped around Rowan's waist, holding her back flush to his body, while the other held her head to the side. Rivulets of blood dripped down her pale skin, soaking into the red silk of her nightgown as he feasted on her. Her eyes were wide and unseeing, her hands limp at her sides like a doll's.

Conor wanted to scream, to rip Valen limb from limb, but he also knew the vampire was hopped-up on a heavy dose of Rowan's life force, and he wasn't confident that he could take him out easily.

Valen pulled away from her neck to laugh. "Your new Red is fucking delicious. Best one yet." His mouth was stained scarlet and his eyes glowed with power.

Rowan's gaze cleared, and her fearful eyes met Conor's. She mouthed his name, reaching for him feebly.

"Not so fast, sweet thing. Don't you want to stay with me longer?" Valen taunted.

Conor recognized the compulsion magic in the air before it hit Rowan. She cocked her head to look at Valen.

"Of course," she murmured, even as blood trickled from the wound in her neck, pooling between her breasts and disappearing into the lace neckline of her nightgown. Her voice was so small Conor struggled to hear it over the wind.

"I want her back...alive," Conor barked.

"She seems perfectly happy right here. Aren't you happy, love?" Valen goaded. He whispered something in her ear that was lost in the wind. She blushed and nodded. "Tell him what you want. Tell your big, bad Wolf."

"I want Valen to suck the life out of me. Then I want him to make me one of his wives so he can keep me forever," she said dreamily.

Conor couldn't stand the vacant look in her eyes. He hated that someone was hurting her, and he could do nothing to stop it.

"You know the rules, Con," Valen laughed. "The Maiden gets to choose which god of death she serves. Perhaps it's finally time to give rise to a new one. I thought Elder Garrett would be the one to deliver her to me, but you did it yourself. You gods are so foolish. You and the way you think you can hold this power. The Mother and the way she thinks she can use me, while I used her elders to strip her of power and grow stronger. Now I will take your place, and then I will wipe the Mother off the map until this world is full of darkness."

So that's what the Mother had been up to. Conor had his suspicions, but now it was confirmed.

Charlie looked to Conor for guidance on what to do, but Valen was right. Conor had created the rule about new gods rising so he'd someday have a way out if he wanted it. Being eternal was overwhelming. It never occurred to him that he might end up in this exact predicament. He'd been the most powerful being in the Dark Wood for centuries. Now the balance of the world was in the hands of a half-conscious Maiden whom Conor was desperate to save.

He'd seen the way Valen's "wives," as he called them, were mindless husks of the women they'd been when they lived. He couldn't stomach that fate for Rowan.

"Rowan, listen to me," Conor begged. "Don't give in to him. I care about you. I lied before when I said I didn't. I should have just told you the truth. That song was for you. I've never written one for anyone else. It was exactly what I feel. I've never shared anything like that with someone before. I've never felt this before. You scare me to death."

Rowan's head rolled back against Valen's shoulder sleepily.

"You're so beautiful, so angry, so damn stubborn," Conor continued. "I need you to be strong now. I need you to fight him. I'm so sorry I made you believe I didn't care."

"Aw, did you melt the heart of the big, bad Wolf?" Valen taunted.

Rowan groaned, her head lolling to the side as she tried to focus on Conor.

"You know I care for you. I know you felt it tonight. I am afraid I have little practice sharing my feelings, but I assure you that I'm crazy about you," Conor said desperately. "Please fight. You are stronger than his magic. I know you are."

Rowan's eyes locked on his and narrowed. A crease formed between her brows as her eyes focused.

"Please, Rowan," Conor insisted. "You are the best part of my week. I hate that I hurt you. I felt every second of it, and I wasn't telling you that tonight to tease you. I was telling you that I understand—that I felt the same."

Valen tried to draw her gaze from Conor, but her green eyes began to clear.

"That's it, love. Just look at my eyes and see that it's true," Conor pleaded.

Rowan's eyes squeezed shut, and she winced in pain.

"Love is what holds back the dark." Her voice was a raspy whisper, but the relief nearly knocked Conor over.

"Fight, Rowan. Fight him."

She focused on Conor as she opened her mouth and started to sing.

30

ROWAN

S he didn't fight with words. Instead, Rowan opened her mouth and sang, and the forest came furiously to life. She felt it stir the moment she'd walked into it half-conscious. The Dark Wood was happy to welcome her. It wanted to help. She felt the symphony of the foliage underneath the snow, its melody brushing her back. Its brambles and vines had snagged her ankles to try to slow her down —to try to help her fight the urge to rush into Valen's waiting arms. It had been trying to warn her, to protect her, but she hadn't been strong enough to resist.

She'd attempted to reach the dagger on her thigh because it hadn't occurred to her that she could sing to the Dark Wood and the Dark Wood would rush to her aid. But the moment Conor had appeared with his words that sliced through Valen's magic, Rowan knew that anything was possible.

She sang as loud as she could manage, and the Dark Wood stirred toward her, ready to assist.

None of them had time to react as branches shot forward from all sides. Valen was so startled that he let go of Rowan. She tumbled forward. Before Conor could catch her, the forest cut him off and formed a ferny pillow to break her fall. Fresh roots and large green leaves wrapped around her like a protective bubble as she continued to sing.

It wasn't like her usual magic. With other plants, her magic was a coaxing call and a tentative response, but calling the Dark Wood felt instinctual, like it knew what she needed before she ever reached out, and it was there waiting.

The whole forest groaned as roots and branches shot from all over, gruesomely impaling Valen. The vampire's eyes went wide in shock as one sharp root penetrated his heart, and he burst into dust.

Rowan let out a startled, horrified breath and stopped singing.

"It's fine. I'm fine," she whispered. The forest seemed to sputter a relieved sigh in response.

Charlie pulled back the leaves around her, staring wide-eyed at Rowan. "What in the name of darkness just happened?"

Conor knelt beside her. She blinked up at him, her eyes narrowed.

"Thank you for waking me up, but I still don't like you," she murmured, her eyelids growing heavy and her head lolling against the leafy pillow.

Conor barked out a laugh. "Honestly, I'm not my biggest fan at the moment either, lass," he whispered.

She shivered, and he removed his cloak, wrapping it around her. He scooped her into his arms.

"Where do you want to go? I'll take you anywhere you like," Conor whispered.

"Take me to the keep," she said.

Charlie sidled up beside them and fell into step. "So when were you planning to tell us that you can weaponize the Dark Wood like that, lass?"

Rowan smiled. "I didn't know that I could."

"I've never seen anything like that," he sighed.

Conor curled her protectively against his body, and she grumbled.

"What's that?" Conor asked.

"I'm still mad at you," she rasped.

"Be as mad as you want, love. As long as you're in my arms when you do it."

He tore through the Dark Wood as quickly as he could, careful not to jostle her too much. She faded in and out of consciousness against his shoulder. It was hard to stay awake for long. She began to worry she'd lost too much blood.

"You're mine, Rowan," Conor whispered as they passed through the keep gates.

"And what if I don't want to be?" she rasped. "What if I want you to be mine instead?"

"Can we not say both are true?" Conor challenged.

"I'm not sure we can," she sighed as they stepped inside the warmth of the foyer. She looked up at him. "I may not have you yet, but I will."

Conor didn't disagree as he climbed the stairs and carried her into her room.

He doted on Rowan as one of his ghostly servants drew her a hot bath. He knelt in front of her, rubbing her small, cold hands between his much larger, warmer ones.

She didn't want to meet his eyes. Whatever he'd said when he thought he would lose her was irrelevant. He told her what he needed to manipulate her at the moment. It didn't mean anything. It was just a strategy. She felt like she had whiplash from being pulled so close, tossed away, then pulled close again. She didn't want to give him anything more of herself. She didn't want to think about the way Sarai's words reverberated through her head when she saw the distraught look on Conor's face.

Love is what holds back the dark.

Was it love for Conor that helped her break through Valen's control? She didn't want it to be true. Love was not something she could afford. So she kept her eyes fixed on where Conor held her hands.

"Rowan, look at me," he pleaded softly. The desperation in his voice was compelling.

She shook her head as he switched to warming her bare feet between his palms.

"Fine," he sighed. "I'll clean you up and put you to bed."

He helped her to her feet and into the washroom. The servant left them alone, and exhaustion pressed down hard on Rowan. She leaned into Conor involuntarily. He gestured for her to lift her arms, and she didn't argue as he slipped off her red silk nightgown. Finally, she met his eyes and he held her gaze, not even daring a glance at her body.

She stepped into the tub and sank into the blissfully hot water. She leaned her head back against the tub and sleep instantly threatened to drag her under.

"Conor, I might—"

"It's all right. I won't let you fall asleep. I have you, Rowan," he whispered as he wrapped an arm around her shoulders.

He used a warm cloth to carefully clean the blood from her neck and chest before washing her hair. It felt divine and strangely intimate to let him bathe her. It was unnatural, and she felt exposed beyond her bare skin.

When he was finished, he helped her out of the tub, now full of water pinked with her blood. Conor patted her hair dry before helping her into a clean nightgown and tucking her into bed.

He lay beside her, his hand resting on her chest, thumb gently stroking her collarbone.

"You have a lot of explaining to do," Rowan sighed. Her eyelids fluttered and her head nodded against the pillow. Fatigue and anger warred in her, and she wasn't sure which would win.

"Rest, Rowan. I'll be here for you to yell at when you wake up," he said, brushing a lock of hair back from her forehead.

"I'm scared," she whispered as her head lolled and her eyes fluttered closed.

"Don't worry, lass. I won't let you sleepwalk again," Conor assured her.

Rowan didn't have the energy to tell him that she wasn't afraid of sleepwalking into the Dark Wood. She was scared of *him*, but for none of the reasons she should have been. Her anger was the only barrier holding back the feelings that would shatter the delicate truce they'd reached. She was scared of what she felt and what it was becoming.

Sarai was wrong. Love wasn't what held back the dark—it was what waited in the shadows to devour her.

Rowan woke disoriented, her head pounding like her brain was trying to escape her skull. Trying unsuccessfully to roll over, she groaned. It took her a moment to realize the reason she couldn't move was that Conor was holding her too tightly against his body.

"Take it easy, lass. We don't know how much blood you lost. Let me get you some water," he said as he reached for a glass on the nightstand. He helped her sit so she could sip the water.

Slowly, her senses returned, and she laughed when she realized how out of place Conor looked in the frilly garden bedroom she'd come to love. His quiet, concerned brooding was in stark contrast to the sheer embroidered floral hangings around the canopy bed and the soft green curtains.

"What's so funny?" he asked.

"Nothing," she said between sips of water.

A smile broke over his face like the sunrise over the sea. Rowan tried to ignore the swell in her chest at the sight of it. He was always handsome, but his smiles were a rare treat, and the warmth that buzzed through her when she earned one sent her reeling every time.

It would be best for her to get back to Ballybrine sooner rather than later. Her gaze shot to the windows. She watched through the spiderwebs of frost on the glass as dawn reluctantly pulled back the heavy curtain of night, revealing a vibrant sunrise. Rowan instinctively slid her hand into Conor's. She was alarmed at how natural it was to want to share every beautiful, wondrous thing with him.

He watched the sunrise with the same intensity she did. How

many sunrises had he seen? Still, he managed to look as full of awe as she felt.

Forgetting herself, forgetting her anger, forgetting reason altogether, she leaned over and pulled him into a gentle kiss.

"The ease with which you separate me from good sense is alarming," Conor sighed against her lips. "I hope that it never fades."

His admission warmed her. It was easy to look at Conor and see a powerful being—the god of death, the Wolf—but he seemed just as in need of gentleness as anyone. Rowan understood. When the world saw fierceness, they assumed that was all that existed.

Guilt crept in, snapping her out of her revelry. She'd walked out of Maiden's Tower in the middle of the night, leaving no note or sign of where she'd gone. When Aeoife woke, she'd be worried sick. Mrs. Teverin and the elders would likely see her footprints and expect the worst.

"I have to get home," she said, standing and nearly falling over from the rush of blood to her head.

"Easy, lass," Conor said, steadying her. He helped her put on a dressing gown before walking her down to the dining room, where breakfast was set on the table.

"We still need to talk," Conor said.

Rowan's eyes narrowed, and all at once, she was happy to reacquaint herself with her anger. She wore it like a cloak to protect her from the chill of heartbreak. Any barrier she could place between herself and Conor was a welcome one.

Even with her lack of experience, she knew what haunted her heart. Love had no instructions, no rules, no reason, but it was the kind of thing that she didn't need external confirmation to know she felt. She didn't need a test or guide to know the potency of her emotions.

She willed the feeling to fade as if desire alone could snuff out the warmth that bloomed in her chest. Despite her best efforts to keep herself barren, desolate, and cold, something wild took root. She had better sense than to let hope in, but the frivolous desire tugged at her.

She busied herself by shoving bacon and toast into her mouth before she could say something stupid.

"Why don't I start?" Conor proposed. "I'm sorry that I made you believe for one second that I am anything other than crazy about you. I panicked. It has been a very long time since I've cared so much for someone. To be honest, I don't know if I ever have. I was careless with you, and you deserve better."

"I do," she said, taking a bite of her toast.

"I got caught up in you," Conor started. "You are terribly easy to get lost in, Rowan. You let me be exactly as I am, and I forgot to keep my guard up. I stole life force from you, and that's why you slept so long. It's why I panicked and sent you away."

Rowan swallowed hard. Everything finally made sense.

"Why didn't you just tell me what you did? We could have figured it out together," she said.

"Because I knew you would say that. I knew you wouldn't leave me if I didn't make you," he said, shaking his head. "You have been taught to put yourself last at every turn, and I won't be another person who asks that of you. I knew that getting closer to you would only mean our mutual destruction." He scrubbed his hand over his face. "Rowan, I don't want to live in a world without you in it. I hate that I took something from you. I hate that I couldn't help myself. I hate that I'm so overwhelmed around you I have no control. My entire existence has been about control, and just a few weeks with you, and I've lost my mind."

"But I'm okay now?" she asked tentatively.

Conor nodded. "I don't quite understand it, but Charlie confirmed that your aura was back to its usual brightness before Valen attacked you. It's as if it never happened."

"So what's the problem, then?"

"How are you not angry that I stole your very life force from you?" Conor asked, his voice taking on a hint of anger. His eyes darkened, the gray and blue swirling like storm clouds. "The problem is that I took it to begin with. That I didn't even notice until Charlie pointed it out. Even if you're better now, I don't understand how that is, and I don't feel confident that it won't happen again. I can't be someone else in this world who is content to take from you."

Rowan chucked a muffin at him. "I'm angry because you didn't trust me to be able to handle a conversation about it. You didn't trust me to be reasonable."

"Would you have left me alone if I'd told you?" Conor asked.

"No, but I still deserved to know the truth. You hurt me on purpose. You knew how vulnerable I was, and you chose to hurt me instead of trusting that I could handle the truth."

Conor looked down at his hands. For the first time, the air around him filled with a discordant melody. *Shame. That's what shame sounds like.*

"I know. I should have. I should have handled this very differently. I could have spared you getting hurt like this again. When I saw him with you, I went a little mad. When I think of Valen's hands on you, I cannot breathe."

Rowan flushed as she remembered the way she'd been compelled by Valen's words. She remembered the way she was desperate for his touch, desperate for more than that. She was so utterly exhausted of people taking power away from her, using her to prop up outdated beliefs and worldviews, using her life force as a power source, making decisions as if they knew better than her. The town of Ballybrine needed her where she was to protect their old traditions. To hold up a world that wouldn't let Sarai love who she loved, even as she prepared to be their next Crone. Rowan was so tired of being a tool in someone else's game.

"You have to stop deciding for me. You have to let me make my own choices, or you are the same as everyone else," she said.

"Rowan, I have centuries of experience, and you won't listen to me. What else am I supposed to do?"

"You're supposed to trust me."

"I do," he insisted.

"Then tell me why you're so afraid."

Conor hesitated for only a moment. "Because I killed Lorna."

Rowan froze. Lorna was the Red Maiden before Evelyn.

"I may not have killed Orla or Evie. But I killed every Maiden before them."

Rowan swallowed hard. The thought had always tugged at the back of her mind, especially after the day Conor brought her down to his temple to see the shrines to each of the Maidens. He'd told her of nothing but his monstrosity. He'd never lied about that. He'd warned her over and over. Beyond that, his insistence on avoiding her, being cold, trying to scare her away...all of it took on a new meaning.

He was a god trying to make things right, and giving her up was his penance.

"How?" The question slipped out of her mouth unbidden.

"I fucked her and drained all of her life force. There was more to it, though," he sighed.

Rowan winced at the loud, keening music that cut through the air.

Conor studied her. "What is it?"

"I can hear you. It's a song that sounds like mourning," she said.

He swallowed. "Lo," he murmured. "That's what I called her. She was not meant for this life," he sighed, a half-laugh tailing the words. "She was much like you in that way. Not exactly a pliant girl. The elders couldn't stand her. You would have been young, so you probably don't remember her well."

"I remember a little, but she wasn't around much," Rowan admitted.

"Yes, she stayed with me most of the time." He paused, looking into the fire. "She was brilliant, kind, and also full of righteous anger. We played chess. We talked about literature. She was honestly one of the first friends I had in centuries, with the exception of Charlie, of course."

He fell silent, and Rowan said nothing. She didn't even move for fear he would stop telling her the story.

"I tried to just take sips of her life force, thinking it wouldn't be so bad. Demon's breath, Rowan, it was like a drug. I could not get enough of her."

Rowan still said nothing. The words were both devastating and not entirely surprising. He'd never lied about it. He told her that he was a monster from the beginning. Still, his grief formed a somber song that broke through the air around them.

"She was in love with me, and I took advantage of that love."

"You didn't care for her?" Rowan asked. "The song around you says otherwise."

"Of course I cared. But I cared for a fix of her more than *her*. I lost control, and I killed her. I've gone over and over that day hundreds of times. I relive it daily. I think of what I could have and should have done differently. And that is why I scared you away. That is why I chased you from me."

"Because you feel the same way about me?" Rowan asked.

"No, because I feel more. I—"

Rowan held her breath.

Conor cleared his throat and met her eyes. "I cannot do that again. I cannot look into the lifeless eyes of someone I care about and know that I am responsible for taking someone beautiful and kind from this world. I will not, Rowan. I am begging you not to let me. I am begging you to stay away. I'd rather live in a world and know you're in it safe and far from me than live with the grief of truly losing you. Forever is a long time to mourn. It is a long time to carry the weight of your wrongs."

"You can't die?" Rowan asked, playing ignorant.

"I can, but I am very hard to kill."

Rowan frowned, the truth finally dawning on her. "You can lose your power. You *are* losing your power."

"I am. The blight grew from here and spread because I cannot hold back the souls who have crossed *and* keep the forest alive. Beasts fill these woods because I can no longer keep every tortured soul and demon in the Underlands. Losing my power only makes it harder to resist you because if I drained you dry, I could regain control. It is yet another reason why you need to stay away from me, Rowan. Please. I'll throw myself at your mercy and beg you to leave me because I cannot do that again."

Rowan shook her head. "It can't ever be about what *I* want, can it?"

"Rowan, you know well the cost of that. I already stole from you once, and we got away with it. I don't know what would happen again. Are you willing to risk that this could all fall to Aeoife?"

Aeoife was the one pure thing in Rowan's whole world. She didn't want to admit that she and Conor had come to the end of the line. She'd have to act much sooner than she wanted to, and Conor did her the favor of reminding her exactly what she had to lose.

"You need to understand," Conor started. "Before Lorna, I was different. Truly monstrous. I did not care for any of them. I held out as long as I could, but I killed them all. I used them all, and I didn't feel bad about it. I wish I could say differently, but it's the truth, Rowan. I was angry about the deal I made, and I took that anger out on the Maidens. It was cruel and horrible of me, but you ought to know who I am."

"What changed?"

Conor shrugged. "I think I got old. I got tired. The monotony of it all—the endless cycle of it—got to me. When Lorna arrived, she was the first person to ever truly try to fight back. Other Maidens had run, but she fought back enough to startle me. She stabbed me the first night with a broken cider glass. She wanted to live enough that I started talking to her."

"Am I just a replacement for her?" Rowan hated the jealousy in her voice.

Conor shook his head. "No, Rowan. You're not. You have things in common with her, but you're so much softer. So very different, and I never felt with her what I do with you. I swear."

Rowan worried her lower lip between her teeth as he continued.

"At first, I was just fascinated, and I wanted to see what she would do, but over time it grew into more. It was the first time I realized I was capable of more than just taking, but the end result was the same as the rest. Still, I know that no matter how much I don't want to be, I'm doomed to repeat the pattern."

Rowan sighed. He'd clearly strengthened his restraint since he hadn't killed Evelyn or Orla, and they'd been around him for nearly five years each. Still, Conor was telling the truth, and if he didn't have the confidence in himself, there was no way for her to summon it for him. The only way forward—the only way to guarantee her and Aeoife's safety—was to kill him. The only way forward was for the Mother to make a better deal with a new god of death.

They stood in silence—the longing in both of them reaching out toward the other across what felt like a cavern of space.

Rowan sighed, all the air rushing out of her as she made the decision. It felt like the walls of her heart were caving in on themselves.

She would do what she had to. She always knew she would need to, and she couldn't pretend anymore that there was another option. The Mother told her. The Wolf told her. She needed to stop pretending there was another choice because the longer she did, the more likely it was that she'd be the one to die. She'd nearly died last night.

Beyond that, she'd promised Sarai that she'd find a way to break their world to make it more equitable for all of them and this might be the only way she could do that.

Rowan wasn't sure if she could live with herself if she killed Conor. For her whole life, everything had been controlled, and for the first time, she wished she could opt out of making a decision and surrender her agency to someone else. She couldn't help but wonder if it was easier to live with herself when she thought she had no choice.

Because the choice she knew she had to make at that moment was the one that would shatter her heart.

She'd tried to find a way for both of them to survive, but the fact remained—they were mutually destructive. There was no avoiding it. No postponing it. They'd passed the point of no return, and no matter what she felt for him, she owed it to herself to want more for her life than anyone else would.

It wasn't that she didn't trust Conor. She knew he didn't want to hurt her. Felt it in her bones, in her heart, in the pulse that passed between them when they stood so close. She just knew that they were all bound by the magic that ruled their world, and as much as he wanted to fight it when the time came, he'd be powerless against it, even if it broke his heart.

So she made the choice to protect herself; to protect Aeoife. It wasn't fair that no one else would do it, but she was used to life's inequity. It was a brutal sacrifice, but she'd make it for Aeoife. She'd make it for herself, even if doing so broke her heart.

"Fine," Rowan sighed. "But I want something first."

Conor nodded. "Anything."

The words almost froze in her mouth before she could get them out. Her heart ached miserably in her chest, so full of unspent love and dread she thought she might collapse.

She met Conor's eyes and forced herself to speak. "Take me to bed one more time."

31

ROWAN

Rowan expected more resistance to her request, but the moment she asked Conor to take her to bed, he seemed desperate to do just that.

He lifted her into his arms immediately and kissed her. She wrapped her legs around his waist and threaded her fingers through his hair, trying to ground herself with his touch.

"Take me to my bed," she whispered, her lips grazing his ear.

He fumbled his way out of the dining room without putting her down. He was so frantic that he paused to kiss her up against the wall several times in the hall before they reached her room, where he tossed her onto the bed. He stripped her out of her nightgown with not a word spoken.

His hands and lips on her skin drove her wild as he nipped and kissed up her inner thighs. Every kiss was a prayer, his mouth filled with worship.

"I'm sorry," he whispered as he descended on her in a frenzy.

Her back arched instantly, and she squirmed under the intensity of his attention. Conor pinned her hips to the bed with his hands as he worked her relentlessly. There was nothing but his touch, the wet slide of his tongue, and his sweet, affectionate whispers against her skin.

"I don't think I've ever enjoyed this as much as I do with you," he breathed before continuing his ministrations.

Her fingers threaded through his hair idly as he licked and kissed her. She climbed higher and higher, afraid she'd break apart if he held her on the edge any longer. Finally, a light hum from his lips sent her screaming over the brink.

Still, Conor stayed put, as if trying to display his contrition exclusively through pleasuring her. She was surprised when the tension started to climb again. She mumbled a curse, panted and writhed, her nails digging into his forearms. Nothing had ever felt so good. He slid a finger inside of her, and every muscle clenched around it, her body desperate for more of him.

"Mother slay me, Rowan. You're so good," he whispered, his breath tickling her skin. He slid a second finger inside of her, and she whimpered.

More—she needed more. She needed him as close as possible.

Every muscle below her waist clenched. Her pleasure climbed and climbed as he worked her with his fingers and mouth. All at once, the tension snapped, and she screamed as she came undone again. Wave after wave of pleasure whipped through her.

She relaxed back down to the bed, and Conor kissed his way up her body torturously slowly. She tried to focus her mind, but it was still buzzing from pleasure, and her thoughts floated away like wild butterflies. She tried to ignore the growing swell of emotion in her chest.

You need to kill him, Rowan. Get the dagger.

Rowan reached blindly, stretching her hand beneath the pillow where she'd stashed it. Her fingertips grazed the cool metal. She gripped the dagger in her sweaty palm as Conor continued kissing up her chest.

Finally, Conor met her lips, drawing her into a scorching kiss. She squeezed the hilt of the dagger in her palm, trying to use it to ground her from the spinning, fluttering sensation in her chest. She reached for him, stroking his length. He groaned, his hips chasing her hand as he thrust forward.

"I should do that for you," she whispered against his lips.

"No, love. As much as I know that I would thoroughly enjoy that, if I don't get inside you now, I'll go mad," Conor murmured. His voice was rough, and it sent warmth pooling low in her belly.

He shifted and she wrapped her legs around his waist as he sank into her. They both groaned.

"There is nothing like the look on your face and the way you moan when I first push inside you, Rowan. Nothing has ever felt so good," Conor rasped.

A strangely prideful satisfaction bolstered her. She had to agree.

It was the dirtiest compliment she'd ever received, and she should have been appalled, but some dark part of her liked it immensely. Her grip on the dagger loosened.

The first time, she had been nervous, shy, and tentative, but now she felt like she'd finally found the place where she could be wild without judgment. She lifted her hips, urging him to move, and he chuckled.

"Slow down," Conor chided. "I'm trying to give you a chance to adjust."

"I'm fine—now move," she said, digging her heels into his rear to urge him on.

He laughed. "I swear, lass, you are out of your mind."

He started to move, and it felt even better than the first time. She'd never felt more comfortable with anyone, even considering the vulnerability of their circumstances.

"Perfect—you are so fucking perfect for me, Rowan," he whispered as he kissed her neck.

Conor moved with her, his eyes locked on hers, oblivious to her plan. She kept her focus on the sensation in her body as he moved so he wouldn't feel her intent. His eyes burned into hers with an intensity that made her squirm. There was no denying it, no mistaking the truth of what she felt. She couldn't escape it any longer.

Rowan was in love with Conor.

The Mother's words were fresh in her mind. "*The moment that he's taking from you, he's vulnerable.*"

Conor was taking her heart, and it might be her last good opportunity to end him before he could end her. She was only pretending she had a choice. He might not want to hurt her, but he would need to. Even if he didn't want to be monstrous, he'd warned her over and over to never forget that he was a monster. His grip on his world was slipping, and eventually, he'd need what only she could give him. She knew that surviving would be messy. She just hadn't counted on this level of devastation.

There was no other way. They were mutually destructive to each other.

Tears blinded Rowan. She'd thought the cruelest part of her life was over, but there always seemed to be one more cruelty for her to suffer. She'd never dared to love like that. Never imagined that it could exist in the life she'd been born into.

She blinked away tears as she met his eyes.

Conor froze. He looked stricken. "What is it, Rowan? Did I hurt you?" he asked. The tenderness in his voice, in his eyes, was not what she deserved.

She shook her head. The dagger slipped in her sweaty palm. She needed to strike now. There was no doubt in her mind what, exactly, he was taking from her. He'd stolen her heart without her permission, despite her best efforts to resist. Why shouldn't he have? He had centuries of experience in stealing hearts, in making women fall in love with him. Why should she be any different?

"Please don't stop," she begged.

Conor hesitated before starting to move again.

She shook as she tightened her grip on the dagger. *You can do this, Rowan. You have to do this. It's you or him. You don't have a choice. It's him or Aeoife. If you can't do it for you, do it for her.*

She moved her hand quickly, pausing with the point of the dagger nearly pressed to the skin of his ribs.

Conor froze above her. His eyes darted to the dagger. She knew she needed to move, but they both held still as statues.

He finally moved, and she flinched, but he stroked her cheek so tenderly.

"And what am I taking from you now, love?" Conor rasped.

She stared up at him, tears streaming down her cheeks. "You know," she mumbled.

"Well, if you're going to kill me, I think I at least deserve to hear it once, Rowan," he said.

She bit her trembling lip. The dagger shook in her hand.

"My heart."

It was barely audible, but Conor looked as if she'd punched him in the gut.

"I hate that you made me love you," she sobbed, "but I hate it more that it means I can kill you."

Conor swallowed hard, holding perfectly still as the point of the dagger pressed into his chest.

She hesitated. Her eyes darted around wildly as she tried to summon.

"Before you strike, Rowan, you should know that I have been in love with you for quite some time now. Your love is a beautiful weapon that I feel unworthy of. I can think of no better way to go."

The words devastated her. Her whole world narrowed to the sincerity of his voice and the look on his face.

"Go on, love. Better me than you," Conor whispered.

She still couldn't make herself move.

Conor brushed her hair back from her face tenderly, as if she'd offered him her heart instead of a blade to his chest. "Death is easy. Living is hard. You've already made the hardest choice, my fierce little Red."

They both held completely still, poised on the edge of the abyss. There was no turning back. She couldn't stop loving him, couldn't escape the fact that she owed it to herself, at the very least, to put her needs first. So many people had let her down, and she'd long since learned that she was the only person she could truly count on. Still, at that moment, she was also confronted with the fact that she very much did not want to kill the first man she ever loved.

Rowan didn't want to stop seeing the hungry way Conor looked at her. Didn't want to stop feeling surprised when she woke up in his arms. Didn't want to confront the fact that no one had ever made her feel so simultaneously safe and out of control.

"Rowan," he whispered. "It's okay."

She shook her head. She knew the moment he looked at her that way, she wouldn't be able to do it.

"I can't," she sobbed. The dagger fell from her hand, landing with a soft thud in the linens. Conor batted it away, and it landed on the floor with a loud clang.

"I hate you," she whispered.

He chuckled as he kissed away her tears. "Oh, love, I think we both know that's not true at all."

"It's not," she gasped.

Conor pulled her into a slow kiss.

"I need you," she whispered.

He understood what was said and what wasn't. He understood what she needed to feel instinctively.

"You are beautiful and kind. All will be well. Now, I've never had a way with words, so let me show you how I feel."

He moved with a new urgency, covering every inch of skin he could reach with kisses until Rowan couldn't stop moaning; until her heart thundered in her chest; until everything frozen in her thawed and heated.

Tension wound in her body like a coiled snake. It wasn't enough. She wanted more. More of Conor, more feeling. She wanted to consume him the way he had her. She wanted to have some sort of ownership over him. She wanted proof of what existed between them —as if love was a thing she could hold in her hands.

She rolled so suddenly that she caught Conor off guard as she positioned herself on top of him and sank down. She threw her head back and groaned as Conor bit out a curse. She paused, meeting his eyes.

"Go on, then, lass, take what you want," he said with a smirk. His hands gripped her hips like she was the only thing anchoring him to the world.

It took her a moment to get her bearings, but the friction and control felt amazing once she did. She rolled her hips, building a rhythm that stoked the kindling fire within her to an inferno.

Conor met her movements with a gentle thrust of his hips. The tension in her was so close to breaking. She raked her fingernails down Conor's chest, and he groaned in satisfaction. She'd never felt so sexy and free as she did with his heated gaze locked on her.

"Please," she whimpered, more to herself than to Conor.

Still, he picked up the pace of his movement, his hand dropping between their bodies to rub against her. She looked into his eyes—eyes that reflected the love she felt so acutely—as she let go. Her climax crashed over her in waves, and she rode it out breathlessly.

She smiled at Conor as the feeling faded, slumping forward.

"Tired yourself out, lass?" he taunted.

Rowan frowned. "Absolutely not."

"Good, because I am not nearly done with you." Conor grinned. He rolled her onto her hands and knees before taking her hips in his hands and sliding back inside of her.

She cursed as she dropped her head to the bed, panting. Conor bent over her so that his chest was flush to her back. He wrapped an arm around her waist and thrust into her.

"Do you like that, Rowan?" he asked.

She couldn't even speak around the sensation. She could only nod. She blocked out everything else but the feeling of him. His whole body shook as she moved to meet him.

"Stop holding back," she grunted.

"Is that what you want, lass? You like when I take control? You like that I want you so much I'm shaking?"

"I like when you don't hold back," she rasped.

The words broke his restraint. He shoved her onto her stomach, and the new angle stopped all rational thought in her head. One of his hands held her hips in place while the other wrapped around her hair and tugged her head back so he could kiss her neck. She reached behind her, gripping his neck. She threaded her fingers through his hair, tugging him toward her. His hips moved harder, more frantic. Their movements took on a rougher, more desperate edge.

"Are you happy now, little Red? You're so tight and slick. I could fuck you like this all night," Conor grunted, nipping at her earlobe.

She whimpered his name. He slid his hand between her legs so he could rub her along with each thrust. Her hand slapped down to the bed, tangling in the sheets as her legs trembled.

Everything spun out of control, the two of them driven to a fever pitch. He kissed over the mark Valen had left on her neck, and then she felt the sharp glide of his teeth over the same spot. It was primal and possessive, like he was trying to wipe out the memory of what had happened—like he wanted to leave his own mark on her.

"Yes," she murmured.

He bit down, not enough to break her skin but enough to send a spike of startling pain through her that drove her into such an intense climax that her toes cramped and her whole body trembled violently. Conor kissed away the pain from the spot as he continued to move.

Perhaps it was just the magic, but Rowan wanted to be consumed. She wanted him to touch and own every part of her, and she wanted that same ownership over him.

"Rowan," he croaked. His voice had a panicked edge, and she knew he was fighting devouring her.

"Don't fight," she said. "Take what you need."

He cupped her face, pulling her into a kiss as he moved.

"I can't," he sighed, tucking his face into her neck.

"I want you to. I'm giving it willingly," she said.

In her heart, she meant it. She trusted that he wouldn't take too much, but beyond that, she wanted to prove to Conor and to the world that he could change. She didn't want the world to define them —Conor a villain and she a martyr. She wanted both of them to live and fight another day.

She wanted to live to see Sarai happy with her love in a world that could not hurt them. Rowan wanted to help her friend break their fractured world completely and rebuild it better. They couldn't do any of those things if another god of death came to power. If Conor couldn't contain whatever sinister force was rising, the world wouldn't be a place worth saving anyway.

Magic pulsed around them, but instead of his usual silence, a strange, mournful melody buzzed around him. She felt a sharp tug on her own magic, the same magic that pulsed through her when she sang. Her impulse was to cling to it, to fight, but she forced herself to let go and give it willingly, and the melody shifted as it ran through both of them. It flowed between them like a song she'd always known, familiar and lovely. Instead of feeling drained, she felt soothed, energized, and powerfully connected.

Conor's movement became jerky, and he groaned her name as he pulsed inside her. He quickly rolled off of her and turned her over so he could kiss her.

"Are you well?" His face was pinched with concern.

She laughed at how serious he looked. "I'm fine. Honestly, I feel pretty amazing." She stretched and felt pleasant, shaky fatigue in her muscles, but her body buzzed with a strange, ecstatic energy.

"You don't feel tired?" He looked her over as though trying to see through her.

"No more than I should be, considering," she teased.

He kissed her, weaving his hands through her hair. "You are something else. I swear you have no sense of self-preservation," he said, shaking his head between kisses. "Are you sure that you're okay?"

She smiled. "I think you know I am very okay."

"How can that be?" he marveled. He drew back, staring at her as if he was trying to see some definitive sign that she was really okay.

"Conor, I'm fine. I swear. I'm just a little hungry."

Conor sprang out of bed and threw on his pants, kissing her again before he disappeared into the hallway. He came back a few moments later and tossed her his robe. "Put this on. I want Charlie to look at you. He'll be able to see if your aura is faded."

Rowan nodded as she pulled on the robe.

Charlie appeared at the door a moment later with a tray of food in his hands and a sly grin on his face. "Oh, hello there, lass. Happy to see you're in one piece. I wasn't so sure with all the screaming," he teased.

Rowan covered her face with her hands, feeling the heat of her cheeks.

"Well?" Conor asked impatiently.

Charlie studied her carefully. "Are you sure you took something?"

Conor nodded. "Positive."

"Well, she looks fine," Charlie confirmed. "She's just as bright as always."

Rowan smiled at him as she swiped a biscuit from the tray. "Goddess above, I'm starving!" she said as she sank into the chair by the fire.

She hadn't realized until she saw the food just how hungry she was, but she found herself hoping that Charlie would bring another tray because she was ready to eat all that he'd brought for the two of them.

When she looked up, both Charlie and Conor were staring at her as she shoveled food into her mouth. "What?"

"You're just a bit of a puzzle, love," Conor stated. "We don't understand how I could have taken something from you, and yet you're fine already. You should be exhausted. Last time you slept for a day."

"What was different this time?" Charlie asked.

Rowan flushed with heat, unable to meet his eyes. She went back over everything in her head. The position was different, as was the intensity between them.

"I told her I loved her," Conor said quietly.

Charlie didn't seem the slightest bit surprised. "And here I thought that was something only I would ever know," he laughed. "I'm impressed. He's stubborn as a mule, and yet you've moved that icy old heart. And did you say it back, Rowan?"

"Yes, after I told him I hated him," she said, cramming another biscuit into her mouth.

"Of course. Perfectly understandable," Charlie teased. "Perhaps it's that. You've never been in love with one of the Maidens before."

Rowan studied Conor carefully. Something flickered in his eyes that formed a ball of jealousy in her stomach.

"Is that true?" she challenged.

Conor frowned. "Yes."

Rowan narrowed her eyes. She had no right to be jealous. There were many Maidens before her, and Conor had lived for centuries. Of course he had a past. She didn't like the inequity that it created between them—that he was her only love and she wasn't his.

"Are you jealous, little Red?" Conor asked.

"No, why would I be jealous?" she asked, feigning indifference.

He licked his lips, and she knew he was tasting her lie. "I'd be happy to clear things up for you or allow you to work through that jealousy," he said with a feral smile.

"I think it's quite clear. That won't be necessary," Rowan countered. She hated that he could taste her lies, but she felt the same proprietary claim to him that he did to her.

"Your jealousy is delicious," he sighed.

"All right, all right, you two look like you're about two minutes from pouncing on each other again. Focus, please. Now, was anything else different?" Charlie asked.

"She gave me permission to take it," Conor said.

Rowan sat up straighter. "That's right. I gave consent."

Charlie considered. "That's something that never occurred to the elders or us. Perhaps that's the key to this. She's a magical being. If she willingly offers her power to you instead of you just taking it, maybe it creates a different balance. Perhaps that's why she's eating like a wild beast now. Instead of being drained, she's simply able to rebuild with nourishment."

Rowan and Conor stared at each other. Could it be so simple?

"Only one way to find out. You'll have to try it again. Con, if this works, it changes everything." The reaper looked at the god of death and smiled. "You could get control of the Dark Wood again and stop losing power to the Mother."

32

ROWAN

Rowan hesitated on the dock leading up to the Crone's cottage. Faith was new to her, and she struggled to figure out who she could trust with what information. Although she and Conor had tested their theory and proved it held true, she wanted validation and wisdom from the Crone.

The sun was high in the sky, casting blinding light on the lake's surface and warming the cold winter air.

"Are you going to come in or just lurk on the dock like a lost soul?" the Crone asked, cracking the cottage door open.

Rowan smiled at her. "I was hoping you could help me figure out a little mystery."

"Come in," she said, propping the door open with her hip.

Rowan brushed by her into the small cottage. Sarai looked up from her basket of supplies and smiled weakly.

"How's Raya?" Rowan asked.

"She's all right. I'm just getting some things to tend to her lashes," Sarai said.

"How's your research?" Rowan asked.

Sarai's eyes darted to the Crone. "It's been informative."

Rowan was afraid to hope. It was likely safer to be away from

Conor, but it also felt impossible. He'd admitted to being a monster, and she had no idea how to rectify the god she saw now with the careless, icy monster he'd been for centuries. She was unsure if she could forgive him for killing all those Maidens and was afraid what it said about her if she could accept that side of him.

Rowan hugged Sarai. She wanted to say so much but couldn't in front of the Crone.

"I think I have figured out something vital," Rowan whispered. She pulled back from her friend and turned to look at the Crone. "I think I've found a way to keep myself from being devoured and keep the world in balance."

The Crone looked wary but unsurprised. "Leave us, Sarai. You must tend to Raya."

"I should be here to help—" Sarai started.

The Crone held up a hand, and both Sarai and Rowan knew from years of experience there was no use arguing. Sarai left in a huff, and Rowan stood awkwardly in the center of the cottage, waiting for the Crone to speak.

Instead, the maddening woman simply gestured to the empty chair and went to make tea. Rowan wrung her hands in her lap as the Crone portioned out the tea and then set a teacup in front of her.

While Rowan loved tea, she was chronically impatient, taking a sip that burned her tongue so badly she hardly tasted the follow-up sip. That was who she was at heart—a girl who couldn't stop touching something too hot, no matter how it burned.

She squeezed her eyes shut and tried not to think about Conor every time she felt overwhelmed and unmoored. She loved him, and he loved her, but it wasn't the way she expected it to be. When people spoke about love, they made it sound simple. Now that she felt it, it was tangled with the reality of who he was and that, at any moment, the delicate trust between them could easily be broken, and it would cost more than just her heart.

"You've gone and fallen for the Wolf." There was no accusation in the Crone's tone. She was simply stating a fact.

"I'm not certain it's so simple as that," Rowan argued.

"Isn't it? You have the desperate look in your eyes that all the women in the village do when they come to me to help them with some ill-fated love affair," the Crone said with a soft smile that didn't reach her eyes.

Rowan sighed. "Regardless, that's not why I'm here."

"Did you know his blight is still spreading into Ashand Orchards?"

Rowan shook her head. "That doesn't make sense. The Dark Wood is completely healed. Why would he spread it more?"

"Because you've shifted things in favor of the Wolf. It seems it's your destiny to do so."

"That's not true! He—" Rowan stopped herself. The Crone had perked up with interest and she didn't want to share any of Conor's weaknesses.

"Look how you protect him now," the Crone sighed. "There will come a time when you have to choose, Rowan. I thought that you, of all people, would be the first to be wary of the whims of the god of death."

Rowan bit her tongue to keep from snapping. Talking to the Crone was a bit like playing chess with Conor. She needed to think about each move before she made it so that she didn't tip her hand.

She took a long sip of her tea. "How do the gods never die?"

The Crone thought for a moment. "I suppose at some point they were just like us. The oldest of the records we have from the first Crone indicates that the Wolf was once mortal. Belief is what gave him and the Mother power. When you can offer something that people need when they need it, their belief in you is what gives you power."

That lined up with the story Conor had told Rowan.

"So, in theory, they could die?" Rowan pressed.

The Crone frowned. "I suppose. But they've lived quite a long time. I don't imagine that would be a wise plan, girl. The Wolf is known for his viciousness."

Rowan frowned at the Crone. She couldn't tell if she was playing dumb or if she truly didn't know that the Mother had asked Rowan to kill the Wolf. It was possible that she thought Rowan had come up with the idea herself, but the Crone had always been an intermediary between worlds. It was hard to believe that the Mother would keep her in the dark.

Rowan wanted confirmation because a new idea was forming in her mind. What Orla had overheard from the elders was correct. If Conor had once been mortal, then the Mother must have been as well. If belief gave them power, then lack of belief stripped them of it. What Rowan needed to know was how the power was transferred to a new god and what the Mother intended to do now.

"I didn't say I was trying to kill him," Rowan huffed. "I doubt keeping myself as ignorant as the rest of the world has would be wise either."

The Crone pursed her lips and gave a slight nod. It was the most encouragement she'd offer. "Many years ago, there was a prophecy that has since fallen by the wayside. I often wondered how that happened. How could something so important fall out of our contemporary scripture?" She sipped her tea and then continued, "It seemed too convenient that the one who wrote it—my grandmother —died so soon after. The same day she wrote that prophecy, in fact. The elder whom she shared it with also passed very soon after. Typically new writings are given much time and attention. The elders ask the Mother for her inspiration to interpret and spread it. They spend months with the text. But with all of the original participants conveniently dead, the scripture was buried among a stack of newer ones."

Rowan took another long sip of her tea and fiddled with her cup and saucer.

"I discovered the writing years later and couldn't believe it had been missed, but at that time, I was new, and the elders did not yet respect me as they should have. I was forced to study it myself. To try to discern its meaning on my own," the Crone said.

"What's the prophecy?" Rowan asked.

"The prophecy said that someday a great wave would rise in the north, and the balance between worlds would shift. When that happened, a new power would emerge to help reestablish the power between the Mother and the Wolf."

Rowan shrugged. "That doesn't sound so bad. It sounds like a contingency for the new religion."

She brought a hand to her brow. For some reason, the tea seemed to be making her much too hot. The Crone's winter herbs were often warming, but Rowan suddenly felt like she was boiling.

"It doesn't, does it?" The Crone sighed. "I think that you are that power."

Rowan's eyes went wide. She went over her last few conversations with the Crone. She remembered how suspiciously the woman regarded her at her first ceremony and what she'd said to Rowan months before about not knowing what she was. She remembered the books of prophecies scattered on the table the last time she'd visited the cottage.

The room went fuzzy, and Rowan squinted, trying to focus. "Me?" she mumbled. "But I'm just a Red Maiden, a spirit singer." The words sounded slow and strange in her ears.

"The prophecy says the change-maker would be '*the one who gives up her name.*' It's only a matter of time before you give your heart to the Wolf in a more permanent way—before he figures out what you can be to him. I cannot let that happen. The problem, as I see it, is that your love for the Wolf seems to shift the balance toward death, and that's not something I can abide. As the arbiter of this bargain, I must intervene. There are older gods—more vicious than these—who would bring this world to its knees. If the Wolf lets them out, it will be our undoing."

"He won't." Rowan's voice sounded strangely hoarse. Her heart beat an uneven, fluttering pattern in her chest. She tried to take a breath and sputtered into the pungent tea. She knew that scent.

"Mother's Mercy," Rowan mumbled. It was a wild herb that, when taken in small doses, helped with sleep. It was used for those with insomnia or patients who needed wounds mended. But in a large dose, it would put her to sleep permanently. No pain—just death.

The betrayal cut her deep. Sarai had left her alone. After Cade,

Rowan wasn't sure she could survive another betrayal, even if the herb didn't kill her.

"How could you?" she slurred.

The Crone's eyes glazed over. "I didn't want to, girl. All you had to do was your job, but he's drawn you in, and I cannot risk our world if he grows more powerful. My only job is to hold the bargain. If you make him too strong, death will wipe out all life." She shook her head. "I'm so sorry. I had to make an impossible choice between you and our entire village and I could not see another way forward with how dire things are."

She brought her hand to Rowan's cheek, but Rowan swatted it away lazily. Her limbs were already getting heavy. She dragged herself from the chair, knocking over the teacup with a clatter.

"Don't struggle. It will make it worse," the Crone shouted after her, but Rowan tore down the dock with leaden legs and ran to the edge of the Dark Wood.

"Help," she rasped. "Help me, *please*." The words were a weak singsong verse.

She fell to her knees, and the cold ground bit through her dress.

Rowan opened her mouth and sang. The Dark Wood rustled and groaned as she fell forward to her hands. She didn't know why she was still singing. It was simply an instinct.

The rustling of the wood grew louder. She looked up and found a strange-looking plant—red and leafy—next to a Mother's Mercy vine.

The vine stretched toward her, and she cowered as it wrapped around her wrist. There was a sharp pain as it sliced into her skin, but it passed quickly, and Rowan was distracted by the leafy red plant that bloomed, pushing toward her hand.

"I don't understand," Rowan mumbled.

The plant grew taller until it was level with her mouth. The Dark Wood wanted her to eat it. She didn't recognize the plant, but she was already dying. She didn't see what harm it could do.

She pulled off several leaves clumsily. Her coordination was terrible, but she managed to shove them in her mouth and chew. She fell to the ground and rolled onto her back, looking up at the blue sky as she swallowed the red herb.

Rowan's heartbeat was sluggish. Her mind wandered to Conor. She wished he was with her. They'd finally come to a tentative understanding, and now something else was going to take her from this world. Rowan wished he'd find her, kiss her, take care of her. She wasn't sure she truly knew who he was, but she wished for the time to figure it out.

The Mother's Mercy vine itched at her wrist, but she didn't have the energy to scratch it. She blinked up at the sky as blackness funneled her vision down to pinpricks, and she faded into sleep.

33

CONOR

Conor tore through the woods. He sensed Rowan's panic as sharply as her grief and fear. He just needed to get to her, but she was so far from the keep.

The forest parted for him, but he was moving so quickly that branches and thorns snagged at his skin and clothing as he sprinted through. Finally, he came to the end of the Dark Wood and found Rowan in a heap at the very edge of the magical forest.

"Rowan!"

He slid to his knees beside her and almost collapsed from relief when he realized she was breathing. He searched her for wounds but found none. He could find no cause for her sleep.

His eyes passed over the purple stain on her lips. He leaned forward and sniffed it.

Mother's Mercy vine. She must have mistaken it for another plant. He listened to her heartbeat. It was slow but steady.

Then he saw the red plant on the ground beside her—Vibrant Vine, a magical herb specific to the Dark Wood that spiked bursts of energy in the body. When he and Charlie went on patrols, they often chewed it to stay awake.

Why would she have taken two herbs with such opposing effects?

He reached for her hand, and only then did he notice the Mother's Mercy vine wrapped around her wrist. It looked strangely wilted, and the sharp scent of it mixed with the sweet smell of Rowan's blood.

The scene was baffling. The Dark Wood had always reacted to the Maidens, but with Rowan, it felt almost sentient. Perhaps it was simply because he had such strong feelings for her, and the magic was a reflection of his own.

He looked over the scene again. It seemed as if the magic of the Dark Wood had somehow tried to help her.

He looked up at the forest. "Can I move her?"

In response, the Mother's Mercy vine unlatched from her wrist and drew away. Conor scooped Rowan up into his arms. He turned and found the Crone standing just outside her cottage door, watching them. This was her doing.

"I'll be back for you," he said quietly.

Her face betrayed nothing but grim acceptance. She nodded just as a girl who looked about Rowan's age burst out of the Borderwood.

The girl was startled at the sight of the Wolf holding Rowan before her eyes narrowed suspiciously on the Crone.

"You're Conor," she said, her gaze returning to Rowan. "I'm Sarai. Take me with you. I can help."

He recognized the name. She was Rowan's friend, the Crone's daughter.

She turned her accusatory gaze on the Crone. "What did you give her, Mother?" Her tone was clipped, and even without knowing her, Conor read the fury in her eyes.

"Mother's Mercy," the Crone called.

Sarai nodded as she stepped closer to him and brushed Rowan's hair back from her face. "I'm sorry, Rowan. I should have known she was up to something when she sent me away." She felt Rowan's pulse. "I'll be right back."

She scurried into the Crone's cottage before reappearing a few moments later with a bag. "Let's go," she said, a determined set to her shoulders.

"I know you are the Crone's protégé, but you might still struggle in the Dark Wood. Even those with magic struggle to make it to the keep," Conor said.

"Then help me get through because I'm not leaving her right now."

Conor nodded. He liked Rowan's friend already.

SARAI WORKED QUICKLY when they returned to Wolf's Keep, grinding herbs into a tea that Conor helped her feed a barely conscious Rowan. Now, she sat on the edge of the bed, keeping a nervous vigil by checking Rowan's heart rate every few minutes.

"It's still strong," Conor said. "I can hear it all the time. You don't have to keep checking. I will know if she needs us."

Sarai sighed. "I hate waiting. I feel helpless."

"I know," Conor said.

She chewed her fingernails, caught herself, and busied her hands by picking at a thread on her sleeve. "I'm sorry. I should have realized there was a reason my mother was sending me away. I should have paid closer attention. I just never thought she would try to hurt Rowan," she said.

"You can't blame yourself. She's all right now," Conor said.

"I suppose you're also not blaming yourself?"

He sighed. "Fair enough."

Sarai came to sit next to him by the fire. "You're not what I expected."

"And what did you expect?" Conor asked.

She shrugged. "She made you sound more commanding, but right now, you mostly seem terrified."

"Yes, well, it seems that Rowan has softened some of my edges."

"As you've sharpened some of hers," Sarai said.

Conor liked the idea of that—an exchange of sorts. He knew it was true for him. Rowan had softened him immeasurably, but had he really sharpened her, or had he simply allowed her to see herself as she truly was deep down? It was possible Sarai was giving him too much credit.

Rowan groaned, her eyes fluttering. Conor was instantly up and at her side.

"Conor," Rowan said with a smile. "Am I dead?"

He stroked her cheek. "No, love, you saved yourself once again."

Sarai huffed out a breath. "Speak for yourself! You mostly saved yourself, Row. Conor and I helped."

Rowan laughed weakly before her eyes narrowed on Sarai. "Did you know?"

Conor had been wondering the same thing in the back of his mind, but seeing Sarai's growing panic as they waited, he felt only true fear for Rowan's life, not guilt. Centuries of experience taught him the difference.

Sarai's eyes filled with tears. "Row, of course not. I would never do that to you. Not when you found a way to save Raya and help me hide her. You're my dearest friend."

Rowan nodded. Her movements were slow and pained and her skin was alarmingly pale.

"It doesn't make sense the way the magic of the Dark Wood seems sentient and connected to her," Sarai said, meeting Conor's eye. "It stands to reason that if her voice beckons to dead things or acts as a reminder of life, that she could bring back plant life or lure spirits across the forest, but why would the Dark Wood work for her?"

Rowan struggled to push herself up to sitting. "I whispered my name to the Dark Wood. It knows me. I feel this sort of understanding of it."

"When?" Sarai asked.

Rowan laughed and shook her head. "Names have power. Of all the things for my mother to be right about."

"Rowan, you're not making any sense." Conor brought a hand to her forehead, checking for a fever.

"When I was five, I whispered my name to the Dark Wood, and it whispered it back. It was permission of sorts. I didn't realize it at the time. I'd accepted my fate. The same way I've willingly given my power to you," Rowan said.

Conor stared at her. *Consent.* She'd given the Dark Wood and Conor both consent.

Sarai paced the room. "Goddess above! It finally makes sense! The prophecy that made my mother want to kill you. The prophecy about the one who would shift the balance said '*the one who gives up her name.*' We took that to mean a Maiden who married the Wolf—a symbolic way of giving up her name. My mother thought, because you fell for him, that you'd marry him, eventually solidifying his superiority over the Mother, but the reality is that you gave your name to the Dark Wood. In theory, you sacrificed some power over you, and so the Dark Wood gave you some back. You consented to an exchange. A sacrifice given of your own accord would carry more weight than something you're compelled to do. It's why you enchant plants everywhere, but especially the Dark Wood."

"Sarai, we need a plan," Rowan said. "The Crone said that the blight is still spreading in Ballybrine, and I think the Mother is doing it. There must be a way to strip her of power and pass it to someone else, just like she was planning to do with Conor."

Sarai furrowed her brow. "Well, theoretically, the magics are two sides of the same coin. Death is just the pause before life. It's all an endless circle." She leaned back in her chair thoughtfully. "I have an idea, but it's going to be a long shot, and it might not work at all if we don't have enough people to witness the transfer of power. Still, it's our best option."

Conor sat down, and the three of them set about making a new plan.

ROWAN STOOD in front of Orla's shrine, striking a match to light a candle and bowing her head in prayer. The afternoon light pouring through the stained-glass window cast her face in an array of colors.

Conor stood awkwardly off to the side. He'd been following her around all day. Even Sarai teased him about it, but so much had happened in the past day, and he had a strange fear that if he let Rowan out of his sight, she would disappear. Or, worse, change her mind about him.

Rowan had been presented with quite a bit of startling information in the past few days, from the Crone's prophecy to Rowan's ability to control the Dark Wood to the fact that the Mother was still spreading the blight into Ballybrine to the revelation that Conor had killed most of the past Maidens.

She'd been uncommonly quiet and reserved, even when he made love to her that morning. She was more tentative. Her emotions were carefully tucked away from him.

Conor's mind spun wildly. It was the first time he'd been able to see a real way out of the mess he'd made so many years before. The plan that he, Sarai, and Rowan had formed meant that he'd no longer need to be bound by taking Red Maidens. Unfortunately, it also meant that as soon as they handled the Mother, Rowan would no longer be bound to him. She could finally have a life of her own, and as much as he wanted that for her, he didn't want to think about how his days would drag without her.

She lifted her head and sighed, brushing her hair back behind her shoulders as she turned to look at him.

"What's going on in your head?" Conor asked.

A smile tugged at her lips. "I thought you knew now with our bond."

"I know what you feel at times, which is quite a lot, but I have no idea what you think."

Rowan considered it, wringing her hands and twisting them into the skirt of her dark green dress. "I think that I wasn't surprised when you told me about the other Maidens. I wanted not to believe it, even if it's what I suspected. I'm not sure it changed anything, but I can't exactly say that it's comforting."

Conor waited breathlessly for her to say more. He didn't remember ever feeling so terrified. It went far beyond what he felt for her physically. Lorna might have introduced him to compassion, but

Rowan had demanded it. She dazzled him, and now, as all of their truths were borne to each other, he was desperately afraid that she wouldn't want him. He knew asking her to love him still was asking a lot, but he foolishly hoped for it anyway.

"I want to keep you," Conor said desperately.

Rowan's face softened. "Keep me?"

"Yes. Keep you in my arms. Keep you safe. Keep you smiling."

"And if I don't want to be kept?" she challenged.

"Then I want you to keep me," he sighed. "I just want to be with you."

She frowned, and apprehension buzzed through their connection. "But I will continue to age. I will get old and gray, and you'll be just as handsome as you are now."

He was surprised she had thought of such a thing. When they met, she'd seemed so certain of her early death that she hadn't even bothered to think of what she might want if she could decide for herself. Rowan had come such a long way.

"That's not necessarily true, lass. The magic of this place preserves you while you're here."

Rowan's eyes went wide. "So if I stayed here forever and never went back to Ballybrine, I would stay the same age?"

"It's not instant—if you walked back to Ballybrine after a year, you wouldn't instantly age a year. It's simply that when you're in Ballybrine, you age normally, and when you're here, the eternal magic keeps you as you are."

If she was thinking that much about the future, perhaps he had more of a chance than he thought. Perhaps she could love him with the same certainty with which he loved her. Perhaps he could satisfy all of her questions until the only answer she had left was "yes." Could he be so fortunate?

"You know, I would make the whole world dark for you so that you can be the only bright light," Conor said.

She smiled. She'd let him drag her down into the dark, or perhaps she'd always lived there and he simply found her and made her unafraid. She'd lived at odds with her nature, but he wanted to set her free.

"There is an ember in you that glows brightly all the time. To have been hurt and forgotten, to have been wounded and betrayed, and to still do nothing but burn... I am blown away by you, Rowan Cleary."

Conor lowered himself to his knees.

For Rowan alone, he was devout. He had spent centuries as someone who exclusively received reverence and homage, not one who gave it. But Rowan demanded his faith with her very presence, and he never wanted to worship anyone or anything else.

Rowan stared at the monster humbled before her. In the past, Conor would have been humiliated by doing such a thing, but he was bolstered by the hint of satisfaction on her face. The god of death was kneeling in his own temple to her, a girl who'd spent her life feeling powerless. He wanted her to feel strong, loved, perfect exactly as she was—because that was how he truly felt.

"What are you doing?" she rasped.

He took both of her hands in his, kissing her knuckles softly as he held her gaze. "Bind my heart to yours if you deem me worthy. Weave your life with mine."

Rowan went utterly still. He held her hands, kissing each fingertip, her palms, the insides of her wrists. Recognition lit in her eyes, and Conor felt the warmth of her joy and the buzzing of her apprehension in his chest as if they were his own. They were the words of traditional Eireione wedding vows, and it was clear that, despite her sheltered life, she recognized them.

He took a breath and continued, "From my lips may only truth flow. From your heart may only peace grow."

He hugged her around the waist, staring up at her. It was dangerous to share his power. He had no idea what would happen if he took a wife, but in their culture, marriage was a spiritual vow, binding one soul to another forever. Conor hadn't thought about his own soul in quite some time. Perhaps it would act as a millstone for hers, dragging her down to the depths. Perhaps she'd gladly fall. He was far too selfish to feel guilty for it.

He spoke again. "You are the mirror of my heart. You help me see myself even when I want to stay blind."

She blinked back tears.

"From this day until my last, I bend to no one but you, Rowan Cleary."

Rowan held her breath as shock reverberated through their connection. She'd likely never dreamed she would hear those words.

"Say it back, Rowan. I know it's an untraditional proposal. I know it's not really a proposal at all, but please say it back."

In Eireione culture, couples married themselves. They committed their vows either privately or in front of friends and family, but there was no officiant necessary. If she said them back, they'd be so.

Conor felt the impulse to pray, though he had no clue to whom gods were supposed to pray. How did mortals bear the lack of control?

Rowan was still as a statue. Tears streamed down her cheeks. He couldn't tell if they were a product of grief or joy.

There was no accounting for Conor's heart. He loved this woman. Perhaps he'd pushed her too far. Perhaps it was asking far too much. Perhaps the past few days had convinced her how truly unwise it would be to bind herself to him in any significant way. Still, he would not let fear stop him from humbling himself for her.

It astonished Conor that he could still experience new things after his centuries of existence. He wasn't certain Rowan understood what it meant for him to be on his knees and say those words. Even long ago, when he'd been mortal, he'd never had an interest in companionship. He was a warrior first. He was someone who had built his entire existence on certainty.

Now he knelt before a beautiful woman with nothing but uncertainty stretched out before him. The words he'd said to Charlie weeks before came rushing back to him. *"I'll not make hope a noose from which to hang myself."*

He feared he'd done just that.

34

ROWAN

Conor's face was full of fear and longing as he knelt in the center of his temple. Rowan could not believe he'd humbled himself before her. He'd given her what they both thought him incapable of.

Her heart warred with her mind. She wanted to believe that he meant what he was saying, but he could have just as easily been trying to find a way to bind her to him now that she'd be free. But this offer felt less like possession and more like homage.

Her hands trembled as she cupped his face. "Conor—" Her voice broke. He wasn't just offering his heart for a lifetime. He was offering it for an eternity.

He reached to wipe the tears from her cheeks. She looked at the rows of shrines of her fallen sisters and, instead of feeling repulsed by his savagery, she felt suddenly certain that someone tame would never do.

She lowered herself to her knees, meeting his stormy eyes. "Bind my heart to yours. Weave your life with mine."

Conor sagged in relief, squeezing her hands.

"From my lips may only truth flow. From your heart may only peace grow. You are the mirror of my heart. You help me see myself even when I want to stay blind. From this day until my last, I bend to no one but you, Conor—"

"Grey," he supplied.

"Conor Grey," she said with a smile. "Now what?"

Conor kissed her, weaving his fingers through her hair and pulling her body flush to his. "Now, lass, we get to the business of making it official," he whispered against her lips as he guided her down to her back on the cool marble floor.

Hiking up her dress, he bent to kiss her again, brushing his fingers over her thighs.

Pounding footsteps cut through their frenzy as Sarai and Charlie burst into the temple. Charlie paused in the doorway, looking unsurprised.

Sarai drew up short, turning away. "I've had a vision. You must come. Something is very wrong in town. I fear we need to put our plan into action now, or we may lose our chance."

They dashed out of the temple, through the keep, and to the front doors. Charlie took off to gather the reapers as Conor helped Rowan into her cloak and pulled on a leather breastplate marked with the crest of the Wolf.

A furious pounding on the door made them freeze.

Conor pushed Rowan and Sarai behind him and threw open the heavy wooden doors, coming face to face with the Crone.

"We must move fast!" the Crone said. She met Sarai's eye. "Did you see it too?"

Sarai nodded.

"I'm sorry, Rowan," the Crone said, shaking her head. "I know I made a grave mistake. I see the error now. You were meant to right the balance, not ruin it. I only had part of the picture, but I have the whole now. Something is very wrong in town. The anxiety was already through the roof, but there was such a surge of restlessness... I did not receive a full vision, but something is wrong at the tower, and I worry even if we run, we will be too late. I know you have no reason to trust me, but please come quickly."

"It could be a trap," Conor said, glaring at the Crone.

"I swear on my soul," she said meaningfully.

Conor gritted his teeth and nodded.

Sarai stepped forward. "Mother, if you're lying—"

"I swear I'm not, but if you need me to prove it, I will pass along my title to you right now," the Crone said.

Rowan's gaze whipped to Sarai. It was exactly what they'd discussed happening in their plan.

"I've seen all the outcomes," the Crone said. "The plan you have is the only one that has a prayer of working."

A silent understanding passed between Rowan and Sarai.

"All right, let's go. We will transfer the power as we move," Sarai said.

Together, Conor, Rowan, Sarai, and the Crone rushed down the trail toward Ballybrine. Rowan jogged alongside Conor, her hand in his. Behind them, the Crone and Sarai spoke back and forth in incantations. After a few minutes, they went silent and picked up their pace.

Rowan felt a strange hum in the forest, the plants perking up as she walked by. She could sense the song in them in a more vibrant way. Something had shifted, either from her call for help the day before, or from her wedding.

"I'm very proud of you, Sarai," the Crone said.

"Congratulations, Sarai," Rowan said, smiling back at her friend. "Now, whatever is happening at the tower, you need to let Conor and I go first. You hang back because we'll need you both if the Mother appears. You know the plan only works if she doesn't see you coming."

Sarai nodded. "And if we can get witnesses."

They hurried on as the flickering torches of the trailhead came into view.

Loud shouting and the smell of smoke wafted down the trail, and Rowan burst into a full run.

"Rowan, let me go first!" Conor shouted.

"Keep up!" she grunted in reply.

They burst from the trail and Rowan drew up short as Finn came into view, leaning against the wall in front of Maiden's Tower, looking beat-up and dejected. The door of the tower had been battered inward, several bodies strewn about the entryway. Finn's sword dripped with blood and his gaze lifted, colliding with Rowan's.

"Row, I tried—"

"No," Rowan breathed. She tore past him into the tower and came to a stop at the bottom of the stairs, where Mrs. Teverin lay in a pool of blood.

"Mrs. Teverin," Rowan said. Her voice broke. She looked up the stairs. "Aeoife!"

She lurched forward, but Conor caught her hand. "Rowan, perhaps I should go first."

"If she's scared, she won't recognize you. She'll be hiding, waiting for me," Rowan said.

Conor followed behind her. The weight of dread slowed their ascent.

Rowan stopped when she came to the first landing. The sight of Aeoife's small body in a heap stole all the air from Maiden's Tower, leaving her breathless, a silent sob caught in her throat.

"Aeoife," she said finally, falling to her knees beside the little girl.

"Rowie?" Aeoife coughed.

Rowan crawled over to her, pulling the girl into her arms. "I'm here. I'm here, Aeoife."

Aeoife smiled up at her, her eyes full of tears and relief. Rowan tried to ignore the puddle of blood that instantly soaked through her dress, making her knees sticky.

"I fell on the stairs. There were so many men coming, and Mrs. Teverin and Cade tried to get me out, but we made it downstairs too late, and she told me to run," Aeoife said. Her eyes fluttered shut, and she was breathless, as if speaking took great effort.

Rowan realized she must have broken ribs. "You're going to be all right. We're going to get a healer. I just need you to stay awake, Aeoife," she urged, barely able to contain her panic. There was far too much blood pooling around the girl's little body.

"I'll get the healer," Finn said, disappearing down the stairs.

"See, Finn is going to get help. You will be okay, Aeoife. Just look at me, okay?" Rowan pleaded.

Aeoife smiled weakly. "Is that him?" she asked. "Is that the Wolf?"

Rowan followed her gaze to Conor, who was trying to both be supportive and give them privacy.

"Yes, that's Conor," Rowan said.

Conor knelt beside her. "Hello, Lady Aeoife. It's very nice to meet you. I've heard so much about you."

Aeoife smiled. "He's not very scary," she noted, meeting Rowan's eyes again.

Rowan moved her hand and felt that Aeoife's head wound had soaked through her cloak where she held it in place. "That's not true, Aeoife. He's terrifying. It's just that you're very brave."

Aeoife's eyes weren't fully focused. "I know you said not to tell people about what I feel, Rowie, but I can feel how he worries for you. It's like how you worry for me," she whispered. Tears streamed down her cheeks, puddling in her hair. "I think I'm—"

"No! Don't say it," Rowan said. She looked frantically at Conor, but she could tell by the grim line of his mouth that he was seeing something she wasn't.

"Please, Conor. Can you help?" Rowan begged desperately.

"I wish I could, love. But you know that life is not my gift," he said.

Rowan was desolate as she met Aeoife's eyes. "All right, why don't I sing you a song? I'll sing your favorite. The one about the Storm Prince and his princess."

She opened her mouth and sang a song of love and loss, even while knowing it was hopeless. She tried. Rowan pressed her magic into the girl in her arms, willing her back to life—as if it was as simple as bringing back plants. But unlike the fairy tale in the song, Rowan's life turned into a nightmare as Aeoife breathed out in a rattle and her chest refused to rise again.

"No—" Rowan breathed. She felt the moment the life left the little girl who had been a sister to her.

Rowan felt like she was drowning on dry land. She was wild with grief, unmoored, and shredded to pieces.

There was a commotion on the stairs behind her as Finn reappeared with Charlie on his heels. "I couldn't find any healers. Everything is in chaos—" He stopped when he saw Rowan's face. "Rowan, I swear I tried to keep them back. There were just too many of them."

Rowan blinked, trying to clear away the visual of Aeoife's lifeless body.

It was impossible for someone so full of life to be gone. She couldn't wrap her head around the loss. It wasn't a pit like she'd felt for Orla. It was a dark star that sucked in everything else. It was a vortex that split wide with depths that went on forever into the dark.

Something stirred in Rowan. Something burgeoned from the depths of her grief. She felt the Dark Wood reaching toward her for comfort. She felt its power in her bones, in her heart, in her hands. She felt the stirring of a rage that could swallow up the sun.

"I need a white sheet for a shroud," she whispered.

Conor disappeared and returned a moment later with the sheet. "What can I do?" he whispered as he knelt beside her, resting a hand on Rowan's shoulder.

She didn't have words to tell him that was what she needed—him beside her, sharing her grief, unafraid of her growing rage.

"She was going to be eleven next week," Rowan whispered. "She loved fancy pink dresses and romantic fairy tales. I was going to bring her to the keep next ceremony so she would be safe. She hated sleeping in her room alone, and she was afraid of the dark."

She brushed Aeoife's hair back from her face and carefully placed her body on the sheet, tucking the ends around her reverently and covering her sweet face last.

"She'll never hold my hand again. She'll never sleep in my bed. We'll never have sticky buns together on Sunday mornings. We'll never look at dresses in the windows of shops in town and say which one we like best. She'll never grow up," she rasped. Conor wrapped his arms around Rowan, and she leaned into him. "She was supposed to *live*."

"I know, love. I am so, so sorry," Conor whispered.

Rowan brushed away her tears and steadied herself. "I have to bring her to her mother. Their house isn't far from here."

Conor nodded and helped her stand with the body in her arms.

"I can carry her, love," he said softly.

"No, I have to do it," Rowan insisted.

Conor sighed and turned his gaze on Finn. "Did you see who was responsible?"

"I did," Finn said, eyeing Conor warily.

"Charlie, please gather those men for us. We will be back soon," Conor said. With that, he guided Rowan out of Maiden's Tower.

Rowan led him down several streets before she came to a stop outside of Aeoife's family's cottage. They'd chosen to stay where they had always lived even after Aeoife was taken as a Maiden since they were a middle-class family to begin with. The house was charming, with a thatched roof and a white fence surrounding the yard.

Rowan hesitated on the walkway up to the house.

"What's wrong?" Conor asked.

She swallowed hard. "I just wanted to give them one more minute of peace before I tear their world apart. Just one more minute, and then we'll knock," she said, blinking back tears.

Rowan didn't say that she also wasn't ready to let Aeoife go yet. She'd had no time to make peace with the sudden loss of the one person she'd promised to protect. The failure threatened to bring her to her knees. Rowan knew Aeoife was already gone, but there was a finality to handing her over to her family that she couldn't wrap her mind around.

The door opened, and Aeoife's mother was startled at the sight of Rowan and Conor just a few feet away. Her eyes went instantly to the white bundle in Rowan's arms.

"No. No, no, no. It can't be," Aeoife's mother said. She fell to her knees in agony as she looked at the white shroud.

Rowan bent toward her and placed Aeoife in her arms.

"You promised you would protect her!" Aeoife's mother screamed, clinging to the body cradled against her.

"I know," Rowan breathed. "I'm sorry."

"You've done enough!" the woman shouted. Her grief was so profound that Rowan was certain people could feel it blocks away.

Conor stiffened beside her, but Rowan settled a hand on his arm. "It's okay. She's just grieving."

"She shouldn't talk to you that way," he whispered. "You did your best."

Rowan looked at him. "I'm the only one she can talk to that way. I am the only one who can share her grief with her. It's far too much to bear alone."

She turned back to Aeoife's mother, who looked furious and broken. The woman had tried to hide her magical daughter from an unimaginable fate, and she'd failed. She'd been dragged away from Maiden's Tower sobbing the day Aeoife was given over. Of course she was angry, and she could not yell at the elders or the men who'd hurt her daughter for fear of the same violence befalling her or her other children. She could only rage against someone who loved Aeoife just as much.

"There is no way to fix this, but I will see justice done. Stay inside tonight and keep your loved ones close. I will not let this go unpunished," Rowan said.

Aeoife's mother nodded, her lip trembling and her gaze fierce with shared conviction. "You show them the same mercy they showed my beautiful girl," she rasped. Then she turned and disappeared inside with Aeoife's body, leaving Rowan feeling empty and too weighed down to move.

"Rowan, I'm so sorry," Conor said. "There aren't words for her loss. I know you loved her very much."

Rowan turned to face him, unable to make out his expression through her tears. "She was good. She was supposed to be okay. She was supposed to still be here after me. I was going to stay forever if I could. I was going to make sure she never had to do what I did. It was supposed to—"

She couldn't breathe around the loss. She felt like her chest had been torn open.

"It was all supposed to be worth it for her," Rowan gasped.

The truth was devastating. Above everything else in Rowan's life, her love for Aeoife—her desire to protect the girl from suffering the same fate—had been the one thing that sustained her. Now she felt lost at sea with no purpose or direction and no way to steer the ship.

Conor pulled her into his arms, and she buried her face in his chest and cried. "I wish that I could take this grief from you. I wish I could save you from it, but it's simply love that you had left to spend, and you always have so much love to give."

He rubbed her back in soft, soothing circles as they walked away from Aeoife's house. As they cut down the street, the grief abated, swallowed by a fresh wave of anger. By the time they reached the trailhead at Maiden's Tower, she was propelled purely by fury.

Charlie had gathered the men responsible, and they all knelt in a line on the dais outside the Temple of the Mother where the weekly Gratitude and Grieving Ceremony was held. Rowan had expected to see Finn, but he was nowhere to be found.

"These are all the ones that the demon and Finn could identify," Charlie said solemnly.

"The demon?" Rowan asked.

"Your friend, Cade," Charlie said. "He and the hunter tried to hold off the crowd."

Rowan swallowed hard. Despite all that had happened, she was relieved that at least Cade had been there to try to protect Aeoife. What had really broken Rowan was the thought of Aeoife being terrified and alone.

Rowan felt sick as she looked at the men. Some she recognized from prominent houses in Ballybrine.

"And what did you hope to gain, chasing down a child? Trampling an old woman?" Rowan demanded.

None of the men spoke.

Conor stepped up beside Rowan. "Speak or die," he ordered.

The men trembled at the sight of him, and Rowan wondered what they were seeing.

Rowan laughed bitterly. "Oh, is that the problem? Am I not frightening enough? That can be remedied."

She tugged on the tether between herself and the Dark Wood, and the forest rushed over its boundary, pressing out behind the men. The temple groaned and stained glass shattered as the enchanted vines and roots burst through the walls. In moments, the temple was in ruins, and the edge of the Dark Wood loomed right behind the group of men.

Rowan tugged again at the magic, and the men cried out in fear and surprise as their hands were roughly dragged overhead, bound by roots and vines.

"We didn't hurt her. She just fell!" one of the men shouted.

"She fell because you were chasing her. Do you have any idea what it would be like for a young girl to be chased by a mob of angry grown men? What was she supposed to do after you'd killed her tutor?" Rowan screamed.

She opened her mouth and sang, tugging on the tether between her and the Dark Wood. The forest ran a large root through the man's heart. A sickening gargle burst from his lips and blood covered the ground. Rowan should have been horrified, but she only felt bone-deep rage and grief. Killing him did nothing to lessen her burden, but it felt good to be able to do something.

"Please, Lady Rowan. Mercy, please," another man said, hanging his head.

Rowan faltered. These were someone's husbands, fathers, sons. She could tell by their clothing that they were common men, stirred into a frenzy by a fanatical religion. Killing them wouldn't alleviate her pain. It would just spread it around.

She looked to Conor.

"It is *enough*, love. You have given them enough. They do not get your mercy," he said.

Rowan considered if she had more to extend them. More patience. More understanding. More of herself. But there was none. There was only the emptiness of losing Aeoife and new rage burning through her blood. Rowan did not care for mercy when she could have vengeance.

Conor was right. They would never stop asking for more. She'd sacrificed most of herself to them and it still had not been enough. It never would be. As long as she had breath in her lungs, they'd ask for more.

It was for her to decide now, and it was finally enough.

So she sang a different song—one of rage and fury—and the Dark Wood stretched out its roots and ripped the men to shreds. After just a few moments, the blood that flooded the cobblestones was the only sign that the men had ever existed.

The entire Dark Wood rumbled and stretched, tearing into Bally-brine like a beast ripping chunks from its prey. People screamed and fled as nature took over.

Rowan turned toward the town and walked into the havoc with death at her back and the Dark Wood at her beck and call. The townsfolk ran screaming, but she did not care. She'd spent her life bending for them, and they'd finally broken her, and if they stood in her way, she'd break them right back.

Rowan had been taught it was right to always give more—to always think of the Mother's mercy—but the Mother had never shown her any. In fact, the Mother had taught her that mercy was a weakness. Rowan felt no guilt for showing the same mercy she'd been granted her whole life.

Grief was an anchor. She could let it drag her down into the depths, or she could see it as fuel and transform it into vengeance. Rowan was ready to spend all of it at once. Maybe it wouldn't make her feel any better, but at least it gave her something to do. At least she could make the people who thought it was okay to attack a young girl regret being so heartless.

She turned and caught Conor watching her. He looked fully in awe.

"You are exquisite," he sighed, pulling her into a vicious kiss that stole her breath.

When she met his eyes, her desire for revenge was reflected on his face. Fear and hurt and pain all razed down to simple vengeance.

"Love, when you're done ruining them, I'm going to make our

vows official on the altar of the fucking Temple of the Mother," he growled, kissing her again.

The words sent a surge of heat through her body.

"I look forward to it," she said breathlessly.

She smiled as she drew away and turned her attention back to the town. How far could she push the Dark Wood? How far would her rage carry her? To the square? All the way to the sea? How far did she *want* it to carry her?

She didn't know. All she knew was that she wasn't dead yet.

Conor followed behind her with Charlie and a flood of reapers on his heels.

"Demon's breath, lass! You know how to make an entrance," the reaper said. "And I thought you were intense, Con."

The Dark Wood pulsed around them—the new growth eager to spread into town.

"When I met you, I was afraid you were too soft. Now I think perhaps you're more fierce than even I am," Conor said.

Rowan soaked in the awe in his gaze.

"All right, I get it. You're in love. Can we keep going? We have a job to do and not much time to do it. The new refugees just arrived from the north. It's now or never," Charlie said.

Rowan took a breath and closed her eyes. Grief rose like a great tide. Conor's hand slid to her lower back, and she knew he felt it through their bond. She forced herself to march on, dragging the Dark Wood with her as people fled.

Those people would never understand what it was to be raised as an object. They wouldn't understand the grief of loving two beautiful Maidens who should have had their whole lives ahead of them. They didn't understand the frustration of having no control over your life and fate. They didn't understand what it was to want desperately to live when you knew you would die.

Rowan was happy to give them a lesson. She thought perhaps she would mourn the sweet girl she used to be. So many times in the past few months, she'd killed off and buried new versions of herself. Reinvention required what was dead in her to stay dead, allowing what was left to rise like a phoenix and burn the world down for killing her in the first place.

She knew what people would say—that she'd allowed the Wolf to drag her down into the dark. The truth was that she'd spent her life in the dark, and he was the first person who allowed her to be exactly as she was.

"I know we had discussed a more subtle approach, but obviously, we'll have to act now with what little bit of the plan we have," Conor said as they walked.

Rowan nodded. They had no idea if their plan would work. With Conor's power waning, they couldn't be certain he was even really immortal anymore. There were many points of failure. They could both be hurt and gone in an instant, but they had to try.

Rowan would try for Orla and Aeoife—for all the Maidens who had come before her. She would try for Sarai, who deserved to love who she loved and live a life that allowed her to be who she truly was. She would try for their small, sheltered village that needed to acknowledge the damage done, grow from their mistakes, and never forget them so that they would not be repeated.

Most of all, Rowan would try for herself. She'd been alone her whole life, but she wasn't anymore, and she never would be again, because the forest had always been listening, and it knew her pain well.

Rowan began to sing, pulling hard on the magic, and the Dark Wood grew around her like a green tide.

35

ROWAN

Rowan was a storm tearing through the village with all the fury of an unwilling sacrifice. It felt good to be taking action instead of waiting for her life to happen to her, and regardless of how things turned out, she felt immense gratitude to Conor for empowering her. The only way out was through, so she walked into town, dragging the Dark Wood behind her.

Rowan, Conor, and Charlie clamored into the town square. People ran screaming in different directions, fights breaking out on every street corner. It was complete chaos, and at the center of it all, the Elder Tree was burning.

"I always hated that thing," Rowan said dryly. It was macabre to have a tree transplanted from the Dark Wood that bled whenever a Red Maiden died. "Maybe it's time for some old things to burn."

She shook her head, looking back at the chaos. "All of this because people were afraid of the blight. All of this hurt, all of this loss. Will men never cease to spread misery rather than dealing with their own hurts?"

Finn burst around the corner like a storybook hero in his white tunic and golden cloak embroidered with the symbol of the Mother and surrounded by the flames of the burning village. He looked more vital than he had at Maiden's Tower, as if something supernatural bolstered him and, taking in his new regalia, Rowan wondered if the Mother was close by.

Finn's cheeks were smeared with soot, and his hand was poised on the hilt of his sword, ready to stand and fight. He stopped short when he saw Rowan's hand in Conor's.

Finn swallowed hard. "You have to stop destroying the town. I'm not your enemy, Rowan. I'm on your side, but this has gone too far."

"And what side is that?" she asked. Some foolish part of her held out hope that he could really learn—that he'd somehow see the error of his ways and actually listen to her for once—that he'd seen the violence in the tower and would fight for what was right instead of upholding more outdated ideas and principles.

"The side of what's good and right," Finn replied.

"You mean the side who let me walk into the Dark Wood to service the god of death? The side who unnecessarily kept me from having a family and friends? The side who let a mob of people kill a ten-year-old girl out of some mistaken sense of duty?"

The Elder Tree shuddered in response to the anger that rose in Rowan. Finn looked from her to the tree in confusion. She wanted so badly to display her strength for the man who'd refused to think of her as anything other than someone who needed saving, but she reminded herself that he had fought for Aeoife.

She pitied Finn. He'd never bothered to break the mold their world cast for him. She'd tried to make him see, and he'd still insisted he knew what was best. He thought it was well-meaning, even while ignoring how patronizing it felt to be on the receiving end of his good deeds.

Conor squeezed Rowan's hand. "I assume you're the one who wanted to take my lovely Rowan from me," he said to Finn.

Finn drew his sword and took a step toward her and the Wolf. Rowan had to hand it to Finn—he was as brave as he was stupid.

"May I, love?" Conor kissed her hand tenderly.

"Take what you need," Rowan whispered.

Conor tugged on her magic, and she let it go. The sweetest

melodic magic buzzed through them as their power married in a glowing blueish light that flowed between them with ease.

"Rowan, stop! What are you doing? He'll kill you!" Finn's panicked shout rose above the melody.

Conor gently drew his hand away. He cupped Rowan's face in his hands. "Are you all right?"

She smiled up at him. "I feel fine."

"Charlie?" Conor called without turning away from Rowan.

"She looks just as bright as always," Charlie confirmed.

Conor's shoulders relaxed and he pulled her into a kiss. Relief flooded Rowan's body, pulsing out through her limbs. She fisted her hands in his shirt and pulled him closer. Their plan was very risky. It relied heavily on speculation. If this was their last kiss, she wanted to make it good. She lost herself in the feeling of his hands on her, the whiskey taste of him, and the warmth and love that tingled in her body.

Finally, Conor drew away. "I hope you're not trying to kiss me goodbye, love," he whispered.

She brushed his hair back from his forehead. "I like to be prepared for anything. There's more where that came from later."

Conor chuckled. "I'll hold you to that." His smile was a beautiful threat that she hoped he delivered on.

"Go. I can handle Finn," she said, waving her hand.

Conor hesitated. She knew he wanted to protect her, but she also knew she'd made the right choice when he nodded and left her to take care of herself anyway.

She turned back to face Finn. "Finn, please just go. I do care for you. Maybe not in the way you want me to, but I still don't want anything bad to happen to you. I know you tried to save Aeoife. I know that you're a good person at your core, even if you lack imagination."

"You want to destroy our world. Our way of life!" Finn barked.

"I do." She nodded.

"But this is my city—my life, Row."

"Yes," Rowan started, "a whole city of people who were happy to have me hold up their world on my back. I've tired of doing so, and I'd like to make a world where that responsibility is shared among all instead of those born unlucky enough to become a sacrifice. I refuse to go willingly to my death for those who wouldn't give me a second thought. I will be the last Red Maiden."

"Rowan, I know you were unhappy, but this—" Finn looked around at the flaming buildings and overgrown forest. "This isn't you."

Her laughter turned bitter. "And who am I, Finn? Do you even know? My whole life has been struggle to crush the largeness in me down so that it could fit into the shadow of my responsibilities. You can't pretend to understand that. You got to choose your path. You had the privilege of money, access, training, time. I only had the ability to see and talk to the dead. I was ripped away from my family and treated as an object my whole life."

"I never treated you that way," Finn insisted.

"You didn't?" she asked. "Did you ever even ask me if I *wanted* to marry you? You just assumed that I was a poor little curse girl who would be would be delighted with your charity. You didn't care about what I wanted and you only liked me weak."

Finn looked stricken. "That's not true."

"Then fight for me now. Trust me to know my own mind. Trust that I don't want to be saved. I only ever wanted an opportunity to save myself."

"But you had one!" Finn shouted. "You could have killed him. It's all you had to do, Rowan."

She shook her head. Apparently the Mother had shared her plans with Finn. "And then what? The world requires balance, Finn. You can't just have no god of death. There would be a new god of death— one who killed Orla and tried to kill me twice, so I killed him instead. But now there isn't a good option. Thanks to the Mother."

Finn paled at her words. "He tried to kill you?"

"Not Conor. The vampire, Valen, whom she wanted to take my power and Orla's so he could overthrow Conor. The Mother is not who she wants us all to believe. She's losing power, and she's just trying to find a way to steal it from the Wolf. The Mother is causing the blight in your orchards. It's just a way for her to cultivate your alliance and influence in town."

"That doesn't make sense," Finn said, though she saw the hint of doubt in his eyes.

"Doesn't it? The new religion in the north is affecting both of them. Gods get their power from faith. The fewer people that believe in them, the less power they have. The less they can control, the less people believe in them. It's a vicious cycle. So she's been stealing from the Wolf. He's held his power, because what does everyone believe in and fear more than death? She's found small ways to siphon off his power through the monsters in his Dark Wood, who give some of it back to her. Now she's floundering because I killed her little minion."

Finn shook his head in disbelief, but Rowan could see the cracks in his resolve.

"Think about it, Finn. You're smart. You've always been a believer, and I know how hard it is. Trust me. No one was more disappointed than I was to find out her promise of salvation was just a twisted game," Rowan said, swallowing the lump in her throat.

A bright flash of light burst in front of them, blinding Rowan temporarily. When her eyes adjusted, the Mother stood between her and Finn with Cade at her side. She wore a golden gown with a shiny gold breastplate and sword at her hip, her blonde hair pinned on top of her head in a crown of curls.

"My dear, it seems you've failed us again," the Mother chided. She shook her head as if Rowan refusing to kill the Wolf was terribly naughty.

"I couldn't do it," Rowan said. "And I'm not sorry. Maybe I should have, but there has to be another way."

"Oh, you sweet, foolish, sheltered girl, there is no other way," the Mother said. "I really thought you were the one, Rowan. I could tell the first time I laid eyes on you that you had a tenacity, a fortitude that all the others lacked. Beyond that, I knew you were a bitter little thing."

Rowan's anger flared like a bonfire in her chest. Her gaze flicked to

Finn, who stood to the Mother's right, before landing on Cade, who stood to her left.

"You know, I expected it of Finn, but not you, Cade," Rowan said bitterly.

"Sorry, Row. You have multiple shots at redemption, and I only have one," Cade sighed.

Rowan tried not to be disappointed, but that was the thing about letting people close; you gave them the means with which to wound you. She had to take the bitter with the sweet.

Finn shifted beside the Mother. Rowan could practically see the gears turning in his head. He was clearly uncomfortable with the Mother befriending a demon and even more uncomfortable that he could now see said demon.

Rowan almost laughed. All she'd wanted most of her life was for others to see Cade so she didn't have to constantly pretend she didn't see or hear him. Now she wished he'd go away.

Instead, Cade stepped forward and grabbed her. She tried to pry her arm from his grip, but it was no use. She was stuck. She prayed that what she'd passed of her power to Conor would be enough. She wasn't certain where her prayers floated off to, but she hoped Conor would somehow hear them.

"Now Finn, my brave warrior. Tell me how the Wolf pulled from her," the Mother said. "Short-sighted of me not to realize you could be a constant source of power."

Horror squeezed the air from Rowan's lungs. The Mother wanted to steal Rowan's power. The goddess had always been driven by power. Rowan should have anticipated the move sooner and made herself scarce.

Finn hesitated, his eyes flashing from the Mother to Rowan. "He just took her hand and then..." He trailed off as his eyes met Rowan's.

"This is your shot, Finn. You can make a difference. You want to save me so badly? Shut your stupid mouth," Rowan said, gesturing to the surrounding chaos.

All around them, huntsmen were engaged in fights with Conor's reapers. There was the clang of metal against metal and grunts of pain, and the air was thick with the smell of smoke and blood.

Finn stared at the ground.

"What's a matter, lover boy?" Cade taunted. "All those proclamations. I guess it's easy to make big promises when you think no one else is there to hear them. I heard you promise to protect her, but actions speak louder than words. Especially when it comes to letting the woman you proclaim to love be sucked dry of her power by the Mother."

The Mother grimaced at Cade. "What are you doing, you little devil?"

"I'm reminding this idiot that actions speak louder than words and past mistakes. He claims to want a chance to be a hero, but every time it's handed to him on a platter, he tosses it away," Cade quipped.

Rowan saw it—the moment that Finn decided to be who he always should have been. His eyes locked on hers and his throat bobbed. He didn't need to say it for her to know he was sorry.

He swung his sword suddenly, but the Mother anticipated the move. Throwing out her hand, she blasted Finn back with a bright ball of light. He landed several yards away, unconscious.

Rowan turned to run, but the Mother appeared suddenly in front of her.

"I'm not a prisoner you want to take," Rowan warned. She'd never felt such a sense of certainty. A new idea bloomed in her mind.

"We'll just see about that, won't we?" the Mother taunted. She tore the sleeve of Rowan's dress and cloak, gripping her skin.

Rowan shoved at the Mother, trying to escape her loud cacophony of magic. The goddess's hand burned into her forearm, scalding her skin. All around them, reapers fought off huntsmen, but Conor was nowhere in sight.

The vicious ache in her arm honed Rowan's focus. She just needed to hold out a little longer until the Mother was distracted. She hoped that Sarai and the Crone were close.

Rowan stopped fighting the tug of the Mother's magic. Instead, she let hers slip. She reached into the vibrant, angry chaos of the Mother's magic and tugged—hard.

The Mother's eyes went wide in shock as her magic rushed into Rowan. It burned all the way down like her body was full of a vicious poison, but she didn't let go.

The Mother took a step back, but Rowan clamped her hand down, holding fast to the goddess.

A flurry of movement to her left drew her focus. Conor stepped out from the shadows like a dark knight in his hunter-green tunic and leather breastplate. The space between them was too great. There were dozens of huntsmen engaged with Conor's reapers scattered throughout the square between them. He shouted something that she couldn't hear but still knew what it was. *Let go.*

Rowan locked eyes with Conor over the melee—the pain on his face a mirror of her own. They were out of time, and they both knew it.

She had known the moment would come. She simply hoped it wouldn't be so soon. Time had always been her most limited resource, and she'd desperately tried to fit as much as she could into what little she had. The rapid passage of it had stirred panic in her when she was younger, but now that she had even more to lose, a strange calm settled in her stomach.

Chaos reigned around them, but between Rowan and Conor, there was only the stillness of knowing something dreadful and imminent. A single moment stretched out between them, suspended by the weight of their desire. Perhaps loving someone so much made small moments larger. All the love and joy and loss—every sweet thing, every anger, every heartbreak—and a desperate longing for more filled that moment until it was bursting at the seams.

Rowan reminded herself it would never have felt like enough. *Enough* was a concept Conor lived outside the boundaries of.

She'd spent her life in the shadow of an hourglass, trying to grasp the moments as they slipped through her fingers like sand, so she'd filled what little time she had with small rebellions and little connec-

369

tion so it wouldn't be too hard to disappear. All of that, and it still didn't seem like enough.

It wasn't that she wanted things to be fair. *Fair* was a child's word. The world was a cruel and inequitable place, and it didn't owe her anything, and she wasn't foolish enough to ever expect fairness. Still, she felt that she'd sacrificed more than most.

But magic was a thing that required balance, and she felt betrayed by that concept as every bit of favor seemed to land on the Mother's side.

Perhaps it would have been easier if she hadn't fallen for Conor, if she and Sarai were content to sit prettily in their roles, pawns for a society that was happy to trade them and their futures in exchange for peace of mind.

Conor nodded to Rowan, and she tried to smile but only succeeded in frowning as she let go of the Mother and stumbled back.

He charged toward Rowan, stepping between her and the Mother just as a shout stole Rowan's attention.

"Rowan!"

She spun and found Sarai, who was gesturing wildly. A flood of people was making its way up the street. "New refugees! Several boat-loads! Give them a good show!"

Rowan nodded, turning her attention back to Conor and the Mother, who were trading vicious magical blows. Conor's glowing blue magic clashed with the Mother's golden light.

On the far edge of the square, several elders knelt, their heads bowed in prayer. Rowan tugged on her magic and had them strangled with Dark Wood vines, but it was too late. They'd given the Mother the advantage, and she had her hands around Conor's throat. She was pulling the power right out of him.

"Sorry, Con. It's been a long time coming. This is a whole new world, and there will be only one now," the Mother said with a vicious smile.

Rowan charged toward her, her dagger in hand, and the Mother laughed.

"I'm doing you a favor. What on earth am I taking from you, you ungrateful little brat?" she growled.

"You're trying to take my husband," Rowan said.

"Husband?" the Mother said as her eyes snapped to Conor.

One moment of disorientation was all Rowan needed. She plunged the dagger into the Mother's chest. The goddess let out a keening wail.

"Now, Sarai!" Rowan shouted over the noise. She tugged on the Dark Wood, and it pinned the Mother in place with roots and vines.

Sarai dashed forward with her mother on her heels. She placed a hand on the goddess's back and the other on the former Crone's chest. Conor scrambled beside them, pressing his hand to Sarai's back.

A loud, sweeping symphony of magic whirled up through the air, drowning out everything else. Rowan stumbled back as she covered her ears against the assault. Conor steadied her with his free arm as they watched the transfer of power unfold.

The Mother howled as Sarai spoke in a hushed tone, pushing the goddess's power into her own mother. A golden light grew around the three of them, pulsing until it was so glaring Rowan had to shield her eyes.

After a few long, blind moments, the melody of the magic ceased, and Rowan blinked her eyes open. Conor stood panting next to a wide-eyed Sarai and a glowing Crone Mother.

The former goddess appeared to collapse in on herself. She aged before their eyes, crumpling inward as if her bones were deteriorating right beneath her skin. "How?" she rasped as she writhed on the ground. "I should have just been able to use you. How did you figure it out?"

"Death is just the pause before life starts again. Life and death were always made of the same magic," Rowan said. "It made sense that if you could create a new Wolf, he could create a new Mother."

With one last huff, the goddess disintegrated into ash before their eyes.

The new Crone Mother looked to Conor.

"The nightmare is still gone?" she asked.

Conor closed his eyes and a blue aura swelled around him. After a long moment, his shoulders relaxed, he opened his eyes, and nodded.

The Crone Mother's relief matched his.

"Did it work?" Rowan asked Sarai. "Did we break the world?"

Her friend grinned as her gaze fell on the former Crone. "I think we broke it. What do you think, Crone Mother?"

Sarai's mother, the new goddess, the Crone Mother, turned to look at Rowan. "It seems you could see what the rest of us couldn't. Thank you for not giving up on us, even when we gave up on you."

"Now what?" Sarai said. She turned and tipped her head toward the wide-eyed refugees filling the square.

"I think you're supposed to tell us that, O wise one," Rowan taunted. "What's the new bargain? How do we rebuild?"

Sarai took a few breaths, turning to face the murmuring crowd as Conor made his way to Rowan.

He stood in front of her, looking bruised and exhausted, but he was still standing, and so was Rowan. She threw herself into his waiting arms, and he rained kisses all over her face and held her close.

Out of the corner of her eye, Rowan saw the confusion of the crowd gathered in the streets. They seemed shocked to see the Wolf showing such tenderness, especially toward a Red Maiden. They gave her and Conor a long look, their eyes narrowing in puzzlement as they took in her tattered red cloak and Conor's ominous presence.

"I'm so glad you're okay," Rowan whispered, brushing Conor's hair back from his forehead. "It's a good thing you love me."

"I'm not the hero, love. You are," Conor laughed.

"Ugh, I'm glad we won and all, but you two are becoming insufferable," Charlie griped beside them.

Rowan grinned and kissed Conor again before turning to face Sarai. Her friend gave her a questioning look, but she just waved her hand, encouraging the new Crone to address the people.

Sarai turned to the crowd. "Be well, be well, all. I am the Crone of

Ballybrine, and I'll be taking my rightful place once and for all as the voice and scribe of the Mother's scriptures. The elders are no more. The power of prayer has been given back to you, the people. I will be here for counsel and to hold the weekly Gratitude and Grieving Ceremony, but the rest of your devotion belongs to you. We'll return to the old ways."

It was exactly as they'd planned. Sarai turned and took Conor's hand in one of hers, the Crone Mother's in the other.

"Behold a new deal between gods," Sarai continued. "The goddess above—the Crone Mother—and the god of death—the Wolf. They hold the balance between them. The keys of life and the keys of death. Both are important. Both agree to uphold the balance; to seek no more than the necessary power; to keep us all safe from threats both living and dead."

She met Rowan's eye, and Rowan nodded.

"Our last Red Maiden is gone. The passage of the dead will be managed by the god of death and Lady Rowan Cleary. Together they will lead the souls of the departed to rest," Sarai said. "As long as you believe you'll have protection and peace."

The people murmured among themselves before several of them folded their hands across their hearts and held their hands out in a sign of reverence. Several fell to their knees and bowed their heads.

"The fight is over. The Dark Wood will recede to its former borders, and as long as you stay steady and faithful, we will thrive together," Sarai said. "Please, if you can spare the space and resources, we have new refugees and people who need shelter while we rebuild."

The people nodded faithfully and pushed forward to brush their hands over Sarai's and the Crone Mother's and, to Rowan's surprise, hers and Conor's as well. Conor looked stunned by the recognition, and she supposed it made sense. For the first time ever, the people saw him not as a monster but as a necessary balance in their world.

Rowan studied her husband's stunned face as the people murmured their appreciation. After a long while, the crowd dispersed, and people turned back to town to rebuild and take in the new refugees.

As the crowd grew thin, her eyes fell on Cade. He walked toward her, pausing tentatively a few feet away.

"I'm really sorry, Row," he whispered. "I wanted to tell you what I was for so long, and even more than that, I wanted to save Aeoife."

Her demon friend looked uncharacteristically emotional.

"She was a sweet girl, and I miss her already," he said.

Rowan nodded, blinking away tears. "I'm sorry that you didn't get what you hoped for."

"It's all right. There are worse fates than being what I've always been. I just feel bad for letting you down. Do you think—" Cade swallowed hard. "Do you think we could go back to being friends? I know I don't deserve your trust, but I miss you."

Rowan knew she needed to forgive him. It wasn't his fault he couldn't save Aeoife from an angry mob.

"Love," Conor said, placing a hand on her back. "It can be very compelling when someone offers you a way out of the pit. Perhaps give him another chance."

Rowan frowned. "Magnanimous of you."

All of them did their best, and still, they'd all failed in their own ways. It cost them all something, though it cost Aeoife the most.

Rowan nodded.

Conor took a step toward Cade. "I'd like to extend an offer for you to join my reapers. It wouldn't make you good, but it would make you neutral and give you something productive to do with all your energy."

"I'd be honored," Cade said.

Conor placed a hand on Cade's forehead, and a soft blue glow flowed from his hand into Cade's skin. A swell of hushed whispers rose as a blue aura formed around him. His eyes glowed a pale blue color before settling back to their usual hazel.

"Charlie, you'll show him back and get him settled?" Conor asked.

Charlie nodded and led Cade away from the gawking crowd.

"I'm tired of being stared at. Let's go home," Rowan whispered, leaning her head against Conor's chest.

"Now, my love, as I remember, I told you that I would make this marriage official on the altar of the Temple of the Mother if we made it out of this alive, and I'm nothing if not a man of my word." Conor grinned.

Rowan arched an eyebrow. "Well, if you insist. It might no longer be my job, but I'd still prefer to keep the Wolf happy."

"And I you," he said, sweeping her up into his arms as she laughed and carrying her back toward the wreckage of the Temple of the Mother.

Rowan leaned her head against Conor's shoulder and smiled to herself. She'd broken every rule and lived in full rebellion, and she'd been lucky enough to live to tell the tale. She'd make the most of her life for Orla and Aeoife and every Maiden that came before them. She made a silent promise to herself that she'd stay wild enough for all of them.

36

CONOR

Six Months Later

Conor's boot slid in a mud puddle while his wife was greeted with a path of ferns to cushion her bare feet. The forest sprouted flowers around her path, pressing them to caress her arms, branches bending low to comb her hair. The affectionate way the Dark Wood responded to her still shocked Conor.

A bush of wild roses shot up from the side of the trail. They bloomed rapidly and sent a rush of sweetness into the air.

"Thank you. They're beautiful," Rowan murmured, bending to breathe them in, her unbound hair falling in front of her shoulders.

"Sure, give her roses while you give me mud," Conor grumbled.

Rowan giggled. "Is it roses you want, my love? I'm sure the forest will accommodate."

The branches and bushes around them shuddered before climbing vines of bloodred roses shot up the tree trunk beside Conor.

The Dark Wood might have been an extension of his magic, but it was Rowan's care that brought it to life. It was the way she'd secretly poured all of her love and hurt and hope into it. It was the magic in her heart. Of course it liked her better.

She continued walking, passing through the gates of Wolf's Keep, which were now girdled in vines of climbing florals. She walked into the Dark Garden, singing a soft lullaby, her voice floating through the flowers and shrubs, carried on a spring breeze that ruffled her hair and the hem of her pale green dress.

Conor wrapped his arms around her from behind and kissed the top of her head, and she sighed into the end of the song. Never could he have predicted being so undone by a woman.

"Don't stop on my account," he said.

Rowan sighed in satisfaction and leaned against him. She'd already lost focus as his fingers slid down her bare arms.

"You just like to distract me," she murmured as Conor's lips brushed her neck.

"It's only because you smell like dessert," he teased. "It makes me want to check if you taste as sweet as your scent suggests."

Rowan shivered, pressing her back against him harder as his hand ran down the front of her body.

"Conor! Behave yourself," she said, craning her neck to look at him. Her tone was scolding, but her eyes were bright with delight.

"Impossible when you're so tempting, lass," he said. Her hand cupped his face as he lifted her into a kiss, and she wrapped her legs around his waist.

Conor was happily lost in her, but Rowan pulled away before things became too intense.

"You have to stop seducing me in the garden. If Charlie or Cade catch us out here again, they are going to move out of the keep," she murmured.

Her resolve crumbled as Conor went on kissing her. He loved having that power over her but loved it more that she had the same power over him. His wife was a goddess, both in his mind and in the minds of the people of Ballybrine, though they argued over her true title.

Was she the goddess of death? Goddess of balance? Goddess of the woods? Goddess of rebirth?

Perhaps she was all of those things, but to Conor, she would always be the only goddess he ever wanted to worship, and her power grew as tales of her courage spread.

After Rowan and Conor fought for Ballybrine and the ships full of refugees poured in, faith was at an all-time high. The people had borne witness to a new deal between the Crone Mother and the Wolf. There would be no more spirit singers sacrificed to the god of death. It was too late for Orla and Aeoife, but they would be the last to pay too high a price for Conor's youthful foolishness. But as long as the people believed, the Wolf and his red-cloaked wife would carry the souls of their loved ones from the realm of the living to the realm of the dead.

He wasn't sure what they'd done would be enough. His dreams had not stopped, but they also hadn't become worse, so perhaps it was enough for now.

Rowan pulled away and met Conor's gaze, her verdant eyes shining. "Say it."

"I love you, Rowan Cleary," he whispered against her lips.

She loved to hear him say the name she'd feared would be forgotten long ago. Now it would be remembered forever, both by him and by all of Ballybrine.

"I recall a day when you told me quite gruffly that you were not somebody who could love me—that there was nothing but darkness where your heart should be," she said.

Conor grinned at her. "It seems I was mistaken."

"I thought you were the all-knowing god of death," she taunted, running her fingers through his hair.

"I think, at that moment, I was simply a common liar," he sighed.

"And what are you now?" Rowan asked.

"Just another poor sap helpless to a beautiful woman," Conor said.

Rowan laughed. "Perfect! I finally have you right where I want you." She kissed him again, and he lowered to his knees, laying her gently down into the soft grass.

He lay beside her, looking up at the large, fluffy clouds in the bright blue sky.

"It's a beautiful day to live in a Red Maiden-less world," Rowan sighed dreamily. She slid her hand into his.

Conor's powers were restored, and the monsters of the Dark Wood were once again banished to the Underlands and the nightmare was secure. Together, Conor and Rowan saw to the dead and spent their days playing music, walking the woods, and gardening. Conor had never imagined such a simple life could feel so full, but he was happy to have been proven wrong.

EPILOGUE

The Dark Wood was a wild place, unnavigable and impassable to even those who dared to enter and explore. The only ones who easily navigated it were a man made of shadows and a woman in a red cloak. They appeared once a week, the forest parting around them like a wide green sea, so that they could lead the souls of the departed from Ballybrine to the realm of the dead.

There would be no more Red Maidens, but all the Maidens who had come before lived on in stories told in the village by the sea. They spoke of girls in red cloaks who braved late-night walks through a magical wood to please the god of death.

Some nights, when it was particularly quiet, a melody could be heard, carried forth on an enchanted breeze from the Dark Wood all the way to the sea. It was a mournful and triumphant song, tinkling piano mixed with an angelic voice that sang about the courage of the Red Maidens of old and the price they paid.

And not a single name was forgotten.

Thank you for reading
SONG OF THE DARK WOOD

Did you like it? Love it?
Read it because you needed a standalone to hit your Goodreads goal for the year?

However you feel about it, I would be so grateful if you would **REVIEW** it on Amazon. Reviews help indie authors like myself reach new readers and they help readers determine if this book is for them.

Please take a moment to write a short review.
THANK YOU!

Scan code or visit site to review

https://www.amazon.com/dp/B0D1M81771

* * * * * * * * * * * * * * * *

Get your BONUS CHAPTER by scanning this code:

ACKNOWLEDGMENTS

This book was in my mind for a good year before I finally had the chance to write it. I've always wanted to write a story about music-based magic and a girl who can see the dead. From there, it grew into a tense love story between a woman and her power, a god and a maiden, and a witch and her best friend who wanted to break the world that fed on them. I wanted to examine how common monstrosity is ignored for a selective version of "the greater good", how we come to redefine acceptable losses, and how feminine rage transforms in moments when the world badly needs reinvention.

This book is dedicated to my grandmothers. They would probably be a bit horrified by the spice and witchy content, but proud that their courage inspired the story. I've done my share of braving the dark so I hope I've done a justice to their legacy.

A massive thank you to Tanya Grant, who has been behind me since day one. Thanks for tirelessly reading the worst drafts of all my books, and for hours on the phone talking through the chaos that is my writing mind.

Special thanks to my writing wife, Liz Leiby. I'm so glad I forced you to be my friend and critique partner—no takebacks. You are a top-notch structure witch—and I have always said that.

To Mike, who is always one of my earliest readers and asks the best questions about the logical parts of the world I've created, while ignoring the romance. Thanks for letting me disappear with my stories for hours at a time, and for pulling me out of my writer cave every once in a while.

Thanks to my Montco writers group for your encouragement and word sprint companionship, without which I might never have finished this draft.

To my indie writer friends - Em, Helen, Kara, Les, Nicole, Penn, Tay, Vanessa, Courtney, Callie, and Jenessa. And to all the other indies who have shared their wisdom and expertise with me. Thanks for helping me build something.

To Erin - Thank you for letting me feed you my books nonstop this year, for putting so much energy into each one, and for validating my loose story threads.

To Tabs - Thanks for the commas and the raw reactions.

To Andrea - This cover is a work of art. Thank you for being so patient with me. I am so lucky to have you.

To Charlotte - Thanks for your brilliant storybook depictions of these characters, for doing it in a time crunch, and for not being thrown when the time zone difference means you're getting my uncaffeinated, unhinged early morning art feedback.

To my Beta Readers - Megan, Alicia, Maddie, Michelle, and Lydia, your feedback shaped the threads of this story into something I'm incredibly proud of.

To my business witches - Your magic and rage are woven into this story alongside mine. Thank you for your wisdom and grace, and for sharing your gifts.

To my family and friends - thank you for supporting all my stories.

To my street team- All of you bring so much joy to every release and keep me from taking myself too seriously. Thank you for making this job so much fun.

To all of my readers. Thank you for walking through the dark with me. Thank you for giving all of my stories new life. And just remember: You are never alone. There are always ghosts.

Finally, to all the spiritual teachers who taught me to understand the hum of energy I hear in the world. Thank you for throwing on the lights for this haunted girl.

ABOUT THE AUTHOR

SONG OF THE DARK WOOD is Sheila Masterson's fifth novel. When she's not writing fantasy romance novels, you can find Sheila practicing yoga, or curled up reading tarot or a book. She lives outside of Philadelphia with her fiancé and way too many houseplants. You can keep up with her online at sheilamasterson.com.

instagram.com/sheilareadsandwrites

Milton Keynes UK
Ingram Content Group UK Ltd.
UKHW030624200924
448496UK00017B/172/J

9 781960 416148